ORIGINS

THE COMPOUND

Aaron and Diane,

Thank you so, so much for supporting me and helping make my dream reality!

All my love,

Kempton

By Noah Kempton

First paperback edition August 2021

Book cover art by Delaney Allen
Map by Noah Kempton

ISBN: 979-8-4553-8020-4 (paperback)

Published by Noah Kempton
noahkempton@gmail.com

Table of Contents

Foreword

I will be brief in this, for I know that many of you are as excited to read this as I am to finally allow the world to see it. I began writing this novel in 2015 at Harford Community College where it was originally a writing exercise. After the assignment, I found that I was still thinking about it. So I added to it and added to it until what began as twenty-or-so pages grew, over the course of five years, to become what you are about to read. Many people have been of service to me, and I would like to thank them all right now. Jade Raccioppi, you were one of the very first to read this novel's earliest iterations. Your words of encouragement and praise meant a lot to me and told me that I was doing something worth while. To my father, thank you for instilling in me the virtues on which many of these characters were based… and for letting me watch Lord of the Rings when I was probably way too young to do so. To my mama Sandy, my grandmother and grandfather, Sylvia and Jerry respectively, thank you for being there for me when I had questions of spelling and the like. Your support and critical analysis of my words helped me sharpen this body of work. Thank you to Victoria Flickinger for guiding me and showing me that it is sometimes better to cut than to add. Thank you Kathleen Dempko, Rosanne and Jeff Taylor for being of similar service in regards to plot and spelling. Thank you to Delaney Allen for creating such a wonderful piece of art for the cover of this book. It means everything to me that you helped me bring this thing that has been living in my head for years out into reality.

Since I was a freshmen in high school, I wanted to be a storyteller, someone who could invoke real emotion in their readers, just as J.R.R Tolkien did for me, and herein you may see some similarities.

That all being said, I really don't care if you like it, because I totally do.

All my love,

Noah Kempton

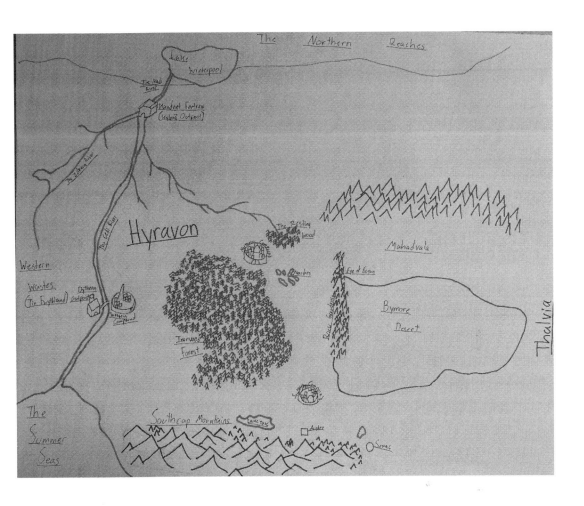

Viper's Map of the World. Scale and geographical
locations subject to change

PROLOGUE

Junn pushes through pine branches as he struggles against the cold and wet on his way to shining light ahead. For most men, this sort of environment would be deterrent enough, but he served with the Black Flag and they are a breed apart. The forest floor crunches with twig and needle as Junn breaks through the last of the trees and stands before the circle of huddled men. All are dressed in dark, hooded cloaks that glisten with rain. All carry swords, drawn and sharp. All, save for one. As Junn looks upon the group, he imagines himself in a time before when things were different, safer. Back then, he and Grimhild the giant would have been smiling ear-to-ear, giddy with the excitement of another adventure. Times changed and now he, Grimhild, and the other members of the Black Flag are more or less forced to stay close to the Compound. The Bandits are growing to be a more dangerous problem, and tonight is no different.

"Where did it happen?" Junn asks.

"This way," says Marcus, the swordless man.

"Marcus," Junn says. "Be ready for what you might see. Bandit attacks can be… extreme."

Marcus stops and looks at Junn with haunted eyes.

"I am prepared," he replies. "Let's get to it."

Marcus steps out of the circle, immediately followed by a tall, brawny man with an unpleasant grimace on his face; Junn comes in stride next to him.

"Carver," Junn says in a low voice. "The last time Bandits—"

"I don't need your *wisdom*," Carver interrupts. "Just because you're in the Black Flag doesn't make you better than me."

Junn tries to reply, but Carver picks up his pace and walks out of earshot. Junn stares at the back of his head and follows as the group heads deeper into the forest.

Junn remembers a time when Carver was… well, he has never been what you call kind, but one could withstand his naturally aggressive personality for a short while. He doesn't know whether it's due to terrible weather or the pressure the Bandits put in Carver, but these days he's nearly as vicious.

"After all these years and you still haven't learned," someone says.

Junn turns his head with a start. He looks behind him and finds a man of strong physique approaching him. His short brown hair is matted down on his forehead.

"Quit creeping up on me like that, Dale," Junn exhales in relief.

"Don't tell me that you didn't hear me coming," Dale chuckles.

"Is the murder of our people amusing you?" Carver barks.

Dale and Junn lower their voices as they march through pine and bush, ever towards the Bandit incursion.

"What kept you so long?" Junn asks.

"I lost track of you lot going through the ford a little ways back," Dale says. "On top of that, I can hardly see my hand in front of my face in this blasted rain and dark."

Junn is always a little surprised how his years in the Flag changed him, especially when he is in the company of his brother, in the field once again. He and Tegan would often spend days on end meticulously and sometimes mind-numbingly hunting their next meal. Too often their rewards for that hard work would be ridiculed by Grimhild who's appetite rivals that of a bear fattening itself to sleep through winter. Those endless nights gave him an advantage over most men, but Dale has always been a quick learner. Ever since they were children.

Dale and Junn follow behind Marcus and Carver through the shimmering trees in single file. In the embrace of the Ironwood Forest, the broad world narrows. All that is seen, heard, and smelled is your new world, and the senses that guide you through it is all that matters. Especially at night.

"Here! Here!" a man cries. "I've found them! Someone is still breathing."

Junn and Dale rush to the shouting voice, battering branches away from whipping their faces in their haste. The lantern light ahead grows brighter until they reach the man to which the voice belongs. He stands in the midst of a glade, enclosed by thick tree trunks and made smaller still by the veil of night; a brook runs along the edge, disappearing in and out of the trees. Splayed around the men are bodies, their once proud uniforms covered in visceral lacerations, splattered with blood. Guts and limbs strewn about the glade pile their horrid stench into Junn's nose as he looks upon it with emotionless eyes. One among them still draws breath in choked gulps. Marcus drops to his knees beside him.

"H-help…" the wounded man gasps.

"Don't talk, son. The more you speak, the less time I have." Marcus whips phials and bandages out of his satchel and treats his injuries. "You can tell me what happened after you're back at the Compound."

The man reaches up with his blood stained hand and clutches at the collar of Marcus' cloak, his eyes desperate.

"I don't want to die…" the man convulses in a spell of violent and bloody coughs.

Marcus shushes and tries to stop the bleeding, but the man draws one last rattling breath and then lies still. Marcus stops and curses, pounding the ground with his fist.

"The damn fools," Carver says. "Why did they come this far? And over foreigners to boot!"

Junn inspects the massacre more closely. He sees it, too, and kicks himself mentally for not being the most observant. Perhaps Carver deserves more respect than it seems. Perhaps. But like it or no, he is right. These bodies, some of them, are dressed in attire uncommon in Hyravon. These are the garbs of a noble house, no doubt hailing from Thalvia on the other side of the Bymore Desert. Junn stands beside one of the dismembered corpses and uncovers a sigil from underneath the stained uniform. It is a bronze flower with silver petals. Junn does not recognize the symbol as one of the Four Houses. He replaces the folds of stained cloth and notices something else. He would have never noticed it if he had not knelt down so close. It is a small hole, a puncture wound that is nearly invisible through the splattering of dark red blood. Someone went through a lot of trouble to make sure these deaths were at the hands of Bandits. But who and why? Junn stands and carefully inspects the remains of the other slain men. Sure enough, all of them share the same wound, even the few of the Strong Men from the Compound. Junn reaches to the bloody side of a body and plucks a tiny, pointed barb. These men were poisoned, and it acted quickly. The killer, or killers — for it is difficult to be certain — was highly skilled if they eliminated these soldiers so swiftly.

"In your expert opinion," Carver exudes sarcasm, "would you say they're dead? Or have you found something?"

Junn drops the barb and raises to his feet.

"I am only thinking."

"Junn," Marcus says. "You're the expert here. Find where these Bandits went. They will pay for this."

Junn notices Carver's ugly look. He glances at Dale; Dale nods back. Without a word, the two men walk among the slain, scouring the ground for any telltale signs of the 'Bandits', the print of a boot, disturbed trees. Junn stops beside the brook, bends down close, and touches the bank with the tip of his finger. He draws it back red. Junn stands and jerks his head in the direction of the brook's flow. Dale follows as Junn steps into the forest. They only come a short distance when Junn comes to a halt before a short cave into which the brook vanishes. Junn bends once more and peers into the recess, the flow of water echoing inside the cave.

"Bring that lantern closer," Junn says. "I think I see something."

"Be careful," Dale warns. "Snakes like to live in places like this."

Dale passes the lantern to his brother. Junn takes it and pours its light into the dark cave. The space is claustrophobic and deep. The brook cut a trench into the earth, leaving narrow strips of dry land on either side as it continues its path into the uncharted depths. Junn pushes in his prying light and it shines on a small figure pressed tight against the wall of the cave; it retreats further into the cave as though the light sears it. It is a boy, half starved and shivering.

"Hey now," Junn comforts. "It's alright. I'm not here to hurt you. You're safe."

Junn reaches out his hand and the boy eyes it warily.

The child's chest heaves with rapid breaths, his hair is plastered to his face and small bits of twigs and leaves cling to it, giving him a feral look. But the smart gleam in his eye tells Junn that he is intelligent.

"What's down there?" Dale asks.

"It's a little boy. Can't be older than fifteen-years."

Junn goes back to coaxing the child out of the cave. His soothing voice gradually brings the boy closer and closer to his out stretched hand until a smaller, cold damp hand grasps his.

"I've gotcha, little man. I've gotcha."

Junn takes the boy's withered body in his arms and goes to stand, but before he does, he notices something reflecting the light from his lantern, close to the mouth of the cave. Junn reaches for it.

"Did you drop somethin'?" he picks it up and discovers that it is a long bladed knife with a bright silver grip, adorned with strange symbols.

Junn tucks the knife into his belt and stands next to Dale.

"How in the hell did he end up there?" Dale asks, incredulously.

"Beats me," Junn says. "I don't think the blood on his clothes belongs to him. He seems unharmed. Could use a hot meal by the looks of him. I wonder if he was with the group that got attacked."

"What are you going to do with it?" Dal's asks.

"This is a person, not an object," Junn corrects. "And I'm not sure. I know that he can't stay here."

"I don't think that—"

A noise of crunching foliage and scrapping branches comes from the site of the attack as Marcus and Carver emerge from the trees.

"What have you found?" Marcus asks. "Have you found the Bandits?"

"We found someone, but he is no Bandit," Junn turns and reveals the frail boy cradled in his arms.

"Just leave him be," Carver says. "He looks far too weak to live any longer than the journey back to the Compound."

"He does look like a runt," Dale agrees. "It's better that we don't trouble ourselves with him."

"I would not be so quick to judge," Marcus counters. "Just look at those eyes. He has fight in him yet. I am sure that Malory will be quite able to nurture him to health."

"If you want to take him back, he'll be your problem," Dale grumbles.

"I will bear this burden gladly," Junn announces. "I have not the heart to abandon him to the wilderness. And if he's going to be a part of the family, he deserves a name. Since we found him in the home for serpents, I will call him... Viper. May he live long and healthy."

"Do you know what you're getting into?" Dale asks.

"Not a clue," Junn answers. "But this boy deserves better than this fate. And if I can do something to change it, by damn I'll do what I can. You never know. You might like him."

Carver scoffs, Dale rolls his eyes; Marcus smiles and turns away to start the trek back to the Compound.

CHAPTER 1

— Brothers —

A bird, feathers as red as the setting sun, flutters down from a branch overhead and lands on the toe of my worn boot. Its wings throw turbulence through the plume of smoke wafting out of my pipe, tossing the aroma of White Sage and mint back at me. I have been laying still for a few hours now in the grass underneath the twisted trunks of three trees that have grown entangled in one another. The bird must not realize that I am an animate thing, or it might remember that I am no threat to it or its home from my constant visit here, on the Hill. I remember when I first discovered this place after escaping from the Compound and all its judgments of me. But now I come for the peace. I instantly fell in love with the quiet streams and the docile creatures that live in the meadows and the light spacing of strong trees. Those things for one, and the strange nature of these three trees for another; I've never seen anything like them, and I lived in the wilderness before Junn and Marcus took me in. The trees are not even in the same family. One is an oak, broad and powerful in its age. The second is a cherry blossom whose beautiful flowering often sprinkles the grass below. And the last is a magnolia, and its white buds mingle with those of the cherry blossom, and in the height of spring, the two together create a kaleidoscope of vibrant color through which the sun shines down from a blue sky. Needless to say, most of my days since being adopted into the Compound have been spent in this immaculate solitude.

I don't know how these trees have come to find themselves grown together or who could have planted them. But I thank whatever the cause day and night. Speaking of night, I should be going back soon, before sunset. With all of

Marcus' leadership, Carver's small army of Strong Men, and the proficient knowledge of the Black Flag, the Bandits still rule the night. Yes, I should get back as soon as possible. I've heard enough stories about those skeletal demons to make me never want to see them with my own eyes. I gently sway my foot back and forth and the red bird flies away with flapping wings and cathartic singing. I sit up, supported by my elbows and savor my last few seconds before I stand and head for home.

My route back takes me through flat, grassy fields and rolling hills dotted with dandelions, all cut into unfair portions by gently flowing streams. At the point where the Compound is a few miles away, the stream widens somewhat, becoming wider, spanning eighteen yards in width, though not much deeper than where the stream is thin. I come to where I routinely ford the water, but when I step from scattered trees I come to a complete stand still. Up ahead, on the stream's opposite bank, are a herd of deer, does, bucks and their fawns. The sun, on its path to sink into the western horizon, hangs low in the sky and shines through emerald leaves and onto blades of grass, igniting their tips with golden light. The does and their young cross first, splashing through the water, their white speckled brown coats shimmering as they catch the light reflecting off the stream's surface. Behind them follow the bucks, their many-pointed horns growing wide and proud from the crowns of their heads; moss clings to some of them, giving them the appearance of being the spirit guardians of the forest. I crouch down and look in awe of this rare spectacle. They all make it to the other side and, together, disappear from sight. I remain still for a few moments more, listening to the babbling stream.

"They truly are magnificent creatures, aren't they?" Junn says, quietly.

I turn with a start at his voice. I didn't even hear him approach, but that's Junn for you. He's always been light on his feet, but you would never guess that by looking at him. He pushes his tall, well-built stature through the thin wall of tree branches and tucks his black hair behind his ear as he kneels down beside me.

"Almost make you wonder if they're animals at all and not spirits of the forest."

I turn back to look at the deer and smile. I think the exact same thing.

"Where have you been off to this time?" I ask. "Overthrow a lord and take his castle?"

"Nothing so glamorous," Junn smiles at me. "Rather tedious, actually. Spent most of the time watching, waiting… But, tell me, have you been practicing the forms I showed you?"

The deer ahead vanish from sight as they venture down the grassy slopes of the field. The truth is, I would have easily mastered the stances if Dale had agreed to spar with me. But it seems that his grudges are not easily shaken. Ever since I came to the Compound, Dale has been wary of me. And now that Junn has been teaching me the sword over the last few months, Dale's dislike of me has catalyzed.

"I've done what I can," I answer. "But—"

"But you've got no one to help you. I figured as much," Junn sighs. "No matter. You will learn, and learn quickly. I know you've got the talent for it, all you need is a little time. We should be getting back. Sun's going down."

Junn stands up and I join him as we trek the last two miles to the Compound.

*

It is a grand sight to be sure, not because of its beauty, but because of its sheer size. The walls of the Northern Compound are as tall as they are thick. Towering grey blocks that make you feel so small when you stand against them. I've walked the circumference once before, and if I counted my steps right, it's about three miles all the way round. The massive fortifications look so terribly unfriendly, not at all like the two men that stand watch at the huge gate, slightly open.

"You two are cutting it close this evening," Gale says.

"And don't think just because Junn's with you that we wouldn't lock you out," says Fen.

Junn and I share a laugh with the watchmen. They've always been a pleasant sight and always in good spirits, though I have no idea how, especially lately.

"Where've you been this time?" Fen asks. "The Flag keeping you busy?"

"I'm afraid so," Junn replies. "Work that's none too interesting, but I like to think that every bit helps."

"I dare say I believe you," Gale says. "You are a braver man than I. I don't think I'd last more than three breaths against the Bandits in the wild. You share some… terribly interesting company with the Flag. The others got back just a few hours ago. That big one gives me the shivers."

"He's not so bad once you get to know him," Junn chuckles.

"Right you are," nods Gale.

"Better be coming inside," Fen says. "If Carver catches us with the gates still open, there'll be hell to pay."

Junn and I mutter our agreement and head inside, saying our goodbyes as the gate thuds shut. Just like the walls, the buildings and paved roads in the Compound are nothing to look at. But they are strong, safe, home.

"I've got to head off and settle a few things with the Flag," Junn says. "I'll come find you when I'm through with it."

Junn departs and takes the street to the left and becomes lost by the people finishing the last of their daily business. I can almost see his destination from where I stand. The black and tattered flag of the old barracks flaps in and out of view from behind the tops of roofs. Even though some people still distrust them, they feel safer with the Black Flag tucked away, under the marker of a retired building for which the group is named. I continue to walk in no particular direction as the night descends, the windows of the shops and homes fill with candlelight and the engineers ignite the street lamps with long, slender rods. I notice a woman hefting a large bag that scrapes against the ground in rhythm with her step.

I would recognize that blue ribbon tied around her grey hair from a mile away. Next to the love from Junn, her's is a close second, if not dead-even. She is the mother I never had.

"Malory!" I greet.

"Viper!" Malory slumps the bag to the ground and turns at the sound of my voice. "Don't tell me that you were wandering outside the walls this late."

"I was, but hurried back to help you with that bag of yours," I smile.

"It seems to never end," she gives the bag a vengeful kick. "But I do it gladly."

"I don't know what Marcus would do without you."

"I don't think he would either," Malory laughs in a bright, yet sad way. "Viper, I have something that's been on my mind. You and—"

"It's been ten years," I know what she's going to say. "If he could change, I think he would by now."

"You know as well as I how Dale can be. But these jokes you and Junn play on him… I don't suspect they help your cause. Since their parents died of sickness I have taken care of them, just like you. Dale and Junn have always been inseparable and all each other had. Now you're here, taking what was once all Dale's."

"But that's—"

"And that's not your fault," Malory finishes. "Give it more time. All you can do is *be kind* and you'll have to trust he'll do the same. Now, you know what you have to do, don't you?"

I nod and lift my head to meet her aging green eyes.

"Off you go, then."

I hate that she's right. Playing pranks on people is so much easier than talking about how you feel.

"I love you, Viper, and so does Dale. Just make him see it."

Malory calls out a few last words as I take off in search of Dale. I can feel my heart begin beating faster. Why am I so nervous? It's not like I don't know what's about to happen. I'll be the bigger nam and try to smooth things over and Dale will act indignant and defensive. Junn usually is the one that breaks up the bickering when things get out off hand. It wasn't always this way, though. We used to get along and have fun together. I remember one summer spent in the streams and fields by the Resting Wood. Just the three of us.

I pass by Tao's workshop and take a detour in hopes that Dale is working with Tao on some project. I suspect that they are, judging by the smoke snaking out of the stout chimney. I walk towards the metal-bound door and I am hesitant to knock. This workshop is all Dale has to escape the world. That's exactly what he did after Bandits killed his friends in the platoon of Strong Men during their mission to protect the exterior farms' harvest. I've never set foot in Tao's workshop out of respect, but I feel like I am left no choice. I knock on the door. Tao soon opens the entrance and his grimy face breaks into a friendly smile when he sees me, the lines around his mouth and eyes showing cleaner skin.

The Compound's lead engineer is a kind, gruff looking fellow with a scraggly beard and hairy arms. He is a genius in his work and is the reason the streets are lit at night. Something about oil and pipes under the stone-paved roads. I don't pretend to understand it.

"Look who it is," Tao says. "What can I do ya for, Vipe?".

"Hey," I say. "Have you seen Dale around? I've gotta talk to him about something."

"Yeah. Actually, he's just about done putting the final touches on his new invention."

Tao steps aside, but I remain on the threshold.

"What's the matter?" Tao asks.

"It's nothing," I say.

I enter his workshop. It is very warm inside, and all over the broad workbenches and hangers attached to the grimy brick walls are Tao's contraptions and the tools he used to make them.

"What have you been working on?" I gingerly pick up a ring of sharp blades on a nearby table.

"I've been experimenting with a few things lately," Tao takes the ring of blades from me and returns them to the table. "And trust me, *that* is not ready. As I said, it's actually Dale who has come up with something very promising. I tell you what, he can surprise even myself."

"What is it?" I ask.

"It'll be better if you see it for yourself. Come, he's just through here."

Tao heads for a heavy leather curtain at the back of the room that divides the front and rear of the shop. And, once again, I hesitate. Behind that divide is the lion's den. As Malory used to say, the best way to confront your fears is to confront them. I head towards the curtain and duck through it after Tao. Behind the curtain is a large room with four more workbenches, some strewn with unidentified pieces of metal, and others with more fully formed projects. Dale stands hunched over one such bench.

"Welp, I think it's done!" Dale says, not turning away from his work. "It was tricky to have them spin inside the box without the tips breaking off. But by making the case just a hair bigger, I think I've done it."

Dale straightens up and drags his burly arm across his forehead, smearing sweat and grime all over. His proud smile vanishes when he notices me with Tao.

"What are you doing here?" he demands. "I thought this was the only place I could be rid of you. But I guess that you had to ruin that as well."

"If you'd just give me a chance to talk I wouldn't have to *contaminate* your alone time," I say.

"It's not what you say. It's what you do," Dale turns and washes his hands clean in a basin of water.

"Oh, come on. It was a prank!"

"How would you like it if I threw all your clothes in cow shit? Not so much, I imagine."

"First of all, it was the pig-pen. Second, it was only your shoes, and those wash out easy."

"It was every damn pair!"

"Alright," Tao intervenes, "enough with the shouting. Viper only came by to have a conversation with you. I asked him back here to show-off what you've been working on. So, if you please, would you kindly show it to him?"

Dale huffs.

He whips the hand towel to the floor and walks to the workbench and picks up a small box of a rich, dark wood. The corners and edges are plated with metal and shined and polished so finely that I can see my distorted reflection in them. The whole thing is put together beautifully and carefully.

"You open it like this. Matches are on a wheel. Wheel turns, scrape against the starter, they light."

Dale drops the device back on the table with that brief explanation and pushes by Tao and I.

Tao watches as Dale smacks the curtain aside. He turns towards me with raised eyebrows and gives a low whistle.

"That went well," he says.

"I was only trying to have a bit of fun. It was Junn's idea in the first place."

"As funny as that is, Vipe, I think that you just poked the bear. You never poke the bear."

"Clearly," I sigh.

"You should probably go after him and settle this before things really start to get out of hand."

First Malory, now Tao? This is not the first time advice like this has been given to me, but it is the first time I actually feel compelled to genuinely act on it. Could it be that I am growing up, maturing? Tossing Dale's boots in shit hardly speaks to maturity. No, I suppose it is high time that I leave that part of my life behind me. Be the bigger man.

I leave Tao's workshop and hurry over to Hector's Tavern. If I know Dale, this is the only other place he would be. I see him just before he places his hand on the front door. I call over to him. He looks over his shoulder, shoves the door open, and steps inside.

I chase after him and push through the doors. The interior of the tavern is tall and welcoming, well lit by candles and warm fire burning in the wide hearth at the far end of the hall. A scattered few patrons sit in sturdy and worn wooden chairs along even more worn tables. Their happy voices fill the room and echo among the rafters. I spot Dale sitting alone at a table, nodding his thanks to Hector as he places a mug in front of him. Hector is a large man with an even larger belly. His thick forearms ripple as he removes his fingers from Dale's mug. I step towards Dale as I piece together what I want to say.

"I've nothing to say to you," Dale buries himself into his drink.

"Good, that'll make this easier," I pause for a moment and prepare myself. "Listen, we have to get over this problem you have with me. I didn't do anything —"

"And that's just it, isn't it?" Looks like he does have something to say. "You *never* do anything wrong!" Dale bursts. "When you break the rules, everyone just goes along with it because you're the 'miracle child.'"

"And who says that? I'm no different from you… though I do appear to have more sense."

Dale shoots to his feet and knocks over his chair.

"Say that again!"

The scattered few around stop what they are doing and turn to watch us. The room falls silent.

"You think you're so great, don't you?" Dale spits.

"I didn't ask for this, you know!" I retort. "I never asked for Junn to help me. But you know what? He did anyway. He cared enough to burden himself with some kid on the side of the road."

Dale's nostrils flare as he opens his mouth to shout once again, but loses the words.

I speak quickly to calm him down.

"We used to have fun together, we used to talk to each other. All I want is to go back to that. I'm sorry."

The vein throbbing in Dale's temple beats slower. He bends and picks up his chair to sit.

"Damnit," he says. He takes three big gulps of hot mead and wipes his mouth.

"Do you—"

"Just shut up for a minute while I think."

I gingerly take a seat on my side of the table, purposefully not sitting directly across from him.

"Damnit!" He says again and downs the last of the mead. He finally looks at me. "You're a real pain in my ass. Look, it's not my place to decide if what Junn did was wrong. What's done is done. All I wanted after that night was to return to my life as usual. But you—"

"I—"

"But you," Dale holds up a finger, "have a mind of your own. You're clever, too much for your own good if you ask me. And I can't say that the jokes you play aren't totally without humor, I'd be a hypocrite if I believed that. I guess what I'm trying to say is that I never truly got used to you. Always hoping 'normal' was around the corner."

"This does my heart good."

Dale and I both turn to look up and see Junn approaching our table.

"Sneaking about, are we?" I say.

"I wanted to see where that was going," Junn smiles as he joins us, tucking combed, black hair behind his ear. "Does this mean the two of you've made up?"

"It was nearing something like that," Dale says, shyly.

"Well, from what I heard, it sounds promising. He may not be of our blood, but he's family. And kin always sticks with kin. When bones break, they grow back all the stronger. You know this from Malory, I'm sure — and I've seen the two of you break dozens of times. And this time, you'll mend stronger still.

Dale looks up at me, his eyes holding the light of Junn's truth.

"Well," Dale sighs. "If I can't get rid of you, then I'll just have to tolerate you."

"Fantastic!" Junn exclaims and slaps Dale on the back. "This calls for a drink!"

"I did see a couple of Hector's kitchen hands rolling in new barrels of his Mill House Ale a few days back. Maybe he's still got some with our name on it," I suggest.

"I do love his brews," Junn licks his lips. "What say you, Dale?"

"I wouldn't mind having a mug or two," He answers.

"Right," Junn claps his hands. "Let's get celebrating."

Junn takes a comical look around and stands up, casually walking over to the swing door that leads to the kitchen. He pokes the door open and takes a brief look inside. He then turns smiling to us, motions for us to follow, and disappears into the back.

Dale stands and, just as smoothly as Junn, vanishes through the door.

I stand to follow, but a familiar voice holds me still.

It is Carver and his cronies. They crash through the front door and overwhelm the interior with their presence, occupying an entire table. Carver proceeds to loudly share a tale of the cruel apprehension and killing of a buck and doe on the outskirts of the woods.

I never liked him.

I take a readying breath, stand, and briskly walk towards the kitchen. No one takes notice.

"I could just barely make out its shape in the dark," Carver boasts. "But all I needed in the end was this arrow to kill the beast!"

I stop in my tracks and turn to see Carver flourishing the arrow in question with a stupid grin plaster across his face.

"Now, it didn't die instantly, mind you," he continues. "Had to track it down a little ways into the Resting. But I found 'em alright."

Bragging about himself is true to his character, but Carver is not adept with bow and arrow. Ask any of our hunters and they'd tell you Carver is to archery as an infant is to riding a horse. Why would he make up fables about shooting a deer in the dark? It would give him an excuse for being outside the walls past curfew. But that just raises more questions. Questions that I don't have time for. I turn away from Carver's ramblings and search for Dale and Junn.

"It's about time! Forget how to use a door?" Dale laughs and downs what I can only imagine is not his first pint of ale.

"Don't worry about it," I respond, my words dampened against the wood reinforced clay walls of the cellar.

Junn and Dale sit on either side of a keg of Hector's Mill House Ale. They take turns filling their mugs and consuming the delicious amber contents in no time flat. Dale belches loud and I can smell the hops on his breath.

"Here ya go, brother," Junn swings an adjacent stool over to me.

Dale tosses me a pint glass as I take a seat between them. I lean forward and hold the mug under the tap and fill it with the sweet, malty liquid that froths at the top and spills over the brim.

"I guess this means you and I are stuck with each other," Dale points his freshly topped cup at me.

"Here, here," Junn takes a swig.

I stare down into the pint in my hands and memories of isolation fill my mind. I do not recall much of anything before Junn found me, but I do remember having nothing. I had not a home nor sure place to lay my head at night, only what I was able to take for myself to help me survive. As I give my thoughts to the swirling liquid, flashes of disconnected memory leap to the surface of my mind: encamping in verdant fields, running through the woods, propelled by the fear of death. But all that has changed.

"You can't get drunk by staring at it! You gotta do this!" Dale leans his head back and drinks the rest of his ale.

I join them at last and take a drink, feeling the sensation of alcohol running down my throat and warming my fingers; relaxing my tongue.

"Gods, I don't know how Hector does it," Dale says as ale dribbles down his chin. "I have half a mind to apprentice with that man just so I can learn his recipe."

Junn and I share a look and laugh.

"What's so funny?"

"If I had a silver piece for every time you've said that, I could buy you his recipe," I say.

"That's not fair!" Dale says. "I happen to recall Junn-boy over here promising to show me how to do that sword trick of his."

"Then you should also recall that I said I would only show you after you beat me, and," Junn motions with his hand in the absence of such a feat, "I have yet to see it."

"I would be more than happy to show you," I say.

"Dale turns his incredulous eye on me and gasps at Junn.

"What can I say?" Junn leans back casually. "Viper is a great student."

"We'll see how great he is!"

Junn and I both laugh at the look of surprise plastered across Dale's face. I almost don't hear the sound of Carver's voice above our heads.

"Did you hear that?" I ask. I am barely loud enough over Dale's drunken volume for them to hear me.

"Hey!" I say again, nudging Junn to get his attention. "I think Carver is coming."

"Pfft, who cares," Dale scoffs.

"I do. That guy gives me a bad feeling."

"Alright," Junn reasons, "if it'll make you feel better, we'll get outta here. Should be a way through here."

Junn rises to his feet and walks over to the stairs.

"But that's the way we came in! He'll see us," I protest.

"Ah, but what you didn't see is… this!" he leans his weight against a beam that holds up the ceiling.

The wood holds fast for an agonizing moment as I hear the steps above come closer, but gives way with a short thud and reveals a very narrow passageway, too low to walk through upright.

"Pretty cool, huh?" Dale says, noticing my look of surprise.

"Ladies first," Junn holds out his arm, gesturing for Dale to lead.

"Oh, my stars. You flatter me," Dale plays along.

"Let's get going. I don't want to—"

Carver's voice comes from the top of the stairs. I look up in horror and see Hector open the door and leading the perpetually dissatisfied Carver.

"Yes, yes. I have more down here," Hector says, apologetically. "Made a fresh batch the other d – what are you lot doing down here! You little thieves!" he shouts, rapidly coming towards us.

I look at Dale and Junn in a panic.

"Run!"

The three of us duck into the claustrophobic tunnel, away from Hector's enraged bellows. Dirt from the walls scrape off and gets in my eyes with every motion and idle spider webs only serve to add to our frenzied escape. After I sputter and nearly crawl through the tunnel for what feels like hours, we emerge into an equally cramped space, whose main decoration is a spindly metal ladder that ascends into the ceiling, capped by a circular hatch ringed with bronze light. Dale climbs up first, taking his time to keep his balance from the effects of the unlawful consumption of ale. He opens the way and lets the light of lanterns pour into the hole. Junn follows and I quickly take up the rear.

I reach the top and see that the hidden tunnel leads to Tao's workshop.

"Do I even want to know why there's a secret passage from here to the cellar?" I inquire.

"Sure ya do," Dale answers, enthusiastically. "Sometimes when I get particularly bored, I like to have a drink to get the ol' brain movin'. Helps to get projects thought of. And yes, Tao does know about it. Hell, he's the one who put it here," he laughs.

The Compound's warning bell suddenly rings loud and puts an end to our excursion, bringing our high spirits crashing back down to bleak reality.

A word cuts through the air. It rattles us from relaxations into attention like ice water as it goes through the Compound: Bandits.

"Keep Dale inside," Junn orders. "He's in no shape to fight."

"I will. Wait for me. I'll come back to help."

"No offense, Vipe, but you do not have the know-how to be of use. Take Dale and wait for things to clear up."

Junn takes off running out of Tao's workshop and joins a group of battle-ready men to meet and drive off the Bandits. I reluctantly escort Dale out of Tao's towards the Great Hall as he drunkenly mumbles to himself.

I soon have Dale on the wide steps to the Great Hall, a large and simple building with many windows along its broad side. Many of the Compound's children are shepherded here from the street where they played; I can see their little faces pressed against the windows, hoping to see what is going on. One of them looks at me as I climb the stairs. I wave at him and he ducks down out of sight. He peeks back up slowly when he thinks I am no longer paying attention. I shove open the heavy wooden door, studded with metal, with Dale on my arm. He fumbles with his feet, and I do my best to keep him from falling. I want to say that I laid him down on a soft bed before he collapsed. But saying that would make me a liar. Dale slips from my supporting hold and tumbles to the hard, flagstone floor next to a group of young boys and girls who are now scattering to avoid his falling body. He hits the floor and bounces from the impact. I wince hearing the sound as it echos comically through the deep hall and apologetically rearrange his body to a more… dignified position.

Now that Dale is situated comfortably, I stand and see a circle of staring eyes peering at me. They sit in a ring around Marcus who appears haggard with the arduous task of reacquiring the young ones' attention.

The role of leadership of the Compound comes with it many taxing and hair-greying responsibilities, but volunteering his time like this is not one of them. He does a very fine job at it. I remember when I sat around him like that outside the wall with a roaring bon fire to warm our bodies and stories of grandeur to fill our ears. My favorite stories were about battle and valor, he'd even sometimes mention the Black Flag, and those were my favorite of all. I would run back home and tell Malory all about it, but the person I really wanted to tell was Junn. But of course, he would be off with the Flag on one mission or another. He doesn't care much for storytelling.

"Donovan, Beth, you're going to miss tonight's story!" Marcus pleads. "Come, turn around and listen."

I find a secluded seat in the Hall and sit. With me out of sight, I quickly am out of mind, and the children turn back to Marcus and slowly settle down enough for story time.

"Good, very good," Marcus says. "This, as I said, is about your home and why you are here. It wasn't always like this, you see. Long ago, when the land was young and peaceful, and plentiful and green, we had no need of these walls that now keep us safe."

"Did we not want to be safe back then?" a little boy interrupts.

"Of course we wanted to be safe, Bernard. But safety meant something different back then – you'll understand better if you hear the rest. We lived in a similar way as we do now: farming, raising animals for food and trading with the other peoples of the land for anything else we needed, like medicine or tools we couldn't make ourselves. Our closest trading friends were a wise and noble people called the Pau'larin. They lived in the land across the River to the west, where the sun goes to sleep, and there they made great cities and roads to trade on. The Pau'larin taught us some useful things like how to store food so that it wouldn't spoil and the best way to tell if a snake is friendly or poisonous. But, I am afraid that much of the Pau'larin's history has become lost or forgotten. The world went on like that for year after year, trading, learning and living, until something happened," Marcus says eerily; some of the children gasp.

"An evil that slept in the far north started to make itself known, up where frozen water falls from the sky and where the ground is white instead of green. The Pau'larin saw it coming first and warned us about it so that we could be ready, but we told them that, if the evil came down for us, we would not be able to protect ourselves. So, the Pau'larin, with a great gift, saved us. While they kept the evil in the north from coming down, they made for us the Compounds, walls to keep us safe. For years, we, alongside the Pau'larin, worked day and night until the Compounds were finished, enough to shelter all of us that lived between the River and the towers of the Bymore Desert to the east. There are, as you might already know, two Compounds: one in the north, where we are now and one to the south, near the Southcap Mountains. By the time the Compounds were finished and all of us were safely inside them, the Pau'larin and their homeland of Tir Fwythland had suffered greatly. We have not seen or heard from the Pau'larin since then, over a hundred years ago. But we still have hope to see them and our other friends one day," Marcus stops and looks out of the windows at the dark night's sky. "That's all for tonight, everyone. I'm sorry that this story isn't like the ones that Malory usually tells you. But, it's good to know where you came from."

The kids barely hear Marcus' last words before they start talking, laughing and yelling, wandering around the hall. Marcus runs his hand through his aging hair, smiling to himself as he watches the children do what they do best. He starts to walk towards a door at the back of the Hall, but I stop him before he goes.

"Oh, hello, Viper," he greets. "I don't suppose that you are here for my old tales, are you?"

"I couldn't help but to hear it, actually. And I am curious."

"That is a natural reaction to hearing how things used to be compared to how they are now."

"No, not that," I say. "I am curious that you didn't tell them about the Bandits, how they sacrifice people to their gods, and wear their bones to homage them. Chalking all that up to 'an evil in the north' is an insult to the people that died to protect us from them. They deserve to know—"

"Hold on," Marcus raises his hand and furrows his brow. "You think that a bunch of children, whose only concern in the world is where they'll get into trouble next, should know the horrors of the truth? A truth that, just moments ago, attacked us at our home? Not one of them would be without nightmares if they knew that those bone-wearing savages came so close to where they lie down at night. I know that you lived out there in the wild for a time before we took you in, but not all of us have had that kind of upbringing. Look at them," he gestures to where a few kids are playing with a broomstick and some chairs, "you would have them grow up in an instant and forsake the precious years that they're allowed to spend in blissful ignorance?"

"They'll have to understand some time."

"They will. But until that fateful day, let them be happy and free of worry. Mature years come for all of us. It is the unfair nature of the world we live in that leads that maturity to some of us faster than others. Count yourself lucky, Viper. We sometimes go through difficulty not for ourselves, but for others so that when they are without answers we will be there to guide them."

Marcus turns back to the door and steps through it. I stand motionless on the outside of the door as it shuts in my face. I turn on my heel and walk out of the Great Hall, my feet thudding loudly as I march out. I am not trusted with defending my home from the Bandits. I'm not allowed to share the truth of the world. Too old to relate, too young to be a warrior. I step by where Dale lies, still unconscious, and see a group of the Compound's Strong Men returning from outside the walls, bearing fresh marks from the incursion; they are carrying stretchers towards the infirmary. The bloody men on them do not move or howl in pain. I see Junn walking in the back with a woman with thick braided hair as red as copper. She departs before I can make it to Junn's side.

"How many this time?" I ask, looking as the woman disappears around a building. I haven't seen her in a long while, but I'm sure that was Harlow.

"Six," Junn answers. "They're getting braver. They actually made it around the Ironwood Forest and raided one of our exterior storehouses; made off with our raw materials, mostly wood and iron ore. For some reason, Marcus ordered them there to set a trap for the Bandits. Didn't go well."

"Why would he want to make a trap for them?" I ask. I turn and walk with Junn back to our home and see worried people huddle in their windows and door frames to get a look at the aftermath.

"My guess is that he wanted to show that he's still in control. But everyday proves that the Bandits are gaining," he wipes his chin. "If you ask me, I suspect they're being ordered."

"Who do you think is leading them?"

"It's impossible to say. All that matters is what we can do about it, and we're running out of options."

"Surely the Black Flag has some ideas."

Junn walks on in silence for a moment.

"I fear that the people would be happier to die on their own than turn to the Flag."

"Why would you say that? They like you well enough, and I've seen Harlow get along with them before."

"People's minds are hard to change. Once the first thing they hear takes hold, the roots almost never come out."

As much as I dislike the thought, I believe Junn is right. Only when times are desperate have I seen the Compound lean on the Flag for help. A tool to discard after its usefulness; ready to be used again when the time comes. They sure came in handy when the frost of winter came early and destroyed the autumn harvest. And I would think that we would lean on them once again as the Bandits loom all around us.

"What's going to happen next?" I ask.

"We get through the day as best we can," Junn throws his arm around my shoulder, "and we protect each other."

The streets are empty and quiet

*

The next day brings with it an atmosphere of doubt and worry under the grey sky. The Bandit attack last night is all that's talked about, and so soon after the last one. I go about my morning chores and overhear some of their concerns. Concerns I, too, share. It will be a miracle if we are able to harvest this year's crop, especially the exterior farms, if there's anything left of it. The Compound's gardens, tucked safe within the walls are large indeed, but not enough to feed everyone. This will be a winter of rations and tightened belts for sure.

I hear a resounding ring as the bell tolls twice, the signal for a gathering. I recall just a small handful of times when that bell meant celebration, like the time when Dale and Junn brought in that haul of boar. I can almost taste the smokey meat at the thought of it. I finish my task and fall in with the stream of people as we head for the Great Hall. A chill wind blows.

"Okay, everyone, listen up!" Carver shouts over the crowd of people assembled in the Square. "Quiet down!" He looks pale and nervous. A sheen of sweat shines across his forehead from the cloud-covered late morning sun.

"That will suffice," Marcus says as he walks by Carver to take his place on the top step of the Great Hall. "As you all witnessed yesterday, we were attacked by the Bandits. They are roaming in the Ironwood in the south and the Resting Wood in the north. They raided one of our storehouses and took all of the supplies inside. So, in light of the growing Bandit threat, we are leaving for the safety of the Southern Compound."

Many voice their disappointment.

"How will we be safe on the road?"

"It's nearly winter!"

"This is entirely for your own benefit!" Marcus explains. "I have already sent a raven to Byron of the Southern Compound and he has agreed to take us in. We are expected within a fortnight."

"Will there even be enough room for us?" a woman calls.

"Of course! The southern Compound is larger, there will be a place for us in the West District. It will be a tight fit, but fit we shall."

"Will we actually be safe there?" I hear Hector ask. "I will not go through a move just so my last son can be taken from me!"

"Nothing is certain," Marcus answers. "But, as I see it, we will have safety among numbers. I hear that their militia under the command of Byron is not something to be trifled with. Together, we and those of the Southern Compound will make the Bandits think twice before attacking us again."

Marcus concludes his announcement and retreats inside the Great Hall. People remain and shout their questions and fears after him. Over the discourse, I see a disturbance at one side of the Square. I turn my head and see Junn standing with two others, Harlow and another who's hooded cloak hides his features. But he is a giant of a man. People swarm them as I approach the group.

"Ask all you like," Junn says, "but one at a time, and civilly."

"The lot of you are bastards for letting this happen!" An angry young man shouts. "You cannot force us to leave our homes and our lives!"

"That's not a question, but thank you for the input," Junn says, calmly. "Listen to me. I know that the Black Flag's reputation brings mixed feelings, but you know us. And you have to trust that we will continue to protect you as we make the transition to the Southern Compound. Your life will be as it has been, just with different scenery."

"My Da says the Flag's just a band of killers just like the Bandits," the young man declares. "He's in the Strong Men. He's seen what they can do to a man." He looks up at the giant with a mix of disgust and fear.

"If you've seen what we can do, then I'd watch what you say," Harlow snaps.

"Easy now," Junn rests a hand on sturdy shoulder. "Your father should also know that we fight with you, not against."

The giant remains in a menacing silence.

"I know that many of you are scared, I am, too. But you have to trust that we are no threat to you. Every single one of us will lay our lives down for your own if it comes to it. You, and the rest of the Compound are family."

Family. I remember that cold and rainy night I spent in that uncharted cave. The fear I felt when I heard the screams of death. I didn't believe I would make it to see the sunrise. Then, I remember how that fear and worry melted away. Family is a warm hearth and Junn has tended his well. He means what he says, and the frustrated young man resentfully accepts that. The crowd eventually disperse and whisper their shared distaste for the proposed plan as they head back to their homes. I wish I could be so strong as Junn, but I agree with the young man on one point he so poignantly made. I will miss hearing the birds singing and the cool spring air blowing on the Hill in the Resting Wood.

"If they're through with complaining, big guy here and I are off," Harlow abruptly announces and at once departs.

Junn gives a small grunt of understanding and rubs his eyes with this thumb and forefinger. He looks at me with sagging eyes.

"What do you think of all this?" He asks.

"A little nervous," I answer. "But how bad can it be, right?"

"How bad, indeed."

*

"Keep your wrist locked! Feet apart! Feet apart! They're keeping you planted so you don't get blown away in the wind!" Dale orders as our sparring metal clinks together.

Sweat mats my hair on my forehead, runs down my neck and plasters the shirt to my back. We've been at it since breakfast and now the sun bears down on me from the absolute clear sky above the yard behind the barracks. It's an unusually hot day. Dale pivots forward and brings his sword crashing against mine, and for the hundredth time today, my blunted weapon falls and skips across the ground. My hand stings and vibrates from Dale's hit, my shoulders ache and my legs throb with the effort of keeping my body upright.

"I said keep your wrist locked," Dale leans against his sword, casually.

"I can see why Junn was so keen to help you. You're pitiful."

I side-eye Dale as I stoop down to retrieve my sparring metal. He looks quite the smug idiot with his broad physique supported by a toothpick of an object like that. I thought that I had a good grasp at swordsmanship. I also thought that Dale was supposed to *help* me and not slowly bludgeon me to an early grave. I suppose I had this coming to be honest. If this helps him get over his grudges with me, then I am his punching bag.

"The position of your body is just as important as the thing you use to defend it," Dale recites. "It's just like a breastplate. When there is a weak point, the armor will shatter under pressure."

"I'd be able to keep the damn thing in my hands more often if you didn't treat me like a heated steel meant for shaping," I instantly regret what I just said.

"But that is exactly what you are! You are in need of a lot of shaping, that much is clear to see. Not even that, do you think that Bandits are less brutal than I am? If you think that I'm giving you a pounding, then they'll crush you."

I drag the round point of the sword through the dirt as I trudge towards the bench with my water skin. I drink deeply to replace all that I've sweated out. I'm feeling the onset of a headache coming thumping against my eyes.

"Don't look so discouraged," Dale says. "You'll get better."

I look up at him. He looks uncomfortable. Dale's not used to being nurturing and supportive, at least not with words. He's more accustomed to showing those sorts of things with the things he does, and just by being here with me, I know he means it.

"I should count myself lucky," I take the water and pour some over my neck. "At least you're forced to use these things and not that hammer of yours."

"Right you are," Dale laughs. "That hammer's meant for killing."

We stand and rest for a moment t. Now that I'm still, I can feel the subtle wind cooling me.

"Alright, break's over. Let's get back to it."

I've never in my life felt more exhausted. Dale certainly made good on his promise and put me through the ringer. I can barely feel the sensation of walking as my sore feet carry me out of the yard and back to the bed that awaits me. Footwork, stances, sore. That's all the day was composed of, but I don't care. All I want is to be good enough to maybe one day go off with Junn and the Flag to explore the world. That singular goal propels me through the street towards home, through the bedroom door and onto the mattress at last. I don't even bother to bathe.

*

Shouting wakes me from deep sleep. I rub my eyes awake, sit up and look out the window. I almost topple over from yesterday's punishing exercise. Others have been disturbed by the commotion. I see their pale faces at their own windows. The voices outside grow louder as their owners come barreling down the streets, proclaiming tragedy has struck this night.

"Murder!" A running woman cries. "The Black Flag have turned on us! Murder!"

Unable to process what is happening from the inside of my isolated room, I speed out into the quickly filling street. I flow with the people heading towards the Great Hall. I hear snippets of conversation attempting to string together a rational explanation to the actions of the Flag as I try to avoid stumbling over those around me. Some say that Marcus ordered them to kill, others say that the Black Flag have grown bored and decided to keep their skills sharp by killing a man in his own bed.

"Junn! Hey, Junn!" I see him walking with the crowd up ahead. He turns his head and his eyes find me and my waving hand. He steps to the side so I can catch up to him.

"Do you believe what these people are saying?" I ask. "The Black Flag wouldn't just kill, would they?"

Junn proceeds in a telling silence. He doesn't turn to look at me as he eventually gives an answer.

"The Flag's only job is to protect us. Anyone else that says different don't know what they're talking about."

"If they're protecting us, then why would Marcus have them kill a man? What do they know that we don't?" I ask more urgently. "Answer me! What's going on?"

"Wait and see for yourself."

The people funnel into the Square from various avenues, filling it faster than a cup dipping into a water basin; the Great Hall sits like an island in the sea of people lapping against its walls. On the top step stands Marcus with Carver very close behind, around whom stands a ring of protective bodies, shielding him. Carver pushes them aside to address the mob.

"People," he booms over the ocean of voices. "What you heard is true!"

The shouting redoubles. The scene is utterly chaotic. I look at Junn, but the steadfast expression on his face reveals nothing.

"A man in black, an assassin, crept into my home and attempted to take my life. I woke just in time to see his long, evil knife above my chest! I overpowered the would-be killer, but the coward managed to slink back into the pits at the old barracks before I could apprehend him."

What proof of this could Carver possibly have? Sure, Carver is an ass at the best of times, but enough so to warrant this? Carver continues to speak and answers my unasked question.

"Before he escaped, I was able to get a look at the coward's face. He had dead, black eyes! Who other than the Black Flag would harbor such a wretched creature?" He spits the words out as if they are as bitter as lemon."

"I say we get rid of the lot of 'em!"

The people burst out once more in incoherent accusations and words of damnation for trusting the Black Flag in the first place. I look to Junn again for any telltale signs of his thoughts, but he remains stoic as a rock as he turns his attention to Marcus as he wrestles the mob into quiet.

"Please, everyone, settle down!" Marcus pleads, desperate to restore order. "The Black Flag are, and have always been, the Compound's defenders."

The crowd roars.

"But!" Marcus holds up both hands. "But, it appears that they have now abandoned that role. Even though their motives are unclear, what is plain is that we can no longer place our lives in their hands. And as a result, I say that they will not be accompanying us to the Southern Compound in just a few day's time. If they hope that this attack and betrayal of trust will derail our plans, we must now show them our strength and resilience that comes with our unity. We are strong when we stand together as one!"

"Who will protect us if not the Flag?" someone shouts.

"The Black Flag should not be allowed to stay here! Kick them out, I say. Let them roam in the wild!"

"When we are gone, there will not be enough people to hold the Bandits at bay," Marcus answers. "Death by the Bandits will be punishment enough. Resume your preparations to leave and we will arrive at the southern Compound as though nothing at all happened."

Marcus and Carver retreat inside the Great Hall and the mob disperses. Junn turns and leaves. People avoid him like the plague, but most have sympathy in their eyes. I follow after him.

"Can you tell me what all that was about?" I ask. "You know the Flag better than anyone. Would they really do this?"

"They do not do anything without good reason," he answers.

"What reason would they have to kill Carver? That makes no sense," I say. "I never liked him, but still."

"Just because I am a member doesn't mean that they are obligated to tell me everything."

"Would you cut the cryptic answers and just be honest?"

Junn stops cold and faces me.

"Some things are bigger than you, Viper. Bigger than all of us. The Black Flag were here to hunt and bring in food when we were in need, they were there when the Bandits came knocking time and time again, and they have been there at every turn since. Some things, Viper, are not supposed to be known."

With that, Junn leaves and I do not follow.

Something about this is not right. Junn would never allow something like this to happen. Either the Black Flag knows something we do not, or Junn is hiding something. I return to my room and hope that Marcus is right about how everything will go back to normal.

CHAPTER 2

— Departure —

The Compound hums with activity as we prepare for the trek to the Southern Compound tomorrow. Lines of people carry their possessions to the train of canvas covered wagons and wide-bed carts outside the walls. Some haul chests and burlap sacks while others have rolled all they own inside large pieces of cloth tied with course twine. Sweat builds on my brow as I help those who have packed bags too heavy to carry on their own, glad that Dale, Junn and I finished loading out packs this morning. The carts are filling quickly, and there is not room for all that remains.

"Shouldn't we only bring the necessities?" I say to Dale.

"It never gets any better, I'll say that much. People always think their junk is vital for survival," Dale ignores a woman's rude stare. She hands her things over to Dale and he tosses it on the heap of people's possessions inside the covered wagon. "The only things you *need* are clothes and something to defend yourself with. We already have shelter, and food we can hunt. But they don't seem to get that."

"Some people are more sentimental than you, Dale," Junn says as he arrives at the end of the line with a red-haired woman, both carrying the last of the things to load. "I believe you both know of her, but I'd like you to meet officially. Viper, Dale, this is Harlow. She'll be joining us."

"Are you sure that's a good idea?" Dale asks. "The Flag is hardly on the best of terms with everyone. How can you trust them after what happened?"

"If you'd let him finish you'd have your answer," Harlow retorts.

I turn to look at Harlow. She is tall, standing equal to Junn, and by the way she tosses the last of the heavy bags past Dale and into the cart, strong too. She brushes back her thick braided, copper hair and puts her hands on her hips. Dale ignores the challenge.

"As I was saying," Junn continues, "both she and I agree that the Black Flag needs to show our loyalty to the people. Her presence in the caravan will undoubtedly ruffle some feathers, but it's a very long way to the Southern Compound. If all goes well, we should make the journey in less than four days. All I ask is that you treat her no differently than you do myself."

"And this runt will be joining us too?" Harlow says, looking at me.

"What did I just say?" Junn sighs.

"I don't want him getting in the way."

"Don't be too fast to judge," says Dale. "Sure, he's a pain in the ass, but he can handle himself."

I smile at Dale, but he looks away when we make eye contact.

"Alright," Harlow says. "But if he lags behind, know that I told you so."

Harlow turns and goes back inside the Compound.

"Just give her some time," Junn says. "She's rough around the edges, but I've known her for many years. I trust her with my life."

"She's okay in my book," I say. "Anyone that sticks it to Dale is an automatic friend of mine."

Dale shoves me as he hops out of the cart. We walk back through the gates together.

"Get one last look, boys," Junn says. "It's going to be a while before we come back."

*

Halfway to our new Compound, we have our first delay when one of the carts with the livestock hits a rock and breaks one of its wheels. The animals scatter and we spend over three hours chasing and corralling chickens and goats back into their cages. I would have suspected this event to generate more annoyance and frustration, but Junn helped make a game of it. Even as we walk the wild land, he is keeping spirits high. Not only him, but Harlow quickly proved her worth when she stopped a fight over which path to take through the Ironwood at an unplanned fork. I believe she takes most men by surprise as she roared above their quarreling. I know Carver can't stand her, mostly I suspect because she comes from the Flag, but the most obvious reason is due to a good deal of the Strong Men flocking to her leadership. I think they respect her direct words and find her a refreshing change from Carver's iron-handed control.

Dusk settles at the end of the sixth day. Feet thump on the lightly traveled dirt road, wheels dig trenches as they go, and a horse occasionally huffs and billows hot air in the chilly evening. Some scattered voices try at making conversation, but one can only talk about the weather or sore feet so many times before the topic is as dull and uninteresting as a wet blanket. I walk at the front of the caravan, easily able to keep pace with the horses as they slow from endless hours of work.

"Viper," Dale shouts at me.

"What's up?" I call back, not even turning to look.

"Stop getting so far ahead! It's difficult to watch everyone with you playing lead dog."

"And everyone knows that's your job, Dale," Junn says from beside a wagon a few spots from the front. That gets a laugh. It feels good to laugh; it eases the crippling disquiet.

"Sorry, I'll hang back," I say, stopping to wait for Dale and Junn to catch up.

"I know you're adventurous," Dale says, "but I don't want you getting yourself killed, understand? This isn't like that Hill of yours."

"He reminds me of you," Junn says, taking a large bite out of an apple. "Could never keep you out of trouble."

"Trouble, more often than not, you led me to," says Dale with a sly smile. "Remember when we walked over that mostly frozen river?"

Junn laughs and apple juice shoots from his mouth.

"I couldn't believe there was ice at all that late in winter, let alone enough for us to cross."

"It was do or die at one point, halfway across. Say, where'd they keep those apples?"

"Right behind the cart with the ducks in it," Junn jerks his thumb behind him. "In a wicker basket."

"Want one?" Dale says to me over his shoulder.

I nod enthusiastically.

"He really does remind me of you," Junn says, again. "When I returned from my voyage with the Black Flag over the Summer Sea, I remember Dale waiting for me with the horses on the outskirts of the port-city of Darpas. He brought something with him, a gift in a box. He handed it to me and I opened it. And when I did, the spring-loaded box launched spoiled cream all over my face. Harlow, of course, was very sympathetic and nearly fell over laughing. But when I wiped my face, I saw that there was something actually inside the box. Dale made a leather belt to hold my knives for me."

"And that makes you think of me?" I look over at him.

"Absolutely," he looks back at me with warm eyes. "A true jokester, but genuinely thoughtful at heart."

Dale returns to the front of the caravan with a crisp, green apple for the both of us. He tosses one to me. I catch it and sink my teeth into its skin. It's tart flavor makes my mouth water. The three of us walk onward with the caravan in a comfortable silence. I finish the apple and throw it into the trees.

"I'm going to get some rest," I say. "I've had enough time on my feet today."

I'll go with you," Junn says.

Junn and I step out of the caravan, allowing the horses and carts to pass.

"Why do the biggest carts have to be at the very end?" I joke.

"Because they'd know it'd upset you," Junn laughs. "I am very glad to see you and Dale getting alone again. He's a tough one to break, but once you're in, you're in for life."

"It took long enough. I never thought someone could hold a grudge for that long."

"Dale has always been set in his way. When we were young, before you and I met, he got in trouble because he wouldn't let the other kids use his little tools and Malory had to make him share."

"I can't imagine Dale using anything little."

"He used to be normal sized," Junn chuckles. "It wasn't until he started working with Tao that he got so muscular. Here we are," he says as the carts finally pull up. "Okay, Vipe, get some rest. I'll be just outside if you need anything."

I smile as I jump on the back of the slowly moving covered cart, duck under the heavy curtain and promptly pass out on a lumpy sack of hay.

*

I wake to the sound of raised voices, seething with malice. Voices that are getting louder. I bolt upright and spring out of the cart to see what is going on. Bandits. I can see them pouring out of the treelike on our right. They are wearing some kind of white armor that shines like pearls in the very last flames of the setting sun. They are sprinting out of the wood, waving swords and shields above their heads, emitting heart-chilling wails all the while. The Strong Men gather, forming a line of protection in front of the caravan. One of the Bandits poises his sword and leaps forward to strike, the blow piercing a Strong Man through the neck. Blood jets from the gaping wound and pools at his feet. Choked gurgles are all the man can muster before he collapses to the ground. The Bandit raises his weapon and lets out a nightmarish war cry. As the sunlight fades into darkness, the rays catch his sword and illuminate it just enough so I can get a proper look. It is bone, filed to a point with the entire length of one side sharpened. The armor he is wearing is bone, too, human or otherwise I cannot tell. The torso is made from another creature's ribcage; pieces of rotting flesh still hang from it. Gripped with terror, I can do nothing but stand and watch as the Bandits massacre the people around me. The victorious Bandit captures my gaze, eyes shining red from under his helm. He charges towards me. I cannot move. I can smell his foul breath as he screams.

"Get away from him!" Dale roars, leaping out from behind a wagon and smashing his hammer down on the Bandit's head. I can hear his skull giving way to Dale's blow, his bones splintering under the force. "Stay. Away. From. My. Friends!" Dale yells in righteous fury, accentuating each work with a strike from his hammer.

I am entranced by the sheer ferocity of Dale's attack. He was right, that hammer is for killing. By the time I am able to think he already dragged me away from the fighting, far up the line of the caravan. We stop running only when the sound has died down to a chorus of muffled screams. Dale sits me down behind the cover of a nearby wagon.

"What the hell is going on?" I hiss.

"I had to get you out of harm's way," Dale responds.

"Not that! Why are we being attacked?" I say, a little louder. "They'll die if we're not there to help."

"Keep a level head," Dale says, raising a finger at me. "They'll be fine. Junn and Harlow are with them, and they're both better fighters than I am." Crouching down, he sneaks to the corner of the wagon and checks the area. "Okay, Vipe, I'm going back. You stay here and watch our backs."

"And what am I supposed to do if I see someone?"

"Do what we taught you," he replies, leaving me in the horrid echo of death.

What am I going to do now?

Frustrated, I glance at my surroundings. Seeing no immediate danger, I shift along the length of the wagon and peek out from behind it. With the sun no longer in the sky, it is difficult to make out what I am looking at — save for the silhouettes against distant torch light. Standing up, I take a long, hard survey of the area. Not a soul in sight.

If he thinks he can just leave me here, he has another thing coming.

I sneak closer to the fray and the sounds of battle are becoming clearer. I can distinguish between individual voices, along with their anguished screaming. My hold closes on the grip of my knife as fear grows with each step. Apprehension makes me forget to breathe. The epicenter of the skirmish is quite near now and the sounds and cries of battle stay my already-hesitant pace. The ground I tread on is slick with mud and the scent of gore overwhelms me. I cannot see it, but I know the soil runs red. The stench paints my nostrils and clings to the back of my throat, causing me to gag and retch. I peer over the final wagon between the melee and myself and stare horror struck at Dale and Junn standing back-to-back, surrounded by at least three dozen bone-clad Bandits. They close in on my friends, their blood-stained swords illuminated in sharp contrast by the lead wagon's torches.

Letting out a barbaric bellow, one of the Bandits springs forward at Dale. Reacting in an instant, Dale counters the strike with his hammer and reaches over the guard of his shield. He stabs the Bandit's arm with the hammer's claw and, using his other hand, brings the Bandit up and over his head. Junn darts through the gap toward the line of savages. The moment before he makes contact, Dale throws the Bandit's body into the bloodthirsty wall of foes facing Junn, toppling them under the weight of their maimed comrade. Junn jams his heel onto the neck of one of the fallen Bandits and crushes his spine, then kicks up a shield and launches it at another Bandit's exposed throat. The jagged edge of the bone shield shreds their neck; crimson gushes down his torso. Junn whips around, plucks a small knife from one of the many hidden pockets, and throws it at a Bandit racing toward Dale.

Covered in blood and continuing to hammer at any Bandit that comes too close, Dale hurls an idle bone-helm into the crowd. The force of the impact knocks one's head back. Junn steps forward, snatches a sword from a dead Bandit's hands, and punctures the heart of the stunned foe.

I hear a battle cry and turn to see a tornado of copper hair tossing in the frenzy of battle. Armed with her battle staff, Harlow single-handedly fends off a small group of Bandits closing in on civilians. She rams her steel-capped weapon into a Bandit's jaw. A fraction of a second later I hear a stomach-turning squelch as it exits the back of his skull. Harlow doesn't even look as she shepherds the defenseless people away from danger, Harlow retreats out of sight. I am so preoccupied by the gruesome spectacle I almost tune out the footsteps creeping up from behind me.

I slowly look back to find a towering figure brandishing an enormous sword blocking my view. I scramble away and try to maintain a defensive posture, but I cannot get my knife up fast enough to deter his colossal hand reaching for my throat.

The giant Bandit takes the final step towards me, feet digging trenches in the slippery mud as he approaches, and slaps my weapon from my grasp. His calloused fingers wrap around my neck and squeeze with overwhelming force. Crusted black lips curl into a sneer as he lifts me off my feet. I fruitlessly kick my legs as my vision goes dark; the thud of my slowing heartbeat fills my ears. I pound as hard as I can on the crook of his arm, but it has no effect. In desperation, I reach out with both arms for the Bandit's disgusting face. Stretched as far as they can go, my hands make it to the Bandit's head and I dig my fingers into his eyes. He roars in pain and I feel the warm jelly as his eyeballs rupture. He drops me and covers his face with his hands. I hit the ground, free from his grasp, and frantically lash out with my foot, bashing the giant's ankle. The towering Bandit staggers from my blow and before he finds his balance, I strike again. He slips on the glossy terrain, topples over and slams onto the ground. I scramble to my feet, scoop my knife out of the mud and pounce on him, burying my blade into his chest. The giant lets out a final monstrous, tortured howl before the light leaves his eyes.

"Viper! Viper, where are you?" Dale calls.

I stand and run to the sound, but my feet catch on something hidden in the dark and I lurch headfirst into the hard wheel of a wagon.

CHAPTER 3

— Arrival —

The aroma of wood smoke and the concert of crackling timber stirs me from my fevered slumber. I hear hushed whispers, barely audible above the fire. I open my eyes and see a warm blaze beside me, and ones similar dotting the side of the caravan. The bodies around them are still and grim. I shift my eye to those around me and see the outline of Harlow's copper braids silhouetted against the fire with Dale and Marcus sitting opposite her, hard shadows cast across harder faces.

"Dale… Where am I?" I ask.

I sit up and immediately press my palm against my throbbing temple.

"Whoa, there. You took a pretty nasty knock to the head," Dale gently lays me back down. "Best you get some rest now."

"What happened? Why did those Bandits attack us?" I stammer, death still fresh in my mind.

"We had to cross hostile territory, as you know. Bandits don't take too kindly to trespassers," Dale answers.

"How many of us died?" I ask, flatly.

"We lost some good people, Francis and his three boys, Abby's sister and her husband, Bernard from the steel mill, and others. But thankfully, because of Junn and Harlow's quick thinking, we were able to hide all the civilians in the wagons and drive off the Bandits."

"And where is Junn now?" I sit up again and look around.

"He is why you and I are here right now." Harlow says.

"What happened to Junn?" I ask.

"In order for the rest of us to get away, there had to be a distraction. Junn was that distraction. He offered himself and killed or drove off the remaining Bandits. But enemy reinforcements arrived and they captured him, along with several others. We couldn't do anything to save him," Dale says.

"So why are we sitting here doing nothing? We have to go after them!" I protest.

"That would be unwise," Marcus says from across the fire. "Now that we are so close to the Southern Compound, the first order of business is to set up a preliminary defense, and establish control over the immediate area."

"How can you abandon Junn like this? He saved all our lives! If it wasn't for him—"

"That's enough, Viper," Dale says, quietly.

"Don't tell me that you're taking his side, too. We can't just sit here while those savages have Junn!" I scream in his face.

"And how the hell do you think I feel about this, huh? You think I *want* to be here while those monsters have our brother? You think that I am *choosing* to abandon him while his absence is tearing me up inside? No. I do this because it is what I – what we all -- *must* do."

"Dale is right, Viper," Marcus stands up. "In order to protect the collective, it may become necessary to sacrifice a piece of that collective to insure the safety of the remaining whole." Marcus addresses everyone. "Now, those of you who are not on first watch, get some sleep. We have much to do and still far to go once day breaks."

*

Three days. Three days of freezing rain, gloom and misery. It took us a whole day to bury the dead as best we could. We couldn't even send them away with the customary lanterns. After that, no one spoke, and I can barely sleep. I close my eyes and see demons leaping through smoke and fire. I cannot believe I thought I was ready to join the Black Flag, go off with Junn and see the world. I had no clue how terrifying the world can be.

But, as time goes ever on, the rain clouds break on the fourth day, and what a day it is. It's perfect, actually. The warm sun shines through puffy white clouds floating along the crisp blue sky. If only I had the heart to enjoy it. I turn my eye away from the migrating birds and look lazily at Malory and Dale as their heads bob in time with the jostling wagon. Dale stares down at his travel-stained boots with a faraway look; Malory meets me eye. She musters a smile.

"Nice to see the sun again," she says. "Sure could use it after…" her voice trails off; Dale crosses his arms. "How do you feel?"

"I've been better," I rub the back of my neck. "I miss him."

"I know, Viper. I know," says Malory. "Dale, are you doing okay?"

"Never been better," Dale stands up and hops out of the back of the covered wagon.

The cart's rumbling wheels and the thump of horses fill the silence.

"I can't imagine what he's going through," I eventually say.

"He lost a big part of his life," Malory says. "He has every right to be sullen."

"Everyone lost something. How are you taking it?"

"I'm sad. I'm saddened in a way I can't describe. But I am proud, too. What Junn did was brave and selfless to the utmost and I am so very thankful he was a man of such valor."

"Is," I correct. "He's still alive. I know it."

"Yes, of course he is," she wipes away a tear.

Before I respond I hear an excited commotion sweep through the caravan.

I hop off the wagon and hear people around me exchanging words of relief, others turn to the sky and thank the hidden stars for delivering them to safety. The Southern Compound is in sight. We come around a long bend in the road and the cliffside on our right recedes as the Compound's walls come into view. It looks quite the same as the one in the north, but even from here, I can tell it is much larger. I look above its solid walls and see, far away in the hazy horizon, the peaks of the Bymore Desert poking their heads over the ramparts, upon which the Compound's sentinels patrol. One of them spots us and a bell sounds loud and deep. I rush to the forefront of the caravan. There I find Marcus and Carver on horseback; Dale dangles his feet as he steers the lead wagon. I come in-stride beside him.

"We're finally here," I say up to him.

Dale does not turn his eyes away from the road; doesn't say a word.

"I hope that the West District is big enough for us."

No response.

"Say, Marcus," I call over to him. I glance at Dale, still stoic.

"What is it?" he turns his ear to me.

"Will Byron help us track down the Bandits that attacked us?"

Marcus turns his eyes to me; Dale's body goes rigid.

"Byron's first concern should be getting you people inside the Compound," Carver answers.

"I think that there is much to do before we hold discussions about the Bandits," Marcus says. "Rest assured, Viper. Something will be done."

"When?" Dale challenges.

"Soon, soon," Marcus tries to smile. "But like Carver said, first we—"

"That's what I thought," Dale huffs.

"What did you say?" Carver stands in his stirrups.

Dale glares at him and says nothing.

"And that's what *I* thought. Better watch what you say," he sits back down.

"Keep a cool head," Marcus says. "We are guests here, so if I hear any trouble, from either of you, I will leave you to Byron's judgement."

Marcus looks ahead as the Compound's gate opens and a short man with a bald head and bushy brown beard emerges on horseback, accompanied by four armed men.

"Welcome, our northern neighbors!" the short man greets. "I am Byron, commander of the Southern Compound."

"Hail!" Carver responds.

"I trust that your journey has been both swift and pleasurable?" Byron asks and approaches the head of the caravan.

"Sadly, it was neither," Marcus answers. "We had a bit of trouble—"

"We were all nearly slaughtered by Bandits," Dale interrupts.

We all turn to Dale as he dismounts the wagon.

"Tell me, Byron. Do you have any love for the Bandits?"

"Of course not!" he answers, taken aback. "I don't see why you even need to —"

"And do you have any love for your countrymen?" Dale continues.

"I told you to shut it," Carver hisses.

"Come now, Dale," Marcus says. "We can discuss this matter at a later date."

"If you do have any compassion for your fellow man," Dale looks Byron dead in the eye, "then help me get revenge for my brother, and the other men they stole."

"I am starting to see now," Byron strokes his beard. "Your brother was killed by the Bandits."

"Not killed," I answer. "Captured."

"Ah. How dreadful. I offer my sincerest condolences."

"Do not talk as if he *is* dead," Dale growls.

"Alright," Marcus intervenes. "It is high time we end our journey. We have kept everyone waiting long enough. Byron, would you mind escorting us into the Compound?"

"Yes, of course!" he claps his hands, turns the horse around, and leads us through the broad gates.

Carver and Marcus dismount and cross the threshold on foot; Carver glances at Dale and spits on the ground.

"Putrid man," Dale says under his breath.

"Let's go," I say. "Getting off the road and cleaning yourself up will do you good."

We follow Byron and his soldiers into the spacious courtyard, around which the people of the Southern Compound gather. Some whisper to their neighbor as our procession enters and fewer still shout welcome. Our wagons and carts quickly fill the courtyard and we begin unloading them; some are still stuck beyond the gate. Byron climbs onto the wagon at the center of the masses and opens his arms wide.

"Welcome, our northern neighbors! Allow me to be the first to say that we are glad to have you. You will find the West District through that way," he gestures to the paths and roads with his right hand. "It will be enough to house all of you. However, many will need to double-up on rooms for all to have a roof over their heads. Please, make yourselves at home, and do not feel a stranger and ask either Marcus or myself about anything that you might need."

Byron hops back to the ground and walks over to Marcus and Carver; the people of the Northern Compound filter through the streets with their possessions towards the West District, led by this Compound's humble soldiers.

"Marcus," Byron says. "Could you by chance spare someone to aid me? We ran into an issue with our forge and my engineer, Haedrig, cannot figure it out. And it is over my head as well."

"Absolutely. Anything to repay your generosity. I am sure that Tao will be more than up to the challenge."

"Splendid!" Byron exclaims. "Have him—"

"Someone talking about me?" Tao smiles as he appears from the bustling crowd.

"Speak of the devil and he shall appear," Byron says. "Yes, I was just mentioning to Marcus about a special problem that demands a man with a skillset such as yours."

"Oh, wonderful! It's been long enough since I had something to tinker with. Say, Dale, care to join me?"

Dale turns his weary head to meet Tao's happy expression.

"Why not," he replies.

I watch as Byron shows Tao and Dale the way to the forge. Tao pats Dale on the back. They vanish behind the buildings and I return my attention to unpacking and moving chests, bags, and bundles of others' possessions to the West District. I follow the stream of people along a broad street, enclosed on either side by tall structures of tan and grey stone; some hold signs that tell their business or trade: the bakers, craft stores, and inns. The street goes on and the buildings fall away as I enter the Compound's Square, at the forefront of which lies the Great Hall. Just like the one I have known my whole life in the north, this Hall is of impressive size and humble design. Tall windows poke through into the interior and a wide stair leads to the two dark wooden doors. The Square has additional similarities as well: stalls and awnings stand in front of the buildings around the perimeter, housing stores of various trinkets, food, or trades. A low rising wall and stout architecture divide the Square along the edge so as to provide a sense of order once people give patronage to these shops, and the ground is paved with smooth, grey stone, all of which is centered around a well, wider and taller than the one I am accustomed to. The stream of people carries on through the Square, down roads to the left, and eventually ending in the West District. I set my eyes on one of the buildings set aside for our housing and quickly enter so that I can secure a space for both Dale and I. I walk through the front doors and poke my head into the rooms along the first floor hallways. I get lucky and find two small, unoccupied rooms. I lay my things on one bed, then walk next door to claim the other and return to the courtyard for a second load.

I shuffle through the congested streets and see Tao speaking to Dale. It doesn't look like the repairs to the forge had any effect on him. I make my way over to them.

"Hey, Dale! I saved us some rooms," I say.

"I should find some space, too," Tao says, "before I'm stuck sleeping on the floor."

"Great. Where?" Dale asks.

"Three buildings to the right once you enter the West District."

"Thanks."

Dale trudges by me and becomes lost in the throng.

"I've never seen anyone so depressed," Tao comments. "It's not as if he has not earned the right, though. I don't know if I could handle it any better if I were him."

"He's having a rough time at it," I respond. "Did fixing the issue with the forge help at all?"

"No, sadly. He didn't say a word the entire time. May as well have been a walking tool chest."

"I wonder if Marcus or Byron have anything for him to do. Even if it's menial, he needs something else to concentrate on."

"I'm pretty sure I saw them heading for the Great Hall. Might still be there."

"Thanks, Tao."

I head for the Hall, climb the stairs, and step through the open doors. The air inside is cool and lanterns hanging on thin chains from the ceiling light the interior. At the back of the room is a raised shelf with a long table, presiding over the whole of the Hall; I see Marcus, Byron, and Carver sitting there. I can hear some of what they are saying.

"How terrible," Byron laments. "Ambushed? I had no idea that the Bandits moved so far south."

"They are becoming more of a presence in these latter years," Marcus says. "And I am indebted to you for sheltering us. I don't know how much more my people could take."

"It was the moral thing to do," Byron says, dismissively. "I will be sure to double our guards to prevent any more attacks."

"You'll need to do more than that," Carver says. "The Bandits are ruthless and have to be dealt with directly. Sitting here passively is only begging for trouble. Appoint me Vanguard Captain and I'll deal with them."

"Don't be rash," Marcus says. "We've only just begun to settle in the Compound and all of us could benefit from a respite."

"It sounds to me that you would allow the Bandits to be all: judge, jury, and executioner. Give me the soldiers and let us be the ones that judge!"

"It would be wise to keep your tongue in-check, Carver," Byron says, firmly. "You are guests here. Do not let your head get too big for the rest of your body."

"At least *my* head has hair!" Carver shoots to his feet, his chair clatters to the floor.

"Carver, enough!" Marcus demands. "Sit down. You're making a fool of yourself."

Carver looks over the room at the handful of people watching him. His face grimaces when his eyes find me. He aggressively picks up his chair and throws himself into it; I approach the table.

"Viper," Marcus exclaims. "What brings you here?"

"I was just curious if there was anything I could do to help."

"This young lad of yours has a generous heart, Marcus," Byron comments.

"He's always had a mind for others."

"It's just that my brother, Dale, he's been very gloomy recently… ever since the caravan. I want to know if there's anything you could have him do to take his mind off things."

"The man with Tao?" Byron says.

"Yes, sir."

"I do believe there is something that he can handle for me. I was going to have Haedrig take care of it, but since it appears that another would benefit more, I suppose Dale can do it instead."

"Thank you, sir—"

"Please, there is no need to be so formal. I insist you call me Byron. 'Sir' is so pretentious," he laughs.

"Thank you, Byron," I correct. "What is it that you have for us?"

"It's a very simple task, but one that requires a good deal of physical strength. I need a team to go out into the Ironwood and gather timber for both our newly repaired forge and other venues. But, since the sun is setting, nothing need be done until the 'morrow. I'll have Haedrig tell Tao the details. He is going to be a very busy man."

"Thank you again," I say.

"Think nothing of it," Byron says with a wave of his hand.

I turn around and exit the Hall. Dusk settles over the Compound and I head straight for the West District. I come to the building and walk the hall until I reach my room. I have my hand on the doorknob, but before I push the door open, I stop and open Dale's instead. It glides open and I see him lying on the bed, fully clothed and snoring. I smile and gently close the door. I guess all of the day's stress tired him out. I hope that the morning brings a better mood.

CHAPTER 4

— Questions and Enemies —

Autumn chill creeps into my bedroom and stretches its cold fingers under my blankets. I wake up and for a moment I forget where I am. Then, the memories flashback in their horrible sequence. I lie on my back and stare up at the boring plaster ceiling, not wanting for anything but to go back in time. I take a long breath through my nose and stretch out my legs as far as they can go and hold that position till I feel light in the head; I let go, roll out of bed, and dress.

I shuffle into the hall and stand in front of Dale's room. So many times before I have done this happily and with a lighter heart. Junn was often standing close by, ready for the three of us to hunt, drink, or just waste time together. I raise my hand and knock, knowing that this day will bring none of those things. I wait a moment but he doesn't answer. I open the door anyway. He is still laying in the same position as I found him last night, a dark circle on his pillow from where he drooled in his sleep.

"Dale," I say softly. "Dale, get up. We've got chores to do."

He rolls over.

"What are you talking about?" he grumbles.

"Byron gave us a special job. Come on."

Dale groans and buries his face into his pillow.

"I'll be out in less than a half hour," he mumbles.

"Alright," I close the door.

I head out of the building and go in search of Haedrig while I wait for Dale to become human again. The sun begins its course across the sky, shining through dawn's wispy clouds and turning them a translucent, burnt orange. The open spaces in the West District are empty at this hour. Nearly a week on the road with a Bandit raid is hardly the recipe to put a spring in your step. I walk the streets and more lively sounds come to my ear as I near the Compound's Square and I ask around for Haedrig's smithy.

"Oh, he just passed a moment ago," a man with less than all his teeth says. "Went down that way. No need to hurry and catch him, he's slow enough these days."

I thank the man and follow the direction where he pointed with his chin. Soon enough I see a slim man with a slightly hunched back and silver blonde hair that appears to have been in a fierce battle with a tempest, though no wind is blowing. Hoping he is my man, I approach him.

"Hello," I say. "I'm looking for Haedrig. Do you know where I might find him?"

The man stops and turns at my voice and I see his face. He has thin eyebrows, a thin nose and almost no lips at all. He has deep cut lines around his very light colored eyes and more lines in the youth of their formation everywhere else. The man looks terrible.

"Look no more, I am he," Haedrig says.

I look at him dumbly, not realizing that my mouth is wide-open.

"Is something the matter?"

"Oh, sorry," I say. "I wasn't—"

"Expecting this?" He holds his arms away from his weird body. "I'm afraid no one does. Truth be told, I never wanted this job. If anything good came of the Bandits, Tao's arrival is surely one."

I am still held in a silent shock, this time, mouth closed.

"You'll find him down that way, round the corner to the right and onward a few dozen paces," Haedrig turns and hobbles away. "Thank god for Tao."

I stare after him and utter confusion, but soon collect myself and follow his directions. I find the smithy, a two-story structure with a very large circular chimney and thick panes of glass. A tent is erected before the building with a few dirty men hefting crates from a mule drawn cart. I approach the workers and hear Tao's voice issuing his commands.

"Set that down here, carefully — carefully! These are very delicate instruments," he says to a hazy-eyed man. "You may not care for them but they are irreplaceable!"

"Things going well?" I ask.

"They are going, but in what direction is yet to be seen," Tao massages his eyes. "Haedrig mentioned you would be coming."

"I ran into him a moment ago. Is he alright?"

"I dare say he is now — for the love of god, gently!" Tao barks, losing his patience. "Honestly, it's a marvel Old Haedrig got anything done with these donkey-brains," the cart mule turns his head as if he heard and understood the insult; it swishes its tail.

"Regardless," Tao continues, "to answer you: yes. It turns out the man you and I met is Haedrig II. His father, the first, died a few months ago and the stress of the job was running his son ragged. So, he gave full ownership of his workshop to me, and what hell it's been already."

"You mean, besides all this?" I gesture to the large piles and stacks of Tao's relocated tools.

"You don't even know the half of it. Nearly everything in the workshop needs tending to from the amount of negligence, the chimney is all stuffed with squirrels and shit, the Compound southern wall has a crack in it. A crack! Can you believe it?" He massages his eyes again, cursing quietly to himself.

"Byron said that there was firewood to be gathered," I say. "Maybe that being checked off the list will get rid of your headache."

"Yes, of course," he says. "Come this way. I'll show you where to go."

Tao walks to the back side of the tent to a table with papers strewn about its surface.

"Right here," Tao jabs his finger onto a circle drawn on the map.

"Okay, I'm here," we both hear Dale say as he enters the tent.

"Splendid!" Says Tao. "Just in time. I was just beginning to show Vipe the way to the firewood."

"So I've heard. Where is the wood that you need?"

"It's an especially tough wood called Rock Elm. It burns twice as hot as the wood I usually have. You'll have to go about five miles into the Ironwood to find the bulk of it. I'll need as much of that as you can bring back," Tao hands me the map. "I've already spoken with Haedrig and he agreed to set aside three of those big wagons and some extra hands. That should be enough."

"Why do you need special wood?" I ask.

"For weapons," Tao says. "Since Bandits are making more trouble, Byron says make as many blades and shields I can. I hope we're ready."

"Ready for what?" I laugh, nervously; no one joins me. "You think they would attack the Compound? Do you see how thick these walls are?"

Tao leans and stretches his back. "Who the hell knows."

"Don't worry. We'll get what you need."

Tao pulls his lips into a tight smile; Dale remains quiet.

"Alright, let's go already," Dale steps forward and snatches the map from my loose grip. "It's about time I hit something."

He heads straight for the stables. Tao and I share a look, both signaling the same thing: this oughta be good.

*

It takes us a little over an hour to reach the location marked on Tao's map, and the sun has just about made it to its peak. We brought two of Haedrig's old apprentices — now under the tutelage of Tao, Henry and Shane. The two resemble nothing of their old master. Both are brawny, hairy-armed men, one with a bushy beard and the other wears his shoulder-length dark brown hair in an iron-laced braid. They keep their eyes focused on the shifting trees, scanning between their shadows. Dale draws the horse to heel and our train of wagons rumbles to a halt. Our boots thud and crunch on the forest floor and as we collect our gear. I glance around and noticed that all the trees here look frighteningly like the ones I saw on the way from the Compound. Uniform, steel gray trunks all as thick as a wagon wheel or larger.

"We'll go in groups," Dale takes charge. "You two go to the north and east. Viper and I will go west and south. Let's not take too long out here. No telling if Bandits have come this close to the Southcap Mountains. So watch each other's backs. Meet here in four hours."

It is eerily quiet as Dale and I weave through the strong trees. I am so used to hearing the chirping of the birds or the scamper and chatter of squirrels. This far south and this late in the year looks to have driven both from the forest and the usual sounds are replaced by the crackling of the map as Dale checks it occasionally. Soon, the trees part and reveal a shallow clearing that houses a tiny shed, a few sawhorses and rusty looking chains and hooks under the shelter. Dale makes for the shed, opens the lock and takes out a beaten sled.

"Let's get to it," Dale says.

I follow him back into the trees and we begin hacking away at the tree trunks, taking turns swinging, wrenching free the buried hatchet and repeating until the timber cracks like lightning and comes thundering down to the cold earth. We take the tandem saw from the sled and rake it back-and-forth across the wood until the sled is piled with manageable pieces. Dale drops the saw to the ground and heaves the chunks of Ironwood back to the clearing. Veins spider across his arms and his face reddens from the strain of it. But his years in the forge and Tao's workshop have prepared him and he pulls like a workhorse and, by himself, has the wood to the sawhorses and begins splitting the wood with great and powerful swings. He hacks and drives his hatchet into the wood again and again, each swing looking stronger than the last. Dale raises the sharp edge of the hatchet high above his head and brings it streaking down and chops through everything, the wood, the saw table, all of it; even his hatchet snaps from the force. Dale beats the defenseless wood with his headless ax and bellows in frustration. I know better and stand aside, waiting for him to tire himself out. He whacks the wood once more and hurls the ax handle deep into the woods. He finally throws himself down, sitting on the pile on the sled brought low from our efforts, breathing heavily.

"I'll kill all of them."

I walk over to the split wood scattered about the clearing and stack it neatly off to the side. I say nothing. What more is there to say? No. The only remedy for him is action, reckless or otherwise, it doesn't matter.

Dale stands up, finds something else to cut with, and goes back into the forest. I finish stacking the wood and go after him. It's a few hours before silence is eventually broken.

"One more trip to go," I look from our dwindling pile of wood over to Dale. He returns my gaze with a gaunt look.

I stack the split pile of timber in my arms and place them on the sled. I turn back for more and see Dale duck down fast.

"What's up, Dale?" I drop to one knee.

Dale mimes for me to be quiet and points ahead to a spot a few meters away. I crouch-walk beside him and look through thick tree trunks and grizzly bushes and see Carver walking alone through the forest. What in the hell is he doing here? Surely he's not here to help us. Carver keeps moving, looking angry and bemused, and becomes lost in the maze of trees. Dale creeps after him. I follow. What else is there to do? There's no stopping Dale. He found his action. We keep our safe distance and come to a pause behind mossy rocks and prickly bark of the trees as Carver approaches someone waiting for him. A Bandit. He stands expectantly, wrapped in bones, and holds a vertebra of some unfortunate creature in his hand, tipped with jagged metal. Carver stands before the Bandit and crosses his arms.

"What's going on here?" I whisper, but my query is met with cold silence as Dale monitors the exchange. The distance between them and us makes it difficult to hear what the two are saying, and I dare not move closer. But from the Bandit's aggressive stance, and Carver's stormy attitude, there seems to be a problem.

Carver uncrosses his arms and jabs his index and middle fingers square in the Bandit's chest, raising his voice at him.

"But you weren't supposed to take Junn!"

My heart jumps into my throat.

I can see Dale shuddering with vehemence at Carver's words. He goes to stand, but I hastily pull him back down.

"What the hell are you doing?" I hiss.

"Are you deaf? Junn might still be alive!"

"And you won't be if you go out there. What would you do anyway? Neither of them would tell you anything."

"I'll rip the answers out of 'em," Dale says, absolutely overcome.

"Listen to me," I take a worried glance towards the angry pair, but they haven't noticed us. "Carver is Marcus' right-hand man, if we are caught spying on him talking with a Bandit it would mean the death of the both of us. You think that Carver will believe that we found him by chance?" Dale's body relaxes, only slightly.

"Bloody hellfire, why do you have to be right?" Dale says.

"Let's finish up and get this wood back to Tao. Figure out what we're going to do," I sneak away back to the wagon. Dale hesitates, still deadly focused on the Bandit. Eventually, he follows and I see color returning to his face as the fire of his will reignites in his eyes.

*

Our full wagons dig deep trenches in the ground as we near the edge of the Ironwood Forest. Henry and Shane talk between themselves, but I cannot discern their words over the whirring hum in my mind. I see Dale's jaw muscles clench and unclench as his eyes are fixed on the trail before him. I always disliked Carver, but to be vindicated in this manner does not give me the pleasure my imagination once prescribed. I glance over my shoulder at the talking men. Once I determine they're paying us no mind, I scoot up to the front beside Dale.

"What do you think we should do?" I ask.

"I don't know."

"Well, we can't do nothing."

"I'm aware of that. I just don't know what to do *yet.*"

I look up towards the setting sun, at the skeletal trees, cast in a hard and brilliant golden outline, and at the last flocks of birds moving out for winter. A scuffling sound of scampering feet draws my attention away from the sky. I turn just in time to see a white, cottontail retreating to the safety of a thicket, hiding from our approaching wagons.

"When we were ambushed by those Bandits, how many did we lose?"

"Why ask that all of a sudden?" he raises an eyebrow.

"Since we saw Carver, I've been running the ambush over and over in my head, and I think something is off."

"Oh?" Dale says. "And what's that?"

I pause for a moment.

"Remember when I went to take a nap at dusk, and Junn went with me?"

"Yeah?"

"And where were Marcus and Carver?"

"They… I think they were in the third – no, second wagon from the front," he answers, tentatively.

"Far away from where Junn was, right?"

"Yes," he furrows his brow. "Where are you going with this?"

"I think that maybe it wasn't chance that the Bandits attacked us."

"What are you saying, Vipe?" Dale asks, stern and serious.

I ignore his probing and press on. "Who did the report say was taken along with Junn?"

"Let's see…" he scratches his stubbly chin to recall the information. "John, Mortdecai, Clive, Ray, Cayde, Deklen, Fen, and Gale are all the names I remember… And they were all in the same group as Junn," Dale's face twists into an angry scowl. "You're not saying that the Bandits were targeting his group specifically, are you?"

"I think it's too convenient to assume otherwise," I respond.

"Hang on a minute. If you say that the Bandits targeted Junn's group on purpose, why would Carver be upset about his capture? Was that not the point?"

"I also thought that was strange. There must have been a last minute change of plans and the Bandits didn't tell Carver, or Junn was just at the wrong place at the wrong time."

"Why would the Bandits want to capture Junn in the first place?"

"To get him away from the Compound? To weaken us, demoralize us?" I say. "But that points to some kind of actual leadership in the Bandit ranks, and you and I both know following orders is not one of their strengths."

"Just more questions and more enemies," Dale says, distastefully.

"All that we know as fact is that Carver and possibly Marcus are somehow tangled up with the Bandits. They're up to something and that cannot be good for anyone."

As I finish speaking we emerge from the trees and the Compound's grey walls come into view. Disquiet and trepidation fall on me like a load of bricks as I think about who is lurking inside. For now, I have to keep this a secret between Dale and I, or else we may be the next target on Carver's list.

*

"Thank you! Ah, finally we've got some warmth!" Tao stretches his palms out towards the roaring furnaces. "With this burning hotter than the Bymore in summer, we'll have the Compound armed before you know it," he wipes his hand off on his already filthy pants and extends it to Dale. "Once again, I owe you one."

"If it's not too much to ask," Dale shakes his hand, "then I'd like to call in one of those favors."

"Alright, Whatcha need? Stronger hammer? Two hammers?"

"I want to know what you saw during the attack on our caravan."

Tao cocks his head slightly, but obliges.

"I was in one of the covered wagons in the middle of the caravan. Got as far as I could from the Bandits when they came at us," Tao scratches his head.

"And what about Carver? Was he there, too?" Dale asks, eagerly.

"Yes, he and Marcus were inseparable the whole time leading up to the ambush," Tao replies.

"And after?"

"Well, after that I didn't see much of anything. Like I said, I was hiding with the rest of the people. I admit now I'm ashamed I was too scared to fight," Tao answers, bluntly.

"Damn," Dale says under his breath.

"Although, after we recovered from the battle, I did happen to hear Marcus saying that he was upset about the Bandits."

Dale's eyes lit up.

"Who was he talking to?" I blurt out.

"I couldn't see, most likely that Carver fellow," he admits.

Dale shoots me a knowing look.

"Well, thank you for your answers. That's all I wanted to know," Dale nods at Tao and gestures for me to follow him out of the forge.

"I was serious about making you that hammer if you change your mind," Tao calls after us.

"Maybe," Dale closes the door.

CHAPTER 5

— Tireless Lessons —

"Viper, wake up," I hear a voice calling me from somewhere outside the miasma of my mind. "Wake up," the voice repeats more gruffly.

"Alright, I'm up. What?" I groan.

I blink and rub my eyes awake and see a brawny, square-jawed man standing in my open door. I recognize the man through hazy vision as one of the Strong Men from the caravan that left Carver's leadership.

"Harlow says she needs you," the man announces.

Whatever she is doing, she can probably do it by herself. I reluctantly tear myself out of bed and dress, fearing the consequences for ignoring Harlow's commands.

The freshly risen sun dazzles my eyes as I step outside. I shade against the rays and try to scan the open space of the West District for Harlow. She is nowhere I can see. You would think she would at least have the courtesy to meet me out here. I walk through the district to the Square and trudge over to a working crew gathering around the wide mouth of the well. I see the brawny man among them.

"Hey!" I call to him. "Have you seen Harlow?"

"She was here a moment ago," he says. "But he might."

I follow the direction of the man's hand and my heart violently skips a beat.

Carver is towering over me and carries an enormous digging bar over his shoulder.

"That vicious harpy is at the gate," he says, tersely and shoves by me.

I do not even pause to thank him before I start running for the gate, hoping that Harlow is not the kind of person that views punctuality as a virtue…. And to get away from Carver.

The gate comes into view and I see Harlow leaning casually against the wall.

"You're late," she states.

"It would've helped if you told me where you were," I retort.

She stands up straight and uncrosses her toned arms.

"If I wanted a smartass, I would have asked – either way, I still would've ended up with you," she laughs and slaps me on the back.

"What do you want?" I ask, a touch irritated.

"You and I," she rubs her hands together slyly, "are going hunting."

"Hunting what? Most of the animals worth hunting are gone for the winter."

"Don't worry your little head with the details, just do what I say. The first thing you'll need is a sturdy pair of boots because it's a long walk to the mountains."

"Walk?" I ask, incredulously. "We have horses for a reason, you know."

"And why would we ride a horse? That would only rob you of the perfect opportunity to put some real muscle on your bones."

"Do you even know how far the Southcap Mountains are from here? Is it even safe for us to be traveling in the open for so long?"

"Yes and no," she replies. "But that won't matter. Just gather your things and we'll be off. But pack light! You'll be carrying my things as well."

"Oh, come on!"

"Do not raise your voice to your teacher!" Harlow puts her hands on her hips.

"What do you mean 'teacher'?"

"You have Dale to blame for that. Now, stop wasting my time and get moving!"

*

I think I am dying. It's only been three days since all of us came south from the Northern Compound and I was finally getting comfortable with the new accommodations. Now here I am on the road once again, and with far less entertaining company. During our first day of travel I attempted to ask Harlow questions about herself, questions about the Black Flag and Junn, but she has yet to answer any query. When she doesn't outright ignore me, she gives some sarcastic reply: "how do you keep your tongue from falling out with your questions," or "are you writing a book about me," but "shut up" is my favorite yet. My company aside, and the permanent bend in my spine from muling both our packs, the weather has been gratefully forgiving. The warm sun, as faint as it is, has kept the chill wind at bay. Its weak rays filter down through the withered branches of the trees and fall on the leaf-carpeted ground, crunching and scraping with every stride.

After four arduous, draining days of walking through and around the Ironwood, I finally see our destination. The snowy heights of the Southcap Mountains stretch into the hazy sky, their peaks mostly obstructed by clouds. Daunting pillars of earth. I've never seen them before. How can something be this massive without crumbling under its own weight? Harlow, walking ever ahead of me, pauses at a rocky outcropping. She puts her foot on a knee-high rock and waits for me to catch up.

"Viper," she announces.

"What?" I wheeze.

"Catch your breath, pansy. You'll have to do better than this if you're going to be successful."

"Successful at what?"

"You, my little Viper, are going to hunt a boar," she smiles.

I am stunned into silence, completely staggered by Harlow's statement.

"As you are well aware, both Dale and Junn have done this in spades. You are going to do the same at Dale's specific request."

"Did he actually say that?" I protest.

"He asked me to train you after your helplessness during the caravan ambush," she answers.

"He didn't tell you about that giant Bandit I killed?"

"He may have. But that does not change the fact that you're next to useless in a fight."

I glare at her with indignation and wait for her to give me direction.

"You will first find a boar, then stalk and kill it using only this," she tosses me a knife.

"Wait, this is my knife. How did you—"

"And start!" she shouts, shoving me into the trees. "And watch out for poisonous barbed vines!"

*

It has been a few hours and I still have not seen anything even close to resembling a boar. I've hidden in prickly brambles, up a tree, behind a boulder in the river and now I lay spread-eagled in the mud, caked with the stuff. I've all but exhausted the knowledge Dale and Junn passed onto me. Did it even occur to anyone that, just maybe, all the game moved on for winter?

I curse my foul luck, smearing mud all over my face as I vainly try to wipe it off. Then, as if things could get any worse, I hear a light pitter-patter all around me. It starts slow, but within a few seconds, the light tapping grows into heavy splashes as the heavens open wide and unleashes a deluge upon my head. While the last remnants of my sanity fades away I hear a deep and vibrating snort of an animal approaching. I wriggle down into the mud and make myself as small as possible, scanning the environment for a glimpse of what I hope is my quarry. There!

The beast's black hide is scarcely visible through the overgrown tree trunks and the sheets of falling rain. The creature has its back to me as it moves through the mud patty and heads for the trees at the other side. It's head is broad and thick. I can see the sinew of its ropes of muscle move as it scrapes its deadly tusks over the drenched ground. All of my want and desire is calling me to leap out of the mud and end this hunt, here and now. But there is no way that I'd be able to reach it in time before it either escapes or decides to put up a fight. I eye its tusks and guess that it would be a fight I would lose. I bide my time. I see the branches around my target separate When it moves farther into the wood. I inch my way up and out of the mud.

All I can think about as I trudge quietly through the trees is how much easier Dale and Junn had it during their hunt. They had broad daylight and time to prepare; I had to walk sixty miles and have no idea what I'm doing. But I haven't lost sight of the boar. Yet. It seems, as I continue to follow, that it walks a trail, something of a regular route by the way the grass has been trodden down into bare earth. I guess that my luck has not entirely expired that I happened upon it. I wonder if it is heading back to its den? The boar keeps its pace and leads me to a narrow clearing in the path. On my left, the woods sprawl over the unleveled landscape and hide the mountain range that looms above the reach of the treetops. To the right is a shallow ravine with large clumps of thin vines clinging to the slick walls. There are not any barbs on them. I have to keep waiting for my chance to get close enough to use my knife.

I push through tight-knit trees and clawing branches, constantly battling with thick raindrops falling onto my face. I come to a bend in the path and see the boar's hind legs disappearing behind the little gully. Every step I take towards my pray elevates my yearning to succeed, my desire to prove to Harlow that I am not the helpless fool she believes me to be. I round the bend and see a divide in the path. Right leads farther down into the ravine, flooded with muddy water, the left leads up and over it. Suddenly, a deafening clap of thunder sunders the air, immediately followed by an immense, forked bolt of lightning that, for a brief moment, illuminates the grey sky and soaked earth. I see the boar descend right, barreling through the water. I clench my knife tight and tail it from higher ground. My prey remains on its course, boxed in on both sides. I duck down low and quicken my stride. I look ahead of the boar's trajectory and see that the trench narrows into a bottleneck, though still wide enough to squeeze through. Perfect. I pick up a small stone as I go and swiftly dash a few feet in front of the boar, stopping right above the small gap in the boar's path. I poise to lob the stone.

Lightning flashes and thunder booms a second time. Out of the corner of my eye I see a dark shape moving but I keep my focus on the boar below me. Nothing is more important than getting my quarry and getting out of the rain. I lift the stone above my head and I hear a deep, harsh snorting as a second boar charges me. I try to turn, try to guard, but too late. The boar rams into my side and launches me down into the ravine. Pain spider-webs all over my body from the point of impact, and the air is knocked out of me as I hit the opposite wall and roll into the opaque water. The first boar squeals in surprise and rears up, shaking its deadly tusks in the air before he stomps down where I lay. I roll backwards, scrambling to my feet and avoid powerful hooves pounding down. Sparing no time, the boar lowers its broad head and charges, swiping its tusks over the water. I wait for it to get closer, bending slightly at my knees. Just before it is in arm's reach, I leap in the air and jump off the ravine's slick sides. I land behind the boar and it comes to a splashing halt. In the same moment, I hear something land behind me. I whip around and see the second boar coming back to its feet from the short drop. I turn my head as I back away and see the first boar also closing in. This is not good. As the boars come nearer, I feel the wind pick up. It gusts overhead and blasts through the ravine fast enough to cause me to lean into it to keep my balance.

I weigh my knife and the stone in either hand, looking at the wall, the vines… thinking of a plan. The boar in front of me lets out a snort, steam shooting from its flared nostrils, and it charges forward. I leap out of the way, trying not to cut myself in the disorienting weather, and land on its back, using the extra height to help me reach the vines hanging down from the edge of the walls. I take one in my hands, holding my knife in my teeth, and heave myself up and out of the ravine. I stand to look at the brutish animals while they pace frantically back and forth, sometimes attempting to climb the slick walls, always resulting in failure. I still need to finish this hunt, but how? I look down and smile. I have the rock in my off-hand; knife still secured in my mouth. I look back over the edge at the boars still trying to climb out. Just as one jumps and begins to slide back, I hop down, grab a handful of vines in my right hand, and tangle them around the boar's tusks. The boar squeals and jerks its head ferociously against the vines, some break and snap loudly, but they hold the creature fast. I land in the muddy water and hurl the stone at the second boar that is moving to attack. The rock glances off its thick forehead, but it is enough to force it to turn away. With its eyes averted, I weave my way around its blind side and run my knife along the boar's throat. I lift my eyes and see the second boar struggling with the vines clinging to its tusks, completely unwilling to be shaken off. Before it realizes what is happening, I march towards it and slice through its large neck. It collapses lifeless to the ground and all is still. All but the pounding rain, of course.

*

I finally breach the tree-line, wet and exhausted, out into the clearing where Harlow began my torture, out of breath from hauling not one, but two enormous carcasses out of the wood. But where is she now? I hardly suspected that she would have the decency to wait for me, but to abandon me completely was… well, it's what I should have expected from the beginning. I continue to trudge along, cursing Harlow's insensitivity. The only merciful thing about all this is that the storm has moved on, but left behind everything cold and drenched.

"Hey, you've finally made it," the sound of Harlow's distinct sarcastic tone draws my attention to the south where I see her sitting amidst a small campsite. "Oh, surely you can move faster than that!"

Then you can get your ass over here and help me.

"Please, don't get up on my account," I say, aloud. "It's not like I didn't just find, stalk *and* kill both of these beast with my knife," I shout back, heaving the boundless weight of the creatures over to Harlow. "And next time you want me to do something like this, give me some proper gear," I lay the boars out for Harlow to see.

"Don't get all whinny. You did it, right?" Harlow's eyes widen at the game I managed to score. "Impressive," she whistles. "With kills like these you could feed Grimhild for a week!" She looks at me proudly and gives me a hardy slap on the back, "But I only asked for one. Do it again."

I whip my head up to look at her, my eyes pleading for her to be jesting. "You can't be serious! It's nearly dusk, and by the time I find another, the sun –

"Settle down, I'm only kidding. Learn to take a joke," she laughs. "Now, start preparing them for supper."

By the time I have both of the boars skinned and dug clean of their insides, the sun has gone down and a frigid air descended from the mountain tops. I can see my breath, billowing like the clouds that are covering the stars. Harlow stands idly by the fire that she somehow managed to get started, arms crossed and staring into the flames. I stand from my completed work and Harlow looks up.

"So," I say, "what did you mean when you said 'watch out for barbed vines'?"

"I meant watch out for them," she answers, simply.

"Care to elaborate?"

Harlow walks over to a small stack of sticks elevated slightly above the damp earth, picks one up, and takes out her knife and files down its tip to a sharp point.

"I was referring to the Scorpion's Sting vine," Harlow blows on the tip of the skewer. "It is incredibly poisonous."

"What does it look like? I don't think there was any growing in there."

"It has flaky brown bark and real pointy barbs that you don't want anywhere near your skin," she puts down her completed skewer and reaches for a second. "Good thing you didn't run into any."

"Does it grow in these mountains?"

"It can. It can grow anywhere. But, depending on where it grows decides how deadly it is. Here, in the cold and wet, Scorpion's Sting is only a problem for small animals, but a prick from one of those will paralyze you for a few hours. In other places though, if the poison gets in your blood it can kill a grown man," she tosses me the second skewer. "Ready to eat?"

Harlow stands and walks over to the pile of meat laying on my cloak and spears a piece with her skewer. She faces the fire and sits, resting the stick in the crook of her arm so that the boar meat hangs above the fire; a few moments later, it starts to crackle as it cooks. I do the same and join her at the fireside.

"So," I say, "the weather is pretty fickle around here, huh? It was pouring earlier today and now I feel like it's about to snow." I look over at her and show a weak smile. Harlow ignores me and spins her skewer for an even roast. "You should have seen how I hunted them. After finally finding the first one, the other appeared out of thin air and attacked me."

Harlow pulls in her skewer and inspects the meat. It is a golden brown; steam wafts from the tender flesh. She twists her lips in a subtle gesture of approval and takes a bite. I look at my own just as it catches fire. I curse and frantically pull the charred piece of boar from the fire and blow it out. It's ruined.

"Hunting is more than just killing," Harlow says with her mouth full. "It's about patience and one's willingness to do whatever it takes to complete the hunt. And it seems that you understand that. However," she swallows and looks at me, "it also seems that you have no idea how to make use of that talent."

"What do you mean by that?" I ask, leaning over to the pile for a new piece of meat.

"I mean you can't cook to save your life! How can you show respect to the animal – the living thing that died to give you something – when you just go and burn it to a crisp? Here, give me that."

Harlow snatches the skewer from my hand and holds it over the fire.

"Look. See what I'm doing? You have to keep your eyes on it as you turn it over the fire. Otherwise, you just get a lump of coal like you just did. This goes for most everything else you cook: keep watch and know the easiest way to get the best result."

"That's all very helpful," I take back my skewer, "but what does that have to do with making me a better fighter? Isn't that why I'm here in the first place?"

"It's got everything to do with it! In fighting, just as in hunting, cooking and whatever else, you have to respect your opponent. Not them themselves, but what they stand for in that moment. Meaning," she sighs, noticing my confusion, "that the boars you hunted symbolized our dinner. A symbol you tarnished by turning it into ashes."

"How are you supposed to apply that to the Bandits?" I counter. "It seems to me that they don't give a damn about whatever they kill."

"That's because they don't have the heart of a true warrior," she taps her chest. "Part of the reason they do what they do is because they gave both mind and heart to Merr'tyura, their god. And the reason why I, why you, do not dishonor our foes is because we understand what it means to give something for the sake of another. To sacrifice."

"You mean I understand death?"

"If that's how you see it, then I suppose yes. You understand."

I take my skewer from the fire and it shows a crisp brown in the flickering light.

"Lesson one: respect," Harlow states.

She stands and tosses her skewer into the fire before putting away the extra meat.

"Finish cooking the rest of the meat so it doesn't spoil and then get some rest. Lesson two starts at dawn."

CHAPTER 6

— Know Thy Master —

By the time I wake, the sun has not yet risen, and I can see my breath clouding on the air. I look next to me and see that Harlow already left the tent. I get out of the tent and try to find a trace of her but to no avail. It appears that my predictions about the weather last night were true, for a thin layer of snow blankets the surrounding area. The frost on the grass causes my footfalls to crunch as I step out of the comfort of the tent. Feeling quite dismayed, I turn to walk back into the soothing, warm mouth of my shelter. Turning to go back inside, I notice a loose scrap of fabric lethargically waving in the slight breeze. I tear it from where it hangs and inspect the writing:

"Find me."

"Find me?" I say, aloud. She really likes to keep things easy, doesn't she?

I gaze longingly at the opening of the tent, wanting to just go back to sleep, and I see this time that the uniform, frosty-white scene around me is broken. A small patch of ice and snow has been knocked off just behind the camp. She must have headed in that direction. I duck back in and put on warmer clothes and my knife and step back outside, resigning myself to the task at hand.

I pull the hood of my cloak tight around my head, raise my arms against the stiff branches of pine trees, and force my way through their crystallized needles. I brush off as I exit the opposite side and scan for remnants of Harlow's passage.

There are a few things Junn told me to look out for when you attempt to track: any depressions in the earth, no matter how shallow. Be aware of disturbances. It could be that the wildlife have gone silent, or the environment itself has been altered in some way…

For the few visible meters in front of me, I notice that more ice and snow have been knocked off, but when I follow the trail, it vanishes. I look at the white-dusted ground, but nothing is there. No footprints, nothing to follow. I crane my neck to look at the tree tops. If I can't see anything from the ground, maybe I can up there. I find a tree that is both tall and sturdy enough for the branches to hold my weight and climb to the top. At this new height – what I guess to be at least thirty meters above the snowy earth – I see the Southcap Mountains stretching over the grey horizon and frost-crusted trees dressing its steep slopes; the frozen surface of Lake Tave to the west. I turn to face the south-east and see a plume of smoke rising from the pristine white landscape. I wonder if that's Harlow. Only one way to find out.

Memorizing the direction of the smoke before I come back down, I am soon stepping through the trees once more.

As the day wears on the sun shines brighter and hotter and it clears away the thin snow; I can see the bark of the trees darken from the melting frost. It also reveals something on the ground. Footprints. The size tells me a full-grown man made them.

I kneel down to study them properly and my mind flashes back to the night where our caravan was attacked… The same prints were present when the Bandits came. Peering more closely, I realize something that stifles my breath and brings a cold sweat to my brow. The edges of the dirt around the prints themselves are held in sharp relief. These are fresh, no more than a day old.

From the amount of footprints and the rate of them overlapping, I surmise there are at most ten of them. Then again, what if they're not Bandits? Who else would be wondering around this far from the Compound? What if I could find them, get them to tell me where Junn is… I am completely torn between finding Harlow and completing my training and following a pack of Bandits. Hardly my best set of options. What should I do?

I stand back up and resolve my course of action. But even before I can move more than three steps a massive, blunt force comes crashing down on my head. The world reels around me and then goes black.

*

When I finally come to the edges of my vision are black and clouded and my head throbs in time with my heartbeat.

What happened?

The fiery pain radiating from the trauma's point of contact keeps me from piecing together the events that have led me here. Dizziness at last fading, I try to stand, but hard knots tied around both my hands and ankles keep me down. I can feel the hard floor on which I lie sapping me of warmth. From the damp stench and jagged surfaces, I can tell that I am in a cave or somewhere underground. Then I notice the smell. Thick and putrid, it clogs my sinuses and forces tears to my eyes. Sight returns to my misty irises and I see a faint glow off to my left, glistening on the rough, moist walls. I hear an echoing scuffle very close to me and I freeze. A low and disgruntled moan comes from the corner of the claustrophobic room.

"Is anyone there?" the moaning voice whispers.

Confounded, I remain silent

"I can hear you breathing," the voice continues. "So just say something, would ya?" The blunt and gruff demand floods me with relief.

"Harlow, is that you?" I gasp.

"Hot damn, they got you too, huh?"

"I didn't even hear them coming. All I remember is being bashed on the head and waking up here," I answer, shifting my position on the cave floor. "What happened to you?"

"A group of Bandits found the shack where I was waiting and burned the place down," she admits. "I was caught off-guard."

"Never thought I'd see the day," I laugh despite myself.

"Shut it, worm. You should focus on getting loose instead of snickering at your master. You're still not done training," she retorts. "Get started before they come back for us."

I force myself into a sitting position and try to find my knife, but it is nowhere to be found. The Bandits must have stripped both of us down and removed anything they deemed to be threatening. As I move around, my foot knocks against a rock protruding from the cave floor, sticking out just a few inches. I pivot around and maneuver my wrists on to the rock and saw off the course binds.

Cutting the constraints generates a deep, rattling clamor. I keep pace back and forth on the stone and I feel the rope loosen, strand by strand. With my hands freed, I perform the same action on the restraints around my legs, and a short time later, I am fully mobile. I move to Harlow to untie her, but footfalls bouncing off the walls make its way to my ears.

"Viper, get back down," Harlow orders.

"But I can get you out," I protest, continuing to fumble with the rope around her legs.

"Guess what, genius, that won't matter if we're both killed for trying to escape!"

I pay her distress no mind and carry on untying her. I can feel the tight knots give some slack when the approaching steps bring with them shadows on the wall.

"I told you to get down," Harlow says, her tone deadly serious.

I ignore her again, but this time she pushes me away hard with both legs locked at the heel and I topple backward.

Seconds after I slam on the ground, three figures appear in the mouth of the room. Bandits.

As my eyes dart from them to where Harlow lays silent, her stare locks-on to mine, voicelessly commanding my utmost compliance.

"There's a lot of movin' around noise comin' from 'n 'ere," the low voice of one of the Bandits speaks.

"That's right," another chimes.

"Shut it!" the first voice shouts. His irate outburst is preceded by a whoosh of air and the sound of the second voice's body hitting the ground.

Harlow maintains her calm demeanor.

"We're movin' a'long now," the first Bandit continues. "An' that means you're comin' wiff us," he nods to the third Bandit who moves towards me.

I lie still, waiting for the Bandit to grab me up; waiting for Harlow to act.

The first Bandit goes to claim Harlow, who is spouting ill wishes onto his pathetic comrade. His profane monologue swiftly silences as my peripheral vision catches a blur of movement over where Harlow is laying. The Bandit approaching me stops and turns at the abrupt lack of speech, but is too late to react to a roundhouse kick delivered by Harlow's leg. Her crushing blow violently lurches the Bandit's head back and shatters his neck. The momentum of the strike lifts him off his feet and launches his lifeless corpse against the stone, which then collapses to the ground like a saturated rag thrown against a wall.

All I can do is gawk at her display of power.

"Don't just sit there!" Harlow growls, tucks her head in and shoulder-rams the second Bandit hard into the wall. He folds back to the ground and Harlow stomps on his vulnerable neck. "Make yourself useful."

I give no audible acquiescence to her demand and move over to the Bandit that had been sent slamming into the wall. The stench emanating from his broken body is overwhelming. I cover my nose and stoop down to the carcass, but the smell still perforates my defensive hand.

After a few moments of searching, I am rewarded by the touch of something solid, hidden deep in the folds of the Bandit's person, and the scent that will follow me into my nightmares. Exhilaration courses through my veins as I remove the curious item and pull it into the cave's feeble light.

It's a cylindrical tube constructed from a very dense and dark wood. I notice a narrow seam at one end and I grab hold of it, twist and the end softly pops open; I look inside and examine the contents. Within the container rests a wad of paper. Wonderment peaked, I pull it out and unravel it from its crumpled state.

Staring at the unfolded paper, I try to make sense of the unintelligible scribbles – haphazardly drawn lines going this way and that, words unrecognizable in the poor lighting. I am absolutely perplexed... Until.

"Harlow," I call.

"What?"

"Come have a look at this," I can hear Harlow's obvious annoyance as she stands.

"What is it?"

I hold out the page for her.

"What the hell is thi—"she starts to say, but stops when she understands what is written there. Her face lights up in a deviant way. "Well done, Viper," she praises. "I hoped that they would be kind enough to carry around a map with them."

"Could we find Junn with this?" I ask.

"Yes," Harlow admits, slowly. "But we're not out of shit creek yet," she says, glancing at the cave's entrance.

Shadows are once again dancing on the cold stone.

I look from Harlow to the shadows, and back to Harlow again. I begin to speak, but her sweaty, dirt coated hands clasp my partially open mouth. She takes me over to the opening of the room and crouches us down on the right side.

As their flickering shadows move from wall to floor, Harlow shoves me away from her and whispers,

"You handle this one."

Completely taken aback by this blatant betrayal of my trust, my frenzied state of mind is not benefited in the slightest as I stumble in front of two more Bandits, one carrying a lit torch. The Bandits roar and they charge towards me. I take the map's case and pitch it with all my might at the leading Bandit's face. The hard cylinder impedes his furious progress towards me, causing him to shield his face from harm. I rush the parrying Bandit in his moment of blindness and ram his body into the wall's impermeable surface; the force of the impact drives the Bandit's head against the rock. Not giving him even a moment to draw breath, I secure his chin in my grip and suddenly smash his skull against the wall again and again until his body flops to the ground. The muffled crunching of bones does not even fade into an echo before I snatch up the Bandit's torch. I dash to where the other Bandit stands and raise the fire high, its light immortalizing his look of horror; I bring the flame crashing down into his eyes. Overcome with agony, the Bandit clutches at his searing wound and backs away; dropping to his knees. I step towards him as he growls and bares his jagged teeth in pain. I make a grab for his throat, but the Bandit surges forward. He leaps at me with a furious bellow and has me in a crushing bear-hug before I can react. I lose balance and fall to the floor, right onto the pool of blood draining from the other Bandit's shattered skull. I try to roll and shake myself free, but I am held tight. The Bandit brandishes his teeth, reels back his head and lunges to bite at my face. I lean hard right and my head bumps against the cylinder; the Bandit's teeth snap at empty air. If he was not angry before, he surely is now. The Bandit releases his hold on me, slides a knife of bone out from his boot, and lifts it high. I feel around the right of my head frantically, heart racing, and my fingers find the hard case. The knife comes tearing down and it stabs through the wood of the case. I twist it and disarm the Bandit; smash it against his head once, twice and he falls back. I scurry upright and jump on top of him, ram the case into his scorched, bleeding face, and finish the job.

I drop the blood-splattered case to the rocky floor and sigh in relief at my victory.

My adrenalin now seeks a new target.

"Harlow!" I yell. "What in the hell were you thinking? I could've been killed!"

"But you weren't," she replies with a chuckle at my aggravated state.

"You're going to have to stop using that as an excuse for your reckless behavior," I retaliate.

"How are you supposed to learn if *I* handle every fight you encounter? Besides, that was the last of 'em."

"And how do you know that?"

"Because, that's how many brought me here. If I had been ready for them, it would have taken twice that number," she says as an aside to herself. "Now, let's get a move on," she walks by me, "and be sure to find our things before you follow me out."

*

Over the past several weeks, getting a camp together has now become routine. Harlow and I are able to gather the wood – both for burning and shelter, dry leaves for sleeping on, and locating a source of water in half the time. We settle around the radiance of the fire that melts a radius of snow around it, creating a barrier between the elements and us.

"Tell me your story," Harlow's abrupt inquiry breaks me away from the flames' trance.

"What's my what?" I babble.

She shakes her head but asks again.

"I want you to tell me your story."

I stare at her in disbelief.

"Well?" Harlow probes for a third time.

"I guess my story started when I was taken in by Junn and Marcus. I was little and alone when they found me in the cave. I don't know how I ended up in that way or who my parents are, or were. For all I know they're both dead. I can't tell you how long I lived that way, all by myself. But I've always had this," I slide my ornate knife out of its sheath, its engraved silver grip and sharp blade mirror the flames spectacularly.

"May I?" Harlow holds out her hand.

"Of course."

I hand the knife to her and she brings it close, trying to make sense of the etches that run up the masterfully crafted blade. She spins it in her hands, balancing the leather wrapped handle on her finger. She flips it up, catches it and presents it for me to take back.

"It's a wonderful piece," she admires. "But it's a bit too long to be called a knife, I think. It's almost as long as your forearm."

"Do you know what these markings mean?" I ask.

"I can't say that I do," she admits. "What do they mean?"

"I haven't the slightest," I laugh. "Marcus, Junn, everyone that's seen them can't make heads or tails of it. Junn said that whoever gave it to me or made it must know. But I don't know where I would look for them. Anyway, this knife has always been with me. I remember one time, after I came to the Compound, I used it to fend off a snake. I drove it off, but it still managed to bite me. I hurt a lot, but its venom didn't kill me, as Malory said it should have. Junn said that it was my guardian spirit protecting me."

Harlow stands and grabs her staff and uses it to rearrange the burning logs.

"I always figured Junn to be your guardian spirit."

"That's not too far from the truth," I say. "He did save me life…"

"Oh?" Harlow looks at me as she leans her weight on her staff.

"It was nearly ten years ago when it happened," I lean back on my elbows. "I had just finished with the daily chores and was eager to go to the Hill. Marcus told me I could go, just be back before the sun went down. I felt particularly adventurous and brave that day, so I ventured past the brook and the Hill to a place I'd never been before. The land beyond was unfamiliar and exhilarating. Every bright color on the flowers, the calls of the animals, even the trees seemed to hold new, fantastic traits that I somehow overlooked until that very moment. I remember following the path of the stream farther and farther away from the Compound, forgetting to keep an eye out for landmarks to help me find my way back. I soon came to an open field with Blue Flag Iris flowers, and I raced towards them. I was a few feet away from the flower patch when I started to feel my footfalls on the earth begin to stick and squelch. It was too late when I noticed that my calf was deep in the mud and slowly sinking.

I panicked. I was in an unfamiliar marsh, and no one knew where I was. I struggled for a while against the mud, but every effort I made only drug me farther down. I lost hope. But then I heard a voice; felt my body lift out of the marsh. Junn spoke to me. 'I've gotcha, Vipe. Don't worry, I've gotcha.' I looked up and saw his black silhouette against the overcast sky, and his face appeared soft and kind. Eventually I managed to ask him how he knew where I was, and he replied 'I'll always know where you are.' He said that Dale and I are his family, and kin always looks after kin.'"

I sit up and stare into the fire.

"And I've let him down. He found me and I have no clue where to look for him… To tell you the truth, I still find it hard to believe Junn was so ready to accept me. Why would anyone want to take on such a burden?"

"Have you been?"

"What?" I look at her shimmering eyes from across the fire.

"A burden," she answers.

I sit in silence and ponder her question, once again captivated by the fire's glow.

"No," I finally respond. "Of course, there have been moments where I have gotten in their way. But, I can solemnly say that all of our lives being brought together has yielded nothing but good."

Harlow looks at me approvingly.

"Okay," she says with a huff. "I suppose it's only fair that this relationship continues to be give-and-take," Harlow walks over to the pile of wood we collected and returns with a few large pieces, casually laying them on our little inferno. She takes her staff and again optimally arranges the logs. Satisfied with her efforts, Harlow turns her steely eyes to meet mine.

"I am sure you've been dying to know more about me. Am I right?"

I give her an energetic nod and she continues.

"I haven't always been with the Compound and Marcus' group. Before I was acquainted with all of them, I was a mercenary. We called ourselves The Black Flag, perhaps you heard of us? There was our leader, Contil, me, the brawler, Vincent and Teagen, the hunters, and five others made up our close-quarters fighters – Nalu, Grimhild, Haebur, Amour and Riston," she rubs her chin with her thumb. "Amour was–"

"You didn't have any medics with you?" I interrupt.

Harlow grins with pride.

"No. You see, as a prerequisite, all aspiring members had to have an understanding of our great Mother Nature," Harlow continues, seeing my befuddled expression. "Meaning, before any was allowed to call themselves a member, they first had to be able to administer first-aid at a moment's notice using the things around them. This served to weed out the weak and incapable. Anyway, I traveled around with them for a few years; acting as a hitman or a guide. Since the rising Bandit threat, I've mostly been a guard on various expeditions. Contil was a good leader and saw us through more than one tight spot. The most vivid memory I have of him is how he used to fight," Harlow sets down her staff and returns to her seat.

"None among the Flag would dare test their mettle against his. Thinking about it now, I can fully appreciate that apprehension. Contil would never make the first move, unless that was the most fortuitous action. Allowing the advisory the initial strike opened a window for him to counter. Seldom did Contil's engagements last passed that second move."

"What did he do that made him so effective?"

"Many consider that a mystery, but I have my own guess. I did once ask about his technique, but he greeted my curiosity with a simple line: *I will not say. For if there comes a day where we no longer find ourselves in accordance, I shall have the upper hand.*"

"What eventually made you join us?"

"Well, after the years of gallivanting around with the Black Flag, all our hands became stained, and some among us developed a hunger for it. Their insatiable thirst soon began to show in their work; the before routine job started to get a little too messy, leaving no witnesses where in the past we had spared lives."

"Did Contil do anything to punish those people?"

Harlow lets out a hard laugh, "No. He was the one who started that murderous trend."

"What do you mean?"

"All I will say is that Contil was bored of all the little menial jobs the Flag was taking on. He wanted to do something bigger."

"And did he?"

"After seeing his bloodlust," she continues, brushing over my question. "I, along with all save for three, decided to disband and sell our skills on our own. Amour thought that Contil's new way of doing things was giving us a bad reputation, so she stupidly decided to go after him, convince him of the error of his ways. A mistake she wishes she could take back," she stares into the fire, lost in past memories. "It wasn't long after that when I was approached by Marcus to guard some farmers. I decided to stay-put for a while after that and over a few years, the other members of the Flag reunited and we've been at the Compound ever since. But, that's enough history," Harlow says, quickly noticing my thirst for more answers. "Tomorrow we go over your swordsmanship."

CHAPTER 7

— Eyes of a Warrior —

An object lands on my chest and I bolt upright. I look down through the veil of very, very early morning and see a crudely carved wooden sword laying on the ground next to me.

"Time to wake up," Harlow says. "Come on! Get up, pick up your weapon and let's see what you've got!"

I give her a puzzled look and take my sparring sword as I stand, still groggy from waking before the dawn.

"Is that your stance?" Harlow berates. "Your feet are so close together you could be knocked over by the wind! Look at me: shoulders squared, knees slightly bent, feet planted, one in front of the other. Try again."

I mirror Harlow, but she slacks her arms and groans.

"No, no, no. That's not even close."

"I did exactly what you said!"

"Sure you did," she walks over to me and arranges my body into the proper posture.

After she finishes, she goes back and resumes her stance.

"Alright. Now, show me what you got."

I step forward and Harlow instantly stops me.

"Wrong again. How do you expect to win a fight by walking slowly at your opponent? In a real fight to the death, you'd lose in a heartbeat."

"I have been in a fight to the death! You were there!"

Harlow dismisses my argument with a wave of her hand.

"Not a real fight. I'm talking about when you're facing down another trained swordsman. Go back and try again, but this time attack like your life depends on it."

I do as she asks, arrange myself back into the stance, and try again. I lunge forward, bending my leading leg and thrusting the point of the sparring sword at Harlow. She swats my attack away with her own sword, clacking together sharply.

"That's better. Go back, and this time, follow up the thrust with a second attack."

I resume my stance and attack, following up the initial thrust with a slash. My second hit brushes Harlow's sleeve and she calls a halt.

"Well done. It's imperative to always be acting. Whether it be on the defensive or otherwise. Of course, to every rule there follows an exception, and it is up to you to decide in the moment if it is permissible to break that rule. And remember, most fights are all about a warrior's awareness and ability."

"Junn used to say that," I remark.

"Who do you think I learned it from? Now, go back and keep your feet moving."

Harlow continues to run me through drill after drill until the sun rises and makes the sweat all over my body glisten. After the rigorous sparring, she calls for a respite. As Harlow sets down her practice sword she rolls her shoulders and neck and takes her water skin from her pack, drinking in large gulps. I eagerly drink from my own and it spills from the corners of my mouth, trickling down my chin. I take the water skin from my lips and my stomach growls. This attracts Harlow's attention.

"Do you hear something?" she mocks. "Sounds like a bear is around."

I rummage around for the extra boar meat from two days prior, finding it rolled in cloth and glazed with salt, techniques learned from Harlow. I bring the lot of it over to the pile of charcoal that is our fire pit and go in search of new wood to cook the meat. After a few minutes, I take a seat and devour the pork as though I have not eaten in days. Harlow joins me and we eat in silent fellowship as squirrels chatter and rattle sparse leaves overhead. I glance over at her. She is looking thoughtfully up at the hidden wildlife, slowly chewing lean meat.

"Can you answer a question for me?" I ask.

Harlow continues chewing and looking up at the trees, shifting her eyes towards new sounds as they come. She finally swallows and looks down at me.

"It's possible."

"Can you tell me why you're the only one of the Black Flag that came with our caravan?"

Harlow takes another chunk out of her meal and goes back to gazing upward.

"Of course," I babble, "If that's something you're not allowed to talk about I understand. If you're bound to loyalty towards them and for that reason you can't say, I respect that. I'm sure I would feel the same way. I don't think that—"

"For the love of all that is silent, quite your rambling!" Harlow shouts. "I'll tell you if you'd only give me a moment."

I avert my eyes from Harlow and feel my cheeks flush. I sit completely still and wait for an answer in her own good time. She takes another bite and turns from me. She eats, she looks, she swallows; she then stands.

"The reason why only I accompanied the caravan," Harlow finally answers, "is because the others among us felt that they had a conflict of interests with the Compound's influential members."

"Do you mean Marcus?"

"They felt that the way certain things were being handled reminded them too much of Contil."

"Does that have anything to do with Carver speaking to the Bandits?"

Harlow pauses at the question. "You know too, huh?"

"You know?" I furrow my brow at her. "How come you didn't say anything about it?"

"That sort of information in the wrong hands wouldn't do any good for anyone. How do you think the people of the Compound would react if they knew their leaders are conspiring against them?"

"Dale and I handled it well," I counter. "We kept it to ourselves and thought of what to do about it."

"And that was a wise decision," Harlow picks up her sparring sword and swats me in the arm with it. "No more questions. Back to training."

I reluctantly pick up my own sword and stand, my hunger for knowledge more ravenous than ever. Harlow recommences sparring and the hours roll by and night falls over the trees of the Southcap Mountains.

The following morning I wake up sore and poorly rested, but gratefully *after* the sun has risen. During the night the wind picked up and brought with it the chill of the mountain tops and the closing winter. Now, the sun is bright and shining and I notice Harlow is missing. I get up and search for her, walking through the trees until their trunks block the camp from view. I come to a narrow clearing that runs along the edge of a cliff, dizzyingly high, and find her sitting on the ground with her legs dangling off the brink. I approach and join her, though I sit safely away from the ledge.

"What do you see?" she asks, her back still facing me.

I crane my neck and look out over the precipice and see a pale green valley cradled between the white-capped, sloping mountains; dark boughs of the evergreens dress the land around the valley and the surface of Lake Tave and its tributaries shimmers off in the distance. All of which is speckled by the shadows of clouds drifting overhead.

"Nothing special," I respond.

Harlow turns her head and looks at me.

"Look again and think harder. Tell me what you see."

I sigh and observe the land a second time. But just like the first, I come to the same conclusion.

"You're really not getting this, are you?"

"Unless you have a sixth sense, what is there to see?" I retort.

"I suppose you might call it a sixth sense," she turns back and casts her gaze over the sprawling land.

"And what do you see that I can't?"

Harlow points her finger to the east, "do you see how the mountains enclose the valley? How rivers running from Lake Tave wind through that valley and cut off the western portion from escape? That valley is a death-trap. The ensuing battle would be short and bloody. However, there's a way to avoid that. The rivers have carved out the mountains over countless years and made caverns that burrow deep underground, exiting far to the south and depositing into the ocean. If the ambushees knew of this, they could save entire battalions of soldiers by using those caverns to hide and plan a counter-attack, or use that time to escape battle entirely. On the other hand, if the ambushers scouted the terrain of battle before and knew of these caverns, then the tide of war would swing back in their favor," she glances over her shoulder, "do you see now? Being a soldier, a warrior, is more than swinging a sword or fighting for one's virtues. It's about being a sound tactician in battle; to know from where to strike and where to avoid or retreat."

I follow her stare and see the world through her discerning eyes.

"What about those times then you have no time to prepare and are forced into the unfamiliar?"

"In those instances, the best course of action is to rely on instinct. If you know the ins and outs of battle, the places to avoid and where to hide, then there is really no place that will be foreign to you."

I ponder her answer, wondering of the times where she had to take her own advice.

Harlow stands up and stretches her arms above her head.

"As my teacher once said to me: 'don't be an idiot.'"

"Who was that?" I stand with her.

"A very wise, very dead man," she answers and walks back in the direction of our camp.

I roll my eyes at her steadfastness towards dodging questions and follow her back.

"Before I forget," Harlow says, "when you've finished your training, you'll be returning to the Compound alone."

"What for?" I jog up to her side.

"There's… something I need to take care of."

"Why did I even bother asking."

"That is something I will always wonder," she chuckles. "It's good that you have an inquisitive mind. I prefer that a student of mine is constantly thinking rather than taking things at face-value. At any rate, there are still many things you need to learn before then."

We return to our camp and begin drilling with the wooden swords while Harlow goes over combat strategy. The days go by and she fills my head with knowledge of swordsmanship; weeks go by and what I learned is becoming second nature to me. And although Harlow remains secretive, I can tell by her tone and the new and complicated ideas and techniques she is teaching me, she is proud of me and my progress. After three months, I have mastered the basics and am adept at the more complex ideas. And in the dead of winter, it is time for me to return to the Compound.

CHAPTER 8

— A Kingly Meal & A Lone Candle —

I never want to walk another step again. I want to sit by a fire — indoors — with a pint of mead in one hand and a smoking pipe in another and have nothing to look forward to but just doing the same thing again. At least the return journey from the Southcap Mountains was a good deal warmer than my outset. The frost and ice crusting the earth and trees is melting and the snowdrifts piled high against the rising and falling ground and the broad tree trunks are dwindling. With the midday sun overhead and my feet begging for relief, the Compound's walls come into view.

I step by the last of the trees of the Ironwood and onto the road to the gates. There is a quarter mile stretch of clean and open land around the whole of the Compound, and after a few moments treading upon it, I hear a bell tolling; a few moments after that I see the shapes of armed men gathering atop the ramparts. I come to a halt, now within earshot of the sentinels shouting down at me.

"Who goes there, traveler?"

"It's Viper," I shout back. "Coming back from the Southcap Mountains."

"Where's Harlow?"

I shrug my shoulders. That seems to be enough of an answer for the sentinel. He lowers his guard, waves his hand to someone out of sight and I see the gates opening.

After what I just went through with Harlow, the training, the hunting, the being hunted, I had it in my mind that there would be some kind of grand reception for me. But as I walk through the gate, I see absolutely nothing out of the ordinary, just weary and haggard looking people going about their business.

"Hey, you," I hear Dale's voice.

I turn to the sound and see him leaning against the wall, one foot up, head leaned back. He must figure himself something slick.

"You're coming with me."

"Am I?" I say.

Dale pushes himself away from the wall with his foot and comes towards me.

"That you are. You have quite the knack for coming back once all the hard work is done."

"Hard work?" I laugh. "You do know who I was with for three months, don't you? She isn't exactly what I would call a relaxed person."

"It wasn't all fun and games here while you were away with that ape of a woman," Dale nudges me with his elbow. "Had a nasty run-in with a pack of wolves while out hunting. One of Carver's men got bit on the arm and another still hasn't gotten out of the infirmary. But besides that, it's been smooth."

"If everything's gone so well, then why is it that everyone looks so glum?"

"Rationing," Dale says, simply. "With the Compound packed near to breaking, food and water are as precious as diamonds nowadays. That, and Carver is still challenging Marcus and Byron at every turn."

"What's he been doing exactly?"

"Not what you're thinking," Dale rubs the back of his neck. "We haven't seen even a hair of the Bandits, but that hasn't stopped Carver from butting heads over them, always shouting about cowardice and death. Most of these southerners don't care a shit for him, and I can't blame them. But he is growing in popularity among our own people."

"I'm sure that eventually he'll finally say or do something that will get him in trouble," I reply.

"That's what I thought, too. But he went behind everyone's backs and took a squad of guards out beyond the wall to hunt Bandits. He still thinks he has the run of the place. If you ask me, I think we should just lock him up and be done with it.

But enough of doom and gloom, I'm starving. And after the hell you've been through, you must be, too."

"Took the words right out of my mouth."

I continue to follow Dale through the streets and we eventually come to the tavern.

We push open the doors and enter a tall room with the familiar long, wooden tables, sturdy chairs and benches, and the small clumps of patrons scattered throughout. We take a seat out of the way of the rest of the people and Dale gives a subtle nod. A short moment later Hector stands before us.

"Viper, Dale, very good to see you again," Hector says in his large voice. "This means it's time?"

"I dare say it does," Dale replies.

"Time for what?" I look between the pair of them.

Hector taps his nose with his meaty index finger and heads into the kitchen; Dale rests his elbows on the table.

"You're not going to tell me, are you?"

"Not a chance," Dale winks.

We talk candidly about our time apart and the details about my training with Harlow, but I make it a point not to mention the Bandit's map in mixed company. His eyes light up with pride as I tell him about the boars; head shakes when I mention my capture. I flex my arm for him while I recap my sparring lessons with Harlow and Dale gives it an approving squeeze, but still mocks me as he presents his own thick arms.

"Two meals for two kings," Hector says as he returns, two heaping plates in his strong hands.

He sets them down in front of the both of us and I stare dumbly down at it. It's positively a mountain of food. Potatoes and greens covered in butter, large cuts of tender pork slathered with Hector's special sauce who's familiar, savory aroma makes my mouth water. There are also loaves of bread painted all over with more butter and a tall tankard of hot, spiced wine beside.

"Stars above!" I breathe. "I thought you said that we were rationing."

"That we are," Hector says. "But this one here has been setting aside some of it and hunting extra, so don't feel shy about it. He's earned it," he gives Dale an approving, fatherly look and departs, leaving the decanter of wine on the table.

I look up at Dale.

"I don't know what you're waiting for," he smiles. "Dig in."

"And that, Viper, is how you welcome home family!" Dale punctuates his statement by slamming down his emptied tankard on the oak table.

I finish my own drink and my head swims from the copious amount of food and wine that I just consumed. I belch loudly and Dale laughs.

"Good one! But next time…" he burps even louder and longer, causing other patrons to turn in their seats to stare at him, "…do it like that!"

"That's just gross," I smile and shake my head at him.

"Looks like going through hell with Harlow gave you a man's appetite."

"Seems so. And thank you for that, by the way. I would have been very happy to stay here."

"You have to admit that you needed *some* teaching if we're going to get Junn back."

"I will say in hindsight that I'm a much better fighter now than I was three months ago," I agree.

"And stronger, too," Dale observes. "You look like a proper fighter now. I suppose I should teach you how to shave. Or has Harlow already taken care of that?"

I throw a bone at him as Dale roars with laughter. We ate and spoke so long I didn't even notice nightfall. The hearth's warm light bathes the hall and sends flickering shadows up the walls. The sky outside darkened and became painted with pastels, the descent of the sun bringing forth hues of mandarin and crimson at first, followed by dark blues and purples as the night deepened and the constellations supplementing the sun's absence.

"I must say," Dale says, "It was a good idea sending you out with Harlow after all."

"Even though you should have told me about it first," I say. "But yes. I suppose it was."

I yawn long and hard and rub my eyes with my knuckles.

"You've earned a long night's rest," Dale stands. "Come with me. There's one more piece of business I want to discuss."

I rise and Dale escorts me from the warm tavern and out into the somewhat colder streets. What other surprise does Dale have planned? Is Junn waiting for me somewhere, ready to leap out and apologize for this ill-thought joke?

I follow Dale through the Square back to the West District and he leads us to our housing. Before he enters he takes a cautious look down the streets, quickly retreats inside, and briskly walks to his room, closing the door and shutting out the light in the hall. I don't think Junn is here. Dale's boots clomp on the floor as he walks to the other side of the room. He returns and sits at the small, square table, lighting a candle with his brand new lighting tool. This is fixing to be less of a happy surprise by the moment.

The candle's warm flame casts Dale's room in an ominous light. The spokes of the chair's back send fingerlike shadows against the wall, wavering and scratching as if they are trying to escape into the darkness outside the window. Dale's eyes reciprocate the mood set by this lone spark of light.

"Viper," Dale says, "I have a plane to get Junn back."

"What?" My heart feels as though someone grabbed hold of it and will not let go.

"To find Junn. I think I found a way," he repeats. "But, we're going to have to go back to the Northern Compound."

"Is that safe?"

"Of course it isn't safe," Dale waves his hand dismissively. "But we… *I* can't stay here any longer. Doing nothing."

I can see the iron determination in his face; feel it in his words.

"And we are going to need some help."

"What kind of help?"

Dale leans back in his chair and takes a deep breath, the wooden limbs creak.

"Well, for starters, I don't exactly know where the Bandits have him, or if he's even still alive—"

"Don't say that! He is! He has to be!" I say, appalled.

"We have to be prepared for every eventuality," Dale reasons.

A silence falls over us. I think about the possibility that our rescue attempt may be made in vain.

"That being said, I am not giving up hope in him or the Black Flag. If anyone knows anything about the Bandits, it's them."

"And they might know how to read this," I pull out the poorly kept Bandit map.

Dale takes a careful look over the map in the meager light.

"How did you get this?"

"I took it from one of the Bandits that captured me."

"Did Harlow see it, too?"

"She did. She couldn't read it either."

"Then reaching the Black Flag is more important than ever," Dale scratches his stubbly chin, thoughtfully.

"How do you plan on reaching the Northern Compound?" I ask. "The main road through the Ironwood is probably swarming with Bandits, and I don't think we could afford the time to go all the way around it."

Dale stands and walks to the cabinet next to the slightly cracked window. Following a short moment of rummaging around, he returns to his seat with a fresh candlestick.

"I've given that some thought," he holds the new wick over its predecessor's flame. "The only other option is through the Rock Gardens to the east."

"The what?" I gasp. "You don't mean the desert, do you?

"I wouldn't suggest it if there were another path. But the heat beside, the Alnnasi that live there are no less friendly than the Bandits. But there is a greater probability of finding Bandits in the woods, so I'll take my chances," he says quickly, noticing my shock.

"How long will that route take?"

"If nothing happens, I would guess only a few weeks. Beats the promise of a month going around the Ironwood, and more if we run into Bandits."

"What could Carver do to the Compound if we're gone that long?"

"It's a risk we're going to have to take," Dale stands again and stops beside the bedroom door.

"When do we leave?" I join him by the door.

"I'd prefer that we leave with Harlow, but who knows where in the hell she is," Dale shrugs. "I will gather our supplies and send for you, and if Harlow still isn't back by morning, we'll head for the Gardens."

I nod my agreement and go to leave.

"Dale," I say with my hand on the door.

"What is it?"

"Can you tell me how Junn was captured?"

"Not now, Viper."

I turn around. Dale strokes his chin and avoids my eyes. I let go of the door and take a step towards him.

"I deserve to know."

Dale goes and shuts the window.

"You should go get some rest. The Rock Gardens are unforgiving."

He blows out the candle.

CHAPTER 9

— The Rock Gardens —

"Time to go. Tao is waiting for us," Dale says, a little loudly to wake me.

In reality, I hardly ever shut my eyes. Couldn't stop thinking of all the nightmares Junn is going through. Why won't Dale tell me what happened?

"And Harlow isn't back," Dale goes on. "So let's get us gone. I don't want to wait around."

The clomping and stomping of Tao's horse echoes eerily through the early morning air; the tossing of its head rattles the cart it leads. Dale and I clamor into the flatbed of the uncovered cart and Tao urges the horse forward. We arrive at the gate and a sentinel stops us.

"Ho there, my good man," Tao says, reigning in the horse. "Just popping out for some supplies."

"Little early for that, I reckon," the young sentinel observes. "Where you be going?"

"Just a stone's throw into the Ironwood," he jerks his thumb in my direction. "The lad left something valuable behind at the logging site a wee bit ago."

"Funny that. I'd warrant that Carver ordered the teams going outside the walls be no less than five. And if I'm still sane, I only count three."

"We won't be longer than a fart in the wind," Tao smiles, nervously. "No need for—"

"Wait here while I tell Carver."

"Now, there's no need for that."

"What's the hold up here?" A second sentinel comes to stand beside the younger one.

The young man salutes, back bolt-straight at attention.

"I was instructing these men of the five man rule, sir," he states.

"Carver," the old sentinel spits in the dirt, "putrid man he is. Let these fine working men pass."

"But, Carver—"

"I don't care a damn what Carver ordered. He's not in charge here, Byron is. And last I checked, he made me Sentinel Captain. Now, let these men through before I make you spit-shine the entire armory!"

The young sentinel nearly pokes his eye out with his rigid salute. He scurries to the gatehouse and shortly after, one of the gates clinks and clanks open.

"Well, that was almost a right pain in the ass," Tao laughs as we pass out of earshot. "Right bastard that Carver's turned into. Stirring up trouble, sticking his nose into everyone's business…ack! Tell me" he slightly turns his head to Dale and I, "why might you lot be going back to the Black Flag?"

"How in the hell do you know where we're going?" Dale asks.

"What other use is going up north?" He shifts in his seat to look us in the eye. "Am I right?"

"You're smarter than you look," Dale huffs.

"Oh, don't be upset," Tao laughs again. "I've known you long enough to know what you're thinking, and what you mean to keep from me."

I look at the familiar scene of trees around me as Tao takes us farther east. In the distance, even standing from the walls of the Compound, one could see the towers of the Rock Gardens standing tall over the trees, but this close to them reveals their true size. And we haven't even stepped foot in the desert.

"I don't suppose you'll tell me why you don't want a soul to know where you're going?" Tao says after the long silence.

"Makes things easier," says Dale.

"I hope you know what you're doing. It may be nearing the end of winter, but it's an eternal summer in the desert.

"We have what we need."

I look over the cart, passed the horse and beyond, over the crest of the hills to the tips of the Gardens. Mile after mile rolls by, the sun rises and the air grows hot. By midmorning, the sun bathes the land, but the jagged barrier of the Garden's spires shields us from the heat also showers us with blinding light that reflects brilliantly from their tops like a mirror. The cart rumbles to a halt.

"Alright, we're here," Tao announces. "Get the hell out of my cart."

Dale and I gather our things and hop out, landing on parched soil; it clouds around our boots.

"Thanks for the ride," I say.

"Think nothing of it," Tao smiles. "And don't worry, I'll keep you secret."

Tao spurs the horse on, turns the cart around and clomps and stomps and rumbles back towards the Southern Compound. I hike my pack high on my back, the contents inside rattle. Dale stands beside me and we stare ahead at the monster before us. The sun does not wait for us and continues to climb higher and higher above the Rock Gardens.

"We better get a move on," Dale starts walking.

I follow him. After an hour of hard walking we take our first step into the Rock Gardens; the blistering heat greets us enthusiastically.

*

I wish I had the wings of an eagle to soar far above the land and never feel the aching muscles in my legs. I wish I had the gills of a mighty fish so that I might swim in deep, cool rivers to escape the heat. All that I have are feet and they're killing me. Every step I take is double the effort it would normally on solid ground. The sand slides and gives way under my weight. It gets in my boots and blows in my hair and eyes. And that's not even the worse part. Noon came swiftly and brought with it an all-consuming heat. It distorts the tan horizon and evaporates my sweat before it has the chance to drench me.

After a few more agonizing hours, and many draughts of water later, I breathe a heavy sigh of relief. The gentle, rolling dunes of the Bymore that have been my constant companion are beginning to flatten and sprout towering spires of rock that make the earth mercifully solid. I could always see them in the distance, but now that I'm up close to them I see how enormous they actually are. I pass in and out of their shade and feel the temperature fall and rise with their shadow. I look up and see a shape ahead of me that still dominates the spires even at its greater distance; its apex burns with the ferocity of the sun, dwarfing the height and shine of its neighbors.

Dale and I make faster progress now inside the Rock Gardens. For all the challenges to navigation the spires impose, the gargantuan spire to the north is our guide amidst the maze. In the somewhat cooler atmosphere, time passes and the sun dips below the western wall of the Gardens and ignites their glassy tips red in the sunset. Dale and I slide through a narrow trench between shelves of rock, tempered and sharpened by the windswept desert, and come into a small, open area enclosed by a tight ring of stout spires. A few large plants around the fringes jut from the rocky ground, dusted with sand.

I approach one near me. Its limbs are thin and covered in barbs, but also bear bulbous fruits whose skin is leathery and rough, each a size and a half larger than my fist. I pluck one from the plant and give it a sniff. It gives off a faint sour odor and as I bring it to and from my nose, I can feel something moving inside. I take out my knife, cut into it and an opaque liquid spills from the puncture. It drips down my hand and soaks in the thirsty earth. I raise my hand to my lips and dab the liquid with the tip of my tongue. It tastes bitter and stings my mouth. I drop the fruit to the ground and finally sit down and rest my legs. I eagerly drink from my water skin and wearily drop it at my side when I have my fill.

"Dale," I say, "what do you think about resting here for the night?"

Dale stands on the opposite side of the basin of rock and sand, inspecting the surrounding walls. I notice that they are perforated by several small holes.

"Dale," I say again.

"Yeah?"

"We should camp here, I think."

"Agreed. I've done enough walking for one day."

He takes his hand from the rock, slumps to the sand and lets his pack fall from his shoulders.

"The only thing we have to worry about is keeping warm during the night," he says with eyes closed.

"I'm sure we'll be alright," I walk over to him and sit beside him. "It's a desert after all."

"Don't be so sure," he says, opening one eye. "The sun is everything in the Bymore. Without it, nights get colder than you think. But, if we use blankets and sleep close, then yes, we'll be alright."

Dale leans his head back against the wall and shuts his eyes again. I stare up into the darkening sky as the light flees from shadow.

"So, how come you don't want to talk about it?" I say.

Dale remains silent; his breathing deepens.

"I asked you before we left the Compound about what happened to Junn, and you didn't answer."

"And?" Dale gruffs.

"*And* I want you to tell me."

Dale opens his eyes and sits up, running his hand through his dirty hair.

"Why do you have so many questions?"

"Would it surprise you if I told you that Harlow said the same exact thing?"

"Not even a little," Dale chuckles.

"So," I say, "spill it."

There is a long pause as Dale shifts in place.

Cool, white light from the awakened moon comes down to our little circle and turns the tan sand grey and makes it glow; it illuminates just part of Dale's face.

"We were surrounded," he says. "The Bandits caught us by surprise and right from the start we lost so many good people... people I grew up with. The Strong Men didn't stand much of a chance. It was all I could do to keep myself alive, let alone everyone else that couldn't fight. But Junn, like he always does, came up with a plan at the last moment."

Dale pauses. He wipes his nose with his thumb and looks into the darkness.

"He said that, for the caravan to escape, we needed something to lure the Bandits away, to regroup and push back. He volunteered to be that person, but we both knew that such a plan would likely end in death. So I said I would go, but he was hearing none of it. I'll never forget what he said," Dale looks at the sand under his feet.

I dip my head and catch his eye.

"What did he say?"

Dale looks me in the eye. I see a great sadness there; he turns away.

"He said that 'the life of the elder should not witness the death of the young.' That's the last I saw of him. His last words a slap in the face."

"I don't understand."

"And how could you?" Dale snaps. "You never knew him like I did! He always had to be the protective big brother. Always had to do everything himself."

"I don't need to know him to be here now." I say, softly. "But I do know that he is a kind-hearted man and that he is worth saving, no matter what. And I wouldn't be prancing through a desert if I didn't believe that."

Dale says nothing.

"And for what it's worth, there's no one I'd rather take such a journey with."

"Yeah, yeah," Dale lays down on the sand and rests his head on his pack.

I lie out on the ground and cover us both with the blankets. We wait out the night, knowing that soon we will be again subjected to the mercy of the sun.

*

Morning comes with a dry heat. It is early still and the air retains the night's chill. I remove the blanket and sit up. Dale stirs and wakes. He stretches and searches through his pack.

"By all that is holy, where is it?" he mutters.

"What are you looking for?"

"My water skin, I can't find it," he answers. "I swear that I left it in here."

"Here. Use mine. There's still plenty left."

I look around for my own supply and see it moving away from me. I lunge for the container from where I sit and when my fingers take hold and lift it, a half dozen small, black shapes quickly burrow into the sand underneath. I jump with a start at the unexpected discovery, and in my surprise, I manage to unstop the water skin and douse a small radius around me.

"That's not good."

"Please don't tell me…"

"Yes," I shake my completely dry water skin, "it's empty."

"If we don't have water, we're dead!"

"Don't panic just yet," I say. "These weird water fruits don't taste great, but we can use those."

I walk over to the plants, but when I get close, I find that there are little creatures swarming it, tiny lizards with flat, pointy heads and scaly black bodies. They crawl over the bulbous fruits and chew on their stems, dropping them to the sand so that the other lizards can carry them away; they take them in their mouths towards the walls and crawl into those small perforations.

"Well," Dale calls, "what do you have?"

"More bad news, I'm afraid," I turn and face Dale. "Lizards stole our water."

"I'm sorry," Dale laughs, humorlessly. "I thought you said lizards stole our water."

"I did. They must have mistaken our water skins for those fruits and carried them into the holes in the walls."

"All of the water we had was in those!"

"Then we should start walking right away, before it gets too hot. Find water and—"

"Where are we supposed to find water in a place like this?" Dale retorts. "That's why they call it a desert!"

"I'm just trying to help."

"Let's just start moving before something else happens."

We quickly gather our things, shuffle our way back through the trench, and resume our parched trek through the Rock Gardens.

It does not take long for the ground to bake and the air to boil. The sun shines unabated. I can feel my skin burn and my body grow faint. With no water to replace the sweat, my head swims from dehydration and my vision blurs and sways. We trudge through dune and spire, always scanning the shifting horizon for the shimmer of water; the shape of another water plant. But I see no such salvation in this sea of dunes and rock. The only thing that changes is a towering shape far off in the distance. It rises above the spires around it and its peak shines brilliantly as though a star crowns its pinnacle. Its body and base wave in and out of view as the heat haze distorts what I can see over the endless expanse of the Bymore.

My boots are heavy and are increasingly more difficult to pick up again as I continue to march over the shifting sand. The wind does not make the struggle any easier as it periodically gusts and whips grains of sand in my face, getting in my eyes and dried mouth; I cannot even spit it out, though I try. I lift my delirious head and see Dale struggle in my same fashion. His head is bowed and his shoulders are slumped.

Our battle against the desert and our own ravaged bodies is nearing impossible to fight. My lips are cracked, my throat is scorched and my legs burn from shoveling over the sand and stepping over uneven rock. Dale stutters and falls to his knees. I hobble next to him.

"I can't," he gasps. "I can't go any more. Too… too tired."

"We can't stop now," I say, equally as exhausted.

I waddle passed Dale, but I only make it a few steps before my legs give out from under me. The sand sears the palms of my hands as I catch myself. I try to stand back up, but the sand moves under my feet and I collapse fully to the ground. I do not have any strength left to move any more. The sun watches as I fade in and out of consciousness until I give into its black embrace.

CHAPTER 10

— A Cause for Sanatan —

My eyes flutter open. Above me, I do not see the merciless, burning sky. I see the maroon canvas of a tent. I am laying on my back, on the mats covering the floor; a cushion supports my head. Where am I? I push my weary body upright and my head swims as the tent spins violently; I can feel myself about to vomit.

"Mahlaan! Mahlaan hunak!!" a voice says.

I hear scurrying feet, and the next thing I see is a wooden pail placed in front of me moments before my stomach empties bile and what meager food I last ate. I wipe my mouth and look up at the stranger. A man with dark skin. He wears a shabby, brown robe with coarse salt and pepper hair sticking off his head at humorous angles. He holds a gourd and offers it to me, helping me drink from it while supporting the back of my head with gentle hands as I enthusiastically have my fill. He takes the gourd away and I look up at him.

This man is undoubtedly Alnnasi. Was he watching us? Waiting for the desert to take its toll before he swooped in? But why does he look like he's helping me? Didn't Dale say that these people are dangerous?

"There is no need for fear," the Alnnasi says. "You are safe and in friendly company," he sets the gourd down and sits on an adjacent mat, legs crossed under his robe.

I continue to eye the stranger cautiously.

"You have much fortune that we discovered you and your companion when we did," he continues. "You were on verge of never waking."

"We ran out of water," I say. "Tiny lizards."

"Ahha, yes!" He laughs as if we share a secret joke. "The Sahali are a pest in this place, but can be dealt with simply. Though, a pest always."

"Where is Dale? Is he alright?"

"Ahha, yes. He is well and strong as fearsome Batal," he laughs. "Had to fight him a little to bring him here."

"That is good. But," I look around the mostly empty tent, "where is here?"

"You, my friend, are with Alnnasi in Al'hadayiq. What your people call Rock Gardens. Tell me, why do you try to cross the desert? This place does not forgive — I don't know if you are brave or stupid."

"Both, I reckon. We were on a mission, an important one. Dale and I took the desert road to avoid trouble."

"Ahha," the Alnnasi chuckles. "But trouble knows no borders," he springs to his feet, still quite spry in his perceived age. "I am sure you would like to see your friend. Follow me."

He practically skips out of the tent. I get up, still dazed from dehydration. I look down and tentatively bend to retrieve the gourd before I follow the Alnnasi.

As soon as I step out of the tent, I nearly trip over an animal being led by a rope. I apologize as the Alnnasi tugs the animal away. It is a stout creature with a short, black coat and two tightly curled horns coming from the back of his head. The two of them continue walking over the trail through the tents and I lose sight of them. I look around me and see many similarly dressed Alnnasi going about their various business; some carry wooden casks on either end of a pole across the broad of their shoulders, some walk and converse in pairs, speaking in the sharply rising and falling language of the Alnnasi, and others carry bow and quivers of arrows with them. The place is very excited and the air buzzes with anticipation. I take a few curious steps into the encampment and I see my friendly Alnnasi emerging from the tent in front of me. He smiles, holds the tent flap open, and gestures for me to come inside. I follow his direction and find Dale lying inside.

"As you see," the Alnnasi says, "Dale is fine."

Dale sits up on the mat-covered tent with water and food to spare. His lips are chapped and his sand-swept hair is an absolute mess, but besides that he is in perfect health.

"I am so very happy that you both are well, but I must leave you to make preparations."

"Prepare for what?" I ask.

"Well, the festival, of course!" He beams, perfect teeth blinking white in the light creeping in from the fluttering tent flap. "It is Alnnasi tradition to shelter and welcome travelers, and so long has it been."

He departs once more, but I call after him.

"Wait a moment," the Alnnasi pauses on the threshold. "Would you tell me your name so that I can thank you properly?"

"My name is Orbith," he smiles and exits the tent before any thanks can be given.

I turn around and look at Dale.

"How are you feeling?"

"I'm feelin' queasy, but that beats being dead in the desert," he answers. "It is a true miracle that they found is when they did."

"Agreed," I sit beside him. "Have you learned anything interesting from Orbith?"

"Depends on what you find interesting. Said that we're welcome here, no doubt about that; that we're something of a special event for them. He also said not to go north."

"Good thing we're going that way," I shake my head. "Why shouldn't we go that way?"

"Don't know," Dale shrugs. "Kept hissing and tapping his wrists like the thought of it would hurt to speak aloud. But, go that way we must. Guess we'll find what all the trouble is when we get there."

"What a strange people these Alnnasi," I muse. "Almost hard to believe I've lived so close to them without knowing."

"The world is quite the small and large place. You know," Dale says with an air of mystery, "I lived with the Alnnasi for a time."

"Really?"

"For a short while, yeah. I'm surprised Junn never mentioned it before."

"Whenever your name came up," I lean back on my hands, "we just talked about how bad you stink."

Dale throws an idle cushion at me while I laugh at his expense.

"I've spent enough time in this tent," he says. "I need to stretch my legs."

He stands and I rise also, but before I stand all the way, he pushes me over and runs out, giggling like a child. I finally get up and join him outside, in the heat of late afternoon; we begin walking around aimlessly through the Alnnasi conclave. Most of them that we pass give us curious looks and I cannot entirely blame them. I am sure that our lighter skin tone and improper attire stand out quite a bit. We stride past a pen where a man tends to more of those horned animals, both young and old with shaggier coats and much longer horns.

"When did you live with these people?" I ask.

"Long before you came to us," says Dale. "I was…oh," he scratches his chin, "no older than ten at the time. Junn was well on the way to joining the Black Flag, ready to become the youngest member they've had."

"And you wanted something to do?"

"It was by accident, really. I was a lot like you. Always wandering around the trees and streams, looking for something new and exciting. And one day I found a group of them by the northern fringes of the Resting Wood. They were kind. Must've thought I was lost and brought me back with them. Never came down this far south, though."

"How long did you stay?"

"The better part of two years."

"Two years?" I splutter. "Are you joking?"

"You should have seen Malory's face when I got back. Never in my life have I heard her so angry and happy to see me again. Junn almost seemed to expect that's where I've been off to, clever bastard," he tilts his head back in fondness of the far-away memory.

"What else don't I know about you and the Alnnasi?" I ask as we walk passed a couple women with baskets filled with leather water fruit.

"Not much else," he says, simply. "They showed me a lot of how to live in harmony with the environment and people of the land. That used to make sense to me."

"And now?"

"And now I've grown up and seen what the world's really like."

"What's that supposed to mean?"

"C'mon, Vipe. You can't be so innocent."

"Never claimed to be. I just think it's worth it to keep an open mind."

"People all over can be right terrible," Dale lowers his voice a touch. "Never know who's got a knife for your back."

"People all over can be kind and generous," I say. "You, Junn, Harlow, Orbith. I can keep going. My point is that no one can show you their worth if you always keep them out. Take me for example. You used to hate me, now you can't get enough of me."

"Okay, okay. Point taken," he claps me on the back. "Some people are worth all their trouble. But what I'm most concerned about is where a man can find a meal around here."

We continue to meander in the heat while Alnnasi gawk and smile at us. I cannot believe just how large their camp is. We have been sightseeing through maroon tents, stores of tools and supplies of their foreign design, and stockpiles of food and water for the better part of an hour and I still have not seen its end. Perhaps what's more surprising than that is exactly how they've been able to not only build a city of tents in the desert but sustain it, prosperously too. We eventually come to a spacious courtyard with a canopy of beautiful design that shields the ground from the sun. People gather, creating, cooking, weaving, or smoking from long and slender pipes. It takes a good deal of willpower for me not to join them and partake in their native herbs whose scent I can't quite identify.

"Mmm, do you smell that?" Dale closes his eyes and breathes in long and deep. "Something's cooking."

He looks around for the source, eventually noticing a curl of smoke rising above the tents. We walk through the courtyard between a small line of weavers as they work their needles and find ourselves standing in front of a fire pit, over which roasts a large piece of meat; I can see sizzling fat dripping from it. My stomach growls. Orbith notices us from where he peers over the shoulder of the Alnnasi smokemaster and comes over to us.

"Greetings, friends! I see you found where we prepare the Alramal."

"It looks quite good," I say. "Smells like it, too."

"It is indeed!" Orbith says, jovially. "And it is only had when Alnnasi celebrate: The Solstice of Euyun, the first rainfall of the year, and of course, when we are blessed with unexpected company. They are just a few of the traditions we carry on from our brothers and sisters in the east."

"There are more Alnnasi in the Bymore?" Dale asks.

"There are quite a number of us, yes! We come from Mahid, cradle of Alnnasi in the east where most of my people dwell. There are we that stay here, and north," at this Orbith shudders and taps his wrists. "But enough with unpleasant thoughts. Come, I would like for you to meet my family!"

Orbith taps us forward on our backs, taking us back through the courtyard towards the largest tent in the conclave. If you could even call it a tent. It is grand to be certain, buttressed by additional tents that add to its magnitude. Banners of green and gold hang from tall staves in the ground along the front and more from atop the tent sway regally in the small wind. In the space where a door would be is two halves of a curtain of black and gold with beads of multicolor studding its fabric. Orbith strolls to the entrance and holds the way open.

We step inside and stand in a tall space, the roof supported by a large pole in the center, and mats and cushions are placed around its base and in clusters around the edges; low tables as their centerpiece. To the center, left, and right of the space are entrances to separate parts of the tent, capped by more black and beaded curtains; all cast in a maroon light as the sun filters through the tent's red fabric.

"This is incredible, Orbith," I say. "Your family lives here?"

"This is the house of the Zaeim," Orbith explains. "A terrible trouble to keep sand out."

"What is a Zaeim?"

"The Zaeim is the Alnassi leader," Dale answers.

"Very good!" Orbith praises. "You know much of Alnnasi ways?"

"I was taught a few things when I was younger. Enough to know that to become a Zaeim, you have to be exceptionally gifted in leadership, bravery and talented in combat, wise and impartial, and able to command the respect of those they lead. I'm sure that you must be very busy with your duties, Orbith."

"I, Zaeim?" Orbith cackles. "Ahha, no, no. I am no Zaeim. She is my Zawja. My… how you say companion of life."

"Your wife is the Zaeim?" I ask.

"Ahha, wife! Yes, I think that is the name. Wait right here and I will bring her."

Orbith turns on his heel and steps through the middle and largest of the three entrances. I can hear his exuberant voice from the other side as he speaks in his native tongue. Their conversation is short and Orbith returns to Dale and I heralding the arrival of a tall woman with long, crinkly black hair and a gold net of small and ornate chains dressing it.

"Allow me to introduce the Lord Zaeim, Hazin Uwli," Orbith declares. "And also the most beautiful bride!"

"Please, my love. Modesty," says Hazin with a smile. "It is quite wonderful to make your acquaintance."

"We are honored, Lord Zaeim," I bow my head. "Your home and conclave are both very impressive."

"There is no need for that," Hazin tilts my head back up with a gentle finger under my chin. "Only if you were Thalvian would I expect such formality."

"Modesty," Dale whispers and elbows me; he looks at Hazin. "Thank you for your hospitality. We would have been long dead if you hadn't help us."

"It is the right thing to do," Hazin shows her palms in a sign of humble humility. "As Euyun takes us who travel the earth, we, his disciples take in those that travel within our borders. You have made Orbith very happy. We have not held Sanatan since we were children."

"Is that the name of the celebration?" I ask.

"It is indeed," Orbith says. "And there is something very special I would like to show you before we begin the feast at sundown," he springs to Hazin's side and pecks her cheek with a kiss. "Go and finish your many duties, my love. I will be off!"

Hazin smiles at us and ducks back through the beaded curtain. Orbith, his excitement fully invigorated, leads Dale and I out of the Zaeim's tent, through the whole of the conclave, and out into the sand-blown outskirts. We follow him as he weaves and hops his way over and around the rocks and small spires that guard the conclave. Dale and I begin to breathe heavily as we chase after him, not in the least cherishing the thought of becoming lost in the encroaching night. We stumble out of the maze and find Orbith standing triumphantly on the brink of a ridge. I join him and look over the majesty of Orbith's special location. The spires of the Rock Gardens cradle the sand on either side and stretch off into the distant, onyx horizon; the indigo-dyed sand and the canopy of the stars shatter the sky as they chase away the sun.

"This is beautiful, Orbith," Dale says. "I must admit, this place can be incredi—"

"Ahha, this is not Orbith's place," he laughs. "To reach there, you must earn it."

He turns away from the desert expanse and points up at the spires behind us. I follow his finger up to the summit of the spire that looms over the Alnnasi conclave. I look back down at Dale. He looks at me.

"Are you sure this is a good idea?" I ask. "I'm not too familiar with the Rock Gardens, but—"

"Ahha, do not worry!" he bursts. "Trust in your feet and follow me. I know the safe way up."

Orbith nearly skips as he heads in the direction of his spire. We join him at the base and wait for our guide to make the next move. He turns and smiles at us. He faces the spire, pulls up his robes, and slides his bare foot into a vertical slit in the face of the rock.

"Do you see?" he says, "This is not difficult."

Orbith shoots up the side of the spire with surprising speed and agility, reaching out his hands for climbing points; using his legs to push him upward.

"Well, come on," Dale says. "We're gonna lose him if we just stand here."

Dale marches to the starting point and follows in Orbith's footsteps. His progress is slow and labored, but Dale is soon hot on Orbith's heels. I, too, begin the climb. The surface is surprisingly smooth to the touch, but as I go up, my hands become covered in dust. Orbith may have been right to say that this climb is not difficult, and when I glance down to check my progress, I see that falling to my death is also an easy task. I continue to find foot and hand holds, trying to forget how far above the ground I am. I hear Orbith and Dale shouting down at me to hurry up. If it was not for the shade of night, I may already have reached the top, not as if they care to hear my excuses. But I persevere and soon pull myself on to a small shelf a few meters below the very top of the spire.

"Ahha, good! You made it!" Orbith cheers. "Come this way and see!"

He shuffles around the spire to its south face and disappears. Dale follows behind me as I tentatively inch my way around the extremely narrow lip that wraps around the spire, meeting Orbith as he takes a seat with his legs dangling over the edge; he smiles up at me.

"What do you think?" Orbith says.

I look out and see the Alnnasi conclave splayed out beneath me and the hundreds upon hundreds of tents, all glowing red from the twinkling firelight speckling the entire camp. The light is strongest at the spacious area before the grand tent of the Zaeim in the conclave's throbbing heart where they make the last preparations for Sanatan. I look up, past the settlement and over the land through which Dale and I suffered and see just how far into the Rock Gardens we've come; how large the Bymore really is.

The last of the sun slips into darkness in the west, a last red line burning the horizon beyond the spires, and at last night envelopes the world.

"You can see everything up here," I say.

"Euyun has truly blessed me," says Orbith.

"I almost wish that we could stay here longer."

"You are most welcome to."

"As tempting as that offer is," Dale leans his weight against the rock behind him, "we must continue northwards come morning."

Orbith hisses and taps his wrists.

"Why do you do that?" I look down at the Alnnasi.

"It is a foul memory that resides in the north," he answers, mournfully. "A blight on Alnnasi history. Must you go that way?"

"We have no other choice," says Dale.

Orbith heaves a great sigh as he tightly crosses his legs, the dirt-covered pads of his feet showing black in the silver moonlight.

"Then, for your safety, there are things that you must know. Do you see that?" He pivots his torso as he points his long finger at the gargantuan spire jutting from the earth like the very pillar holding up the heavens. "That is the Eye of Euyun. The place where the Baarutal worship madness. Long ago, during the time of the father of fathers, the Alnnasi were one people. But a great war was fought against brother and sister. One side wanted tradition, the other wanted blood. The Zaeim called for help and Thalvian king sent the defeated Alnnasi into banishment, into the Rock Gardens."

I glance over at Dale; he looks back.

"Should that worry us?" I ask.

"Ahha, no my friends," he laughs, but there is no mirth to his voice. "When Baarutal lost the war, they took their evil rituals with them and practiced them without limit. Long has the Eye of Euyun been a symbol of hope for Alnnasi, but Baarutal burrowed into it, tainted it and used its power to further taint themselves. They stood in Euyun's sight directly. It was terrible. Still is. But not for Orbith. I never went through Muruae, evil practice."

"Then, you — all the Alnnasi here are not Baarutal?" I ask.

"Once, we were," Orbith sighs again. "Long after Baarutal corrupted the Eye of Euyun, some Alnnasi that clung to old ways whispered revolution, change things back to the way they were before the war and banishment. Their whispers became shouts of defiance and they challenged the Baarutal, led by T'hanzin, great man; Hazin's great-grandfather. T'hanzin led his people to freedom and we are his children that live in the south."

"We can't catch a break, can we?" Dale says. "Bandits dogging our every step and now we have to cross paths with more insane cultists? Dare I ask if things can get any worse?"

"All is not lost," Orbith rises to his feet and places a hand on our shoulders. "You are in sacred land. Even when Baarutal is corrupt, Euyun is strong. He will watch over and preserve you, you see. He is strength at night and peace to weather the storm. He has sheltered us here and he will shelter you on your journey."

I stare into the deep, black wells of Orbith's eyes and I feel his reassurance warm me like a heavy blanket. I hear drums beating and voices singing down in the conclave.

"Ahha!" Orbith claps his hands. "We talked too long. Come! It is time for the Sanatan!"

*

The fringes of the conclave are totally absent as Orbith escorts us to the celebration. As we move farther in, closer to the tent of the Zaeim, I can hear Alnnasi voices become louder; Orbith cannot stop smiling.

We pass the final row of tents and step into the courtyard, packed to the breaking with Alnnasi who are all dressed differently than before; where once their robes were tan and drab, now they are all shades and hues of red, bright yellows, vibrant oranges, and soulful blues. They dance wildly to the rapid drum beat, black hair and colorful clothes dancing with them. Young children and youths dance in concentric circles, moving in alternating directions and waving long and colorful streamers filling the air with their joy and laughter; the smell of the feast makes my stomach growl. Some of the older men and women rise to their feet from the tables when they see Dale and I.

Orbith enthusiastically waves us forward, and Dale and I follow him around the Alnnasi and the feast splayed before them. I glance down at what is on their plates and see what looks like a ball of twisted roots, hunks of dark bread, slices and chips of meat and more water fruit that are a darker shade of violet and smaller then when I fist saw them the day before. We end up directly in front of the Zaeim's grand tent, in front of which the Zaeim herself sits. She is wearing a simple yet quite large mantle around her neck that covers much of her chest, made up of long, golden rectangular pieces, held together by small, thin chain links, more of which ornament the rest of her dark red robes, speckled with dots of yellow and streaks of orange. The enormous roast that I saw earlier is placed before Hazin and the low burning fire beneath it makes her small chains shimmer and sparkle. Orbith approaches her, kisses her hand, and takes his place beside her. Dale and I follow behind and Hazin raises her right hand to us.

"Welcome," she says. "Please, sit and be fed."

Dale and I gratefully oblige her and sit in front of equally full plates as the ones around us. But before we can take our first bite, the Zaeim stands and all Alnnasi rise with her; the drums cease, the voices silence.

"Alnnasi! Hayaka yoku. This day, Euyun brings two of the Ard to us, and we welcome them. Long are the days since last this happened and long are the days that we keep tradition of sheltering weary travelers. And so it continues. So eat and be glad of Euyun's blessings."

Hazin sits and the gathered Alnnasi sit after she has done so. Dale immediately sets to eating. The food is delicious and surprisingly flavorful. The chips of meat are spicier than the sliced pieces; they are savory and tenderer. The balls of roots have a crunchy skin and a soft inside, not unlike the potatoes we grow at the Compound. The night goes on in high spirits as the Alnnasi and Dale – doing more than his fair share – surely consume every morsel of the feast. I can hear Orbith speaking with Hazin in their own language, but I can understand when he mentions our names. The Zaeim turns to Dale and I.

"I must apologize for not being a good host. I had many duties today," Hazin says. "I trust my Zawja was more than adequate?"

"He certainly kept us entertained," says Dale through a face-full of bread.

"That is wonderful to hear," she smiles. "But I must know, why is it that you come to us? The desert is no easy path."

I look over at Dale; he swallows and nods at me affirmingly. I return Hazin's expectant look.

"We're on a mission to save our brother," I answer. "He was captured by Bandits three months ago."

"Bandits you say," she takes a dainty drink from the water fruit. "This is not the first time I have heard that name, but Euyun has kept them far from us. They are not meant for Bymore sun. I do know their deeds are terrible. I am sorry to say, but your brother has most likely perished."

I look away from Hazin's dark eyes, flickering with firelight. I've been able to keep it out of mind for so long. Pushed it down with every swing of my training sword with Harlow, buried it with every stride through the Bymore desert. But now it is unearthed once again and I cannot deny its crushing weight. He can't be dead. He can't be. The Bandits are changed. They've never taken hostages before, at least not ones that were still alive. Junn is not dead.

"I still think—"

"Pardon me, Lord Zaeim," Dale says.

I glance at him and see his hard face.

"But you don't know my brother. If any can survive, he is the man to do it."

"Of course," Hazin says, gracefully. "Excuse my ignorance. I see now your need for haste. Tell me what you need and it is yours."

Dale coughs up some food; I'm speechless.

"Ahha! Look at them," laughs Orbith. "They cannot believe your offer!"

"That is most generous of you," Dale croaks. "But surely you've done enough for us already."

"Do not be foolish," Hazin waves a dismissive hand. "You will need water, of course, and Adiat to preserve you in the sun. Take also Alramaat to ride."

"You are truly gracious," I say.

"She is as beautiful as she is kind," beams Orbith. "It is a shame that our sons are not here. Ouror knows every stone in every ally of Al'hadayiq. He would be the perfect guide."

"You have children?" Dale asks.

"We do, but to call them children is not the right word," Hazin says. "Ouror is strong and quite resourceful, but Sarian has growing to do."

"It would have been a pleasure to meet them," says Dale. "But I'm afraid that we must be on our way at first light."

"I will have everything prepared for your departure," Orbith says. "When you are satisfied, I will show you where you may rest."

"You read my mind," I say. "Thank you both for your generosity."

"You are most welcome to it," Hazin tips her head, gold chains flashing.

"Come now," Orbith rises. "I will show you the way."

CHAPTER 11

—Fists & Hollows—

Just by looking at these resilient, desert people one would scarcely guess at their genius. The first time I found myself in their tents I experienced the sun's all-consuming heat subdued, when the Alnnasi during Sanatan educated me on how they're able to keep their conclave sustained using deep, deep wells and irrigation, and now I am experiencing a new layer of their ingenuity. This morning, as promised by Hazin, I found an Adiat, resembling the light grey robes all Alnnasi wear, resting folded on the mats beside me. Now that I'm wearing it under the sun, on my way to Hazin's tent, I know beyond doubt to never judge by appearance alone. The exterior of the Adiat's fabric is stiff to the touch and smells like an Alramaat pen, but the inner lining is silky smooth and light as a feather.

I come to the courtyard before the grand tent looking as native and natural as ever, and my skin has become a good deal darker from the outset of my journey, what feels like a lifetime ago. I wave awkwardly at well-wishing Alnnasi as I enter the Zaeim's tent and find Dale, Orbith and Hazin waiting for me.

"Ahha, fair morning to you, friend!" Orbith greets. "I hope that your rest was peaceful?"

"I wouldn't have been disappointed to remain that way longer."

"I gave you an extra hour or two while Orbith and I made the final preparations," Dale says. "And here I'd thought you'd be grateful."

"You have everything in order?" Asks Hazin.

"I believe that we do," Dale pats himself down as he racks his brain. "Nothing left now but the road."

"That is excellent to hear. Might I give you one piece of advice before you depart?"

Dale and I pause on our way to the exit; Orbith has one hand on the flap.

"Please," Dale says.

"Stay away from the Eye of Euyun if at all possible. The Baarutal are not known for their grace in hospitality."

"I pray that you will never know it," Orbith taps his wrists. "But we will hold you no longer. Come, I will show you out."

Dale and I turn to follow Orbith out of the tent, but Hazin places her hand on my shoulder.

"There is one last thing that you must know," she says, her expression deadly serious. "If all else fails, challenge Batal."

"I don't understand," I say over Dale's beckoning voice.

"Challenge them, do not forget," she escorts me outside. "Safe travels, Viper. You are always welcome here."

I thank her and chase after Dale and Orbith, reeling internally from Hazin's ominous farewell. I catch up to Dale as he mounts a large Alramaat with his travel pack and extra supplies from the Alnnasi already slung across its back. Orbith tightens the straps around the second of the two mounts.

"A word of caution about Alramaat," Orbith says, pulling the last strap tight. "Speak to them sternly and strong. Use 'hab' for go, and 'tawa' for stop. Come, Viper, this one is ready. There is plenty of water for you both and with Euyun you will exit Al'hadayiq in three days. Go safe, my friends, and go swift."

He slaps the hind of Dale's Alramaat and spurs it into a brisk trot. I mount my own and encourage it forward with the Alnnasi command. I come in stride beside Dale and together we depart the Alnnasi conclave and dive back into the depths of the Rock Gardens' spires and the Eye of Euyun that is present on the horizon. The wind starts to blow.

*

Our road north, so far, is a narrow and treacherous one. It forces us to weave through the towering spires and they break the curtain of sun into shafts of light and pools through which we periodically pass and feel its punch of heat, though severely lessened by my Adiat. I shield my eyes against the grains of sand carried by the wind as I glance up at the spires, moving from the sun's ruthless stare, and see their black silhouette against the pale sky, the dominance of Euyun's Eye drawing us ever closer, despite our best efforts.

We continue in silence with our heads on a swivel, daring not to speak out of fear from being noticed by unseen ears. Hour after hour pass by. The hooves of our mounts provide a constant tempo that echoes into nothing as it bounces against the columns of rock surrounding us.

The wind has not stopped tearing through our pinched and perilous road or hissing over the sand since we once again entered the thick of the Garden's spires. When the wisps of white that have grown to full-bodied clouds break, I see the solid black shapes of the fence of rock against the dreary sky. Had we not our Adiat to shield us from the biting sand on the rushing air I guess that by now my skin would be torn away from my bones. I can barely see more than twenty or so paces ahead of me and the situation yields no signs of improving, so I trust in Dale and our Alramaat to guide us.

I ride through the swirling maelstrom of sand. It is all I can do to just keep my eyes open so that I don't mistakenly tumble into some unseen rift in the earth, or deviate from Dale's winding course and become hopelessly lost. Even the Alramaat is showing its snorting and huffing discomfort. I spit and sputter and endlessly run my fingers over my eyes to brush away the unceasing stream of sand and grit. Then I see a dark shape looming high overhead.

"Up there!" Dale yells over the surge. "Shelter!"

We aim our mounts towards the promise of respite and the ground beneath begins to dip and slope. It levels out as we reach the base of the spire and the sandstorm rages over our heads. Tendrils of sand snake around the spire visible above as I dismount and lean my weight against it, thankful for clean breath and vision at last.

"I truly despise this place," Dale grimaces as he shakes sand from his hair and clothes.

"Agreed," I turn and rummage around my pack for those water fruits Orbith gave us.

"We're leaving as soon as this storm passes. The sooner the better—"

Dale's voice cuts off short.

I turn my neck to glance behind, guessing that I would see him scraping sand from his tongue. But I don't see that. I don't see anything at all, not Dale or his Alramaat.

"Dale?" I step tentatively towards where he stood.

I look down at the sand-covered, rocky ground and see signs of frantic movement, scuffling feet. What in the hell? I spin around to look for answers, panic rising in my chest. My Alramaat is missing now.

"Dale?" I begin to shout. "Where are—"

A hard, callused hand closes around my mouth from behind and pulls me into the spire's solid stone. Only, it's not solid.

*

I am immersed in complete darkness. Invisible fingers remove my weapons. I feel the disembodied hand's grip around my wrist as it leads me through a narrow passage; my shoulders occasionally knock against rough stone. I try to speak, but dust clogs my lungs.

My eyes adjust to the black around me and pick up a small glimmer of light ahead.

"Who are you?" I ask through cracked lips. "Where am I?" A solemn grunt and a hard tug on my arm meet my query.

We continue to march and the light ahead grows stronger, revealing the complexion of my captor. The light shows the outline of a man with no hair upon his head. In its place, from what I can gather, are pieces of fabric, showing translucent in the dim.

My heart races. I pull and struggle against the strength of the person's grip. He barks at me in his native language and yanks on my arm once again, proceeding along at an accelerated rate.

It is then that we arrive in the full light of our destination.

The size of the passage spoke nothing about the destination, for inside the hollowed spire yields a grand and awesome sight. I stand in the midst of a dark atrium whose ceiling stretches up to the very pinnacle of the spire; wrapping around the circular walls, whose circumference is at least one-hundred strides, are spiral stairs that form landings at regular intervals. Narrow slits are cut into the towering walls and allow the hot Bymore sun to stream through, their beams crossing over one another the entire length of the spire in a mesmerizing helix; red torchlight burns in the shadows. It all makes me momentarily forget about the vice grip around my wrist. But only for a moment. My captor yanks me after him and the Baarutal gathered here take notice of my arrival with glowering stares and harsh sounding words in the language of the Alnnasi.

A commotion far above me draws my curious eyes upward. Marching over the spire's higher level, I see two shadowy figures dragging a third by his arms across the floor. As the Baarutal bring the third closer to their unseen destination, his anxious resistance becomes more and more desperate and vocal. His screams of protest rattle in his voice and bounce around the spire and amplify his terror. A few scream-filled seconds later I hear the deep, echoing boom of a great door closing and all becomes still once more.

I hear Dale's voice emanating from a separate passage.

I turn my head in every direction in search of him and I cry out, but the Baarutal leading me silences me with a fist to my gut. After I get my breath I glare at the back of his head with watery eyes and furious indignation. It is then that I see the full scope of his appearance… And I wish I hadn't. Every square inch of his exposed flesh is horrifically burned and scared; the things I saw in the dark of the passage that looked like fabric clinging to his scalp are actually flakes of decaying flesh, peeling off like the skin of an onion. I turn away my gaze from this nightmare and I see that the skin of his hand gripping my own is no exception from the rest of his body. My stomach turns over and I force down hot spit

The Baarutal leads me to the base of the spiral stair and we climb. We go level after level, each floor resembling the last: plain doors set into stone walls, narrow windows to the outside, and the bystander Baarutal, silently observing me as I head for an unknown destination, and that, above all, scares me the most. Up and up we go, my head reeling with panic, waiting for something to happen, the sure punishment that awaits me. I cry out again, this time in anger.

"Do you plan to kill me through exhaustion?" I pull against the huge weight of the Baarutal. "It's going to take a lot more than that to—"

The Baarutal stops dead in his tracks. He turns round and looks down at me with the joy of inflicting pain upon others glinting in his eyes. He drives his thick and scared fist into my stomach, my jaw, the side of my head. When the rain of blows finally ends I can barely see straight. I feel my numbed body dragging along the floor and suddenly I am weightless as I fly through the air and collide against a rough stone wall, landing in a dark cell lit only by a slit window.

I stumble to my feet and make for the door as it slams in my face. I pound my fist against it, but it is unyielding and offers no promise of escape. I slink to the dirt floor.

CHAPTER 12

— Chains of Metal, Chains of Earth —

What do they plan to do with me? What do they plan to do with Dale? I heard his voice, but that now seems to be an eternity behind me. What if Dale is being tortured right now as I sit here, locked up and useless? I need to get out of this room. I stand up and put my lips close to the gap made by the door ill-fitted to the frame.

"Come on, you bastards!" I shout. "This is how you treat a Zaeim's emissary?"

I am no emissary, but no need to tell them that.

"I demand to be released!"

I wonder if anyone can even understand me. I move away and turn to look out the slit of the window. What I see only adds to my sense of helplessness. From this high above the earth, I have a perfect and unobstructed view of the expanse of spires that stretch to the edge of the Rock Gardens, and onwards to the dunes of the Bymore, who's massive breadth I cannot even begin to fathom. Looks like no escape will be made in that direction either, even if I could slip through the window.

"Hello, are you still there?"

I hear a raspy whisper drift through the door. I press my ear against it.

"Are you from the Alnnasi in South Al'hadayiq?"

"Yes. I mean, no. I came from there, but I am no Alnnasi," I whisper back to the voice from what I suppose is an adjacent cell.

"I knew as much by your voice," the speaker's tone drops. "It was a vain hope. You are not here for Muruae?"

"My friend and I got lost in a sandstorm and we were taken captive."

I hear the speaker mutter something like a chant in his native tongue.

"I am sorry."

"It's not your fault," I know my words sound empty, but what else is there to say?

"I know that you do not know me, stranger. But, will you help carry a message for me? If you make it out?"

I sit in a dumb silence for a moment. If I make it out…

"Of course," my voice cracks.

"Tell my family that I will always be with them and that—"

I hear an approaching parade of footsteps.

"—that they are stronger than they know."

I hear the feet go passed the door. I can't see above their elbows from my angle, but there are five of them. They stop before the cell adjacent to mine; one turns the lock and opens it.

"Euyun bless them!" The speaker is shouting now. His words transform from coherent speech in the Common Tongue to unintelligible babbling and cries for mercy as I see the Baarutal drag him from the cell.

I press my check hard against the door to steal a glance outside. I can just make out the sight of an ornate set of double doors standing black and ominous, blurry through one eye. The group takes the crying man towards them and I hear, for the second time, the echoing boom of their closing. I lean my head back against the cell door. I don't even know who that man was, let alone his family. Just a false promise to a dead man, or soon-to-be dead anyhow.

The door behind me suddenly bursts open. I whip around, preparing for the worst, and I see the most ghastly man that has ever befallen my eyes. He is a mountain of a man, looming over me as he lumbers into my cell. I scramble backwards. His titanic proportions do not solely go up, but outward as well. His wide girth only just fits through the doorway; the vertical beam of sun through the window shines on his skin, another point of fascination — it is not nearly as hideous as the other Baarutal I've seen. The flesh on his head and the blisters across his bear chest are not raw or spitting blood. He must be old, long passed what Orbith and the stranger called Muruae.

"Do you speak, Draimon?" The hulk asks in a deep, abyssal voice; thick vocal cords move under scorched skin. The last word he spits like a curse.

"I do," I say, still pressed against the back wall. "Tell me where my friend is."

"You make demands of me?" He bellows with hideous laughter. "The emissary of Alnnasi have no power over Zaeim-Baarutal!"

So, they did understand me.

"We intend to pass through. That is all."

The Zaeim-Baarutal looks down on me with total disgust, the place where his nose used to be squirms and his scarred hands ball into fists.

"It matters not your intentions!" He roars. "You have defiled sanctity of Euyun! You will die!"

"Then why take me here? Why not just get it over with?"

What am I saying?

"I am protected by the noble Hazin of the Alnnasi and I challenge for Batal!" I say the words with a completely unfounded confidence, hoping to the stars that my voice does not waver.

I do not understand the weight of the words spoken, but they have a perturbed effect over the Zaeim.

"Draimon wishes to become Qintal?" He grunts what I can only imagine to be a curse, lips curling back to show yellowed teeth. "You will soon wish that you were thrown from the spire. Follow."

The Zaeim gives me one last look and thuds out of the cell. Four guards quickly file in and surround me, taking me out into the landing and lead me down. I descend to the ground level and march toward a dark clay path on the floor that leads to a wide, open arch with red torch light around its mouth. I come closer and I can hear the phantom sound of someone's voice clawing its way from the depths to my ears. The Zaeim leads me and his guards through the arch and into the sloping path set within. Soon the light from the atrium fades into the foreboding gloom of the wide tunnel. After a few steps into this dark I feel the path start to turn; a little way further and I feel myself walking in circles.

The torches on the walls fall away slowly as each step I take downward snatches them, one-by-one. All I can see now is the slightly darker, large shape of the Zaeim pressed against the tunnel. The voices I come towards grow more substantial as I am led down through the spire.

The tunnel brightens to a glow at the bottom of the inverted tower, capped in an uncharacteristic, studded metal door. The Zaeim approaches and raps twice upon it, the sound echoing solid and loud back through the tunnel.

I hear metal grinding over metal as the door's heavy bolt slides out of the lock on the opposite side. The way opens and the attending Baarutal steps aside swiftly as the Zaeim shoves by, leading his guard and I in his huge wake. The room I enter is even more poorly lit than the atrium far above me. It is a shallow space with multiple corridors shooting out from it like the spokes of a wheel. The Zaeim barks something at the doorman angrily and jerks his head in my direction. The doorman slides his eye over at me and grunts his understanding to the Zaeim before he disappears into one of the corridors.

I'm left naught to do but stand and wait. I look down at the ragged flagstones and see the red slime of old blood caking the cracks. I hope that doesn't belong to Dale. I hope that Hazin's advice is not also a death sentence. I look around at the small handful of spindly torches hanging from their brackets and wonder what is taking so long. The Zaeim shouts something and his voice bounces around and rattles in my ears. When the ringing subsides I hear the rapid tapping of feet and soon the doorman returns; I can see blood slowly dripping from his fingertips.

The Zaeim pushes by the wounded Baarutal and his guard sweeps me after him. The walk through the corridor is short and I come to another circular chamber, only this one is caged off by thick iron bars, the interior ringed with bright flames on the wall; their light glints on red stains of past battles. The guards take either arm in their harsh grip and throw me through the open gate like trash. I land in the dirt as the exit closes. Isn't this just peachy. Challenge Batal? Why didn't I ask what the hell that meant?

I hear a monstrous cry, faint from its distance and it chills my blood. I notice that the Zaeim and his guard have left. Am I meant to rot here? Was I really so foolish to think that these cultists would honor a challenge by an outsider?

I hear a rumbling, feel the ground quake. I feverishly look around and see dust shaking and cascading from a section of the brick wall as it begins to retract upwards. I take a nervous step away as the opening grows wider; animalistic grunts and snorts emanate from the dark.

Adrenaline pumps through me. I make for the closest torch and brandish it in my hands, waiting for my adversary to reveal himself.

My opponent enters the arena and rewards my anxious patience. The Batal is tall and fearsome, his burned skin stretches across bulging muscles that shine in the fire's light while metal studs, hammered into his flesh, glint like sparks from flint and steel. The rest of his body comes out of the dark and shows thick chains wrapped around the length of both arms; the wall slides back down, closing the only avenue of retreat. The slab of brick gives a muffled boom; the Batal opens his deformed mouth and roars his battle cry.

We stand face-to-face. This is why asking questions is so important.

The Batal charges forward with a terrible roar, bringing his left arm up in a wide arc and the coiled chain follows its path.

I sidestep frantically and dodge the chain as it whistles passed my ear in a whoosh of air before its subsequent thud against the ground. I recover and glance at the Batal in time to catch his second chain ripping through the dust-choked air. I roll and dodge in time, but drop the torch.

While I roll, I scoop a handful of sand and whip it into his eyes. The Batal recoils, snarling furiously. Taking advantage of the warrior's laps in guard, I snatch up the dropped torch, swing it around, and crash it into his skull, sparks and splintered wood scatter against the wall and fall across the floor. The Batal howls, brandishing his yellow teeth in a daunting snarl. The empty pitch behind his eyes glows with a homicidal glint.

I hurry to the next torch to attack once more, not knowing what else to do, but the heavy chain crashes into the wood and smashes it to unusable fragments. The impact not only destroys the torch, but extinguishes the flame as well, reducing the light inside the arena. The pieces of wooden shrapnel do not even have the chance to fall from the air before the Batal brings the second chain up to disintegrate the next torch, and he destroys each light in sequence. All that remains in the new darkness is the Batal's labored breathing and my own, sharp and shallow.

We are shrouded in blackness. I hear the chains slide over the scared floor as they fly towards me. I anticipate its direction and move right to evade, believing that its trajectory to be vertical as before. A sharp and throbbing pain explodes on my ribs as the chain wraps itself around my torso. The Batal bellows and pulls me towards him.

I scramble and pull against the insurmountable force heaving me closer, running my hands along the wall to secure myself, raking my fingers across the sandy floor in desperate hope to find something loose to grab hold of. My hand drags against something buried under the sand. It's solid but I can feel something crumble from it in my palm. Not caring what it might be, I curl my fingers tight around it. I feel a protrusion press against my clenched hand, feel the thing giving way as the Batal heaves his great chain.

I flail my other arm around and take the buried thing in both hands; I feel the protrusion lightly prick the bottom of my finger and I instantly feel the hand grow a fuzzy numbness. I recall Harlow's words like a forgotten song: wafter-like bark, barbed vines, where it grows decides how deadly it is. Strength and courage floods my muscles as I remember. The Batal tugs and pulls on his chain, dragging me towards him, aiding in my effort to uproot the Scorpion's Sting vine. I stop moving and hear the Batal take in a sharp breath. Before he strikes, I lift my legs up over my head and roll backwards, using the significantly loosened Scorpion's Sting as leverage. The floor vibrates from the Batal's missed blow, but I am able completely uproot the long section of vine; the numbness from my left hand creeps to my forearm. Before the Batal can move again, I lunge at him, brandishing a whip of my own. My headstrong push relaxes the tension on the chin and causes the Batal to falter. I raise the vine to swing, but before I feel it connect, the metal studs implanted into his scorched skin catch the meager light from the corridor for a brief moment.

The reflected light broadcasts the Alnnasi's movement and gives me a fraction of a second to duck under his right-hook.

The Batal reels from his missed strike and I circle around him, the metal chain links still wrapped around me clink ominously. The Batal growls his frustration and tries to follow my light-footed evasion. By the time he turns around, I snake around once more. Overcome with rage, the brute thunders with the force of a tempest, flailing his immense arms in the faint light. His flailing fist catches me on my left shoulder and pops the joint out of socket, radiating pain throughout my body. Spots flash across my vision as I recover from the strike; the Batal is still blindly raining his fists and chains.

Guided by the flickering metal studs adorning his seared flesh, I maneuver around his thrashing body, carrying his chain with me. I move closer and closer to the warrior, his raining fists become increasingly difficult to evade; left, right, left and left again I dodge, the occasional blow finding its mark on my back or arm; still, I continue to serpentine through his attacks, weaving his chain in my wake.

The length of his chain diminishes with every circle I complete around the Batal, each pass becoming more and more difficult as the poison from the vine consumes sensation in the whole of my left arm. I am now restricted to a three-foot distance from him; I can smell his putrid breath blowing hot in my grimacing face. Even with his arms fastened to his body he still will not give up the fight. He reels his great, block head back and smashes his thick skull against my own. I would have been sent sprawling on the floor had it not been for the chain holding me upright. The Batal roars, sensing his victory. He readies for a second headbutt and drives his head down to meet mine. Instead of skull crushing against skull, I rip the barbed vine through the air and drag its hard, cutting spikes across the Batal's face. He screams in agony and throws his head from side to side. I break as far away from him as the chain will allow, flourish the vine in my good hand, and swing it whistling through the air. I feel the barbs catch embed themselves into the thick skin around his neck and shoulder. The Batal collapses to his knees with a quaking thud, but I do not relent. I bring the vine down again, hissing in the darkness.

Again. And again.

The tortured cries of the warrior quiet to stifled gurgles, his poison-riddled body, at last, folds into the dirt.

I quickly unravel myself from the metal constraints and I feel fatigue creep into my body, barely able to maintain the will to stand. I look down at my defeated adversary and find a resting place against the wall. I glance down at my dislocated shoulder. I look up at the ceiling and take a deep breath; I grab hold of my wrist and I pull. I grit my teeth against the pain that finds its way through the buzzing numbness. In my delirium I hear the sound or iron grinding against iron.

The Zaeim reveals himself in the corridor outside the arena. In his meaty grasp, he is holding aloft a long metal rod with a flat, circular tip. He glances down disdainfully at his fallen champion, surely hoping to find him standing in my place, and shifts his focus on me; a fire burns behind his eyes.

"Bring wood and oil."

Both unwilling to move a muscle, the Zaeim and I stand locked in an unnerving silence. Two Baarutal guards enter the chamber, one with wood, the other, oil. Placing them at their Zaeim's feet, they exit as swiftly as they entered.

"Place the wood around slain Batal," the Zaeim orders.

Fearing still that something could go awry, I follow his command and arrange the wood around the body.

"Take oil and spill."

I take the clay pitcher of oil and tip it over, spilling its foul smelling contents over the Batal's carcass.

The Zaeim removes a torch from the wall in the corridor and tosses it on the pile. In an instant, bright, hot flames engulf the dead warrior, licking at his chest and arms.

"Outsiders, tested in Maeraka, are to be marked. Show their worth to Euyun and all Alnnasi," he places the tip of the rod into the fire. "To honor Batal, the flames of his soul are burned into the flesh of the victor, proving their worth in the eyes of Euyun."

The Zaeim removes the rod from the flames and brings up its white-hot tip in the shape of a circle crossed with a vertical line, "step forward."

My eyes grow wide and transfix upon the glowing brand.

I take one-step forward.

The fumes emanating off the burning corpse blinds my senses; the heat is stifling.

I take another step.

The searing steel is inches away from my bare arm.

I hope he picks the left arm.

I am enveloped in an all-consuming pain as the Zaeim's brand stamps its mark onto the flesh of my good arm; my skin sizzles and smokes.

I scream out, but I do not hear the sound of anguish, only feeling the Alnnasi tradition of blood and metal searing my skin. My mark of victory.

"You now have approval of Euyun; title of Qintal," the Zaeim speaks, his resonant voice ringing through the arena with a loathsome distaste.

The second time I enter the atrium is far different than the first. When the Baarutal look over at me their sneering eyes are even more hateful when they see the brand on my arm. Their displeasure brings me great happiness as I stride to pass them. I feel totally immune. My spirits soar higher still when I see Dale sitting quietly in the midst of the atrium, looking up towards the dizzyingly high ceiling.

"Dale!" I shout as I run to him.

"Vipe?" He looks around before his eyes find me. "By the stars, you're alright!" He comes to his feet and meets my embrace.

"What happened?" I ask.

"Same thing that happened to you, I reckon," twists his body and shows the similar brand on his upper arm. "This is not the place to talk. These Baarutal don't look happy to see us with these. Come on. We don't have far to go before the Northern Compound."

"How much longer?"

Dale walks for the exit.

"If nothing else goes horribly wrong," he says over his shoulder, "by nightfall tomorrow."

CHAPTER 13

— Stories & Poetry —

One day's walk, just as Dale said. One of the few times where I'm glad he was right. The peak of Euyun's Eye has nearly vanished from the distance and the fence of smaller spires around it. It makes my skin crawl thinking that place was so close to the Northern Compound. But that is of no consequence now. We made it.

The early spring weather paints the earth in green renewal and life returns to the bushes and trees along our path. Pink Ambrose climbs low against the bland stone blocks, emerald blades of grass creep towards the colorless gate and choruses of bird song carry with the aroma of wild flowers on the mild dusk breeze.

"Feels like forever, doesn't it?" I remark.

"That it does, Vipe. That it does," Dale answers after taking in a deep breath. "But, we should remain wary. The Flag have always been the more… cautious type. No need for us to catch an arrow after all the trouble it took to get here."

"After all that I've been through, an arrow would be an improvement."

"Just keep quiet."

Dale and I approach the closed Compound gate. All is still as we come against the entrance. No sound of conversation or settlement emanates from within. I look at Dale and sense that my inkling of trepidation is mutual.

"How do we get in?" I whisper. "It looks like no one is here – maybe the Bandits already got to them."

"Oh, please," Dale scoffs. "It would take an army to kill that many members of the Black Flag."

"That would make me feel better if the Bandit's didn't have an army."

Dale nears the gates.

"Hello?" His voice pierces the majesty of the night. "It's Dale. I need to speak with someone in the Black Flag."

No response.

"We have to talk about the Bandits!" Dale calls a second time.

Silence. The birds even stopped chirping.

Dale turns to me, his eyes haunted by the notion that we have met an end to our endeavor; his shoulders collapse. I search for uplifting words but do not get far before sounds of mechanical clunking comes from the gate and shakes Dale out of his trance. Dale nods sternly at me, communicating to keep my wits about me. The gates creep slowly open, revealing to us the image of a lone man standing in the empty courtyard hooded and cloaked in the encroaching darkness of yet another uncertain night.

I step forward for an introduction, but Dale's arm bars my way. I can see his jaw locked from the tension while he stares down the figure.

"We're here to talk. We're friends."

The mysterious figure shows no acknowledgment of our greeting and continues his unwavering silence.

The wind picks up another scent and it mixes with the sweet fragrance of the flowers ornamenting the walls.

"We're not alone," I breathe.

"How many?" Dale questions, his gaze never swaying from the cloaked man ahead of us.

"If my nose could count I'd tell you."

"Listen," Dale addresses the figure again. "We do not bring any underhanded intentions. We just need some information."

I hear a rustling behind us; see a slight shift in the darkness.

"Dale…"

"We just want to talk."

"Dale, they're moving," disquiet finds its way to my words.

Dale takes a step towards the hooded person, appalled by the egregious breach of etiquette.

"Look here, we didn't come all this way just to be—'

Crack!

The tumultuous noise of snapping branches from the left startles Dale out of his rage and brings his attention to the source.

Crack!

A second signal of fractured timber comes from behind.

"Dale! Watch out behind y—" a cold hand closes around my mouth while the point of a blade rests in the small of my back.

"Move and your friend dies," a man hisses in my ear with the indifference of a hurricane.

Dale whips around and then freezes with his hammer ready as he realizes what is happening. I am voiceless as I watch someone creep up to the oblivious Dale, a long polearm poised to bludgeon him, its metal-capped ends catch the dim glow of the unveiling moon. Just as it is about to come crashing down on Dale's head, it stops. The attacker relaxes their offensive posture, lowers their weapon and takes Dale in a warm embrace.

What in the hell?

"What is the meaning of this?" the man behind me demands. "Just finish him already, Harlow!"

No way.

"This is Dale, you idiot!" Harlow shouts back. "And if Dale is here, that means…" she glances around until her penetrating eyes find me held at knifepoint, "…that Viper isn't far behind."

"You know these two?" The blade on my back falters.

"Have you not listened to a single word I've spoken to you, Tegan?" Harlow rolls her eyes and the words on Tegan's lips sputter into incoherence. "Go and help these two inside. They've traveled far to reach us here."

"You know that's against protocol," Tegan interjects, smugly.

"Grimhild is expecting them. Just go and do it, okay?"

Tegan relinquishes his hold over me and sheaths his blade. He storms off into the Compound, not making eye contact with either Dale or Harlow, muttering under his breath all the while.

"I'd say that you'll have to excuse his behavior, but this is how he usually is," Harlow admits.

"Harlow!" I burst, finally free to speak. "What a relief!"

"Isn't it? Almost took his head off," she says playfully, offering Dale her hand.

Dale and Harlow shake hands in greeting. She pokes fun at the sad state of our desert clothing, escorting us in our old home. Stepping foot into the Compound is like stepping through a doorway to a different time. I almost expect to hear Fen and Gale joking beside the gate as we pass through. But they're long gone. There are no children playing in the streets, no joviality resonating from the banquet hall, just the scattered light of a handful of torches. Solemn and resolute. We pass the hooded character still posted in the entrance. It is only then that I see it's a wooden dummy.

"So, what's that?" I inquire, gesturing back to the mannequin.

"Oh, him? That's Burt. He's a scarecrow, so to speak. Makes it easy for us to surprise visitors."

"Yeah. Worked wonders," Dale says, bitterly. "But we came to talk about Junn."

"I already know," Harlow says. "But that must wait. We're not too keen to do business after nightfall."

"Fine," says Dale. "I'm not known to say no to a bed. Just know that I won't enjoy it."

"Oh, my! The intensity!" Harlow's words drip sarcasm with every syllable. "Rest assured that we will help you once the new day arrives."

Harlow leads Dale and I towards the Great Hall's broad, metal-filigree wooden doors. She raps thrice against the deep, echoing planks, crosses her arms and shifts her weight onto one foot, leaning her head back to look down her nose at Tegan as he opens the way.

"Oh, for the love of—" Harlow begins, raising a disciplinary hand.

"Nalu already sorted out their rooms," Tegan says, defensively, not flinching at Harlow's advance.

"Right. Good work," she moves by Tegan. "You two should go and rest."

*

A bright light jerks me from my slumber. I blink vigorously to shake off the dazzling luminance coming from the window. I see a slender man standing over my bed with black paint around his eyes. Shocked by this demonic apparition, I clamor out of the blankets to my feet, keeping the bed in between us. However, the man offers no signs of aggression or even caring to notice my alarm. He turns away and closes the door softly behind him.

Who was that? Ugh, what these Black Flag members lack in subtlety they more than make up for in sheer unpredictability.

I dress under the assumption that the bizarre man's appearance was a wake-up call and exit the bedroom, following the sound of retreating footsteps.

I enter the main chamber and see the strange man's back just as he disappears through an adjoining door to a separate area. The tall and wide room is just as I remember. The stream of early morning sun bathes the flagstone in a comforting way, crossed with lines from the large window's panes. But there is something here that is not familiar. A man stands before the window, hands clasped neatly behind his back, in front of a beautifully ornate dagger in its scabbard. The warm sun outlines his well-groomed brown hair, tucked smartly behind the ear, his exquisitely tailored maroon tunic, trimmed with silver thread, and down to his polished and shining brown, knee-high boots. He cocks his head back and catches me staring.

"You must be Viper," he says in a clear, strong voice.

He turns from the window and I see his perfectly trimmed goatee around his chin. I've never seen royalty before, but, if I were to guess, I'd say that he is one.

"I am," I answer.

"There is no need to be worried."

"Where is everyone?"

"It appears that it is just you and I that respect punctuality. But fear not, they shall join us in due time. My name is Riston Balroux," he gives a small, graceful bow. "A pleasure to make your acquaintance."

I stand in a dumb silence.

"Come, sit," Riston moves toward one of the chairs situated along the wooden table, singularly grand amongst the rest. "Why stand when one can sit, I say."

I join him at the table, a few spaces away.

"Tell me, young master," he props his feet on the table, "how did you come to be wrapped up in all this?"

"How do you mean?"

"I mean this mess with the Bandits, of course. Harlow hasn't spared a word in the tales about you and her in the Southcap Mountains, nor your visit with the Alnnasi in the desolate Al'hadayiq."

She knew we would go through the Rock Gardens? How? Lucky guess?

"Don't be so surprised," Riston chuckles. "That woman has a way of knowing things some thought were private. I know that as fact."

"Well, I… uh," there is no point in trying to hide anything. He probably already knows the answers. This is a test of honesty. "I was there when the Bandits ambushed the caravan. Dale and I vowed to save Junn who was taken during the attack."

"I see. An admirable goal. Now, answer me this: have you thought about the possibility of Junn being dead? That all of this is for nothing?"

I look at Riston in the eye.

"I have. But thoughts like that don't make reality certain. So I will continue to do all I can."

"A fine answer," Riston swings his feet from the tabletop, leans forward in his chair, and places his elbows on the table's worn surface.

"What about you?" I ask. "What can you tell me about yourself and the other members? I admit that having an audience with anyone from the Black Flag is difficult."

"That is a long story. But, before I can tell you," Riston undoes the clasps of his tunic and opens up the left half, revealing an enormous scar running from the top of his left shoulder and disappearing around his side. "You will first have to hear of this."

My eyes widen. Before I can say a word, he speaks.

"This is from my father, given to me when I was only ten-years-old. My dad, you see, he was a bit of a drinker – putting it delicately – and he had the habit of getting violent. But my dear mother did everything for me. She taught me my letters, instilled the love of music into me with the lullabies she used to sing and the songs she played on this flute," Riston lays a hand on the silver instrument at his hip.

"After too much of protecting me from my father, she decided to get me out of the house, away from the danger my old man posed. But he found out. He was so overcome with rage that she would think to take his blood away from him, his only son, that instead of dispensing his usual beatings, this time he killed her. He came at her, wrapped his filthy fingers around her throat. I couldn't stand and watch, so I grabbed the knife from his belt and stabbed it into his leg. He fell to the floor and I tried to get my mother to safety, but my father reached out and got hold of my ankle before I could get away," Riston refastens his tunic.

"I told her to run, but she wouldn't listen. Instead of escaping, she decided to fend off my drunken father so that *I* could live. It was ugly. I wrestled to get out of his clutches and eventually got free, but he kicked me through the window — earning me this scar — screaming that '*this is her fault anyway.*' The last things I heard from that house was my mother's shrill voice and my father shouting and then silence. I set out on a journey for revenge after that."

"That sounds terrible. Did you ever see him again?"

Riston gives me a sly look.

"Is that how you ended up here?"

"In a sense, yes," he answers. "If it was not for my path of vengeance against my father, I would not have found myself selling my abilities to kill to the highest bidder, and that eventually landed me with the Black Flag."

"How tragic," I'm at a loss for better words.

"Life is always looking to kick you in the teeth," Riston shrugs. "The real tragedy would be not growing from it. Speaking of tragedy, does that bandage around your arm hide a similar story?"

"A little souvenir from the Rock Gardens. Dale and I were captured by the Baarutal and we had to fight a Batal, someone that has both Euyun's blessing and the skill to be undefeated by another aspiring Batal. So, we did and now Dale and I are probably the only people in the world that can call themselves Qintal."

I undo the bandage and reveal the Baarutal's brand: a line enclosed by a circle.

"It's supposed to represent Euyun," I clarify

"You are full of surprises, young master," he whistles. "But if one tale can trump another, Nalu's can surely do it."

"I heard Tegan say that name. Who is he?"

"I believe the two of you have met," he mimes smearing his eyes. "He's the fellow with the paint, and that alone is a sad story."

Riston's eyes become crestfallen. "Nalu belonged to a proud and genius people called the Pau'larin in what was once called Tir Fwythland; now a barren expanse of land, bereft of any significant life."

"Belonged? What happened to them?"

"In a time outside of recorded memory, the Pau'larins held claim over what we now call the Western Wastes. Before the land became blighted it was lush and overflowing with such extravagant life that the pure majesty would bring even the most hardened of men to their knees," Riston explains. "The Pau'larin built sprawling cities but would never use or take beyond what they needed in order to preserve the land. However, one day, as all good things must, the Pau'larin's way of life came to an end."

"But why would anyone want to kill the Pau'larin? If they were as peaceful as you say, what enemies could they have had?" I ask.

"Bandits," Riston answers, simply. "I am sure, at this point, that you are all too aware of the unspeakable atrocities of which the Bandits are capable. They do not revere the sanctity of life, only their own desire to conquer what lies before them and to further their goal to see the world run red."

"So, the Bandits discovered the Pau'larin and outright put them to the sword?"

"In essence, yes. At the beginning of their invasion of Tir Fwythland, the Bandits were an unorganized horde of countless number. They did not stand much of a chance against the organized and elegant Pau'larin. But as the war raged on, the Bandits learned. They realized that the Pau'larin's strength lied in the land; their next course of action became clear: to dam the river Zilvern, a tributary of the Nadi, and starve Tir Fwythland of water. It did not take long after that for the streams to run dry and the trees to turn to ash."

"I cannot believe that even the Bandits are willing to do such a thing!" I gasp. "Is there a chance that the Western Wastes can be restored if the dam were to be broken?"

"That is not the first time that such a thought was conceived," Riston sighs. "Alas, no. I fear that the opening of the dam would merely wash away what is left of the land. It has been so long without water that a torrent of it would only serve to flood and drown. The days of Tir Fwythland and the Pau'larin have been written. A truth a shameful few people know of that extinct people is that they were the ones responsible for the constructions of the three Compounds."

"What did you say?"

"It's true. While they were fending off the Bandits in the north, they simultaneously gave shelter to everyone in Hyravon,."

"No, I know that. I meant about the Compounds. There's only two of them."

"And another piece of history is forgotten…" Riston laments. "It's quite true that there is a third Compound, but for all intents and purposes, it may as well not exist. It lies in the west, very near the Cedi River, the one with which you are most familiar. But, due to its proximity to the Western Wastes, the Bandits – following their conquest of Tir Fwythland, defiled that, too."

"I can't believe that Marcus – that no one – told me about this."

"In addition to eradicating a non-violent people, the Bandits sought to harvest their bodies for an insidious purpose: to honor their god, Merr'tyura. It is a savage piece of Bandit lore. As the story goes, Merr'tyura and her only child and son, Merr'putra, were sailing the ocean — though from whence they came I know not. A terrible storm assailed them and in the raging waters, Merr'putra was lost. Without her son, Merr'tuyra could no longer work her foul magics, so she focused all of what yet resided and called the dead from their graves. She cursed them to search for her son without rest. Or so the story goes."

"That's the reason they murder and cannibalize us?" My mouth goes dry from the realization. "To find a made-up son?"

"I, too, have my doubts," Riston strokes his beard. "But I've learned the hard way to never take anything for what it truly is at first glance. In any case, the fact remains that the Bandits extinguished a flame that burned only to bring light and warmth to the world."

"They obviously were not entirely successful, were they? Or else Nalu wouldn't be here with us," I reason.

"Once again, Viper, you have a sharp mind," Riston praises. "Yes, they were not wholly successful. Although, they soon would be. Not too long ago, but certainly before you were born, one lone group of the once proud people remained, still clinging to their dying way of life. One day, Grimhild was on an assignment from his Caste Elder to recover relics of the Pau'larin for the purpose of recording their existence. It was then that he first met Nalu, surrounded by Bandits that remained from the extermination decades past. Casting aside his own sense of self-preservation, Grimhild, his enormous battle-axe in hand, charged the enemy with such reckless abandon that it opened the ranks of the Bandit hoard."

"Incredible," I breathe.

"With one swing of his weapon, Grimhild sent the heads of scores of Bandits soaring into the air and a red mist clouding the battlefield. He and Nalu made short work of the demoralized Bandits and sent them to meet their comrades. The rest is history," Riston leans back in his chair. "Since then, Nalu and Grimhild have been inseparable, their bond of brotherhood going deeper than shared blood ever could, made absolute through risking one life for another," Riston chuckles to himself. "I do not know if this is true – because he refuses to discuss it – but, according to Grimhild, the black paint around Nalu's eyes are from the ashes of both the members of his clan and the Bandits he slew with his bare hands, so that he never loses sight of his origin or the ones responsible for their demise."

"Your sense of humor worries me, Riston."

"One must laugh off the insanity of tragedy lest they succumb to it," Riston counters.

"Does every member have such a sad story?"

"It seems a cruel joke that such things appear to be a prerequisite. But without them, we would not be speaking right now. Yes, to answer your question. But her's took place where none else could follow. Her name was Amour," Riston answers, despondently. He stands from the chair and walks to stare out of the window, fogged from dew. "She had the most beautiful long and flowing silver hair, and a brilliant mind for music. There was a time when one would hear me profess my undying love for her."

"I am so sorry," I console. "What happened?"

Breathing in deeply, Riston turns away from the window and returns to his seat. "She chased Contil after the rift, saying that she knew him and that she could get him to come to his senses -- an action universally detested by the other Black Flag members. She looked up to him so much, following in his footsteps like a newborn pup. I attempted to go after her, but I wasn't fast enough. That was ten years ago and a memory I have striven to bury under lyric and song," Riston's eyes light up. "Would you entertain me to listen to one?"

"Please, I would be honored."

"Very well!"

Riston takes a few steps from the window, straightens his back, and clears his throat

"She took me to the edge of the cliff, along the coast; it was dark still, but the air vibrated with the eminent light of an impending dawn. We waited there together, on the cusp of daybreak. The radiance of the sun slowly crept above the waves of the sparkling ocean, and rose further still as the watery depths once again released its captive onto the sky.

She spoke,

"My name is Rising Sun. I am the first light of your day. Erasing the darkness of night and replacing it with the hope of a new dawn."

We traveled back down the mountain path and the birds awakened around us. Their music was clear and beautiful. They flew from treetop to treetop, only visible for a moment, appearing as streaks of red, blue, and yellow.

She gestured upwards, towards the avian ballad,

"My name is Bird Song. I am the first tune that fills your ears and the purest of all melodies."

We cleared the trees and were once again on level ground, the emerald plane stretching out before us. The morning sun shone on the blades of grass and seemed to ignite their tips with golden light. It tickled the back of our knees as we traversed the field and we began to laugh when the grass overcame us.

She spoke,

"My name is Innocent Laughter. I bring a joyful tear to your eye; I never fail to make you smile."

The trek to town was peaceful. The landscape changed from the beautiful, empyreal nature-centric scenery to a more cultivated, urbanized one.

She spoke,

"My name is Dynamic. I change from form to form. Though I change, my differing figures are no more or less illustrious than the last."

The day was spent meandering through the town. So much to see and do. Lunch was shortly succeeded with visiting the many stores and markets the town had to offer. Vendors of various trinkets, clothes and food occupied a majority of the market square. The sun, passed its peak in the sky, began its descent towards the horizon. We walked to a weathered wooden bench and sat, watching the people go about their business.

She spoke,

"My name is Joyous Satisfaction. I fill your empty space with my aura and presence. I make you happy and free."

The red light of dusk blanketed the town, reflecting brilliantly off the windowpanes and dazzling our eyes. We left the town and escaped back into the countryside, the clouds bathed in a myriad of colors. Their contours were glowing in white and every shade of red, purple, and orange filled them. We sat together on a boulder, sunken into the earth, and watched as the sun was swallowed up by the trees in the distance.

She spoke,

"My name is Magnificent. I paint my masterpiece on to your life. You look through the abounding flaws in my composition and see me to the core, taking my beauty and my blemish."

Starlight lit our position on the rock when the sun slipped from the sky, the wind brushed the clouds away to awake the moon from its slumber; it's silver essence illuminating the ground with its pale light. The heavens rotated over our heads, sometimes dropping a star, sending it soaring across the night sky. We looked up at the celestial dance and plotted our own constellations, laughing as I held her close.

I whispered, "I found your name."

"What is it?" She whispered back.

"It's Astounding. Your delicacy and strength expounds on your character. You are like the air I breathe, there for me when I need you. You assume the status of grace and compassion."

She spoke,

"My name is Forever. It transcends distance and time. I'll be there with you wherever you or I may roam; you just have to know where to look.""

"That was beautiful," I remark.

"You have my gratitude, Viper," Riston bows his head and flourishes his hand. "Not often do I find myself in a position to share what's in my heart in its raw form. You are a fine audience, and so full of mystery. Tell me, how were you able to live in the wild all on your own? Harlow is known to spin tales of extravagance and exaggerated size, and I wonder if this is true."

"It is, unfortunately," I say.

"So, how did you manage it?"

"I don't remember much of that part of my life. I have images of open sky, a cave, flowing streams, but that's not much to go on. The first real memory I have is the feeling of Junn's hand as he pulled me out of a cave."

"So you say that you did all of that by yourself?"

"I always had the suspicion that someone, or something was watching over me. There was no sign of such a person where they found me, only this," I unsheathe my long knife and lay it gently on the table.

"May I?" Riston leans forward.

I nod and he takes the weapon for closer inspection.

"What do these marks mean?"

"I haven't the faintest. No one I've spoken to could make heads or tails of it. Though, one did say something interesting. He said—"

The doors at the end of the hill carry voices and approaching footsteps.

"Ah, here they come at last," Riston hands the blade back to me. "Our moment of vulnerability is past. How nice of you to return!" he says, opening his arms.

"Oh, stop showboating," Harlow scolds as she walks by him.

"My dearest Harlow, if you keep up that indifferent, leisurely attitude, it will not go away," Riston delivers in a singsong manner.

The other members pass through the large doorway. I recognize Harlow, of course. After her comes Tegan with his shoulder-length black hair pulled into a bunch at the back of his head, then comes the curious man Riston called Nalu, still as ominous as ever with his dark eyes that seem to observe everything. Dale comes through next and his face breaks into a smile as he sits beside me. The final member enters and my eyes linger. He is a hulk of a man, almost as big as the Batal. His head is clean-shaven on both sides, leaving a short strip of obsidian black hair running down the middle. His piercing eyes sweep across the room; he looks down on me over his strong, slightly crooked nose. He speaks from behind his flowing, braided black beard.

"That's enough love talk, you two," the giant says.

I recognize him now, from that day in the Square. The day I learned we would be leaving the Compound. Grimhild.

"There's much to do and precious little time to do it."

The Black Flag take their places around the table. Nalu sits at Grimhild's right hand, Tegan shoots me a dark, untrusting look and crosses his arms; Harlow and Riston look as though they're a family awaiting the promise of a banquet.

"Let us get right to it. Viper," Grimhild's singular focus on me makes me suddenly nervous. "Harlow told me many things about you and your reasons for being here. Rest assured that your goals are mine, also. We will do all we can to get Junn back. She told me of a map. Do you have it?"

"Yes," I fumble clumsily for the crumpled mass of heavy paper and smooth it flat before passing it towards the head of the table.

He pours over the unintelligible scratches and scribbles on the page, thoughtfully stroking his beard. He lifts his eyes.

"You can always trust the Bandits to surprise you."

"Let me see that," Tegan snatches the map from the table and looks over it himself. His brow furrows, the lines growing deeper with suspicion with each passing second. "What is it that we can do with this?"

My heart sinks. That's not what I was hoping to hear.

"This charts the southern territory. Correct me if I'm wrong, but we are in the north. Are we to trust in the Bandits and this map of questionable procurement? I say that we must wait to gather more actionable knowledge."

"If we wait any longer, there's no telling what the Bandits will do to Junn," says Riston.

"What more could they do?" Tegan bites back. "He was taken during the ambush, correct? That was five long months ago. If the Bandits do indeed hold Junn captive, I fear by now they are struggling to find new methods of torture to inflict upon him."

"Who's side are you on?" Harlow shouts.

"I merely state the facts. Do not paint me a villain for recognizing the grave severity of the situation."

"Fighting one another serves no purpose," Grimhild interrupts. "It is true that the likelihood of Junn's survival this long is slim. However, none know as best as us that he's a hard son of a bitch, and even harder to break. And I for one intend to go after the Bandits responsible. My lungs will breathe fire and the mountains will crumble before I abandon one of my own."

"Do you have a plan?" Dale asks, hopefully.

"I'd venture to say that I do," Grimhild's face breaks into a smile.

CHAPTER 14

— Preparations —

The air on the ramparts blows cold and gentle as Dale and I stroll in the midday sun; the sky brushed with thin clouds. I hate waiting, especially after the past weeks of constant moving, fighting for my life, wondering which breath would be my last. The old Viper would be chomping at the bit to be hunting Bandits, but I know what I'm up against now. Too well. Dale and I walk our circuit in silence, just enjoying the company in the pleasure of spring and its scents and sounds.

I hear a pattern of thumps outside the walls, out and down to my left. I peer over the thick blocks and see Tegan walking back from a scarred tree with his hand full of white-feathered arrows. He comes to a stop a good fifty strides away, stowing the retrieved arrows in the quiver at his hip. He unholsters his longbow, glinting dully in the sun, and nocks an arrow to it, standing still for a moment while the wind rattles the trees and tosses his hair. The second stillness resumes, Tegan's body explodes in a blur of movement, firing one, two, five arrows in rapid succession; all find their marks in tight grouping.

"He has a perfect shot, doesn't he?" Riston says.

I look over to see him with his arms resting on the ramparts.

"I've never seen anything like it," I respond. "Has he always been this skilled?"

"The answer you look for first requires a tale's retelling," Riston comes and stands beside Dale and I. "However, I know Tegan to be a sort of secretive man. You'll have to hear it from the source himself. But that is not the reason I sought you out. Grimhild wants to see you both in the armory," at this, Riston rubs his hands together and smiles in a way that can only be described as maniacal, "it's time to go hunting."

I am a touch jittery walking the roads towards the armory. Grimhild must run an extremely tough group if he is already setting his plan in motion. Not that I find it all too surprising.

"How you holdin' up?" Dale asks.

"I'm a little worried," I eventually answer. "I should be ready for this, shouldn't I?"

"I don't remember 'being ready' stopping us from going through the Rock Gardens, or training with Harlow."

"No, but—"

"You're stronger that you're letting yourself believe. The world doesn't care a shit if you're ready or not," Dale says, half trying to convince himself. "You'll never know what you're made of until it's all put to the test."

"Storming a Bandit fortress is some test," I rub the back of my neck. "Can the eight of us pull it off?"

"You heard Grimhild's plan. Sounds like the only real way to go about it. All we have to do is put our trust in them."

"And our lives," I add.

"Like I said," we come round a corner, "we have to just square our shoulders and carry on."

The Compound's armory is housed in a small, unassuming building that, in all regard, is in a real need of renovation. There are no windows, but over time and through the rot of the ages, holes have appeared on the walls and dark green moss grows all around the base. We step inside the humble space, lit by a singular lantern hanging from a hook in the ceiling, and see simple steel swords lining the walls and wooden bows and barrels of arrows lean against the left wall while studded shields rest on racks above it all. The air inside is stale and hot, mirroring the poor state of the arms and armor. Grimhild stands in the middle of the room, waiting expectantly.

"Good, you're here," Grimhild says. "Let's get this done quickly, yeah?" He walks over to a barrel of iron-tipped arrows, reaches in for one of them and pulls it out... only, it doesn't come out, but stops halfway; a sound of stone scraping against stone accompanies the action. Grimhild releases the wooden shaft and takes a step back as a plume of moldy air and dust rush from the crack in the wall. The crack grows wider as the symphony of grinding rock proceeds its dust-stirring din.

Dale stands with his mouth open.

Grimhild looks over his shoulder

"The Flag have caches of arms at each Compound, among other places," his lips curl at Dale's expression. "Here, the Southern Compound, and the western edge of the Southcap Mountains to name a few." Grimhild takes a step into the open maw of the hidden room, taking the lantern off the hook as he moves. "Coming?"

Dale and I exchange excited looks. We quickly follow Grimhild, traverse a lengthy spiral staircase, and soon come to the bottom. It is dark and damp down here, underneath the Compound and the rest of the world. Grimhild steps forward into the darkness and, with a small creak from the lantern's shutter, passes the light from his flame to another lamp, revealing to us the scope of this secret trove. The firelight reflects spectacularly off the polished metal of visored helmets, still holding their shine from their long confinement here. Elaborately embossed breastplates hang on burlap mannequins, winged greaves and sabatons resting at their base. Towering pauldrons, gauntlets and cuirasses lay on shelves bathed in the fire's warm, flickering luminance.

"I never would have imagined something like this was under my feet all this time," Dale says, his voice hushed by the awe of this newly discovered place.

"You have Amour and Barbosa to thank for this," Grimhild responds. "Amour was requisitioned to craft these arms and armor. It all used to be held in the cellars of the Great Hall, but in the Year of Storms, it flooded. However, Amour, alongside Barbosa, the Compound's old blacksmith, built this place. He excavated this lower level to Harland's, the then leader of the Northern Compound, specifications. He built it; Amour filled it."

"She was a fine craftsman," I comment, inspecting a particularly interesting helmet.

"Indeed, she was. Now, it is time to get you two battle-ready. You can forget about that, Viper," Grimhild says as I look longingly at a set of heavy armor. "Speed is vital to our mission. That will just slow you down. Besides, that belongs to me."

I recoil from the set as though it attempted to bite me. I turn to its owner and offer my apologies but Grimhild waves off my profuse reparations.

He motions for me to follow him to an additional room.

"What you need is hardened leather for movement and the ability to hold off the sting of a blade. This one is made from the Rock Garden's Alramaat – the Alnnasi ram. They are bred for withstanding the punishment of the sun, and special tempering makes the edge of a blade slide off."

I try on Grimhild's selection and strut about the room, getting a feel for the fit.

"It's… kinda tight."

Grimhild takes it back and replaces the brown leather armor; reaches for a black set.

"This," he holds up a collection of hardened pads, slick like oil, sewn and laced with strong black cords, "is made from the hide of Tir Fwythland's Western Plain Bull. Its skin is naturally tough and surprisingly light as well."

I take it from him and try again.

"Much more like it," I twist my torso left and right. "What else is there?"

"Your weapon," he walks towards a closed door and opens it, showing swords and knives of various lengths. Some are simple with leather-wrapped grips while others boast hilts and cross guards of magnificent quality. "Your affinity lies with your knife, yes?"

"I've had it all my life," I answer. "Though, I don't suspect it will be enough for war."

"You are correct."

Grimhild pulls out a short sword and presents it to me.

I take the weapon from him and give it a few swings, light flashing off its single, sharp edge. The lightness of the weapon surprises me.

"I can't believe how nimble it is," I say.

"Forged from tempered iron from the frozen veins of the Southcap Mountains. Its triple folded edge ensures that it won't chip, making the metal dense and sharp as it is light. A perfect match."

I give the blade a few more test swings before I turn it around in my hand and present the grip to Grimhild.

"It's too light. I am afraid that I might swing it right out of my hand."

Grimhild retrieves the weapon and combs through the armory's vast selection. I stand behind him and watch as he skims over broadswords and curved daggers alike, passing each one as he judges them wanting. I turn my attention from Grimhild to the rest of the chamber to search myself. I approach the opposite wall and lean over throwing knives and bows of yew and red oak and think of Junn; I pick one up, but put it back. I do not possess that kind of talent. I move on to where long swords rest on mahogany slabs, their sharp edges shine like golden stars in the firelight. I reach down and run my finger along their pummel and grip. These, too, I pass and at last I come to a cabinet removed of its door. I look inside and see a short sword hanging from wooden pegs. Shadows hide its shine, but even in the gloom, I can see that the sword's edge is well kept. The blade's hilt is wrapped in black leather, intertwined with a single vein of silver that goes passed the cross guard to become the blade itself. I walk up to the weapon and reach for it.

"I see you have found something to your liking."

I take the sword from the pegs and feel its weight in my hands, tossing it between them. "I feel as though it is an extension of my arm."

"As all swords should," Grimhild says. "This is in fact a very special sword, wielded by Agonthar the Red, King of Beasts and Slayer of Demons in the Year of Peace."

"Is that true?" I whip around in shock.

"Nay, it is not," Grimhild bellows with laughter as I turn away, slightly ashamed.

"Forgive me, I could not resist the opportunity. But, on my honor as leader of the Black Flag, this weapon is a fine match for you; made from Thalvian steel and refined in special minerals from my homeland in Mahadvala."

I raise the tip of the sword up to my eye and see my distorted reflection running down the length of the blade.

"This will do."

"I dare say you are right," he nods.

We walk back into the main room to find Dale outfitted with a round shield and a warhammer, specialized for breaking bones and smashing skulls. Its haft is over a foot long, and the head, hard and solid beyond measure is etched in runes of foreign design that line the edges. I see that his old, simple forge-hammer is slung at his side. He turns at the sound of our approach, his mail armor clinking as he moves.

"Just can't stay away from hammers, can you?" I smile.

Dale shrugs.

"Hammers, yes. Shields?" He hefts the iron-rimmed circle, "don't think so."

"If you two are finished here," says Grimhild, "it's time that we set out. The trek to the Northern Reaches will not be an easy one. I will meet you at the gates."

*

I see our party waiting for us in a quiet restlessness at the Compound's gate. Riston sits on a stump, methodically running his whetstone down the length of his great sword, humming softly to himself. Harlow walks to stand with Dale and I.

She rests her weight against her metal-ended staff and looks under her furrowed brow at the grey sky. Tegan is pacing in front of the gate, tugging at the string of his bow.

Grimhild and Nalu turn the corner and march toward us. In his armor, Grimhild resembles the gods of wrath from the fairytales I used to hear: broad plated steel stretches across his chest, decorated in scars from past battles; his enormous battle-axe casually thrown over his armored shoulders and in his left hand he carries his helm, polished to a sheen; Nalu proceeds with the smooth elegance of death itself. It appears that his tales of blood and slaughter are not lost on his presence; the shadow of decay looming over his approach.

I turn from his cool menace. Riston lifts his eyes at the coming of our party's last members, puts away his sharpening stone and sheaths his sword. He stands sentinel, placing his hands in the pommel. Tegan ceases his trepidatious tugging and, too, reveres the arrival of our leader. In turn, all of us stand as Grimhild takes his place at the head of our group and opens the gate and the renewing landscape beyond. He turns to face us, his blue eyes preaching strength and courage, a ward against the devils of the world. The braided lengths of this onyx beard sways in the breeze; he inspects his warriors. His friends.

"We stand on the edge of battle," he booms, voice steady and strong like a king to his knights. "Fear and fail, hesitate and fall. This will not be a forgiving fight. Remember to act swift and act deadly, for we fight for the life of another, for the life of one of our own."

Nalu shouts, the pride of the Pau'larin carried in his voice.

"And so we go, into the very bowels of the Bandit's stronghold. Let our spirits blaze. Let us go and accept our fate so that we can send those monsters back to the abyss!"

We speak in one voice as we shout loyalty and courage in the wake of Grimhild's leadership. We file out of the Northern Compound, my home, and set on the path to Kandent Fortress, to the frozen Northern Reaches. To Junn.

CHAPTER 15

— How Names are Given —

The sky turns grey as we come into view of the Cedi river. In the north and west, it is much more wild than it is back home where is flows between hill and tree. But here, so close to the main body of the Nadi, it thunders along the seemingly endless expanse of bleak land, over the sullen earth and shining like steel under the clouds; it goes on into the nearly unbroken horizon. The only feature of note is the range of mountains to the east, their black, craggy peaks piercing the misty sky like the arched back of a terrible monster.

"Marvelous to behold, is it not?" Says Grimhild.

"I've not seen their like before," I say. "Every place I go only reminds me how much I've yet to see."

"Hold on to that feeling. Without it, I would still be living in Mahadvala," he nods his great head towards the desolate mountains.

"You come from that place?"

"It is possible to survive," he stretches and rotates his shoulders. "It is the land of my birth, lying between the Northern border of the Bymore Desert and the fringes of the Northern Reaches."

"What is it like? I can't imagine it being pleasant."

"The desert's arid climate and the frozen bastion of ice in the north wreaks havoc on the seasons," he chuckles. "One evening you might be on a stroll in the valley and the next morning you're stranded in the snow trying to get out your front door."

"—And all the people there look exactly like him," Harlow calls over. "Even the women have beards!"

"They are a fine and resilient people!" Nalu says over our laughing voices.

Grimhild puffs out his chest.

"You do not want me to prove that I am not a woman," he moves by them and resumes walking down the slope to where the Riston and Tegan wait. "Let us be on our way. Night comes fast in the Reaches."

Harlow, Dale and I step down from our elevation and meet the Cedi river at a great bend in its pass to the southwest. As each sequential step brings us further down and closer to the ford, the coarse foliage and patchy brown soil gives way to rocks, small at first but becoming larger until most come up to my elbows. We tread through the field of boulders and the noise of the water's ferocious flow grows, the wind catches the spray of the water and it becomes lost within the maze of stone and it hangs there stagnant.

Grimhild leads us from the buffer of rocks and we step out onto an open patch of shore along the wide branch of the river. He walks up to the edge of the bank and stands still, probing the water with the long grip of his battle-ax, checking its depth. Grimhild retracts his weapon and judges it safe to cross... Safe for our bodies, yes. But when I reach the opposite bank, the dryness of my clothes suffered greatly. We press onward, to the end of the hilly country, and I take the first step as the one farthest away from home.

"Do you know what I can't understand?" Dale asks me. "Why didn't we take horses to the Northern Reaches?"

I struggle to find a witty remark.

"Because," Grimhild says, loud and strong, "none of our horses would bear you all this way."

"What do you mean 'wouldn't bear me'?"

"I asked them and they told me that you were an offense to their sense of smell."

Riston and I burst out laughing, Harlow does a poor job at disguising her smile, and for the first time since our meeting, Nalu laughs along with us; Tegan retains his stoic posture; Dale blushes as he fumbles with his words.

"That can't be the reason."

"He's obviously toying with you," I say.

"The real reason is because I do not trust horses to carry us where we need to go. Even with the river behind us, we are still a fair distance from our destination. But if you cannot walk all the way, I'd be happy to carry you."

Riston chuckles as he licks his lips before he brings up his flute's mouthpiece. He plays a gentle, meandering tune that stops our merriment at Dale's expense. Bright notes cascade from his instrument and disappear in the air of the flat land; they change tone and guide our spirits to melancholy. He starts to sing:

"Be wary of dusk, the end of life.

It comes to all. There is nothing that it can't outlast.

It has many names: pestilence, famine, and strife.

So keep up your guard that you may live long and happy;

That you might wed a goddess and sire a noble family the like that none shall surpass.

But there will come a day when it is your coffin they will carry.

So keep alive in you a heart that's still beating

And treat every moment as your last.

Every moment as fleeting.

Riston finishes his song and the gentle sound of his voice is replaced by the growing wind that blows in from the east; we march on into the Northern Reaches with the violet vapors of the sunset in the west. No one shares a word. As the miles creep by and the clouds of iron grow darker, the chill of the wind seeps into my body.

But, before all light is lost, the barren land sprouts a glade of short trees and skinny bushes, nestled in the soft ridge that forms a small half-circle. Grimhild elects to stop here for the night, and under cover of a joyless evening, we make ready the camp.

Grimhild takes with him Tegan and Riston into the trees to gather wood for fire, enough to last the fast approaching night, leaving Dale, Harlow, Nalu and myself to dig the fire pit and erect the tents. Their expressions are hard and grim. They sit with their backs together when the work is done, silent and watchful.

"You look like you've seen a ghost," I try to smile. "What, are you scared of the dark?"

"Darkness is not an enemy worth fearing," Nalu's eyes scan the encroaching shadows. "What lurks within is something different."

"Different?" Asks Dale. "What could—"

A howling on the cold wind catches the words in Dale's throat. Nalu cranes his neck and strains his ears for the sound. It comes again, the baleful cry chills my blood. Nalu steadily rises to his feet.

"They must have picked up our scent on the wind."

I look up at him and see his silhouette against the last vestiges of light as he draws his curved weapons. The wolves' howls echo over the plains and bounce among the sad trees. It seems to be coming from everywhere at once.

"They come this way."

"We can't wait for Grimhild any longer," Harlow joins Nalu, body rigid, staff poised. "You two, get a fire going."

The howling creeps closer. Louder; it fills the air.

Their haunting voices freezes my legs in place. I can hear my shallow breath hissing between my teeth.

"You deaf? Get moving!"

Dale grabs me by the arm and drags me towards the thin tree line, stumbling around in the pitch dark under the trees.

"Pick up anything you can," Dale orders.

We drop to our knees and scour the ground, praying that our fingers find kindling in the inky blackness. The heralding cries of the wolves motivate us to move faster.

"Are you ready?" Dale asks, breathlessly.

"Will it be enough?" I feel the weight of what little I was able to find.

"It'll have to be."

I lead the way, sprinting back to Nalu and Harlow, the air rushing in my ears.

"Let's go, Dale! Hurry up... Dale?"

I can no longer hear his pounding footsteps trailing me.

I double back to look for him, but Harlow's shouting stops me.

"We need fire!"

Wedged between my loyalty to Harlow and my desire to make sure Dale is all right, I frantically turn my head back and forth to the depths of the night that swallowed Dale and the sounds of padded feet running towards the camp. I shout, turn from the woods, and rush back to the others.

I dump the wood in the fire pit and search for my flint... my flint, my flint. Where is it?

"Nalu, I need your flint!"

"My bag. Second pocket," he says, rotating to follow the wolves lean, shadowy forms surrounding us.

I dive for Nalu's pack and rummage through its contents. My hand closes around the familiar shape and I whip back around to the pit, pulling out my knife and striking the flint. Sparks fly, briefly lighting up the camp in a snapshot of our desperation: Nalu stares straight into the hungry eyes of three wolves the size of small deer, Harlow guards his back. I strike the flint again, and again, each time the scene of impending horror progresses. Snarling growls of the beasts menace in the dark.

Spewing my frustration at the unlit pile of mere sticks, I strike a fourth time and the sparks bathe the kindling in burning shards of fire. The wood and strands of dead grass soak up the ignition and births a small and flickering light, revealing the fangs of a pouncing wolf. I throw myself flat on the ground and Nalu dispatches the lunging beast with his sloping blade, letting it run itself through on the sharp steel. The rest of the pack claw at the ground, their snarling jaws open wide, showing bared teeth. The ranks of the pack make a hole, letting through a wolf with a coat as black as the starless sky; its eyes reflect the fire's glow, making it resemble a demon summoned from the deepest ring of hell. The Alpha rumbles with a deep-throated growl, its hot breath clouds in the cool night air through its fangs and flared nostrils; its dark hide shimmers in the firelight as it lowers its head.

"This doesn't look good," Harlow shifts in place as the pack maneuvers around us.

Two black streaks charge forward on our left and right sides, their claws kicking up the dirt. Harlow and Nalu take out one then the other with merciless retribution. Harlow's staff pulverizes one wolf and there is a grotesque slashing as Nalu deals with the second. Their blood splatters across my face and gets in my mouth through my clenched teeth. I cannot account for the taste before I shout a warning to Harlow.

"More! To the right!"

Her copper braids dance about her, splayed out like the plumage of a dreadful peacock. She brings up her staff to block a third wolf whose snapping jaws close around her weapon. She wrestles with the creature and shakes it off, killing it with a jab of her metal-ended staff, the strident cracking and squelching of its demise draws forth the howls of the pack. The two wolves on either side of the Alpha show their fangs, dripping with murderous desire. They move forward, drawing closer while we continue to fend off other leaping and snapping teeth.

"Argh!" Harlow heaves one of their carcasses off her and it thumps to the ground.

"Harlow, don't!" I cry, but too late.

The dead animal, with the momentum of Harlow's lurch, rolls over our insignificant fire and extinguishes it, plunging us once more into total darkness. I can feel the cold, hard earth under my shaking hands; hear the voices of the pack.

"Callout, where are you?" Nalu says. "Stay close, don't let—" Nalu's cries of pain leech into the night.

I open my mouth to call for Harlow, but before I can make a move, a wolf pounces on me and digs its claws into my chest. The beast's rotten breath makes my eyes water as I attempt to hold its razor-sharp teeth from closing around my neck.

Desperately fending off the wolf with one hand, I fumble for my knife with the other. My fingers are almost completely numb; everything feels the same. Just as an ocean of dread threatens to smother me I remember that I dropped my knife in the fire pit. I reach for it, but the body of the dead wolf laying there covers it. I push hard against the creature snapping at me with wicked teeth while I try to dig my hand into the pit, but it is no use. I cannot do both; I cannot hold off the wolf for much longer.

I hear a whistle shout through the night.

Something strikes against the wolf on top of me. Baying in pain, it keels over.

I heave the carcass off me and plunge my hands into the still hot fire pit for my knife. I ignore the searing pain, hunched over on high alert.

Twice more I hear that sound and twice more the herd of wolves is thinned.

"Is everyone all right?" I ask. I can no longer hear the pack's sinister barking.

"I hate dogs!" Harlow fumes.

"And Nalu?"

"I am fine," he dusts himself off. "You have a fine shot, Tegan. And not a moment to spare."

A few seconds of snapping twigs and rustling branches yields Tegan's wraith-like form, his figure doused in the waving fire of his small lantern.

"Grimhild heard wolves and told me to return to the camp. He and Riston should be back momentarily."

"Really could have used that lantern of yours, Tegan," Harlow utters, caustically.

Tegan turns drearily to look at her, "how was I supposed to gather wood in the pitch dark?"

"Relax," Nalu sighs.

"Dale! I forgot about him. I lost him coming back from the woods!" I cry. "I have to go look for him!"

"Settle yourself," Tegan casually says. "I found him knocked out on my way over here. He ran into a tree."

My panicked state melts into relief as I smirk at Dale's cursed luck.

"I will go for him. You three get this fire going," Nalu walks out of the light's reach.

Tegan and Harlow work in an efficient silence as they throw the dead wolf aside, stack the wood, and spark it into life. Harlow waves me over to her. She kneels down, reaches into her pack, pulls out a square glass phial and a roll of bandages and treats my injuries. The sting of the liquid seems to do more harm than good but soon the medicine relieves the pain of the wolf's claws. I settle onto the tossed soil and soak up the fire's merciful warmth; stretching out my palms and holding them against my cheeks. Nalu returns with Dale half carrying, half dragging him to the camp; Harlow dresses Dale's bloody head wound. He gives a concussed grumble as Harlow ties off the bandage. I rise and lead him to the tents, laying him down inside. He tries to speak but sleep swallows him before the words can leave his lips. I exit the tent and Grimhild greets me, his blood coated axe in one hand, and the tail of a wolf in the other; he drags its body as he and Riston enter our camp

"These pups giving you trouble?" Grimhild chuckles.

"Wouldn't have if we could bloody see," Harlow responds.

"I found their alpha hightailing it over the ridge on my way back. I thought it'd be better suited on a spit roasting over the fire!" he says, lively.

Grimhild allows Nalu to take the wolf from his hands. As Nalu prepares to skin the beast, I now notice that it is missing its head. Nalu removes the hide, Harlow and I clear away the bodies of slain wolves.

With the alpha gutted and ready, Nalu steps into an empty tent and removes its main support beam. He brings it to the body and feeds it through, hoisting it over our growing fire to roast. Unsurprisingly, I have never eaten a wolf before, but simply put, it is completely distasteful, and so lean and muscular that my jaw is soon sore and aching with the effort of chewing it. But I am too hungry to be put off by it. We pick the bones clean, saving some for Dale whenever he wakes, and toss the rest into the fire pit. I stare as the white bones char and turn black, dissolving into the heatwaves and disappearing into the air.

I lean back and prop myself on my elbow, stomach full. The others do likewise as they recover from this hardy, albeit wanting, meal. Grimhild beltches and Riston echoes him. But Harlow rises to her feet and beats both of them with a volume that reverberates over the plains. We laugh and applaud her as she resumes her seat. I find it equally surprising and wonderful that this group can be so candid and relaxed after just coming from a fight. And this is only the first night.

I sit up.

"Can you tell me more about where it is we are going?" I ask to no one in particular.

"It is very cold and there's ice everywhere," Harlow says.

"What kind of place is it?"

"It used to be a hub of trade and travel in the north," Grimhild replies. "Under the name Kylmä Outpost, it housed merchants and travelers from Tir Fwythland to Thalvia on the other side of the Bymore Desert. Lore masters and nobles alike stopped there on their journeys and filled its now cold halls with knowledge and artifacts from the elder days. Or so the stories say."

"I thought you called it Kandent?" I question.

"The Bandits have a way of changing things," Nalu answers. "They take what was once beautiful and rich and twist it into something monstrous. Kandent, my people's word for blighted place, is its name under Bandit occupation. Frozen and stripped of its old glory."

"It has lain abandoned for years before the Bandits arrived," Riston adds, polishing his flute, "the result of the rising Bandit threat a century ago. It was only until recently that the Bandits repurposed the outpost as a means to their vicious end. Ironic that it used to stand vigil against them."

"So, it is a fortress?" I ask.

"It's specific location along the northern road makes it an ideal place for the Bandits," Grimhild says. "It allows them to move freely from their home in the north while also locking off all travel. When the Pau'larin constructed Kylmä Outpost in the days of old, they did so on the brink of Llif Rhew, a waterfall that flows from Lake Winterpool, with only one way in and one way out."

"I still have some worries about how we get inside."

"You heard the plan," Riston says. "Don't trust us yet?"

"Yes — no. I mean, I trust you. I just…"

"Calm yourself, friend," Grimhild rests his broad hand around my neck and shoulder. "This will not be our first time breaking into a fortress. The plan will work," he stirs to his feet. "But now is not the time for tactics. Let us get rest while we can. There is still much road to cover ere the dawn."

*

The chill of early morning drags me into consciousness. I look over and see Dale, still laying spread-eagled. I try to force myself back into sleep, but it's clearly too late. The inside wall of the canvas tent is slick with wet and Dale snores too loudly for me to focus on silence. I leave the tent in hopes to warm myself at the fireside. The separated pieces of wood in the pit still smolder from last night, the grooves in the white charred wood glow faintly with the ghost of ignition. I reconnect the fuel and place more wood atop the old. I revive the flame and revel in the heat that holds back the wind.

It is grey around me. Long tentacles of fog lace themselves over the dead grasslands, the sun appears shadowy and stifled through thin clouds and shows the dry brambles and balding trees that enclose our camp. I blow air into my cupped hands. It leaks out from the spaces between my fingers like white smoke. I rummage around my pack for a loaf of bread, wrapped in brown cloth. It's cloudy and cold. Damn cold. And we still have to go farther north? I can hardly wait.

Feet crunching on frost from behind takes me from my thoughts to where I find Riston and Tegan emerging from their shelter.

"I thought I smelled wood-smoke," says Riston. "Gave me worry that the fire came back to life by itself."

Soon, one-by-one, our Company rejoins at the fireside, lastly joined by Dale, whose dazed expression tells me that he does not remember the night's events. We talk and eat as we regal him at length, with a few jabs at his accident.

"We have been idle long enough," Nalu says. "Let us go."

I douse the fire, help pack the tents, and we file out across plains to rising hills and the growing cold of descending winter.

At times, the wind blows so fiercely that the gusts stagger even the immense Grimhild who must stop to find his footing. By noontime, the stretched out clouds of early morning have gathered more densely and shield us from what little warmth the pale sun provided, and the landscape gives little to distract us from the elements. From our sloping vantage point, I can see naught but dead things and the salvage of winter. The dwindling forest from our camp hides behind the length of our progression some leagues behind us, and all that lays in the west towards the Wastes, and the east where the River snakes, and ahead north is the vision of barren hills and scattered, rocky outcroppings. I am desperate now for the comfort of Hector's Tavern and laughing company. My feet grow heavy and I lag behind. Dale falls instep beside me and he puts his arm around my shoulders, doing his best to help me push through the wind.

We march solemnly onwards and the rolling terrain becomes laden with towering rocks that jut out from the hard ground like hands reaching out from the depths. At first, they appeared in spaced out groups that gave us little hindrance, but as we continue trudging along, they seem to gather before us like a wall. The wind howls ominously between their ragged peaks.

For the most part, the stony towers conceal the low evening sun, but it periodically shows itself dim between them to mock us on our cold and weary plight. Ahead, I see that Nalu stopped and is looking back at us. His mouth moves but the sounds of his words do not reach my ears over the prevailing wind. I look at Dale, but he shakes his head and leads us to the front of the line to gather around Nalu.

"We should rest here and wait for the wind to die down," he says. "There are caves in these towers that face away from the wind."

Shortly after, he finds one of the hollows and our Company takes shelter. The interior of the cave is dark and dry but surprisingly spacious, and the rushing air outside mercifully leaves us be. Harlow and Dale step back outside to search among the bases of the monolithic rocks for wind-swept thistles and bunches of dead leaves caught in the spindly clutches of the sparse, resilient greenery. They return with armfuls of mere kindling, nothing to keep a fire going into the night. I move to speak my concerns, but Grimhild shrugs something off his shoulders and kneels down beside it. He undoes the leather straps and reveals many lengths of wood lashed together into a bundle. Within moments, he builds a wonderfully warming fire around which we unroll our mats and eat a humble supper.

We chew on bland food and huddle around the fire, the circling smoke whisked away by the wind. Grimhild's battle-ax leans against the wall of the cave and its wide head reflects the flames in a bloom of fire.

"Do you like it?" Grimhild asks.

I sputter, realizing I've been caught staring.

"Stronger than any helm or shield that gets in her way."

"It is beautiful," I say.

"Tell him about her name," Riston says. "Such stories are worth a retelling."

"The axe has a name?" Dale asks.

"Of course!" Grimhild laughs. "Weapons that have proven themselves worthy are given names."

"What is it?"

"It is one not given by me. I will let him say," he looks at Nalu seated next to him.

Nalu stirs and glances at Grimhild. He nods his great head and Nalu looks into the embers.

"Its name is Spasiter. It means savior in the tongue of my people. I named it after he saved my life in what is left of Tir Fwythland."

"Riston mentioned as much before we set out." I say. "Truly fortunate that Grimhild was there. But what about you? Do your swords have names?"

"Their names are deeply connected to my culture," Nalu lays one of his curved swords across his knees. "The wielder of the two blades is more than a warrior. He is the arbiter to the gods and their creations. This is Vesindor," he pokes at the displayed sword. "The Western Wind. Una, in the beginning, shaped the land and filled the oceans. With one fist, She struck the formless land and summoned the tides of the sea; made mountains, blew the valleys, and shaped the hills and planes. Beasts of every kind were born from the Western Wind and the spray of the sea, the power of Una," he reaches behind him and shows the second blade still held in its black sheath. "This is Anleg Dau'rün, the Final Death. When life runs its course, Ilithi takes them and makes them ready to be used once more by Una."

"And when one wields them together, he reaps their life with the Final Death and gains their strength with the Western Wind," Riston interrupts. "Such a superstitious people."

"Then what do you call your sword?" Dale asks.

Riston sits up straight and puffs out his chest.

"It is a sorrowful tale of loss and revenge, involving a dashing young man, a flute, and one unlucky night. This flute and I have been in one another's company since I was a lad. It kept the music in my heart and I gave it a voice to sing. One night, in the south of Hyravon near the coast of the Summer Seas, I was beset by a gang of the most unsavory sort. In my sleep, they relieved me of my travel bag, my coin purse and, to my utter dismay, my flute. I spent nearly the whole of the month looking for it, but to no avail. I was inconsolable. I went to an inn to search for the cure to my sullen mood at the bottom of the bottle. I was in a drunken stupor when a group of six men walked in, and I saw my flute sticking out of one of the men's pants. I was so relieved to see that my most cherished possession was not forever lost, but also consumed by anger at the mode of its delivery. I confronted him in the most noble and respectful of fashions, saying: *'you're the bastard that robbed me!'*"

"I grabbed for my flute but did not get farther than that. He beat me to the ground while his friends cheered him on. He looked down at me as I tended to the wound bleeding over my eye and told me to mind my manners. Before I left, I swore that I would track him down and claim what is mine. I searched for a teacher that would show me the way of the blade, for at that time, I knew nothing of real fighting or swordsmanship. Finally, from all of the folktales and dead ends, I came upon my teacher, a nobleman named Sigmund Valar. I was trained in the methods of archery and of swordsmanship, but I found that no combination of feather or steel suited me. Sigmund, in a last and hesitant final effort gave me his own great sword and lo! It fit like a glove. Master Sigmund requisitioned a sword from his family blacksmith and by the time it was ready, he taught me a great deal. But, before my training was utterly complete, I snuck away and found my thief. On that day, I took from him two things: my flute and the man's sword hand. In that moment, my sword was named. For my love of song and for the thief's wailing cries, I named it Melody and I now regard it the same as my flute."

"At times I wish that the man got away," Harlow says. "There is only so much that you can play before we've heard it all."

"Joke all you'd like. I may as well be dead without music."

"The only songs worth hearing time and time again are the ones sung by the enemy as I lay them down. And my staff knows that song's every line."

"Tell Viper about how that started," Riston laughs. "Your master's weapon was once so humble."

Harlow settles her back against the wall of the cave and sets down her water skin.

"It serves a greater purpose than 'Melody' does," she says, sarcastically.

"What was it?" I ask.

"It's a piece of wood that I later used to build a roof."

"I'm sorry, what?" Dale hoots.

"Don't laugh when you haven't heard the full story."

"I'm sure he's sorry," I say. "Go on!"

Harlow smiles.

"I was going to a job with my cart full of lumber that I was using to construct some building when a gang of highwaymen stopped me. They tried to rob me, and my sword was conveniently out of reach. The men went for me, and I went for the wood. They tried to put up a fight, but I soon made them realize that I didn't have anything worth stealing. I'm pretty sure that you can still see the bloodstain on the beam I used to bludgeon them. Ever since, I was never able to go back to using swords. As far as I know, I am the only one that uses something like it. Since that is the case, I had to teach myself how to use it effectively. But, like all things, I mastered it in no time."

"And we're all glad that you're on our side!" Grimhild cheers.

He looks over at Dale.

"You have a strong arm. I'm sure you've used that hammer, though not yet the one you carry from our armory. What do you name it?"

Dale reaches for his simple weapon and rests its hard, grey head in his hands. He sits in stoic silence for a long moment until he eventually says,

"Deep in my heart, I know that without my old hammer I would be long dead. But I also cannot think of any great deeds it allowed me to perform. For now, it is nameless. I'll have to wait and see."

"Aye," Grimhild looks at Dale with shining eyes. "In my country, men that pretend to be of courage and valor are shunned and forgotten. You show your worthy character with your honesty."

Dale turns his bashful face and stares out of our little hollow to the rock speckled land and greying sky; the wind does not blow so severely.

"I fear that I must be the bearer of ill news and say that we must be on the move once more," Grimhild states. "We have enough light left to get us out of this terrain. After that, we will be less than a day from our destination."

We pack our things and trek out into the dying day. The earth smooths as the air grows increasingly frigid. By the time we find a safe place for the night, it starts to snow.

CHAPTER 16

— Blighted Place —

Night seems to arrive quicker the farther north we go, and the only progress we've made is by following the rut Grimhild makes as he shoves through dense snow. No wonder he was against bringing horses. The frigid air bites at the tips of my ears, the point of my nose and stings my eyes; I've all but lost feeling in my poor toes.

The snow stops falling and I can finally see more than ten strides ahead of me. There is a stout spattering of ragged looking trees, overgrown with twisted bushes, all glazed with ice. Grimhild leads us towards it and he keeps the frozen branches open for us to pass through. I take three steps in and I feel an iron grip close around my arm.

"Be wary of your footing, Viper," Grimhild lets me go and points his gloved finger.

I turn to look and see the cause of his alarm. The ground just vanishes not an arm's reach away.

"Thanks," I say, breathlessly.

"Keep focused. This is the very last place to become complacent."

Grimhild gathers us close together.

"This is it, lads. Nalu, Tegan, go now and see if our information is still correct. We will move in sight of the fortress and wait for your signal."

The two men nod and step out from the overlook, becoming lost from view as the white-crusted limbs and bushes shield them from sight.

"The rest of you, this way," he looks at me, "carefully."

I slink along the cliffside, brushing snow from my face when our movement dislodges it. I soon come to a stop with the rest and peer out over the side of the ridge. We are high above the ground, not as high as when Dale and I were with Orbith in his special place, but certainly high enough to generate enough caution to keep me well away from the brink. I look out into the open air and see Lake Winterpool, cupped in the hands of the mountains and the head of the great Nadi river running from it. It cascades over unleveled land and plunges over jagged rocks, flowing and falling until it meets a steep and seemingly bottomless drop. The waterfall, Llif Rhew, thunders down into the desolate lands and shows itself a black ribbon on its course towards the Western Wastes. And sitting perched on the precipice, leering over the frozen land, is Kandent Fortress, a black monolith of unventured evil. A narrow bridge juts out from our side of the Nadi to meet the gates like a slender, beckoning finger.

"Why would anyone build such a thing there?" Dale asks.

"It served a far greater purpose than at present," Riston says.

"It must have taken years, decades."

"That's the Pau'larin for you," says Harlow. "You should know better than most how durable their architecture is. Hope it makes you trust the Compound's walls a little more."

"Aye," Dale says.

"That's enough history," Grimhild says, his steamy breath carried away by the icy air. "Before they give the signal, there is something that I will have you know," he looks at Dale and I most intently. "We have all come far to get here. Know that Junn is in reach. Understand also that recklessness will not just cost your life, but the life of the one beside you. Follow instruction, do not waver."

"You know you can depend on it," Riston states. His eyes turn down to the floor of the river valley. "Looks like we were right after all."

"Appears so," Grimhild glances at the flicker of sparks. "Follow me."

He rises only but to a crouch as he moves towards the steep hill that runs down to the riverbank. He stops suddenly and I walk into him.

"One last thing," he says only to me. "The moment we met, I saw that your love for family was strong. We are alike in that way. To have a hope against the evil of the world is one thing. But to act on that hope, despite all that might stand in your way, is another thing entirely. Just have faith one night longer and you shall be rewarded."

I stare into his assuring face. He winks at me and slides gracefully down the slope.

I meet the rest of the Company at a narrow bank outside of reach of the torchlight adorning Kandent's walls. The sound of the water spilling over the Llif Rhew is quite loud now, like the clashing of a grand army; mist from its plummet appears as white smoke on the brim of the drop. We continue heading towards the bridge, stretching towards the fortress overhead and the river it spans. As we walk underneath the bridge, the tumultuous crashing of water sends echoes bouncing off the arches and pylons.

"How in the hell?" Dale gasps.

What the hell is right. I stop beside Dale and stare as the river surges at our feet. It seems so much wider now that I am right up next to it. I slide my eyes up the opposite side and see the faint outlines of Tegan and Nalu. I look back at the water. How did they get over there?

"Damn this place," Harlow curses.

She takes in deep, sharp breaths and dashes forward. To my relief, she did not vanish into the rushing current, but skips across it on barely visible stepping stones. Riston and Grimhild go quickly after, arms stretched out to secure their balance. They all make it to the opposite bank, nothing but a narrow strip of solid ground upon which the fortress's foundations hold fast against the forces of nature. Without warning, Dale shouts and jumps to the first step. I can hear him cursing each time his feet leave the stones. My turn. The waterfall is all I can think about as I stand locked in place, legs rigid. I look at the surface of the river and red flakes of torchlight from the pillared ramparts and terraces blink back at me. Shit.

I leap after Dale, feeling my stomach drop as I fly through the spray-clogged air. I vault over a mighty bough of a long-felled tree trapped against the sharp, slanted rocks and the relentless current. I take another hopping step onto a glistening, broad stone and another. I land on the other side, heart beating faster than I can breathe. I don't have the time to settle my nerves before Dale's shadow moves away from me.

I meet the group rallied around Nalu and a long metal grate that caps a hole into the fortress, an open mouth swallowing the river. There are a few bars missing. Grimhild steps around it and wrestles the grate open and, one-by-one, we delve into the passage; I keep my feet to the sides of the tunnel to keep out of the water as much as possible. After a short and cramped time I see light ahead. I enter the fortress itself.

We gather on one side of the small but swift waterway. A few meters away is an arched footbridge that connects the two sides, and on the opposite side is a wooden door, its florin spikes dully reflecting the light of a lantern hanging in the middle of the ceiling; the chill of the north permeates through all, rock, metal and flesh.

All eyes turn to Grimhild. He stands proud and determined. He looks over us, our armor and weapons wreathed in shifting shadows as the lantern burns.

"We made it into Kandent's flow chamber," he says. "There are more like this one along the path of the water to make sure its movement is unimpeded, otherwise the entire place would be washed away. Stealth is our best weapon here. With luck, we will get to Junn without detection."

"Luck," Tegan huffs.

"Let's go," Grimhild places his helm upon his head.

He turns, steps across the little bridge, opens the door at the other side, and disappears. We all follow closely behind him, my throbbing heart and our soft footsteps the only sounds over the interior flow of the Nadi.

We walk along a dark corridor from the flow chamber towards a bend in the path. Lanterns hang on regular intervals along the passage, their light struggling to escape their fogged, dirt-encrusted glass. As low and faint as the journey of a still brook, Riston recites a line from a song to himself as we sneak along the corridor:

"Oh, to go where light is dim and hope is spent.

Where angels weep from bowing head

on the path where fools are doomed to tread

And so on, into the dark, the heroes went."

We arrive at a left-leading turn and Grimhild edges his head out around the corner.

Nothing.

We press on and before long, come to a short staircase that leads up to another door.

"This way leads to the Entrance Hall. Beyond it is the way to the cellars. In its time, Kylmä had no use for dungeons, but now with the Bandits occupying Kandent, that is likely where Junn is."

Grimhild cracks the door open and peers inside. After a moment he pushes the way open and waves us forward, silently filing into a moderately sized room, lit by a lone brazier. Moth-eaten tapestries hang from faded gold bars on the grey stone walls, little decorative tables and a beautiful carpet, whose colors have long since withered away, are thrown carelessly to one side of the room. On my left is a high and thick portcullis and its winch, behind which is the only gateway into Kandent, to the right is a second pair of tall, iron-bound doors, only these are open; light from the other side filters through them. Grimhild moves across the room like a shadow and comes to rest next to the door. He pauses, listening, waiting. He looks back at us, shows his hand, then three fingers. I stare at him, blood racing. Then, in a blink, he steals into the Keep.

We come into a cavernous room with a high, vaulted ceiling, shrouded in the dark that the fire from the Bandit torches, rammed into the floor, cannot reach. Directly in front of us is a broad staircase that leads to the upper levels and the balcony that wraps around the room's interior. Bones, some gnarled into splinters and others that withhold their shape, lie strewn about the wet and chipped flagstone floor, collected in mounds off to the side and around the bases of once smooth pillars that hold up the ceiling. I glance to my left. I see the backs of the three Bandits as they wander into a separate passage on the other side to where I see another doorway, sitting deep and black; to my right, beside the broad stair, is a similar door illuminated from behind.

Grimhild takes one look around and goes right. We keep a low profile as we traverse the Keep, taking care to avoid the scattered bones.

Before I enter the lit room, we stop fast, held in place by Grimhild's raised fist.

I look passed him and see a group of three more Bandits, squatting down at the other end of the putrid room. Tegan knocks an arrow but Grimhild shakes his head. One of the Bandits stands from what I can now see is a mound of flesh, human or animal I cannot say. He runs his blood-stained hand across his mouth and starts to turn around. Grimhild shepherds us back before he can see us and takes cover behind the pillars and piles of bones. The Bandits exit the room, one at first, then the other two. As the last's feet cross the threshold, Nalu grabs him, covers his dripping mouth and snaps his neck; he gently lowers the corpse to the floor. Harlow creeps up behind the second to eliminate him, but her feet knock against a loose floor tile, sending fragments skittering loud as a wind chime. The Bandit starts, but Harlow is fast and chops at his throat with the side of her hand. The first Bandit, fully alert at the noises, has his weapon out and ready. He opens his mouth, but before he can shout more than one syllable, Tegan hurls a knife into his neck; Harlow jerks the gasping Bandit's head violently to one side and he falls silent.

"Hide the bodies," Nalu whispers. "Clean the blood."

My nerves are totally on edge as I drag one of the bodies out of sight; Dale scrapes at the small puddle of blood with the Bandit's filthy rags to clean it as best he can. Nalu and Tegan are already moving inside the room as Dale and I catch up to them. I gingerly step over the unidentifiable pile of flesh and the warrior's carcasses without a second thought and follow them through the open arch at the other end of the room.

I step foot in Kandent's Great Hall, cast in the shade of night, but illuminated in pools of cool color as moonlight filters through high, stained glass windows that depict visions of kings and knights. It falls on broad tables, lined with many chairs, though the majority of them lie broken. On the far end of the room, at the center of a table sitting perpendicular to the others, is an elaborate throne dressed in silver on its arms and legs, and at the peak of the backrest a hawk, crafted from silver and green gemstones as eyes, sits with wings spread wide. The aura of this place begets the chill of its ghosts that once passed through; I fear that it is Kandent's doom to never again relive that time. Light from the Keep bleeds into the Hall from behind us, and as we move farther in, the hawk's emerald eyes flash.

"This," Nalu says, voice low and reverent, "is where Kylmä's ruler would host feasts and welcome nobles. What I would give to have been here at its peak; to speak with foreign people," he drops his head. "That is not the fate of my time."

We step carefully over candlesticks and broken plates, skirting around small islands of piled tapestries and hewn chairs. As I traverse this graveyard of a passed era, I cannot help but to hear the murmur and bustling of the people that once sat around these tables. I wonder what they would have to say about what has become of the world. Just as the Pau'larin have been lost to the relentless passage of time and their vast knowledge taken with them, so too have the secrets of Kylmä been taken from us. Perhaps one day, when all of this is over, we will return here and revive the outpost's old splendor, but that—

"Don't fall behind, Vipe," Dale pulls me forward and I remember why I am here.

We follow Grimhild to the back of the Great Hall, into the space that lies behind, and come into the kitchen that lays in ruin. Cupboards and closet doors, hanging from their hinges, are thrown open, rusted cutlery peppers the filthy tiled floor, and a rotting stench hangs in the frigid air. One good thing does remain in this room: behind the kitchen's wreckage is the way down to the cellar. I am so overwhelmed with the desire to finally see Junn, I forget that silence is key. I wade through the debris of the kitchen and send bent metal and ceramic shards scrapping across the floor, piercing the quiet.

"Viper, you idiot!" Harlow says as loud as she dares.

Our group stands as still as stone for an agonizing moment, waiting for the unmistakable sound of pounding feet. But naught can be heard, save for the constant rumbling of water over Llif Rhew.

"Luck seems to favor the foolish and reckless," Harlow scolds.

I am too excited to pay her words any mind as I step towards the stairs and peer into the black descent. A flickering glow at the bottom betrays its depth.

I look at the others.

"We should hurry," Dale looks through the murky window.

I follow his eye and see the stars in the night sky have begun to recede into the west, retreating from the pale violet light of dawn that slowly grows brighter each passing moment.

I look to Grimhild. He nods at me knowingly and I lead the way into Kandent's dungeons.

*

My footsteps on the stairs echo on the grimy walls. Each pace downwards quickens my excited heart. Farther down, the looming light of dawn from atop the stair wanes as one beneath comes nearer. I reach a landing on the descent. To the left is an arched doorway; I can see the forlorn stone floor and the base of bent and gnarled iron bars flickering in amber light. I slowly step forward; the light comes to meet my boots and rises to my knees. I hold my breath. I am coming to the last step. My eyes are fixed on the bars that are steadily revealing themselves with each motion forward.

I step through the arch and make it to level ground. My companions circle behind me, watching. To either side of the doorway hang more hazy lanterns from Kylmä's happier days; barrels of wine and ale stretch into the dark recesses of the cellar, and a wooden bench and table are against the left-hand wall. Though, all I see is what lies ahead. Wedged between floor and ceiling are iron bars; spiders have woven their webs thick and strong in their narrow and crooked margins.

"Junn?" I say, barely over a whisper.

He has to be here. I take a step forward, followed by another. I reach out; the bars are in my quivering fingers. I brush aside the spiders' webs and see a black shape laying on the floor.

"Junn?" I say once more, my words are almost indistinguishable.

I look intently at the dark mass in the cell through blurred eyes; the light behind me sends shadows of my Company across the floor to lap against the opposite wall. The mound stirs and strength leaves my body.

"Junn!" I fall to my knees, holding tight to the ghastly metal.

The mound stirs again and sits up. In this instance, nothing but this figure and I are present. All the hurting of my quest, all the restless miles and sleepless nights evaporate as tears fall and the figure picks itself up.

Even though it is raspy and tortured, I could never forget my brother's voice.

"Is that… It can't be."

Dale kneels down beside me.

"It is, brother," he croaks.

Junn quakes, his shoulders heaving as he sobs. Grimhild orders the gate open and Harlow soon has it swung wide; there is nothing left standing between us. Dale and I rush into the cell and hold the stooping mass of ravaged cloth, and the man inside them, into our arms. Dale holds Junn's head close to his own, their bodies shaking from the weight of their reunion. Junn lifts his head, and I see scars, fresh and old, on his once proud face; his eyes sunken with none of his old spark within them. But he looks at us with such gratefulness and adoration that he cannot help but to laugh as his tears blaze trails through the grim covering his face.

"You came for me," he croaks.

"There was no other choice to be made," Dale replies. "You think it's easy dealing with Vipe by yourself?"

Junn chuckles, though it brings on a spell of rattling coughs.

"We did not do this alone," I look at my companions.

Junn turns from us and looks at the Black Flag. Harlow enters the cell, bends to one knee, and takes Junn's hand in her own. The unbreakable Harlow, too, is in tears. Dale and I pull back and smile wide, laughing as though nothing at all happened over these long months. With Dale's help, I lift Junn's weakened body from the floor and carry him to the bench.

"I am glad to see you well enough," Riston steps aside to allow us out of the cell.

"Aye, it does us good to see you again, old friend," Grimhild places a hand on Junn's shoulder. "Are you able to stand under your own strength? Our load will be lessened if life hasn't left your legs."

"Yes. Give me time and I will be able to walk," Junn says, shakily. "I didn't have much opportunity to keep up my strength after they captured me a second time."

Nalu steps forward and offers him food and drink from his own supply. Junn gratefully accepts and we all wait in silent companionship as Junn has his fill.

"A second time?" I ask.

"You knew I would fight back, didn't you?"

Junn finishes his meal and looks deep into our eyes; his own carrying the flame of the lantern and the blissful joy of reunion.

"I am sure that you have many questions, but I yearn to leave this place and warm myself with fire and ale," he smiles. "I've spent far too long in cold and darkness."

"Indeed," Tegan says. "Celebration must wait until we—"

Echoes come clattering from the stairs. All eyes snap to the doorway that carries sounds of feet and arguing voices. Grimhild hurries to Junn's side and leads him back into the vacant prison. I am about to protest, but Junn shakes his head fervently. I pause, and all of a sudden realize their plan. Grimhild lays Junn down gingerly, swings the gate shut, and ducks behind cover, filling in with the rest of us in hiding. The Bandit's voices grow louder as their quarreling escalates. I hear the clang of plateware and dull thumping when something skips down the steps. A stale roll of bread skids into the cellar and scampering feet come in pursuit. A Bandit reaches the bottom of the stair and bends to pick up the dropped food.

"I'm going!" The Bandit snarls. "Quit shovin'!"

"I've got things to do," the second, more commanding Bandit says, still hidden behind the arch of the doorway. "Feed him. Merr'putra will not be not be denied his sacrifice."

The Bandit stands up and walks right passed us hiding in the shadows of stacked barrels; my breath catches in my throat. He swings the gate of the cell open with a creek and steps inside, kicking Junn hard in the ribs.

"Get up, you lousy wretch!" he drops the tray of disgraceful food on the floor and kicks Junn again as he leaves.

The Bandit slams the gate shut and heads back for the stairs. His black eyes widen in surprise at the sight of Dale hidden beside the arch. The Bandit begins to cry out, but Tegan loses an arrow. It pierces his soft eye and his head jerks back as his body folds to the stone. The second Bandit snarls and steps into the cellar; I see the tip of his sword first, the sharp metal glinting keenly in the light.

Dale bides his time and waits for his arm to follow. The Bandit's ashen grey hand that grasps the sword slides into view, followed closely by his bone-lashed arm.

"What's goin' on?" the Bandit growls. "Come on out, or I'll make you wish you were—"

Dale seizes the Bandit by the arm, whips him around through the musty air and brings him slamming into the unforgiving wall. The Bandit loses grip of his sword and roars in anger, flailing at Dale, but he weathers the Bandit's raining fists. Dale swings his arm at the Bandit and crushes his neck with his elbow. He steps back to allow his adversary to collapse to the floor. In the Bandit's last moments, he looks up at Dale with unfettered rage in the black pits of his eyes right into Dale's burning glare. For a moment, Dale stands with heaving chest and clenched fist, as if he is trying to control his rage and intends to show mercy to a defeated foe. I could not have been more mistaken. Quickly and fluidly, Dale unslings his Warhammer, and with a rush of stale air, he replaces skull and tissue with steel and revenge. Dale raises his hammer again, his chest swells, but he holds himself in-check. Instead, he drops his arms to his side and bows his head, saying in a low voice,

"Now who's the lousy wretch?"

Dale turns from his kill, and with heavy footfalls, returns to Junn's cell, lifts, and carries him up the stairs, calling to us in grim monotone,

"What are you waiting for?"

*

We thunder up the dungeon steps after Dale and emerge from the cellar. I see Dale waiting impatiently with Junn in the door leading to the Great Hall.

"We have to get out of here! I hear Bandits!" Dale urges.

He turns from us again and takes off alone through the Hall, throwing caution and stealth to the wind as we barrel through the detritus of the dead banquet hall. We take flight, knocking our feet against the remnants of Kylmä's dead splendor.

I lose sight of Dale, for he had already made it through the Hall and entered the room off the Keep. The rest of us barge into the room and find Junn on the ground, resting his back against the wall and Dale set in an aggressive stance, facing a lone Bandit. The enemy stands from where he knelt beside his slain allies and reaches for his skeletal weapon, drawing it in a rush when he sees the number of the trespassers multiply. He calls in the tongue of the Enemy and soon more Bandits file in, their various tools of death already held tight in their hands. The

Bandits' dark shapes melts into the dim of the chamber, leaving their bone armor contrasted against the lantern's flame.

They charge.

Dale lifts his Warhammer and swings it wide, bringing it to bear against the lead Bandit's arm. The head of the hammer slams into its target and sunders the bone into splinters. Dale keeps his momentum going and brings the hammer down and to the left, turning it in a tight bend as he brings the hammer flying upwards to meet the Bandit once more. The strike drives into the Bandit's chin and lifts him off his feet, arching his body through the air to land among the other Bandits. They howl and rage, and at once charge Dale, their stained and broken teeth showing behind discolored lips.

Grimhild charges forward with his shoulder down and collides with a Bandit, knocking him to his back. Carried by the momentum of the bull-rush, Grimhild, crying death and destruction, heaves the great head of his axe up and over his head, right into the combatant. The steel sounds off on the flagstone as it cleaves the Bandit through-and-through. He attempts to retract his weapon, but it is stuck in the battered floor; the Bandits notice and one barrels towards him. Before the Bandit reaches Grimhild, Nalu sprints forward, vaults over Grimhild's back, and delivers a spinning kick to the Bandits head. I can hear his neck break as he folds.

I step into the fray to protect Junn, clashing with a Bandit brandishing a flail, its chain made from a spine, laced together with dark metal circlets; its head a five-pointed metal star. He arcs its heavy head towards me and I jump back as the flail pounds the floor, leaving a crater of broken tiles. He swings again and I lunge with my sword, guiding its keen blade in the space between his head and shoulders.

Harlow and Riston battle five Bandits at once, a dancing blur of steel and blood. Riston parries with the length of this great sword while countering decisively with his knife, dispatching them with ease; Harlow twirls her staff, flicks swords from Bandit hands, and decimates them with wood and metal; Tegan delivers an arrow into anyone that is unfortunate enough to enter the room.

Our individual victories leave piles of the slain as we push out of the room and into the Keep. Dale heads the group and lashes out with his Warhammer at the advancing Bandits. I can hear the thunderous footsteps of reinforcements descending the grand stair; see them stationing upon the balcony with bows and black-feathered arrows on their strings.

"Which way?" Dale shouts as he ducks back into the room to avoid a hissing volley of arrows.

"We have to make it back to the flow chamber!" Riston answers.

"There isn't a chance in hell Junn can make it across the River!" Dale looks back at Riston in desperation. "Unless there's another secret way out, the front door is the only option."

"Then let us hold the gate until you can get it open," Grimhild replies.

Before any of us can say otherwise, Grimhild picks up a dead body and charges out of the room while many arrows turn his shield into a pincushion.

Riston and Harlow follow his lead, bursting forward and dispatching the foes Grimhild leaves staggered; Nalu and Tegan protect their flanks.

I run to Junn's side, sling his arm around my shoulders, and pick him up as his feet stumble along next to mine.

Grimhild and the others have pushed through the Keep and secured a perimeter in the Entrance Hall around the gate and winch. As Dale, Junn and I join them, Bandits fill and swarm inside the Keep, pouring from every open door to answer the clash of battle.

"Get a move on!" Harlow yells at Dale as the onslaught beats her back.

"The winch is stuck!" Dale pulls with all his might at the winch's wooden arms.

Nalu backs from the fray and rushes to Dale's aid. Together, they unjam the mechanism and the sound of rattling chains and ancient gears overcome the sounds of battle. I look frantically from the Bandits to the portcullis that steadily rises. Nalu leaves the winch to Dale, ducks under the lifting portcullis, and removes the broad wooden plank barred across the thick doors that lay behind.

With sheer power of will, he lifts the beam, tosses it aside with a ground-shaking crash and opens Kandent's doors, letting in the early morning weather and pale light of dawn.

A roar and a rising chant from the advancing ranks captures my attention. I turn and see a double row of at least ten Bandits bearing large, tower shields and spears, advancing straight for us, shouting a single word: Shalvok. Tegan is able to kill two before they are on top of us, and one more as they make it to the Entrance Hall and engage with Grimhild.

It is all I can do to keep their swords from cutting into me as I try to keep them from reaching Dale and Nalu, who are working desperately to provide our escape.

Our Company unites in a solid front against the darkness, felling Bandits, hewing limbs from their bodies; the war-cries of our defense and of the Bandits mingle to create a dreadful melody that sings over the growing river of blood and carnage. Tegan, all arrows spent, joins the battle with his short blade and throwing knives held in both hands.

The cool touch of morning air on our backs returns strength to our weary limbs as Dale manages to lift the portcullis and Nalu has the large doors open wide enough for us to retreat.

"It's open!" Dale thunders over the booming and crashing of steel, "Grimhild, it's open!"

"Go!" he shouts. "I'll hold them back!"

I take up Junn, and we, one-by-one, retreat out of Kandent and run along its one and only bridge over the rushing tides of the waterfall. Grimhild, true to his word, is the last to exit. In the gap of the open gate, he holds the waves of Bandits at bay with large swings of his battle-axe, felling his enemies like mere saplings. He backs steadily out and at last steps foot on the bridge, turning from the attack to the retreat, making great bounding strides as his beard streams over his shoulders. Junn's slacking pace from his extensive torture and captivity slow me down to just a brisk walk. I grit my teeth and labor on, fearing the shrieking voices of Kandent's Bandits behind me. I glance back and see them spilling out onto the bridge from the gate. They give chase and the sensation of hope fades into the black reaches of despair as the pursuing Bandits stampede across the bridge.

All of a sudden, Junn urgently rouses my attention and stops me fast; the Company stops with me. We gather on the end of the bridge in a horrified circle. Grimhild stands alone at the center of the bridge in the birth of a freshly realized dawn. The golden rays of the sun crest the mountains and cast the Fortress in an impossibly welcoming light, setting the endless spray of Llif Rhew ablaze. Grimhild holds fast with both hands firmly about the haft of his proud axe, his shoulders rising and falling from the exhaustion of combat, helm cast aside leaving his onyx hair to catch the lazy breeze. He stands as an enduring and unfaltering flame set against the blackest night.

"Grimhild, come on!" Nalu cries. "Get out of there! Run!"

"Fly, fools!" Grimhild answers back, his voice carrying solace and courage. "None of these of the abyss shall pass!"

"He cannot fight alone! I must aid him!" Nalu yells.

"Don't!" Tegan says. "We must leave while he holds our escape!"

Hung in the lonely space between heartbeats, we watch Grimhild as he sends foe after foe hurtling down into the wild torrent of water beneath his steadfast feet, showing his defiance and will with every swing. It almost sounds like laughter. Against every fiber of his being, pressed against Tegan's barring arms, Nalu lets go his urge to fight side-by-side, and at last turns. The Bandits overwhelm Grimhild and wrestle him until they tumble from the bridge. Grimhild's ferocious laughter stops, drowned by the sound of falling water as we lose sight of the bridge and Kandent, blocked by the snow-dressed trees and the turning of the road. We do not stop running until the cold air bites hard at our lungs and lament takes us in our own way as the parting of fellowship takes over.

CHAPTER 17

— Colors Upon the Rendering —

I feel lost. I feel lost as one whom relied on mother and father is lost in the wake of their untimely death. My once set course towards the coming days is overcast in shadow and my eyes cannot pierce its gloom.

Tegan halfheartedly, to the surprise of us all, took charge and led us on the long and woeful road back to the Compound.

The flat white plains melt, rise into hills, and the air grows warmer each mile southward. I do not have the mind to notice the passing of time, nor the pain in my sore feet as we march on and on. The sun disappears, the moon slings itself across a star-strewn, obsidian sky, and the process repeats. I do not know where I am until I see, cresting the horizon, the Compound's walls, encircling its buildings in a futile effort to lock out evil. In the rolling land, clad in trees, where once I had not the thought nor care of battle or peril, only the mind for adventure, I can now only conceive the idea of how shortsighted and shut-in I used to be. Of how I let the days slip away, not bothering to plot a future that would lead me into a world in which I could happily reside. Why did I not distress over the state of things? How did I get by amidst all the suffering and loss? I realize now that such mindfulness is a necessary part of survival. So it is to see the coming and going of things. I cannot bear to think of a world without, yet here am I, trapped in just such a place.

The sun sets on the last day before our arrival at the Northern Compound. I look up from the rear of the Company, half expecting to see Grimhild's towering figure leading the way, but all I see is how the nearing of the night splits the world in two, how the fading sunlight falls on only one portion of hill, field, tree, and person.

I stop walking and feel the warm breeze against my skin as I look over the land of my home. What was the point of Grimhild's sacrifice? He left so many behind, left to be haunted with the thought of what might come next.

The Company notices my falling behind and a silhouette comes towards me.

"One of life's terrible truths is that loss never comes easily," Junn says. "It is a struggle. But we must allow ourselves, every day, to forget. Not the person, for that would dishonor their memory, but the memory of their passing. When we finally allow ourselves to see fragments of them in others, we in a way, forget that they were ever gone in the first place."

I look at Junn's scruffy face and try to smile.

"Right now, I see so strongly Grimhild's love for friends in you," he offers his hand to me. "Come on, we're almost home."

No. I am not imprisoned. Grimhild's sacrifice was not hollow, for his blood paved the way for the reclamation of a lost brother, and for that, I am saddened but grateful beyond the usefulness of words. Junn is back. Even though the cataclysm of loss weighs heavy on all our hearts, it is not wholly enough to shroud the exultation of a life and bond restored.

*

Our countless steps from the Northern Reaches bring us at long last to the vine-woven gates of the Compound. In the endless winter of the Reaches, I had quite forgotten that spring was well under way back south. The aloof songs of the returning birds fill the air about the walls, the dark brown tree trunks holding up the emerald canopy stand unchanged, arrayed in the newest part of the year's cycle, and the dirt path leading to the gate is besieged on either side by bright, youthful grass.

Junn closes his eyes and breathes in, long and deep, basking in the aura of his home.

"It is not enough to simply say that this is a sight for sore eyes!" he exclaims, stretching his fully recovered limbs. "What beauty! What splendor!"

Junn's lighthearted return lifts sorrow's veil that has been drawn over our eyes. Seeing him again does not replace he who was taken, but it reminds that he gave his life for the one I now look upon, enveloped in liveliness as he frolics in the lawn. One would never guess that this man just recently emerged from many months of hardship and torment.

"He looks more alive than ever," Dale laughs, looking at the undignified sight of pure joy. "I am glad to have you back."

Junn stops his dancing, walks over to Dale, and wraps his arms around him, "I cannot offer sufficient thanks for what you have done. What you all have done. I can't imagine what formidable lanes you have ventured, but I hope you will fill me in on all of it."

"You would have done the same for us," I say.

"Indeed I would," Junn beams.

"Alright, lovers," Harlow walks passed. "Let's get inside already."

"You can say that again," Tegan adds.

Harlow enters the gatehouse and reaches into a thin recess in the wall, at length resulting in clanking and moaning as the gate drifts open. We talk idly amongst ourselves as we walk into the humble courtyard but cease conversation as we encounter the most unpredictable and reproachable sight of a man, mounted hunched on the back of a grey horse. The sun glints off his metal-bound shield on his back and the pommel of the axe on his waist. The man lifts his hooded head and speaks out from its shadow

"Ere you return at last," he says in a clear, hosting voice, "and with the valiant Junn to boot. When I heard the reports from Kandent, I could hardly believe my ears. Unfortunate that you should come back."

"What is the meaning of this?" Harlow demands and approaches the sinister man. "Who the hell are you and what do you want? Answer swiftly *ere* I let my staff do the questioning!"

"Aggressive as ever, I see," the man laughs. "It does you no fortune to reprise one so high above you in such fashion, Harlow."

Harlow stops in her tracks.

"It does none of you any fortune, for that matter to allow yourselves to become destitute of vision by your own blind loyalty," the man jeers. "Why the Merr'putra has yet to exact his wrath upon you is beyond me. Were it for my will, you would all be right now be put to the sword, just like that bumbling oaf. What was his name again?"

"T'arnarron vetral!" Nalu lurches towards the rider. "You will not speak of him!"

"And here is his pet Pau'larin. A shame that you did not meet the same fate. I imagine that by now that idiotic giant is a bloated corpse, bobbing in the tides of the sea, waiting to be consumed as carrion for the birds."

"Bold words for a man speaking from the anonymity of a hood!" Riston retorts. "Reveal yourself so that we may judge your arrogance rightly!"

The rider unhurriedly raises his hands and folds back his hood. In the light of the sun, the stranger's face looks weathered and desolate, as if unfathomable years have passed him by without the presence of laughter or smile, his red hair, shining more brightly than Harlow's road-weary mane, falls about his broad shoulders fine and smooth. Most notable above all is the scar upon his face, stretching from his left temple to the tip of his clean-shaven chin, standing out clear as snow against his tanned skin.

"Oh, your pretty face get a scrape?" Harlow jeers. "Shame. You were always the pretty one."

"If only you knew the folly of your words, woman," he spits on the ground. "It is a mark of victory from surviving Merr'putra's champion."

"You mean to tell us that you got yourself tossed around by one of your master's pets? How laughable."

"I have come only for a single purpose, which you have generously fulfilled," the rider's face contorts with rage. "Take care not to sleep too soundly."

With that, the man strikes his horse into a gallop and speeds out of the Compound in a cloud of dust that trails behind him.

"What just — who the hell…?" Dale asks.

"That," Harlow responds, "was Haebur."

"Haebur?" I ask. "Are you sure?"

"Beyond question," she grunts. "He has balls for showing himself here, especially after what he did."

"Can someone tell me what's going on?" Dale implores.

"Haebur is a traitor," Harlow answers. "He, along with the other one, Vincent, abandoned us for Contil. He is of the former Black Flag."

"So what does this mean? Has he come to start a fight?"

"No," Junn says. "I fear the fight has already begun."

"It's truly an ill-omen," Riston's freshly washed face and combed hair is perfectly radiant in the sunshine coming through the windows of Hector's Tavern. "And one to arrive at a time all too convenient."

"What is to be done about it?" Asks Tegan.

I sit along the simple, long table with the Black Flag — though Nalu has secluded himself to his room in the Great Hall, leaning my head against the back of my chair as I ponder our situation. Strange that Haebur would be waiting for us, stranger still that he knew so much of our endeavors. Harlow said that Contil was clever and this surely proves it.

"Well, we have to do something," Dale states. "We've got Junn back, we should—"

"Strike while the iron's hot?" Tegan interrupts. "Now is the time for thought, not rash action. We need to consider what we know as fact: the Bandits are organized, suggesting new leadership, they are acting out of character in keeping a live prisoner for as long as they did, and now we know, with Haebur's appearance, that Contil is involved."

"We should think about Carver's hand in all this as well," I suggest.

"It's been a long time since I've thought about that man," Dale's lips curl in contempt.

"He and Marcus have been in league with the Bandits for some time. Remember when we caught Carver and the Bandit in the Ironwood?"

"Aye," Dale nods. "What of it?"

"Who do you think is the one ordering them around? Bandits are behaving oddly, new leadership... From what Harlow told me about his fascination with Bandits, this has Contil written all over it."

"Just as Tegan surmised, and it wouldn't surprise me," Harlow says. "If you can count on anything, bet on that."

"Okay," Dale's eyebrows meet in thought. "So where is he giving orders from? Where do we look?"

"In the Western Compound, obviously," Riston answers.

"The Western what?"

"When the Bandits eradicated the Pau'larin," Riston looks at Dale, "after they ransacked their capital of Aardstav, they destroyed the third Compound as well. Although most people have forgotten it, we believe that it serves a new, dark purpose."

"And with Haebur's unsavory arrival," Harlow grimaces, "it's even more likely that Contil and his followers are still in Hyravon."

"Do we know what he wants? What has he to gain from all this?"

"You're a touch smarter than you look," a smile tugs at the corner of Tegan's mouth. "What indeed. What I know of him leads me to believe it involves a lot of bloodshed."

"If the grass is green," Harlow laughs, grimly, "then Contil is power-hungry. We've all seen it. I bet my life that he plans conquest."

"And the easiest way to weaken resistance is to dissolve it from the inside out," Riston deduces.

The faces of Tao, Malory, Hector, my friends at the Southern Compound flood my mind. What has Contil been able to do to them while we were gone for so long? Are any of them still alive?

"The course of action is clear to me," Junn observes. "We need to return to the Southern Compound and save it."

"I agree. We must help them," Tegan approves. "I also think that rushing into it will only get more people killed."

"So here again are we," Riston vocalizes, "the self-same band who heard our plan to rescue Junn shall now hear of a strategy far greater: the salvation of the Southern Compound."

Tegan laughs in a desperate way.

"And what could we hope to accomplish against such odds? The only thing we will achieve is ornamenting the bodies of Bandits with our bones."

"You doubted our success when we went to Kandent, and look what we were able to do!" Dale says, firmly. "You doubt again?"

"I have difficulty understanding what the strength of seven people can yield," he says, defensively. "What if you all say is true? What if Contil and the Bandits are indeed on the same side? What can we seven do?"

"It is easy for hope to wither when you look into a future not yet realized," Junn counters.

"That may be, but how can we devise a plan without the aid of some foresight? At least we would know the worst-case scenario."

"Fair enough," Junn concedes. "But we cannot let that stop us. This time, more lives than just our own hang in the balance, and the longer we tarry, the more the scales tip in the enemy's favor."

"Aye," Riston says. "With that settled, the next thing we need to do is account for all we have at our disposal. What do we still have in terms of armor and weaponry?"

"The hidden armory in the south and the one here are still stocked, minus what Dale and Viper carry," Harlow notes.

"—provided they haven't been found and ransacked," Tegan utters.

"Right before Vipe set out for the Southcap Mountains with Harlow, Byron commissioned Tao to light the forge and craft arms and armor for his people," Dale rubs at his eyes. "Bah, but we have not an army to make use of them."

"I dare say that we do," Junn asserts.

We all turn to look dumbstruck at him.

"What do you possibly mean?" Tegan asks. "At last count we were just seven, not seven-thousand."

"You forget about our most valuable resource. Marcus has double-crossed them, the Bandits hound them. I am certain that the people will not pass at the chance to change things, to rise up. All we have to do is make it to the Southern Compound and prepare the people for battle."

"This is all too reliant on chance," Tegan says. "But, Marcus and anyone else there will never be prepared for an attack from within."

The westering sun sends its bright rays through the tavern's many windows, bouncing off the worn surface of the table. Dark blue clouds billow in from the southwest and soon cover the sky, bringing swift night. No longer in the sun's care, the chill nighttime air wafts in and nips at my exposed skin, shaking my body with chills. The Company rises from the meeting's adjournment.

"This is all so terribly exciting," Riston says with a bloody smile.

"Again," I say. "Your sense of humor concerns me."

I watch them go out the front door.

Dale, Junn and I are all that remain, sitting soundless, lost in thought.

"Well," I give a long, satisfied sigh, "time to spill it."

"Oh?" Junn raises a dark eyebrow. "Spill what?"

"Come on, you know. How did you manage the Bandits?"

Junn traces a groove in the well-used table. He stops, scratches his clean chin, and looks up.

"I had to be very resourceful."

His short answer makes Dale and I complain.

"Honestly," Dale says. "Escaping captivity surely has its stories."

"After the attack, they were as ruthless as ever. Typical of the Bandits. The others that they took along with me didn't even last a week before dying of their beatings, long marches, or simple lack of food and water."

"How were you able to get away?" I ask.

"Played dead," he smirks. "I realized that I was important to them, so I pretended to have died in my sleep. Worked like a dream, really. I snuck off into the woods and was on the run for a good long while. I managed to make it to Lake Tave before they caught me. It was my own fault. I did not suspect that they went that far south."

"Tell me about it," I groan.

"Well, that's not what I was expecting," Dale gulps down the last of his mead.

"Survival is often a truly dull affair. Although, I did discover something while they brought me to Kandent."

Dale and I lean forward, eyes bright with anticipation. Junn comes closer to a conspiratorial distance.

"They planned to use me in something they called the Awakening."

"Awakening…" Dale ponders it for a moment. "Vipe, any ideas what that could mean?"

"I haven't the slightest," I admit. "But, if it's anything like the other Bandit rituals, it can't be good for us."

"I had the mind to discuss it with Grimhild, for I knew he out of everyone would know the most. A tragedy that he should pass before I had the chance."

"Agreed," Dale and I say in unison.

"Before you rescued me from Kandent, I was to be moved once more. Taken to Merr'putra himself."

"Then it is good that we came when we did," Dale says. "I don't know if we'd be able to find you again."

"I know I restate the obvious," Junn fiddles with his half-full pint, "but I am very thankful for all you've done."

"Literally carried you to safety," Dale laughs.

"I'd do it all again, not that I'd very much like to," I admit. "But it was worth every inch of every mile."

"I promise," Junn claps us both on the arm, "it won't happen again."

*

Soft light filters in through my drawn curtains and bids my eyes to blink themselves awake. I stretch my arms over my head and roll on my side with a great yawn; I can hear the chirping spring birds wafting in my bedroom's open window. I do not want to leave the luxury of my blanket, but upon hearing long strides coming from outside my door, I know that I will — and soon. The door flings open, Harlow's slightly disgruntled figure fills the gap, and polite as ever, she tells me to "get up already" and go to the Hall.

Pulling myself away from bed is the hardest thing to have befallen me yet, and my feet making contact with the cool, rough wooden floor only makes the decision all the more regrettable. I exit my bedroom and am greeted by the hurried sounds of scurrying feet and the brisk packing of bags as I walk towards Dale's room. Dale comes marching out with an armful of clothes, tools and food.

"Why do you keep all that stuff in your room?" I call after him as he rushes outside.

"Couldn't sleep, so I got ready."

Now fully awake and quite intrigued, I head in Dale's direction and find him in the Great Hall across the Compound with the Black Flag. Riston and Tegan stand at the far end of one of the tables, having an animated discussion over a set of baggage.

"Where are the water skins?" Tegan asks.

"You were supposed to remember that! I have the rations!" Says Riston.

Dale dumps his things on a table shared by Harlow and separates the items, placing them in various packs. I walk over to him.

"It's about time we get goin'," Dale pushes wrapped bread and dried meats into an already crammed pack. He turns from his task and smiles a smile that does not reach his eyes. "I did you a favor and got your stuff ready, too"

"Thank you. I don't know how I slept so late," I mumble.

"Probably because you were up all night talking with tweedle-dee and tweedle-dumb," Harlow comments. "Where's Nalu?"

Dale goes back to packing and says in a low voice,

"He's been in Grimhild's room since last night."

"Humf," she says.

Harlow returns to her preparations and fills her bag's last empty place with a phial no bigger than my thumb, containing a dark liquid that shows deep green when it catches the light. She secures the mysterious bottle with a flourish and lays the bags on the floor. Harlow stands, catches my suspicious look and answers simply with a sly wink. There is always something with her. I hear a door slamming open by where Riston and Tegan are arguing. I turn to see Nalu, tall and grim, stomping towards them.

"What are you doing? *These* are mine," Nalu barks.

Tegan and Riston sheepishly back away from Nalu and look around for their misplaced things. Nalu wraps his sword belt around his waist and aggressively finishes off his packing. He does not look up.

Junn walks into the Hall with his bag slung over his shoulder.

"Are we all ready?"

He looks just like the image of him in my head. His brown hair brushed out of his face with a rebellious strand falling to his brow, his stature proud and noble.

"And where is my sword?" He steps towards Dale and I, dropping his things to the floor.

"At last, the two of us are ready!" Riston calls from out of sight.

"As are we," says Dale. "And we should really go."

"Agreed. Have them meet at the gates. And bring me a sword, too!" Junn calls as he departs. Dale follows him. Harlow starts to laugh.

"Stupid man, his sword's right here!" She picks up Junn's blade from the tabletop and tosses it at me. "Go on and get that to him. I'll get these ladies moving. We'll catch up."

The day is still young and the air is cool and new, carrying the scent of the earth, the smell of cold grass, laced with the scent of pink ambrosia climbing low on the walls. Dale and Junn wait for me to catch up and we walk from the Compound together.

"Do we have to go through the Rock Gardens this time?" I ask.

"Definitely not," Dale answers. "Besides, there'll be more than just the two of us this time if the Bandits want to try anything."

"And what about—"

"No to that as well," he sighs. "Our caravan brought with them all the horses that were here. But we will make good time going in a more or less straight line through the forest."

We continue the walk and are now entering the edge of the Ironwood, where trees stand scattered along the road. Ahead, they form a lazy barrier between the distant land and us. Startled blue birds fly away from where they peck at the soft ground into an even bluer sky, where puffy white clouds sail along. The dirt road crunches dully under our boots and kicks up into a small haze as we pass.

"Junn, there's something that's been bothering me since we left Kandent," I say.

"Oh? What's that?"

"Well, when we were in the cellar and Dale killed that Bandit, why did he have a steel sword when all the others have ones made from bone?"

"You have sharp eyes," Junn praises. "The Flag deduced that the Bandits have a hierarchy. Steel determines power in their eyes. I believe the one Dale killed with a single blow the Bandits called Maulner, the commander of Kandent."

"He wasn't so tough," Dale shrugs.

"Rage-induced Dale is stronger than any Bandit," Junn comments.

We all laugh together, our voices slip between the gaps of the tree trunks and reverberate until it dies in the distance. We walk farther into the woods with the sun nearly at the end of its climb to the tip of the sky. Despite all the killing, the worry, anxiety, and the path still before us, I am without thought for defense. Walking between Dale and Junn I feel as though I walk through a deep gorge where towering walls keep guard on either side; walls that keep out the shadows in the night. They help me see color in a grey world, and Harlow and the Black Flag brought their own vivid strokes to the canvas. But there is also blight there. One singular well of black upon the rendering, one which I walk to now and no amount of securing walls can keep that out.

Bright colors do well to distract from the atrocious, but I drift to them still. What if Dale and I were just a little faster and saved Junn during the ambush? Then the Compound might be safe and Grimhild wouldn't have needed to sacrifice himself to rescue Junn. What if we did something the moment Carver's treachery was exposed? How many people could we have saved? How many lives have been lost because of our hesitation? Will there even be a Compound at the end of the road? This blackness, this… void that we head for, can we actually surmount the odds? We have come against the howling unknown before, fought the Bandits again and again, but this seems different. This has everything on the line.

"Hey, Viper. You alright?" You haven't said a word in hours," Junn asks, tenderly.

The ocean of nothingness recedes into a distant singularity and the shadowed forest collapses into view. Dusk is setting in upon the fir trees and grand oaks that encroach upon the path.

"I'm fine," I answer. "Just thinking about what's next."

"If it's rest and camp, you thought right," Dale says. "Let's get a fire so the ones that fell behind know where we stopped."

We veer off the road and place our burdens around the broad trunk of an ancient oak, the lichen hanging from its boughs brush against my head as I pass under them. We go in search of autumn's fallen branches and twigs.

Before everything started, I remember being free to venture to and from these woods at a whim. But now, it is obvious that Bandits roamed in these peaceful towers of wood and leaf and beset it with vengeful wroth. Hacked and cloven tree trunks mark their presence in the pillars of the woods and the green and the brown bedding of their roots. Trees older than I can imagine lay on the ground, and in their descent, they took with them their neighbors who lie dried and dead, riddled with the forests' little creatures. I return to our oak, to where a flickering light has already been sprung into life. Junn builds the fire away from the branches and the lichen dripping from them and is now knelt before it, his head parallel to the ground, blowing steadily at the growing flame. I drop my arm-full of branches at Junn's side and he takes from it a thin branch, snapping it in two across his knee. The fire takes it eagerly and grows in size, increasing its warmth and light. I sit beside Dale on the forest floor while Junn meticulously creates the heart of the camp. The bright light washes out everything around it, reducing the surrounding trees into nothing more than gnarly columns of black against the deep of the woods. Sap trapped in the gathered branches crackles loudly in the quiet. Junn sits in front of the blaze with his hands held together around his knees.

"Do you remember the last time we shared a fire?" Dale asks.

Junn tilts his head back to stare at the leaves shaking in the heat-haze.

"Couldn't have been when we hunted those boars, could it?"

"Couldn't have. Viper wasn't around. When was the last time that we *all* shared a fire?"

"I don't think there ever was a time."

"Well, except now," I reach for my pack for a loaf. "When all of this is over, we should make sure that this is not the only time."

"I would like nothing more," Junn smiles. "Oh, how I love a fire in the woods. It reminds me of a job I had with the Flag in Vaccia."

"Where?" I ask.

"The capital city of Thalvia. Some big, stupid noble families were fighting over the kingdom's next ruler. Anyway, it was the six of us: Harlow, Tegan, Riston, Nalu, myself and Grimhild, may the stars guide his soul. We were charged with aiding the Cromwell's in securing a hold in the foothills, outside of Irwin's Trench, and that night we camped in a forest similar to this one, only it was entirely different."

"That's a little unfair to say," Dale complains. "What was it like?"

"Everything one was to find there, one might also find here. Trees, grass, bushes, that sort of thing. The difference is, that forest did not have leaves of green, but of the most beautiful azure blue I've ever seen. Something in that place changed the color of the leaves, the bushes and every single blade of grass. Oh, and the fragrance! When the warm summer air blew through, it picked up such a sweet aroma, I thought that dear old Malory had set out a blueberry pie to cool. And the way the wind fluttered the boughs and leaves! It was like staring up from the bottom of the sea as crystal-clear blue waves crashed overhead. I wish you two could have been there with me."

"One day we might," Dale says. "I'm usually not one for strange places, but that sounds perfect."

"It does indeed," I agree.

I hear the sound of crunching soil as numerous pairs of feet come towards us. As the sounds reach the ring of light, I see the faces of Harlow, Riston and Tegan.

"We found you faster than I suspected," Harlow says. "I thought that you three had walked at least another ten miles before you gave up."

"You have Dale to blame for that," Junn nods his head at his brother, accusingly. "Couldn't stop talking about wanting rest."

"Should've known," Harlow tosses her pack around the fire and lays to rests her head upon it.

"We were just talking about a job Junn had with you in Thalvia, camping in a blue forest," I say, tossing her some spare bread.

"Oh, yes. I remember," she takes a large chunk out of the bread. "That place was very boring."

"Of course you would say that," Riston says as he sits with us around the fire. "The Sapphire Forest holds such a unique beauty that it moved my heart and inspired a poem. It goes—"

All of us boo him until he gives up on reciting his poetry.

"Well, I dare say that you lot are more or less opposed to a minstrel's ballad."

"More like a jester playing with words," Junn laughs.

"You hurt me deeply," Riston whimpers as he uncorks a flask of wine.

"Now what do we have here?" Dale asks, aroused at the sight of Riston's flask. "Bring some traveling wine, did we?"

"It is merely for the purpose of curing the various ailments of long journeys on foot," he takes a swig.

"Well, come on then. Give it here."

Riston recoils as Dale reaches for the flask.

"I seem to recall a group of ruffians encamped in the woods berating a fellow traveler for attempting to serenade them," he takes another swig; Harlow snatches the flask out of his hand.

"You know what they say about sharing, Riston," she takes a drink.

"You devil-woman!" Riston exclaims.

"Pass it along!" Dale urges.

Riston's flask finds its way to each of us. By the end of its circuit, the flask is empty.

"With friends like these…" Riston shakes his empty flask.

"Say now, where is Nalu?" Junn asks. "I did not see him arrive with you."

"He fell behind, somewhat," Tegan answers. "Didn't seem fond of company."

"Should we look for him?" I ask.

"No, leave him be," Junn says. "Some of us have different ways of doing things."

"Speaking of different ways of doing things," Dale says, hiccuping loudly, "what did you make this wine out of? It's… very strong."

"It is a family secret," Riston holds up a finger to his lips. "I'd be forced to kill you should you discover it."

"If you Thalvians are good at one thing, it's drinking," Tegan comments. "And abusing power."

"I'll have you know that the Balroux family are a respected people in Thalvian court. My old man, may he burn forever, was once the Grand Chancellor to King Edmond Valar. Before he found drinking to be a suitable pass-time, that is."

"Hold on a moment," I cock my head at Riston. "Are you saying that you're royalty?"

"By the stars, no!" Riston scoffs. "Stuffy pigeons the lot of them. No, I am merely a nobleman. Or, I was until I renounced my titles and claims when I joined this band of thugs. I do sometimes wonder what became of things there, who rules and so forth…" he tucks his flute and flask away.

"Kings," Dale shakes his head. "Why would anyone want something like that?"

"People's lives are easier when decisions are made for them," says Tegan. "Even when those decisions make their lives worse than better."

"It would take the world's ending to change that tradition," Riston yawns.

I roll out my mat close to the embers and feel a pleasant weight on my eyes as I lay down. The others' voices sway in and out of comprehension until I fall fully asleep.

CHAPTER 18

— Instruments & Puppets —

Morning comes and with it a cool and gentle breeze. The grey and brown trees down the road are visible in the dawn, receding into the light mist, stacking one atop the other as they have stood for countless years. More than half our journey still lies before us and as we go we talk seldom, for Nalu's stormy mood from the previous day at the Compound has yet to break. He trudges along at the tail-end of our group, his head slightly bowed. I had hoped that with the new and pressing matters besetting us would help take his mind from Grimhild's passing, but all Nalu has yielded yet are cold remarks and touchy silence.

The rows of trees guarding the road fall away as we exit the thick of the woods. I can see the whole of the clear sky up ahead. Towards the east and west, trees clad the land where rocky hills grow before ending up as cliffs before the Southern Compound's walls. Another half mile down the road and I see it, the nightmare I have had so many times, the tree line along the west where Bandits poured out, the patch of road where our people screamed and died, and Junn was taken. I turn and look at Junn to see his reaction. His eyes are hard-set on the road before him and his jaw clenched tight. Dale, having my same thoughts, speaks,

"Junn, isn't this where…"

"Aye, it is," he answers, sternly. "And it is of little consequence to me now. May we walk in peace?"

"Right. Sorry."

I wince at Dale's tactless effort. Behind me, Harlow chuckles to herself; Nalu looks up.

"Do you hid from your past?" he asks.

Junn stops and turns to meet Nalu's eye, "Hide? I do not."

"Then I would hear your thoughts," he says. "I do not pretend to simply forget Grimhild, nor does his ghost haunt me. But yet, I cannot remember to smile."

All of us are now standing around the pair of them.

"So tell me," Nalu plants himself, firm.

Junn stands still, looking hard at Nalu.

"You wish for me to speak about a memory of failure?" Junn asks.

Clouds appear. The wind blows through the leaves and grass.

"Failure?" Says the Pau'larin. "From Harlow and Dale's account it was you that was the hero."

"You call the deaths of my friends a success? My abduction a victory? Not a moment did I see go by without the thought filling my head of those I care about and let down."

"Yet, you were the one that volunteered for that fate. Dale could just as easily have taken your place, just as I could have been the one to fall at Kandent."

"Something had to be—"

"He saved my life." Nalu says, softly. "On the dead plains of Tir Fwythland, I fought against the Bandits of the Western Wastes. They caught me off guard and outnumbered as I scoured the land for some memory of my people. I fought back, but my arms grew weary and the Bandits started gaining ground over me. This," he pulls up his battle raiment and shows waxy scar tissue along his side and across his chest. "This is a trophy of that losing battle. I was on my last breath, a dying man killing over a dead land. Then Grimhild appeared and evened the odds. I have not, nor will I ever forget what he did for me that day. My eyes see it — always," he gestures to the black smeared over his eyes.

Junn relaxes his shoulders.

"So, when we stood together on the bridge…"

"I wanted to repay a life-debt! The man saved me and I watched from afar as he died! So I ask you: why shy from a failure you now walk over while mine imprisons me? At least you are able to find peace from the memory."

"You dishonor Grimhild's sacrifice," Junn looks Nalu in the eye.

"What did you say?" Nalu demands, cocking his head back.

"You haunt yourself by rejecting Grimhild's choice to see us live while he gave everything."

"And I say it needn't have been that way! Do you not see? I willingly would have taken his place!" Nalu takes a step towards Junn.

"It is you that does not see," Junn counters, eyeing Nalu's advance. "He would rather have perished with the knowledge of having given us a chance at life than gone on living with the shadow of any of our deaths hanging over him."

"You disrespect me!" Nalu cries, almost within reach of Junn. "He should have known what I was willing to do!"

"He did. But we all heard him. Did you not hear the laughter? He would not have had it any other way."

"And he could be laughing right now if I... If I!" Nalu stops in front of Junn and raises his fist to strike him, shaking from the rage and sorrow.

Junn does not look away from Nalu's dark eyes. His wavering fist draws back while the other grabs the collar of Junn's shirt. Nalu stands tall over Junn. My wide eyes flick between them, the hand raised in the air, and finally to Nalu's contorted face where the black around his eyes starts to run.

"Why did it have to be him?" he says through gritted teeth.

"It is not for us to know. All we have to know is how to use the time he gave to us."

Nalu's body shudders as though a great chill holds him. His tightly curled fingers unfurl and his arm falls limply to his side as he lets go of Junn. He staggers a few paces back and looks down at his palms, the black paint on his eyes mixing with the teardrops that fall onto his hands.

"How do I carry on?" he asks, no fight left in his words.

"My friend," Junn walks towards him. "You carry on by leaning on the shoulders of you companions. You are not alone."

He puts his hand on the back on Nalu's neck. Nalu looks up into Junn's shining blue eyes staring back with such love and compassion that it causes him to break. Nalu gives in and accepts Junn's embrace, choking back tears.

"Without him…"

"I know."

Riston tenderly goes to their side and, too, comforts his distraught friend.

"He's right. You have all of us here to help you along. To help one another along to whatever end."

Nalu steps out of the embrace and pulls himself together. He walks around and the rest of us fall instep beside him. Never before have I known such love and compassion between friends. We continue in camaraderie as twilight descends on the second day.

*

The moon shines bright through thin clouds that try to cover its face, its pale blood spilling over the grass, trees, and the Southern Compound's walls. Nalu's talk with Junn days ago has given way to pleasant company on our travels here. Now, with the silvered moon slung high across the midnight sky, our Company is far from relaxed. We kneel on the short cliffs overlooking the Compound's northern side. Every building is without candlelight, but are enclosed on all sides by a ring of fire from Bandit torches that stare down from atop the walls like a host of unblinking eyes. Bandits patrol the exterior of the Compound in groups of no less than four. They pass each other and the gate at irregular intervals. It seems that the long hand of Contil's influence has reached the Southern Compound at last.

"It appears that what we feared has come," Tegan says. "This place is a prison."

"One none too carefully guarded, so it seems," Junn studies the lazy patrols.

"So it will be easy to gain entry?" Asks Nalu. "Ropes over the walls?"

I sit and watch as the Bandits continue their endless loops about the ramparts of my home, their occasional barking speech making its way to my hiding place. We definitely should not fight our way in, nor can we just simply walk in. There's only one real option.

"We could force our way in quietly enough," Riston suggests. "And, at least this time, we don't have a waterfall to contend with."

"Not a chance," Harlow gives Riston a perplexed look. "We need to know what we're dealing with before we dive headfirst into it."

"I have a plan," I say.

"Do you?" Harlow turns her surprise to me.

"What do you think?" Dale asks.

"I think that we sneak through the crack in the wall. If Tao didn't end up patching it."

"Don't know if he has," Dale thinks. "Last I remember, he and Byron were looking for the right tools."

"That's our way in. I say that you, Junn, and I get inside to see what's happening."

"And what will be our role?" Tegan asks.

"On our signal, you will need to draw the Bandits's attention away from us while Dale uses his hammer to break in. With his strength and the winter wearing away the stonework, we should be able to get in."

"And what comes after?"

"After that, you will follow us inside. There is a storehouse just beyond the crack for you to hide in and gather the people to fight back while we see what we're up against."

"I like the sound of it," Junn smiles.

"Then let us not delay further," Tegan tugs his bowstring.

Junn, Harlow, everyone looks at me. I feel strange, like I am a fraud that cheated his way to power. But, there's nothing to do about that now but to make sure I earn it.

"Okay, then," my tongue feels thick and clumsy. "Follow me."

I scale down the cliff face and the Company climbs down after. The rocks offer plenty of footholds and our descent is silent and fluid. We gather around the foot of the shelf and watch the Bandits' movements closely from the lurking shadows. I nod to Dale and Junn and we creep along the wall of rock at our backs; Riston and the others fan out and wait for the signal. Now at the end of the cliff's steep rise, my infiltration party crouches anxiously, looking at the gap of wide-open space between us and a thicket of bushes, small magnolia, and shadbushes splayed around the Compound's western side. The Bandits proceed in their duty, unaware of our presence.

I make a break for the next sequence of concealment, the wind rushing in my ears as I bolt across the open terrain. Dale and Junn follow in their own time and moments later we all make it across with the element of surprise intact. We sneak towards the Compound's rear and avoid the Bandits walking in groups. As I brush passed the wide bushes and thin trees, I thank my luck that the crunching and snapping of autumn is behind me. I lead us farther around the circumference of the Compound and I lose sight of the cliffs. Almost there.

With the guidance of the moon, Dale, Junn and I rally around the one fault in the Compound's stonework. No witnesses, no alarms. But, to be honest, to call this a crack is an understatement. The hair-line fracture I was imagining is a lot wider and a good deal deeper. It looks like an angry bolt of forked lightning; I can see through to the other side.

"A crack?"

"Well, I didn't lie about it, did I?" Dale looks at me and shrugs.

"Didn't really tell the truth, either. All the better for us, though."

"Things really must have gotten bad if Tao didn't mend it sooner," Junn says.

He comes next to it and brings his hand up to the split, loose material falls away with the touch of his finger.

"Wonder why no one bothered," Dale hefts his Warhammer. "But, we're not here to mend things, are we?"

"We most definitely are not," I look over at the dark side of Junn's face. "Ready?

He nods back at me, cups his hands to his lips, and calls out into the pastel night in mimic of an owl.

Around the other side of the bend, across the distance we crept, I hear the obtrusive clamor of rustling leaves and scattering of night creatures cutting into the still darkness. The sound wanes as our friends draw the Bandits' attention away from the crashes of our forced entry. Dale's stout, strong legs brace him as he swings his hammer against the weakened masonry, crumbling the stone and widening the gap. He delivers one last blow and the space opens itself to his determination, yielding a hole wide enough for all three of us to pass through. I duck and weave my body between the craggy stone and soon find myself inside the Compound. The sound of my hammering heartbeat pounds in my ears in the foreboding gloom the Bandits have draped over these humble structures.

"Where is everyone?" I whisper.

"Probably locked indoors," Dale says. "If they all haven't already been killed."

"Only one way to discover the answer," Junn says. "It goes without sayin', but keep silent and hidden. There may be more Bandits on patrol within as well as without."

Junn takes his first tentative step into the Compound and we creep onto the captive streets close behind. Passing the storehouse and homes under such pretenses as this makes my stomach squirm. I fear the unknown in this familiar place as one who fears what black shapes their mind conjures in a dark room. I would trade those nightmares with the ones I see stalking the street ahead of us. I cannot fully discern the nature of their gathering but the biggest and ugliest of the large group pounds his bone-armored chest and the Bandits on his side of the two groups shout and yammer. The Bandits stared down by the big, ugly one paces frantically in from of his not-too-excited side. What if we just sit here and let the Bandits kill themselves and save us the trouble? Though, sadly, before any blood can be spilled, another one, bigger and uglier still, orders them around and the whole lot departs.

"They're heading towards the Square," I say. "Let's go."

I step from the alley and tail the Bandits from a safe distance.

A few moments after the last one slips behind the corner, we reach the edge of the building that is cast in harsh shadows from the bright light in the Square. I plant myself flat against the wall, edge out, and see something that I have never seen before. Torches akin to the ones at Kandent are speckled across the Square, speared into the soil, and lit with forlorn fire. Discarded carts and hand-baskets are strewn about, their contents splayed on the ground and pieces of torn cloth cover isolated patches of cold earth. The Compound's Great Hall, laying at the end of the Square, is ablaze with light. I see many shadows cast themselves against the windowpanes. Some are cowering shapes and others stand large and threatening. A large, wooden post, crudely crafted, stands before the doors of the Great Hall and a body hangs from it. Byron. I almost did not recognize his sunken and tormented features but for the sign tied around his neck that reads: this is the fate of traitors. His only crime was to welcome us into his Compound. For a short period, we stand locked in place by this unexpected marvel, wary of what this signifies.

Junn brushes by me, and like smoke on the wind, he vanishes into the hard shadows produced by the breaks of darkness between the light-spewing windows. Dale and I follow, hot on his heels, and find him prying at the glass pane with his small blade. The knife scratches at the corner of the glass, rasping in the quiet outdoors until the window pops open and angles outward on its hinges. Junn waves us next to him. Underneath the small gap of the open window, I can hear the dull murmuring of the people packed inside. One voice suddenly cuts above the rest. One I heard once before speaking with a Bandit in the Ironwood Forest.

"The decision has been made! Take him away!" Carver shouts.

Enraged outcries follow his command. I can hear some of their fervor rise to the top of the commotion and become unintelligible over the cacophony.

"On what grounds?"

"You won't get away with this!"

"Your time will come!"

I crane my neck to get a look at bloodlust and see the swarm of people and Bandits corralled inside, faces contorted with rage and fear. Women cry with bent heads, their young brought close by their shaking hands, men, young and old, stand defiant before their Bandit captors, but are violently beaten into submission.

Three sharp reports of wood striking wood douses the crowd in brooding silence, instantly preceded by Carver's commanding voice.

"The next one to be brought out is..."

I see people shuffling and bumping into one another as they try to get a look at who will be next. I feel the core of my being fiercely shake when I hear the name called:

"…Malory."

"You cannot be serious! What's she done?" a bystander shouts.

The sharp report of wood sounds again.

"Malory," Carver says. "You are charged with aiding a convicted criminal in a plot to overthrow your master."

"I'll kill you! I'll kill you!"

"Enough! Tame that man's tongue," Carver orders.

The people's shouting persists until the sound of something heavy hits the floor. Silence takes the Hall and all I am able to pick up is the thudding and steady footsteps of the Bandits cutting through the throng; heads swivel as he passes through the Hall.

"Now, back to business," Carver resumes. "You have heard your charges and are left with but one choice: will you die or pledge yourself to the Master's will?"

A hush blankets the makeshift court as all collectively hold their breath.

"Well?"

"I choose neither!" Malory states in a strong voice. Though fear is evidently gnawing at her words, she speaks courage. "I know that Viper and Dale are coming back. I know the Black Flag are coming back and soon it will be you that is on trial."

"Such a pity," Carver says, coldly. "Death, then," he strikes the gavel and wrath and indignation heats to the boiling point.

I turn to Dale and Junn, utterly disgusted by what I just witnessed; Junn returns my glance.

"I wondered what Carver's quest for power would produce," I say, brusquely.

He and Marcus both have much answering to do. Where is that bastard anyway? I didn't hear his voice."

The clamor from within the Hall starts up again. The noise begins to fade and then I see the people being wrangled and shoved through the front doors. I follow Junn as he moves along the wall, away from the dispersing crowd, and takes cover behind broken carts and their shattered barrels. I peer out from their splinters and see the hunched shoulders and bowed heads of the people as they go back to their homes. I do not see many Bandits among them, but they are as swift and obedient in their departure as if there were hundreds around, shouting and wailing. As the night again settles back into quiet, I see a dark shape step into the well of light spilling from the Hall's entrance. It shrinks, smaller and smaller, until the man himself strolls into view. Carver's short blond hair is more unkempt than I remember, but the manner in which he carries himself, the way his body tells anyone watching that he is an angry man, is still very much intact. He walks away from where we hide, weaving through the Bandit torches in the Square. Dale makes a move towards him.

"We should go back to the others," I say. "Let them know that—"

"They know the plan," Dale shrugs my hand from his shoulder. "Come with me or not, but I intend to put him on trial."

"I'm with you," Junn says from behind.

"That's settled, then," Dale slinks along the wall after Carver and Junn and I slink after, close in tow.

I see a handful of Bandits lurking inside the Hall as I dart across the Square, but they are enamored in their own brutish in-fighting to pay us any mind. More are scattered amongst the buildings and returning to roam the ramparts. No one expects to find us here and I intend to keep it that way. Carver's shadow leaps from light to dark and back again as we follow him to a two-story building, guarded by spear and ax-wielding Bandits. Carver brushes past and enters the structure.

Dale pauses, circling the building in a wide and cautious arc until we are facing the door and the guards. What are they protecting? Seems strange to station Bandits while the whole Compound is already in lock-down.

"Alright," Dale lets out a long breath, "nothing else for it but to just walk inside, eh?"

"I didn't see anyone watching Carver, or notice the patrols," Junn says. "I'll let you take this one. I can't wait to see what your idea of stealth looks like."

Dale spits into his palms and furiously rubs his hair. He then takes a handful of dirt and smears it over his face. Lastly, he pulls his shirt up above his chin and up the back of his neck. He smirks at us, looking like the perfect lunatic, and limps over towards the Bandits. The act is quite convincing. So convincing in fact that the guards don't take notice of him until he's no less than ten paces away from them. The one with the ax steps forward and pushes Dale hard and he falls over backward. The Bandit turns his back on Dale, thinking the shove enough. But Dale pulls himself back to his feet with an effort and limps towards them once more. This time, the one with the spear tries his hand at getting rid of this old man, but Dale won't be made a fool of twice. I know that all too well. The spear Bandit holds the length of the shaft across his body with both hands and rams it in Dale's chest, but to his obvious surprise, the old man not only withstands the blow but catches it. Dale plants his foot behind the Bandit's and wrenches the spear from his loose grip, tossing his body to the ground as he does. As the ax-Bandit notices what's happening, Dale is on him, turning the blunt end of the spear ripping through the air to crash into his chin. His corpse folds to the earth. It's the turn of the downed Bandit next, whom Dale dispatches with the spear's point quickly and decisively.

He lets the spear fall from his fingers and looks back at us, waiting impatiently.

"I don't know if you've realized this by now," Dale stomps towards the door, "but stealth and I are more or less opposed."

He stops a few steps from the door, puffs out his chest, squares his shoulders, looking determined.

"Are you mad?" I whisper. "Carver doesn't know we're coming."

I reach for the handle and feel it turn in my hand, only I am not the one turning it. Carver stands in the open doorway and looks at us as if he's just seen a ghost. He falters back a step and Dale takes the opportunity to use his shoulder to ram Carver back onto his treacherous ass.

He claws and tries to get away, but there is nowhere for him to run; he wheezes when Dale drives his boot into his guts trying to call for help.

"Set him down there," says Junn.

Dale claps down hard at the loose material of Carver's clothes and nearly throws him into the simple wooden chair in the unembellished dining room. Harsh light from the lone candle on the tabletop casts its flickering shadows on Carver's petrified face.

"You little shit!" Carver hisses, spit flying from his mouth. "I'll—"

"You'll what?" Dale leans his head right in front of Carver's, daring him to finish his sentence.

"You tough, little boy? Strong enough to abandon your people when things go sour? Pathetic—"

Dale smashes his hard head into Carver's nose; I try to pull him away, but Dale takes a swing and I hear a soft pop come from Carver's jaw.

"Enough," Junn steps between them. "He can't talk with a broken mouth, can he?"

"No less than he deserves," Dale sulks away, keeping his rage pointed at the bleeding man in the chair.

Junn looks down at Carver with some disgust.

"How painful this is depends solely on you."

Carver blinks.

Junn leans down close, putting his hands on the arms of the chair.

"How many Bandits are here?"

Carver tilts his head back and spits blood in Junn's face. Dale bolts towards Carver and it takes both Junn and I to keep him from murder.

"Tie down his hands," Junn orders.

I fasten Carver's arms to the chair with his own belt, but I think he's too afraid to move anymore while Dale breathes down his neck like a raging bull.

"I'll ask again: how many Bandits—"

"You're just wasting your time," a voice says from the shadows of the adjacent room.

I flick my eyes in that direction. Gloom lavishes itself upon the small living room. I blink to try and penetrate the darkness and small pinpricks of light reflecting the candle behind me blink back. Then I see a shape coming down the stairs off to the right, hear the panels creaking and snapping in their age as the figure takes his weight from them.

"It's too late to stop what has been set in motion," he sighs, wearily.

He steps into the feeble light and reveals an aged face, head capped with short black hair that grays at the temples, and eyes so pale blue that they appear white pools in sunken sockets.

"Who are you?" Dale demands.

"Don't tell me that you don't recognize me?"

I look more closely at him, at the wrinkles on the skin around his eyes, at the corners of his mouth and in the palms of his outstretched, pleading hands. An image of a man telling stories to children leaps into my mind.

"By the stars, Marcus?" I exclaim.

Marcus shows a relieved smile and steps forward, but the cold head of Dale's warhammer pressed on his chest stops him fast.

"You've got as many reasons to die as this one," Dale growls.

"I dare say you're right," Marcus lets his arms fall limp to his sides. "And I have done much answering, lately," he looks at Junn. "I owe you most of all."

"I dare say you're right," I echo back at him. "Give us a reason not to kill the pair of you."

Marcus lowers his eyes; Carver looks resigned, but his chest heaves with worry.

"There is no redemption for what I've done," Marcus says. "All I want is the Compound's salvation."

"You want to save it?" I shout. "After everything you've done to them?"

"You don't understand, I—"

"I understand perfectly. I know you've been working with the Bandits, I know you had Junn captured," I take out my knife. "So why in the hell should I care a shit about what you want?"

"No, wait!" Marcus throws his hands up. "There is more to this than you know! I can show you!"

"You're a dead man," Carver drools blood.

"Keep your silence," Junn commands. "Show us this proof of yours. Time is running out."

Marcus hurries to the back of the room and returns with a bundle of yellowed pages covered with harsh, angled handwriting.

"These are—"

Junn snatches them from his hand.

"I'll be the judge of that," he begins to read.

The pages crackle as Junn thumbs through them, eyes scanning every word of every line. He hands them to me, no telling expression on his face. I take them and inspect the words.

'If you care about the lives of your people, you will agree to the Master's terms. Deliver the cargo and you and your Compound will live to see another day.'

I look through another page.

'No more tricks! One more stunt like that and you will burn! Double this month's supply or face the Master's wrath!'

'Stay near the head of the caravan. And just because you're moving doesn't mean our arrangement will change. Do not forget that.'

I look at Junn.

"None of that matters now. The Master's plan is already in motion," Carver says. "Kill me, it won't change what's coming."

"It wasn't Marcus's fault," I say in disbelief.

Dale snatches the pages from me and comes to realize the truth.

"No one in this room is innocent," he tosses the paper into the corner of the room. "People are dying right now because of these two, and they've done nothing to stop it!"

"What else was I to do?" Marcus says. "I had my back against the wall. I was made an offer that, if I refused, would have resulted in only more death. Better to save the many than to sacrifice everything for my pride."

"I've heard enough," Junn steps towards Marcus. "What's done is done."

Marcus backs away as Junn comes closer.

"And we, now, have the chance to save the lives you sold."

Marcus bumps into the cupboard, the plateware clinks and rattles.

"But you do not deserve to be a part of that for all the sorrow you've caused," Junn advances farther.

Dale and I watch as Marcus closes his eyes tight, even Carver waits to see what will happen. As Junn stands but a hair's breadth from the shriveled form of Marcus, nothing happens.

"You took more from me than you could ever know," he says through his teeth. "You took a lot from a too many people," he raises a hand to Marcus. "But more blood serves nothing but starting a new cycle of death."

Marcus flinches as Junn rests his hand on his shoulder, knuckles white from restraint.

"Your fate is not solely mine to judge. It belongs to everyone, everyone you've wronged, everyone you made suffer. The people will decide your fate."

Junn turns away and Marcus melts into relief.

"What about this one?" Dale thumps his hammer on Carver's knee.

"Let him go," Junn passes Dale and I. "Let him run back to his master."

He stops at the door.

"Right now, we have more important things to do."

CHAPTER 19

— Bloody Business —

"Listen up, everyone," Harlow addresses the crowd of over three-hundred people. "We have gathered you, we have armed you. Now, all that remains is to take back your home from the Bandits. Their presence here is small, but do not forget their lust for blood as they will not relent until each and every one of you lies dead before them. Act strong, act together, and we shall see the sun dawning upon a liberated Compound."

Dale, Junn and I sift through the throng of men and women, holding sword, spear and ax as they each make themselves ready for bloody business. I do not see a face of excitement for battle nor do I hear a surge of defiant voices. I feel only a simmering wrath finally made to boil from the long and tortured months of occupation. We make it near the front where Harlow and the others stand; Harlow continues to speak, her eyes finding us amongst the crowd.

"Riston and Junn will be in the vanguard. Dale, Tegan and myself, along with Viper and Nalu will take positions on the vanguard's sides. The signal to commence the attack will be three rings of clashing steel. Questions?

Silence.

"Good," Harlow hops down from a crate and we rally around her as the crowd looks for the faces to match the names of the group leaders. "I hope they can handle this," she says to the Black Flag.

"I am sure they will surprise you," Junn brushes hair from his face. "These people are no strangers to battle. All they needed is someone to lift them up."

"Here's hoping," Tegan looks over his person and ensures every knife is sheathed, every arrow is sharp and ready. "Let us not waste another moment before fear takes hold."

He nods to Dale and Harlow and they nod back.

"Nothing else for it than to see it done," Riston heads off with Junn, great sword swinging in its large scabbard.

Nalu and I stand while people shift around us, finding their group. There is more than meets the eye with them. They appear to be just common citizens to a passerby, but they act and move and speak in the parlance of battle-hardened men. After a few minutes, I count around seventy hard faces and expressionless eyes gathered around Nalu and I.

"Let's go," Nalu heads to the left side of Junn's group in the vanguard.

We spill through the streets and around the buildings like a flood from a breached dam; I can see the others from my position, the many helmets and swords shimmer in the glow of the rapidly setting moon. Dawn is coming.

Clang!

Harlow sounds the signal for advance. My heart pounds in my chest. I look at my team. Their faces are hard-set and unwavering.

Clang!

Nalu's black eyes meet my own. He smiles at me.

Clang!

Nalu takes the first steps and our men fall in line behind him.

Marching through the Compound like this seems to change its very nature. Before, the winding streets and the walls enclosing them offered security. Now, they are nothing more than elements of warfare. Friendly, familiar places are ominous and foreboding under the shade of imminent battle. Ahead, Nalu freezes in place and holds up a fist, signaling a halt. He looks to me then jerks his head in the direction of a group of Bandits rounding the corner a short distance away, their attention going back and forth as they search for the source of the racket from Harlow's signal. Our team comes to a standstill behind us while a few move up to crane their necks to get a glimpse at what is impeding progress.

"There are so few!" one burly man says. "We can easily overwhelm them!" He takes a step forward and readies his hatchet.

"No," I say. "Not until the vanguard engages."

"Did you hear what that woman said? Take them out in one go!"

I do not respond and keep watch over the Bandits' progression. I hear the man behind me give a huff and shove by me, joined by another overconfident man. They stomp directly for the unaware Bandits.

The two soldiers approach the enemy and compromise their element of surprise by letting out one sharp whistle, to which the Bandits react at first with shock and then aggressive hostility. They immediately go after the two men with bared teeth and thirsty bone-swords. The first Bandit leaps forward to strike, but his target sidesteps at the last moment and beheads the assailant with two hits to the back of the neck with his hatchet. He spits on the twitching body and dispatches a second foe with the aid of his overzealous ally, successfully followed by a third until the Bandits lie to soak in their own blood.

The hatchet-wielding man turns and looks smugly at me, propping his foot on one of the bodies.

"They're not so tough!" He laughs. "Now, if you're done cowering, let's—"

An arrow buries itself in the back of his skull and its metal head is visible in his mouth as he twists in agony. His horrified companion looks daftly at the fatal wound and the blood coming down like a fountain through his teeth before his body topples to the ground. The second soldier looks away from the body and runs. Before he even takes five paces, there is a low whistle and a dull thump as a black-feathered arrow finds its mark and sends the man to the eternal union of the afterlife.

Panic takes over the ranks of our volunteer soldiers who thought that sharp weapons and plate armor would be enough to deter death. The people nearest the front turn tail and bolt, terrified of an enemy they cannot see. Many towards the back of the group steel themselves against the fleeing men's stricken faces and advance cautiously.

At the fork in the road, where the two dead militiamen lay, shadows stretch their fingers, slowly creeping towards the bodies.

"Nalu," I whisper. "Rotate behind those carts while I sneak around the right."

He does not even turn to look at me before he collects followers with a touch as he moves by them.

I move out and duck low behind a stout wall that is a barrier between the road and a block of houses at my back in the nook of the fork. I peer over the edge of the wall and catch in the faint light a lone bowman. Splinters of bone go from his left hand all the way up his arm to where they array themselves in a skeletal bloom like the feathers of a dreadful peacock. Harsh contrast from the streetlights and the moon rays highlight his muscles as he reveals himself. The Bandit approaches his kills, his bare feet making no sound on the road as he pads towards them. He stops at the bodies and stoops over them, plucking his arrows from the back of one soldier and then from the other, their removal emits a visceral squelching noise. I feel around on the paved walkway with my hand while I keep the bowman in sight. My prying fingers find and grab hold of a piece of pavement dislodged by the weave and tear of time. I weigh it in my hand, then lob the slab of road over the wall in a long arc, sending it to land behind the Bandit.

The fragment of broken street skips and clatters as it lands. The Bandit snaps his focus to the source of the interruption and has his bow ready, arrow notched, in a blink.

Nalu and his handful of followers descend upon the Bandit and cause a commotion to which the bowman responds with cold, murderous intent. The bowman manages to take down three of Nalu's soldiers, notching and releasing his black-feathered arrows almost as fast as Tegan. Though, for all the Bandit's skill, sheer numbers tip the scales in our favor. Nalu sprints at the shooter at full-tilt. He holds one of his curved swords close to his side as he weaves this way and that on his high-speed approach, keeping the arrows from finding him. The Bandit releases two more arrows, ripping through the air towards Nalu. One misses completely and the other grazes his right cheek and sends blood across his face. Nalu closes the gap and slashes his blade in a ferocious uppercut that not only breaks the Bandit's bow asunder, but also removes both of his hands and his right arm up to the elbow. The Bandit falls to his knees as blood gushes out of his wounds. He stares helplessly up at Nalu, his black teeth showing from behind grey lips.

Nalu just stares right back and shakes the blood from his weapon.

"This is for Grimhild," he raises his sword into the air before bringing it down onto his opponent's neck, removing his head in one swoop.

The way forward is clear. From the sounds of raised voices and the clash of swords, it appears that Junn and the vanguard have begun the assault in earnest.

I charge through the remainder of the streets, Nalu, Junn 's vanguard, and Tegan and Dale's group rout the Bandits like vermin fleeing from blinding light. Our militiamen embolden themselves with each hacked Bandits they step over, every building and avenue they reclaim, attracting more members who, at first, were too afraid to heed the call of battle. Now they stand as a wall together, joined by the excitement and chaos of conflict and the prospect that their collective nightmare is finally over.

I stand at the north gate with Dale and the Black Flag as we watch our militiamen hauling something amidst their throbbing masses. Their voices are a mash and tangle of words, sometimes a word or phrase drifts to the top and I comprehend that they've taken a prisoner.

"String him up!" I see Hector raise his bloody butcher's knife above his head.

"Your turn!" I hear another shout.

The crowd breaks and I see the bloodstained figure of Carver on his knees before the seething people. It appears that he was not hasty or crafty enough in his escape.

"Here's the other one!"

Two young men shove Marcus between the gathered bodies and he joins his counterpart in the barren circle. Junn steps forward quickly, sensing the bloodlust.

"Guilty!" The people start chanting. "Guilty! Guilty! Guilty!"

Junn stands with his palms extended towards the throng.

"Please!" He shouts over the tumult.

He waits patiently for the crowd to tire themselves out. Once peace settles over them, Junn paces before Carver and Marcus, both of whom keep their heads bowed.

"Not a chance he'll be able to keep them from killing both of them," Harlow says from the side of her mouth.

"I'm not sure you know my brother," Dale says. "He once convinced me that the world was flat."

"There is blood owed," Riston says as Junn begins speaking. "If I know anything about people, it's that they need balance in one form or another."

"Friends, brothers and sisters," Junn surveys the faces of the crowd. "Today is a dark day. Yes, we have driven out the Bandits. Yes, we have lost and suffered much agony at their hands. And yes, we must now judge what shall be done about the ones heavily responsible. We all once knew Marcus to be a generous and thoughtful man, one that has poured himself into the endless, and sometimes thankless, work of keeping those under his care strong and healthy. But he has sullied himself. He brokered a deal with the Bandits, a plot furthered by Carver. However," he pauses, letting the smothering quiet take hold, "there is a truth that you do not know. This is not the fault of Marcus, but of a man named Contil."

At this a disquiet murmur sweeps through the people, asking who is Contil, and if this new information exonerates or further condemns the guilty party.

"There is no point in trying to reason that this makes Marcus less responsible," Junn continues. "Though, it should make you realize that what he did, he did out of a sense of duty to protect the lives of as many of you as he could. Carver, on the other hand, fully, irrevocably, and under his own volition committed senseless acts of violence against you. These are the facts as I know them. Do with it as you will."

Junn stands firm; Carver and Marcus behind him do not move or utter a sound. Tao steps forward. His grimy face has an anxious expression, as though he yearns to remove a thorn, but is afraid of the pain.

"It's no secret that I've come to hate both of them for what they did," he says at length. "I had a good life back north, many of us did. But I see it as the Bandit's fault more than these two."

The crowd whisper and murmur their assent.

"Who this Contil is I do not know. What I do know is that Carver must pay for what he did. There can be no forgiveness."

"I've known Marcus longer than most," I hear Malory's voice, but cannot see her through the choking bodies. "I know that the Bandits are his mortal enemy, I know that he must have been under tremendous pressure if he made a deal with them. I, for one, forgive him."

I watch Marcus as I see wet drops from his eyes.

Someone in the crowd moves. I drift my gaze across the people and come to rest on a man with a beat-red face and a balding head making his way through the people. We all wait as he reaches the edge, but before he breaches the ring, a little girl steps through. She wears a dirt-covered dress, patches of mismatched fabric sewn in all over. She holds the man's hand but is not led by him, a theory confirmed by the look of anger on his face and the aura of embarrassment coming from him.

The girl lets go of his hand and takes three big steps towards Junn. Looking up at him, she clasps her hands behind her back and says,

"Daddy says that good people can do bad things for a good reason. I think Marcus is a good person so I forgive him, too."

The girl rushes back to her father's side as the crowd fumbles with their understanding and acceptance of what was spoken. If Malory says so, it must be true. But, somehow the unmarked and innocent mind of the child cut through to heart and mind better than any crafted argument ever could.

"What say the rest of you?" Junn asks of them.

"I say spare him," I speak first. "He was one of the only people that gave me a second chance at a better life. I would do the same for him now."

The individuals in the gathering, in their own unique way and separate reasonings and processes, speak in one voice as they find it within themselves to forgive. Marcus finally lifts his red face bright with fresh tears, and stares into his countrymen's eyes, conveying his bottomless gratitude.

"Thank you, all of you!" He cries. "I will never forget this!"

"See that you do not," Malory says, sharply.

"And what about him?" Hector points a thick finger at Carver.

"Someone," Junn says, "go find a rope."

CHAPTER 20

— No Time Left —

Through blood and broken glass, we did it. Victory never seemed a word one would use to describe a fight with the Bandits. Survived, maybe but never victory. Until now. I walk amongst the tired, wounded and bleeding strewn about the infirmary. Malory is darting from bedside to bedside, cot to cot lining the walls to tend to the endless needs of the injured. She's been at it all night, but nothing can stop her. She even found it in herself, against the uproarious complaints of others, to allow Marcus to assist her. But after a few hours of biting pain, people don't care whose hands help stop it. For now, at least.

"Hardly seems real," I say.

"How do you mean?" Junn stands from the stool beside a sleeping soldier, a boy younger than myself.

"We were untouchable in these walls for as long as anyone can remember. Now it's come to this? It's hard to believe that we were able to do anything about it."

"You think we just got lucky?"

I look down at the boy, chest slowly rising and falling underneath the bloody bandages. Luck would be a cruel word to use for this.

"You can't say that we haven't had our fair share of luck over the last few weeks."

"I think we'd have no luck at all if it wasn't for you," Junn walks away from the hurting and crying, and outside into the hazy morning.

"I wasn't the one that led the vanguard," I say, breathing in the crisp air. "I wasn't the one responsible for the surprisingly few Bandits we fought."

"Every tough man, be he king or a simple man, needs someone to lean on now and then."

"I'd suppose Dale would be that person, just one look at him would prove it."

"He's good at breaking and tinkering with things," Junn laughs. "The things you've done are qualities of leadership."

"I did what needed doing. Anyone would've done the same."

"I wouldn't be so sure. Those are no small feats, Vipe. You've become a symbol of change, shown that a broken system can be overthrown, that good can triumph over evil."

"Why should I be the one they admire?" I splutter. "Men better than I have accomplished more. All I wanted was to get you back from the Bandits."

"Don't you see?" Junn exclaims. "That is the very reason you're so adored! You were an outcast, brought to us in fear and speculation. You took all the harsh looks and harsher words and turned them into strength to grow into a man with a heart so full of love that it compelled you from one end of the map to the other just to save someone that anyone else would think to be long dead. And you, just a young man — to their knowledge — single-handedly brought the Black Flag together to end Carver's reign, Marcus's corruption, and their Bandits. Now, look me in the eye and say again that what you've done is of little significance."

I stop and look at his grinning face half-lit by the sun cascading through the distant peaks of the Bymore Desert. I've never thought my actions were anything more than necessary. But to think of them as heroic is almost laughable. Though, none would say it was easy, all the scars I've picked up can attest to that. I turn away from Junn's eye. All these people look up to me? I don't even know their names, who they are. But I suppose that I've got no say in the matter. All I can do is be an example worth following. Nothing else for it.

"I guess that what *we've* done has had some effect on things," I look at the men and women all around, absorbed in their work. "Still don't see why they chose me over you. Doesn't seem right."

"People have a way of surprising you in ways you'd never expect," Junn says. "A way of uniting when things turn sour, of calling a lost boy family in a grey world. And if there is any advice I can give, it'd be this: be wary of the time when you will be challenged and the ones that looked at you with grace will have to reassess the virtue of their hero."

I swallow hard, thinking about how gaunt and defeated Marcus looked when I found him. We walk in silence for a while until we arrive at the tavern. We step inside and I find it a welcoming, familiar place, despite the tortured negligence from Bandit influence. I notice Dale and Riston conversing over heavy, wooden pints.

"Viper!" Riston raises his tankard to me. "I was just talking about you!"

"Nothing bad, I hope," I sit with them.

"Nothing of the sort! I was merely trying to remember a conversation you and I shared at the Northern Compound, before we were interrupted by Grimhild, may the stars guide him. You were talking about the origins of your special knife…"

"I remember. What of it?"

"Would you care to finish your thought?"

I rest my hand on the hilt of my knife, thoughtfully tracing the unknown markings etched into the weapon's sheath.

"An awful long time ago, I heard a story about a traveler far to the east coming to visit on some errand. They say that he knew of all sorts of secret things; said that he might have the answers I'm looking for."

Riston furrows his brow and tugs at his bread.

"My mother used to tell me stories from her homeland about great and wise men and women that could bring the dead back to life and had the knowledge of a thousand lifetimes. People called Sages. But, for all I know, those people are just that: stories."

"Even if that is so, someone has to know the secret behind this knife. I intend to find them."

"And how far are you willing to go for answers?"

"Finding this Sage might reveal the meaning behind my knife, and if that question is answered, then it might also lead me to the person that left it behind."

"Do you know what I think?" Dale says. "I think that you just found something someone dropped one day."

"How can you not find the mystery intriguing?" Riston asks.

"I do hope that you find whatever you're looking for, have no doubt. All I am saying is that you shouldn't let your imagination disappoint you when you eventually find the truth."

"I do truly hate logical reasoning at times," Riston says. "But—"

Riston stops as he sees Tegan barge in the Tavern. His face has a grim expression on it as he hurries to our table.

"Greetings, Tegan," Junn says. "Why the serious look?"

"Junn! Bandits!" he cries, at last standing before him. "Spotted coming from the west, led by a man on horseback."

The tavern falls deathly silent at the mention of Bandits. Junn jumps to his feet, Riston slowly returns his pint to the table.

"So soon?"

I glance around at the horror-stricken faces. You could hear the blood flowing in your own body in this quiet. I rise beside Junn.

"Lead the way."

Tegan takes off. Junn, Dale, Riston, and I follow in tow, cutting through the streets like lightning to reach the western wall.

We arrive to find the Compound's fighters swarming the battlements in preparation for the fight, stretching their heads over their neighbors to see over the parapet. The rising sun streams its light through the spires of the Bymore and paints the tree line to the west in a soft, golden glow. Tegan and Junn put the men into strategic positions and take information from our scouts. Junn rests both hands on the wall and looks out over the quarter mile stretch between the Compound and the edge of the Ironwood Forest.

Multiple sets of feet come charging from the narrow stair to the ramparts, and eventually shows more defenders, along with Harlow, all of whom appear slightly shaken but nonetheless composed for this dire circumstance. Junn greets our last member and brings her up to speed.

"We should send out a group of bowmen to hide in those rocks," Harlow suggests. "Take the Bandits by surprise as they engage the Compound."

"Too risky," Junn answers. "Once they open fire, the Bandits can just turn around and slaughter them."

"Agreed," Riston says. "I think that our archers will be more effective on our walls rather than outside of them."

"Well, we should do something to be one step ahead," Harlow argues. "If we stay cooped up behind these walls, the Bandits will know exactly where to point their swords."

"We haven't the slightest idea what their numbers are, nor are we in a position to launch an offensive," Tegan counters. "Not to mention that we have the walls and they do not."

"He's right," I add. "We'd be sending our men to their deaths."

"I think they accept that as a consequence of fighting a war," Harlow says, drastically.

"You and I both know that is not how we do things here. You're better than that."

She looks at me in a way she has never done before. Her lips slightly open, one eyebrow raised, and her eyes are cold and piercing. She remains in such a state for a while before exhaling hard and dropping her head. Harlow looks back up at me with a look of approval, maybe even pride. It's really hard to tell… sometimes.

"Forgive me," she says, at last. "I did not mean to imply that their lives are worthless. But my concern remains: what are we going to do?"

I look out over the smooth green expanse to the west and see a small black shape rapidly approaching the Compound. As it comes closer, I realize who it is.

"I think we have an answer."

CHAPTER 21

— Awareness & Ability —

Over the song of birds and gently blowing wind, the horses galloping hooves penetrate loud and clear. The light from the sun shines on the rider's face and catches his hair, igniting the flowing copper strands like a smoldering candlewick. The horse stutters to a halt close enough to the wall to allow the rider's voice to carry up to where we stand.

"My master extends his congratulations," Haebur shouts. "It is seldom seen that the plans he sets in motion are put to rest."

"Does he so desire to be exalted that he commands his followers to call him 'master'?" Junn taunts. "Contil is far from deserving of such praise."

"And it is unwise, is it not?" Riston calls. "For a criminal to return to the scene of the crime?"

"One might say that," Haebur answers, his face calm and measured. "But it is the mark of a meticulous man to desire the oversight and fulfillment of the future he has envisioned."

"Oh? And pray tell, what future has his deceit spun, Haebur?" Riston scoffs. "Has he promised peace in exchange for blood? We know that future well, for we live it as we speak."

"Neigh, the Master sees a future far greater," Haebur laughs, coldly. "One in which I, along with my brothers, are anointed and chosen above the rest to preside over the new world. It is a future that burns and creates."

I hear a faint rumbling in the distance. Birds take to the sky like dark clouds.

"You may have thwarted Contil's plans at Kandent," Haebur continues, the rumbling rising like a distant thunder coming nearer. "And you may have momentarily freed your precious Compound, but you have yet to bear witness to the full scope of Contil's future."

Haebur kicks his horse into a gallop and returns, bounding back to the tree line.

"We should put an arrow in his back," I hear someone say.

The quaking stops and all that I can hear is wary voices from our men. Then suddenly, there is an immense *whoosh* from the trees and a split second later panic ensnares the minds of our soldiers when they see Contil's future.

"Take cover!" Junn screams.

He dives to the ground and takes anyone nearby with him to avoid the boulder hurtling through the air. It comes smashing down on the Compound's structures behind us.

The noise and calamity of the projectile's collision shakes the foundations of our fortitude and reduces the courage of our men to absolute zero. Never before have I, nor anyone else, seen such destruction delivered so quickly and without warning. The very air I breathe vibrates with shrieks of panic and shouts of commands. My ears ring and my vision is hazy through the plume of dust and debris erupting from inside the walls. I stumble to my feet, see our defenders scrambling to get off the battlements, others push towards the edge to cry their insults and curses; their voices come to me as though I lay at the bottom of the sea. I look down over the parapet into the Compound and see people hurrying this way and that as they escape the wreckage, trying to understand what is happening.

"Hold! Hold!"

I turn at the familiar sound of Junn's voice and see a scattered few poorly aimed arrows shoot and wobble through the air. I stretch my gaze out past where they land and see Bandits pouring from the trees in far greater force than I've ever seen. More than the caravan ambush, more than Kandent.

"Wait until they're in range!" Junn orders. He holds up a clenched fist, "on my mark."

The Bandits stampede across the clearing from the Ironwood as the thunderous rumbling continues. I notice the trees violently shake, some are even knocked over and the sound of the Bandits comes closer.

"Fire!" Junn throws down his fist.

Hundreds of arrows fill the sky. Many of them find their mark and stop fast the sprinting Bandits. Junn orders a second volley, and another, each sending scores of Bandits to the grave; each failing to stop their ferocious advance.

After being peppered by yet another wave of arrows, the Bandit army splits in two and maneuvers around to the right and left.

"They're going for the gates!" Tegan shouts. "We have to get the civilians to safety!"

I look passed the sea of Bandits to the Forest and see the Bandit's new weapon they brandish against us. It is constructed from great planks and beams of wood and rolls on wide wheels, adorned with the Bandits' signature bone filigree. A long wooden arm with a wide woven metal basket is perpendicular to the ground, but steadily draws back. The war machine's tall wheels bring it crawling forward to a more advantageous position; a dozen or more Bandits push at the rear and pull at the front with ropes. The war machine's arm draws back all the way and the Bandits load a second projectile.

"Shit," Harlow says.

At the sight of the Bandit's reading to take fire, the defenders seek cover. We find it just in time. The enemies launch another enormous boulder at us. It collides with the Compound's wall a few dozen strides from where I stand and sunders the stonework into ruin and smashes open a gap through which the Bandits infiltrate our stronghold and wreak havoc.

My ears ring, clouds of dust choke the air, and pieces of debris rain down. My head is in a daze as I stand. I look on as our defenders follow Junn from the wall and run for the staircase. I storm from the wall after them and sprint for the breach.

Chaos and voices resound through the streets as civilians are shepherded out of danger. Men and women alike rally together in defense of their home and rush to gather at the gate to fend off the enemy, but my destination lies elsewhere.

The scurrying soldiers lead me to where Dale and Nalu, and other brave souls already stand in the breach, slaying Bandits; stemming the relentless tide. Dale's warhammer smashes and cracks bone, swords pierce and disembowel; blood runs freely and mixes with the earth. I race to their aid and brace against the bloodlust of our foe.

"We have to stop them from coming through!" Junn cries. "Do not break!"

I leap into the battle, blade flashing silver, and skewer a Bandit through his breastplate. I shove him off my sword and work together with my countrymen to repel the attack. The war machine launches another boulder and sends it crashing into the Compound, leveling homes and igniting fires from toppled candles and shattered oil canisters.

I duck under a Bandit's serrated bone-sword, grab hold of his arm, and fling him to the ground, stabbing down onto his chest. The rising sun is now above the Bymore's spires and it shines its light on bodies and pools of blood, pools through which our reinforcements arrive.

Tao, brandishing a slingshot of mysterious design on his forearm, spearheads a mass of our militiamen towards the breach, heralding a change in fate. He points his arm towards the Bandits and lobs a transparent sphere at the hoard. Liquid splatters their bodies from the broken glass and causes those touched to writhe and fall; green-tinted smoke emits from their flailing limbs. The reinforcements slam against the Bandit attack with sword and wrath. Bone-swords hack and slash in brutal and rapid strokes, their overpowering strength latches on to the Compound's defenders so they cannot pull away from ripping, gnashing teeth snapping at their unprotected flesh.

Riston and Dale swing their weapons in wide arcs, killing Bandits as a farmer would reap their crop. Junn, Tegan and Nalu push at their backs and keep any from slipping past with blade or arrow.

Others stand atop the broken wall and pepper the Bandits with arrows or pieces of rubble. Their synergy allows us to push back against the onslaught, but it is an advantage short-lived. Over the Bandits' wretched heads, I see one figure above the rest. A towering Bandit whose pale, armored skin shines like the moon and his steel sword, as broad as an oar from a massive warship, cleaves and hacks at man and Bandit alike on his bloodstained approach towards the breach.

I am not alone in my observation of this fearsome newcomer, for the Bandit's attack with vigor redoubled by the arrival of their champion and push forward once more, chanting a word that is indistinguishable above the clash of war. As the hulking Bandit steps closer to the breach, the lesser ones surge and chant louder.

"Shalvok! Shalvok! Shalvok!"

The Bandits' renewed strength forces us to step back, then to retreat entirely into the Compound. We irregularly stop to fight as we wind through the streets to keep from being completely overrun. Each time I do, I see that mountain of a Bandit continuing his advance, the chanting always rising.

Junn, Dale, Riston and I halt at a fork in the road while we cover the retreat led by Tegan, Harlow and Nalu. With the enemy snapping at their heels, we shepherd the wounded and the women and children that have yet to reach safety.

Harlow shouts for my attention. I turn and see her holding out that phial she stowed away at the Northern Compound with its mysterious liquid swirling inside. I take it.

"Coat your blade with it only when it is absolutely necessary," she then moves back to the retreat and disappears.

I see two people in the rear of the withdrawal, an old man and a little boy carried in the man's arms. Bandits are closing in on them. I abandon my position at Dale's side and rush towards the helpless two, wading through felled beast and brother in ny desperation to help them. Dale calls after me to stay put, but I do not listen. I nearly reach them, but a herd of bone-adorned savages come bounding around a corner and head me off. I dispatch them with ease, taking full advantage of the gaps in their defense opened by their lack of swordsmanship, but in the fray, I lose sight of the two civilians.

I head straight for where I last saw them and frantically turn in place searching. I see them alone, rounding yet another bend in the Compound's infrastructure. I immediately give chase. I reach the bend and stop cold. My heart sinks into the soles of my boots.

In the burning circle of buildings, my eyes fall on the old man, laying in a pool of his own blood; his decapitated head rolls on the ground towards me. Standing over the body is the Bandit, Shalvok, his broad frame silhouetted against the fires from the burning buildings behind him. His right arm is fully extended and at its end, clenched tightly in his grasp, is the boy, beside himself with utter terror.

Shalvok turns his black eyes from the squirming boy in my direction as I enter this nightmare. His scarred lips curl back into a diabolical sneer.

"Let the boy go!" I plead. "He's just a child!"

Shalvok laughs a disgusting and guttural laugh and slowly and purposefully raises his blade and runs it through the boy's back, birthing it through his stomach. The crying and screaming stops. The boy's knees buckle as his body drops to the ground. I look back at Shalvok; his sword shining red.

"You aren't even a challenge," he taunts in perfect speech. "Why Merr'putra detests you so is clear. But to send so many of us for this? His reasons escape me." Shalvok steps over the child's corpse; kicks the old man's head out of his way. "What I do understand is that this will be over quickly."

Shalvok leaps towards me, his sword-hand reeled back and eyes wild. I bring up my short sword and parry, the force of his strike drives me to one knee.

Shalvok lifts his sword with both hands to bring it tearing through the air to meet my skull. I roll left and his steel whistles and thumps on the ground as it misses me by mere inches. I bolt to my feet, lashing out as I do so. My attack bounces harmlessly off Shalvok's shin guards. He laughs in that same hellish way and pummels my defense. His terrible strikes against me forces me into a corner of a burning building. My knife pokes me in the back from where it is slung on my belt. The heatwaves coming from the engulfed building distorts my view of Shalvok, making him look more like the apparition of death he truly is. I prepare to take a final stand against this unrelenting force, though I know that I do not have the strength to defeat him.

Then I hear something over the crackle of fire and the clamor of war. It is a small noise. Nevertheless, that small noise grows louder as it finds its voice, just like that day, years ago, when I got lost in the march and my brother saved me.

The light and smoke from the blaze conceals much of Shalvok's body; his hands swing at his side as he strides towards me, peeking through the gloom in rhythm with his approach, his torso and neck hidden in black smoke, showing only his demonic head. I hold out the point of my short sword in a pitiful attempt to prolong my life, to keep this monster away.

Shalvok's black eyes mirror the flames behind me and his mouth opens, showing teeth filed down to points.

The small sound grew – is growing, pulsating. I can no longer distinguish between it and my own throbbing heart.

Shalvok's blood-coated sword raises in the burning dawn and I brace for its impact, of which I feel two. Shalvok's blade smashes against my guard and I can feel my arm break. Pain courses through my body, radiating from my old wound with the Alnnasi on my shoulder, shivering down my legs. The second impact redoubles that pain when Shalvok himself collides against my beaten body. I can see something protruding out of his back. It catches the light through the haze. Shalvok bellows in agony and whips around to see this new threat.

"Only a coward strikes from the shadows!" Shalvok roars. "Come and fight! Come and try to even the odds!" He pulls the object from his back and hurls it away from him. I recognize that blade. One of Junn's knives.

I see a glint, a shard of light ripping through the smoke, heading for the Bandit's exposed chest. The shimmering metal of the throwing knife connects and staggers the brute, furthering his state of torment. Shalvok howls with rage at this hidden attacker, shouting challenges and curses as he scours the area for him. For Junn.

I take advantage of this welcomed distraction and escape from the corner, darting to where I believe Junn hides. With my eyes blind from smoke and my own sweat and blood, I manage to reach the crossroad where I entered. I stumble over the rubble of smashed buildings and look for Junn, but I cannot find him.

I hear Shalvok's words of damnation echoing through the corridor; see his sword in the smoke mirroring the flames. A hand grabs me firmly. The grip steers me farther down the road, away from Shalvok and stops under the doorway of an abandoned shop.

"I can't kill him alone," Junn says. "I will hold him off. Go get Nalu. He's fighting by the bakery."

I don't say anything at first. I look back at Junn, then to Shalvok's writhing silhouette.

How is he going to last against that thing?

"Hey," Junn says, urgency more prevalent in his voice. "Go find Nalu. Go!"

Junn pushes me away and sneaks back through the street to buy me time.

*

I run through the wreckage of the Compound, plunge into the carnage and fear of battle, hot, smoke-filled air scorches my throat as I gulp down air on my way to the North District. I run passed wounded soldiers retreating from the western wall and the breach, carried on the shoulders of those who deserve the same grace. Rubble and bodies of the slain litter the streets. The sun's reflection on thick hazes of dust from the destruction scratch my eyes and clog my vision as I rush through the sheets of light. I am harried and beset by Bandits and terrified defenders, all trying either to kill me or help me to kill, but I cannot stop. I weave around the tangled masses in hysteria. Straining my eyes for the tell-tale signs of a familiar landmark, but all is rendered illegible by the fog of war. I hope I'm getting close.

"Nalu! Nalu!" I shout over the tumult, my voice barely audible to my own ears.

I turn to my right and run until I reach the end of the road. I see someone fall to the ground in their evacuation. The figure quickly springs back up, and comes barreling towards me at the head of a group of blood-splattered men.

A second person detaches from the group and comes to the first's side. They stop before me and I see Nalu in a disconcerted state and Tegan in his footsteps.

"Nalu!" I shout again, struggling for breath. "Junn… fighting Shalvok… we need to help him!"

"Where is he?"

"Close to the breach, far into the south-western side."

Nalu confronts the men gathering behind him,

"Everyone, head for the Square and regroup with Riston, Harlow and the rest of the resistance." He looks back to me, "lead the way."

We barrel around the corner and retrace my steps back to the breach.

"Come on! Almost there."

Please be in time… please be in time… please.

We stutter to a halt. Nalu, Tegan and I stand in the court where Shalvok and Junn are competing for their lives. Junn dashes in under Shalvok's swinging sword and strikes under his guard, stepping back to safety before he is met with retaliation. Shalvok roars, whips his closed fist through the saturated air, and delivers Junn a crushing blow, laughing in the revelry of combat. Junn pulls himself to his feet on one side of the arena, blood flowing from an injury above his eye; Shalvok paces back and forth on the other. The Bandit turns his beastly head towards me and shows his baleful smile.

"Now we can have a fair fight!" He thunders. "Come and test yourselves! See if you are worthy to defeat a king among worms, an anointed by god!"

Ignoring the Bandit, Nalu, Tegan and I circle over to Junn as we keep an eye on the "king."

"We are losing ground," Nalu leans over to speak in Junn's ear. "They need their captain to lead them."

"Nothing can be done about that until he is dead."

"And now we are here! So let's take him down," Tegan says, urgently. "Dale is fighting in the Square with Halow. If we end this here and now, we can get back to them and turn the tide."

"Dale is a formidable man," Junn says. "However, this creature is far more dangerous. Not one of us alone has any chance in single combat, which is why—"

"Is your hope to kill me with old age?" Shalvok shouts. "Face me!"

Junn keeps eye contact with me and continues speaking through the Bandit's taunts.

"Which is why I need you three to do exactly as I say."

Shalvok interrupts again before Junn can issue orders.

"Do not ignore me!" he screams, his loathing for us scorched into his words. "Take me on all at once -- one at a time, it doesn't matter. It will not change the end."

Shalvok comes towards us. I finger the phial in my pocket Harlow gave me; Tegan notches an arrow.

"Your warriors are frail and taste of spoiled meat. The flesh of champions is so delicious."

Tegan shoots his arrow which buries itself in Shalvok's thigh. The Bandit flinches but does not cease in his advance. It only seems to increase his desire to see us lying dead at his feet.

"I think I'll eat the boy first. Always so tender."

Shalvok walks faster and licks old blood off his sword. Tegan readies two arrows at once and releases them. One hits Shalvok's right forearm and the other on his left side. Nalu maneuvers to the right and Junn and I stand our ground. Shalvok breaks the arrow shafts protruding from his ghastly skin and flings them to the ground, deflecting a fourth shot with his sword.

Nalu springs out from the rear and stabs down into Shalvok's back, his sword running clean through his shoulder. The hideous Bandit bellows, reaches behind him, and grabs Nalu, throwing him into the air towards me, but he is up in an instant and charges back toward Shalvok with both curved blades drawn and slashing. I join the fray with both knife and short sword and duck to avoid Shalvok's tree-trunk arms; rolling to dodge his blade.

Our attacks chisel away at his body that is now shining with blood and sweat. My sword arm burns with every strike I deliver and with each blow I manage to barely deflect. My legs only just hanging on. We dance around Shalvok as we sting him with the tips of our swords, taking blows in turn.

In tandem, Junn swings high with all his might while Nalu and I alternate swinging low; every move passes in an instant, every reaction executed in perfect time. Tegan, his arrows now spent, draws his short sword and fights alongside us with more tenacity than I believed this man of reason was capable of. Shalvok swings both his blade and empty fist, lashing out tirelessly and with enormous strength. He bursts with cruel mirth when he delivers a punishing strike, increasing his vigor and zeal to see us suffer under unstoppable force.

"Is this your best?" Shalvok bellows. "I have killed thousands! Slaughtered armies!"

He catches Tegan's sword arm mid-swing and hurls both he and the weapon through the air. I scream out but am knocked to the dirt when I try to retaliate. I gasp for air when I hit the ground.

"Pathetic!" Shavok spits. "Come on! Get back up so I can send you farther down."

Nalu avoids Shalvok's slash but cannot move in time to dodge his fist that drives itself into his stomach. The air is forced out of Nalu's body and Shalvok rams his head against the Pau'larin's, sending him smashing to the ground. I get back to my feet and charge at Shalvok before Junn can help and, I too, am forced out of the battle. I come shooting through the air and land on the ash covered earth. My knife thumps to the ground beside me.

"You underestimate us!" Junn shouts, defiantly. He spins around the brute and gouges a cross into Shalvok's back with his sword. "I have also killed many, and I know exactly how to deal with a wild beast."

Junn leans back and dodges Shalvok's retribution and evades once again by sidestepping masterfully.

"You see, it all comes down to just two things: awareness and ability," Junn says.

Shalvok barks harshly tongue of his kind; his language is the howl in the night, a wretched scar on the land.

"Even as you die you do not accept your fate! Your arrogance is nothing more than a desperate bid before your skull becomes another one of my trophies. Maybe if you give in, I'll show mercy. I am sure that Merr'putra will be interested in the prize that was stolen from him. The living god sees all, is unmatched in power and cannot be stopped. And I, Shalvok the Man-Cleaver, First of the Bandits and Champion of Merr'tyura, will see his god's will carried out."

"I will not beg for mercy to be deceived. I do not believe that you are capable of an act of mercy. The scope of all your deeds is death and misery, all at the behest of your master who would rather pull the strings from the shadows than face his enemy himself," Junn stands strong in the fiery ring of buildings, composed and resilient under the pressure. "Instead, I must fight his dog, and dogs that bark the loudest have the softest bite."

Shalvok's face twists with hate at Junn's words. He lunges at him with his sword.

"A dog am I?" he booms as he rains down blow after blow upon my brother. "Your allies are beaten by this dog, your city burns at this dog's command, and this dog will soon add your corpse to the fire."

He laughs as Junn struggles to fend off the attacks that steadily wear down his strength, blood staining his skin. "See now what your ability and awareness have brought you! See your friends lie slain before you!"

Junn smirks and looks into the Bandit's crazed black eyes with his own, blue and spirited as the sea.

"Your god is a false one. One that offers salvation and glory with one hand while he stabs you in the back with the other. All shall one day stand in judgment. You, myself, everyone."

"I am anointed! When I die I will become the judge that decides your place in the afterlife and there you shall truly suffer!" Shalvok clashes swords with Junn.

"You are all the same: brawn above all else," Junn says in hurried breath. "But strength alone does not decide all things. True strength comes from within. From the bonds you share with others and by putting everything aside to see them grow strong and live long, happy lives. I have spent a lifetime working to see that conviction become reality."

Shalvok pushes against Junn's sword and knocks him back. The Bandit attacks again, and again Junn does not back down. Shalvok does not relent and batters the sword from Junn's grip, smashing his fist against Junn's face, grunting as each blow lands; talking down to his adversary as he is brought to defeat.

"Tell me what those bonds do for you know! You have no weapon, no hope."

"My intention is not to survive, but to save," Junn spits blood out of his mouth. "I, Junn of the Black Flag, have saved this Compound and am at peace."

He spreads his arms wide and accepts what fate has in store for him. Shalvok shows his pointed teeth in a deadly smile and pierces Junn's chest with his sword. Blood shoots from Junn's mouth and Shalvok's eyes glow in the light of his victory. He throws his head back and roars. But his celebration lasts no longer than the beating of a heart.

Junn takes hold of the sword that pierces him and keeps the Bandit from removing it. Shalvok's triumphant pose washes away. Though he tugs and wrenches at the grip of his blade, Junn allows his hands to bleed in payment so that his hold will not loosen.

I glance down at my knife lying next to me.

Junn stares at Shalvok's wretched face and speaks again his words of defiance,

"It all comes down to awareness and ability."

Shalvok bellows his frustration as he continues to struggle against Junn to free his sword. His anger becomes wilder with each second he is denied his weapon.

Junn looks up into the smoke filled sky, blood spilling from his wounds. He removes one hand from Shalvok's blade. One on the sword and the other he stretches out in the air.

I scoop up my knife and toss it to Junn.

My small blade reflects the light from the fires and Junn snatches it with his expectant hand.

Shalvok tears on his sword and pulls it from Junn's chest, bringing it up to strike the killing blow.

Junn meets Shalvok's loathful eyes, "This is for all I love."

Junn thrusts my blade through the Bandit's throat and tears it down to his heart. The gash lets loose a torrent of blood and Shalvok's sword falls from his hands as he daftly grabs at his bleeding neck. Shalvok's mountainous body topples backward and I hear his last gurgling breath.

Junn looks to me from where he stands and smiles weakly. He falls to the ground next to Shalvok's corpse and does not move.

I shout for fear of Junn's life and run to his side, splashing through the red mud. Dropping to me knees, I cradle his head in my arms. My horrified eyes look from the wound to Junn's ghostly white face.

"Hey now, stay with me. Stay with me," I say, trying to sound confident. "You can't die here, not now."

Junn chuckles, but the pain is too great and he coughs up more blood.

"Do not worry about me. Worry for the lives that can still be saved."

"Don't you say that! What will we do without you?"

"You will do as you have done when you were without me," his eyes twinkle and he forces a smile. "You have done grand and impossible things without me and you will continue to accomplish greatness when I am gone."

Junn coughs harder this time. His body convulses as he struggles to breathe and to speak.

A shadow appears across Junn's body. I turn my head and see Nalu and Tegan limping over to where their brother lies. The sun breaks through the haze of battle and shines on Nalu's eyes, brimming with sorrow. He kneels down and gently takes Junn's hand in his own.

"T'un malo se dünba. Sek malo se castra."

Junn looks back into Nalu's black-coated eyes and repeats the Pau'larin's words in the Common Tongue,

"From nothing you came. To nothing you return."

"You have done your part, my friend. Go now and find peace in the Evergreen Pasture."

Junn places one hand on Nalu's cheek and the other around the back of my neck. He looks deeply into my eyes and says all the things in his heart with a look that his body failed to speak. He gasps for air and his eyes drift off my own to stare lifelessly into the burning dawn.

"T'un malo se dünba. Sek malo se castra."

Nalu rises to his feet and stands with Tegan. I do not move.

"Come, Viper," Tegan says, softly. "We have cut off the head of the Bandit's leadership. The body will soon die. Junn will receive a hero's burial, one that will be of such splendor and breathtaking beauty that is deserving of a man both loved and respected by all. But first we have to finish this."

I hold on to Junn for what feels like a lifetime, looking at his face, his vibrant blue eyes and his dark brown hair, forging his features into solid memory, quenching it with the tears streaming down my face.

Nalu stoops next to Shalvok's corpse, hacks his head loose, and carries it with him; it swings at his side as he walks, painting the ground red.

Tegan urges me again to move. I tenderly lay Junn's head to the earth and stand. The three of us depart from the court and the dying flames to bring this war to an end.

CHAPTER 22

— Three Stools, Three Mugs —

There is no more clamor of battle, no more pleas for salvation. A breeze flutters through the Compound like a cool hand across a fevered brow, wafting through the smoldering corridors. I sit on a canvas stool beside Harlow in the Square before the Great Hall. There is an eerie stillness to the place, and even through the cries of the wounded, it persists. I must be in shock. Did that really happen? My eyes look passed the line of beaten, bloody defenders to Shalvok's decapitated head on a spike. I wish I was dreaming, but there it is. His eternal sneering grimace is proof of the waking nightmare. Harlow stretches her arms above her head and cracks her aching neck. I hear crows cawing over me, a dark cloud in an otherwise bright day.

I finish tying a bandage around a young man's arm and send him away with a half-hearted pat on the back; another replaces him.

"I swear," Harlow yawns, "if I've bandaged, sewn, or cut off damaged body parts once, I've done it a thousand times."

The middle-aged man in her care stands and leaves, quickly followed by an elderly fellow with a nasty gash across the top of his chest.

"No, no, no," Harlow stands and holds up her hand. "You need to go to the infirmary, double quick. There's no help for you here, friend."

"But…"

"But nothing! You're still bleeding. Go on, now," she waves over someone helping nearby, "he will take you to Malory. She'll do more than I."

I look across the Square while they depart and see the enormous number still in need of attention. And those fortunate enough to have survived the dawn with flesh wounds have the task of gathering the dead, for burial and burning. One heap of Bandits is already belching its deplorable fragrance into the air with another well on the way.

"I will say," Harlow takes her seat, "killing that big bastard was a stroke of luck."

"Luck, is it?" I respond.

"I don't think we would be here if the sight of his head didn't make the Bandits run away," she looks over at me with an incredulous sort of half-smile on her face.

"What, victory makes you unhappy?"

Happy… I don't know if I know what that's like anymore. I've spent too much time fighting and killing, and now all of that seems like it was a wasted effort. Junn's… he's dead. How can any of this make me happy?

"C'mon, Vipe. What's the—"

Before she can utter the words, she looks down at the hand on her shoulder, then up into Tegan's crestfallen eyes.

"Harlow," he says. "I need to tell you something."

She looks worried as she gets up to follow Tegan. I stay put, mindlessly taking care of one person after another.

I hear Harlow shouting. I look over my shoulder and see Tegan holding her back as she demands that he let her go to exact revenge upon the devils that killed her friend. Tegan's lips quiver as he holds her still and she loses strength and slides to the dirt. They sit for a moment, Tegan resting his head against hers. He gently kisses her forehead.

Tegan takes Harlow's seat and joins me. We work in silence until the line whittles down to just one last person.

"I've got this," he says. "Why don't you find a hot meal and get some sleep, maybe get that shoulder looked at."

I wordlessly take his advice. I trudge along broken roads and pass by Tao's new workshop. Parts of its walls and roof are caved in with one of the war-machine's projectiles in its place. A small train of the badly injured head in my same direction, and we all eventually find our way to the doors of the infirmary.

It doesn't appear to me that anyone bothered to tell the nurses and healers that the battle is over. Frantic, sweat and blood-covered doctors shout and call for medicine, run this way and that to stop the bleeding, to hold somebody down while their legs are taken off. I find some place out of the way to stand and wait, but in the raging ocean of injured, there is no dry ground.

"Viper!"

I look around the musty space for the voice, but over everything I cannot see. It comes again and then I see a powder blue ribbon tied around grey, wiry hair bobbing through the people. I push towards her and feel myself weakening. My tired eyes brim and finally burst when I see Malory coming towards me. I take her in my arms and she takes me in hers and I cry and laugh at the same time.

"Oh, my god! I am so happy to see that you're safe!" She cries. "After the Compound was freed I wanted to find you, but I didn't have the time. Then the attack started and… I thought you might've—"

"I'm safe. I'm here," I pull back and look at her reddened eyes. "Everything is going to be okay."

I see someone move behind her. Malory's expression changes when my hands unintentionally hold her tighter. She turns and follows my eye.

"He's been doing good work here," she looks towards Marcus at a young girl's bedside.

"Everyone's seemed to have forgiven or forgotten. In fact, he's going to perform the Ceremony later. I think they just want to go back to normal."

Marcus exchanges words with a man with a red face and a bald head; he puts his face in his hands as the girl's slowly rising and falling chest stops moving.

"Normal is a long, long way off," I wipe my eyes and nose.

"What about you?" She turns back to me. "Are you hurt?"

"Bumps and bruises," I rotate my aching shoulder. "Nothing herbs and rest won't fix."

"You're just like your brother," she smiles and massages my shoulder. "Tough as an ox he is."

"Have you seen him recently?"

"Dale was here, haven't seen Junn anywhere. Probably off helping others before himself. He's going to get himself killed one day, mark my—"

She notices my expression and stops talking.

"That's the reason I'm looking for him." I say, slowly. "Junn and I got separated from the rest of our men during the fight and were attacked by the Bandit's champion. Junn, he… he died saving my life – all of our lives."

Malory staggers back from learning this dreadful truth, struggling to find words.

"How… where did he… oh, Viper. I'm so sorry."

"I have to find Dale. He deserves to know."

I take her hands and kiss them before I walk back through the infirmary doors. There is only one place Dale could be.

*

The front doors to Hector's Tavern hang broken on their hinges. The room inside is dark and unwelcoming. I walk up the small steps and come inside. The windows have been boarded up and all the wooden tables and chairs are stacked up against every conceivable entrance. Those people must have been terrified as they sheltered here. The floorboards creak and groan familiarly as I move farther inside, passed the barricades and scratched floor to the back where the kitchen is. I open the cellar door and see light at the bottom. I descend the stair that is mirror to the one back north, one that I have descended so many times before. Looking to my right, I see three stools, three mugs and Dale, sitting on the hard dirt floor with his arms over his knees; one of the mugs is in his hand.

I want to say something, but I cannot find the words – any words, for that matter. Instead, I sit on one of the stools situated around a barrel of ale. I reach for the mug and fill it under the tap.

Dale's clothes are smeared with ash and dried blood. The curtain of his dark blond hair conceals his face. He takes a long swig from his mug and throws it across the room, breaking it in two. I jump in my seat, startled at his sudden aggression.

"Why? Why does it always — *always* — have to be him?" Dale yells.

"What do you mean?"

"Don't pretend you haven't noticed!"

He looks up at me; I can see his face. His eyes are red and coarse with veins, his left cheek bears an awful, half-tended to laceration that stretches from his ear to his chin.

"He always takes all the glory for himself."

I am at a loss for words. Is he talking about Junn? How can he even say that? Does he even know what happened? How he sacrificed himself?

"First it was the caravan ambush. Now it's fighting the Bandits. That selfish, arrogant, no good—"

"Stop!" I shout. "Not one more word! How dare you sit here and wallow in self-pity when your brother – *our* brother was just killed."

"*Your* brother? Dale asks, incredulously. "If I'm not mistaken, he shares *my* blood, not yours. You're no brother of mine. The last of my kin died while you sat and watched."

"How could you possibly say that? If it wasn't for Tegan and Nalu, Junn would have never lasted for as long as he did! Let alone taken out that monster with him. If you were there, too, he might still be alive."

Dale shoots to his feet and sways like a tree in the wind.

"Don't pin his death on me! I was busy saving lives while you did nothing!"

"I did plenty—"

"You didn't do enough!" He takes a swing at me.

I sidestep easily and he fumbles to the ground, dust and cups scattering.

"You're drunk. Come find me when you've cleared your head."

"And what do you know of loss? Am I no longer allowed to drink away my grief?"

"I know plenty about loss," I look down at Dale's pitiful state. "More importantly, I know, just like Grimhild, that putting others before yourself is the true expression of love. Grimhild didn't know us very long, but he gave his life for his friends *and* us. And Junn is no exception. Of all people, you should know that. But, by all means, continue to drink yourself stupid. I'm sure that everyone will understand that you'd rather waste away than honor Junn's memory."

Dale's face turns beet red as he stands and searches for the words that match his sorrow. Staggering backwards, he bumps his back against the wall, and sinks back to the floor. He looks away from me and buries his head in his hands.

"Can't you understand the regret I feel?" He says, voice shaking. "There was nowhere that Junn went that I could not follow. Through the springtime meadows, across the mountains to swim in the ocean, over the entire map and back again. But now he has truly abandoned me. For the second time he has abandoned me and I wasn't even there when he left."

I kneel down in front of him.

Dale's shoulders heave as he cries into his hands. I hold onto his arm comfortingly for a long while until he is able to catch his breath.

"I'm sorry. I didn't mean what I said. I just…"

"I know."

I rise to walk out of the cellar.

"Hey," he says, sheepishly. "Tell me when it's time to kill Contil."

*

"At a time like this I would offer congratulations," Tegan's prevailing voice cuts over the discord in the Great Hall. He sits at the broad table in the rear, alongside the remaining members of the Black Flag. "But here is still much to do."

"We need to finish burying the dead!" A man calls out.

More voices echo him. I watch the assembly from the front door, leaning against the wide frame as the defenders and survivors, friends and families, try and put the pieces back together.

"I lost my wife and son in the battle," I recognize Hector's voice. "I will do no work until their spirits are laid to rest."

"And you have every right to do so," Tegan bellows. "But it is important to remember that the Bandits are still—"

"My family is dead, and you want us to…"

The crowd argues and shout to and at one another, crying out justifications for their pain and their want to display it. Their voices peak and loud banging from where Harlow stands brings the noise down.

"Enough! Quiet down!" She pounds the table again and slumps back in her seat. "Do we really have time for this? My heart is full of your pain. But I say let the mourners mourn and the widows weep, but let the fighters fight and repay this atrocity with swift vengeance."

"This is not an issue of battle, but of stability," Riston says. "We will deal with the matter of vengeance once the prevailing issues at our own doorstep are first put to rest. Sorrow has befallen this Compound and its people, and closure is in order."

"I spoke with Malory earlier today," I say from where I lean against the doorframe. "As is our tradition, we will hold the Ceremony of Starlight. Marcus will preside over the sacrament as a gesture of his devotion to those of us he has wronged."

"Does this satisfy you?" Harlow holds out her empty hands towards Hector.

I hear a low grumbling from a group of men where Hector stands.

"With that settled," Harlow resumes, "now we must contend with the matter of the Bandits."

"They're gone!" Someone says. *"Let them rot!"*

"As long as the Master lives," Tegan says, "the Bandits will always be a threat."

"I have an idea," I call out.

All eyes turn to me.

"Step forward and speak," Tegan announces.

The people split to form a path for me to the forefront of the assembly, swallowing that empty space when I pass by. My heart quickens despite myself. Be an example worth following…

"You have fought the Bandits more times than most, Viper," Tegan leans forward on the table. "What do you think we should do?"

"I was there at the breach when the Bandits broke through the walls led by their commander, Shalvok. You all saw how fast they fled after they saw their leader's head on a pike. If that works with the Bandits, then why shouldn't it work with Contil, their Master?"

Disquiet sweeps over the assembly. People ask in many voices who Contil is, where to even look for such a man, and so on.

"Everyone, settle down! Let Viper speak," Riston says over the troubled voices.

"The Black Flag believes that Contil commands the Bandits from the Western Compound…"

The people become restless once more at the mention of a third Compound in existence.

"Yes. There is a third Compound," Tegan arbitrates. "It was thought destroyed during the scourge of Tir Fwythland centuries ago. But, the Black Flag discovered that the Compound is not only intact, but is home to the Bandits' presence in Hyravon. I digress. Viper, please continue."

"From what Harlow told me a long time ago, Contil is a prideful man. We have not only once, but twice faced the lieutenants of the Bandit armies and won. Contil will not want to see us succeed a third time. His pride and proven strength will drive him to accept a challenger, or at the very least, his desire to fight a worthy adversary will give us an opportunity to have an audience with him. I will go and face him alone, both to end this war of ours, and to spare any more of you from experiencing the horrors of battle again."

Tegan looks from me and consults in hushed tones with those sitting around him at the table. The men and women around me whisper their distaste for more bloodshed, about being sick of being scared of the Bandits. After the deliberation, Tegan turns back to me with a slightly exasperated expression.

"As much as your plan goes against everything I believe to be reasonable and safe," he says, begrudgingly. "That may be the best plan we have. We will work out the details later. In the meantime, let us work to make things right here at home."

With that, Tegan stands and dismisses the people. Riston and Nalu rise with him and follow the crowd out through the doors. Harlow remains seated. She looks at me with troubled, maybe even fearful, steely grey eyes. I have never known Harlow to be afraid. Not when we were the Bandit's prisoners, not when we were outnumbered at Kandent. But the look in her eyes now terrifies me more than Shalvok's horrible veracity and even Contil's looming threat. If she is afraid, something bad is about to happen.

I wait in front of Harlow at the table as the last few people shuffle out of the Great Hall. As the last man steps out and closes the doors behind him, the cavernous room quiets except for the sound of Harlow shifting uncomfortably in her seat.

"So," I say. "Do you think we can do this? I mean, we've managed to come this far."

She turns her wandering eyes and looks into mine.

"You remembered what I said to you that night during your training, about Contil searching for an equal?"

"I would not have bothered to ask about him if I did not care to remember it," I say.

Harlow grows even grimmer.

"Then, I suspect that you also remember that no one that has ever faced Contil and lived. How do you think you will beat someone like that? Think about it. At every instance you came against an impossible opponent, you had help. I don't say that to scare or shame you, just to make certain that you understand what's at stake. You won't have an army at the Western Compound."

"I know what will happen if I fail," I approach the table. "And that's not true — me always having help. I fought an Alnnasi Batal in single combat and won."

"Yes, because you used Scorpion's Sting," she argues. "But you cannot keep throwing yourself into those situations and hope to god for a lucky outcome."

"Why are you so intent on worrying and second guessing? Besides, I still have this," I take out the phial she gave me during the battle. I set it down in front of her and the container's thick glass thumps solidly on the oak table. "I'm sure that Contil won't see this coming."

Harlow's fixes her stare upon the phial. She massages her forehead with her left hand, takes a deep breath, and lets it out slowly between her teeth.

"Are you not curious about where I got that phial?"

"I assumed that you made it yourself," I answer. "But, if you didn't make it, where did you get it?"

"I stole it," she says, flatly. "I've had that for a long time. Waiting for the right time to use it."

"Stole it from where?"

"Not from where," she corrects. "From whom."

I give her a confused look.

"What I am about to tell you can never – *never* – leave this room," she says in hushed tones. "Swear to me that you won't ever tell."

"I swear."

She shakes her head, unable to believe that she is about to disclose something so important.

"It used to belong to Contil. This is the secret behind his strength. Contil's Poison. It is the purest extract of a rare plant he calls Mother's Embrace. A name he gave to it in ironic cruelty. I've only seen its symptoms first-hand once. Poor man. Fell to the ground and started convulsing in a few seconds. Had his mouth open like he wanted to scream but nothing came out. The pain looked so incredibly horrible. I swear, he saw hell before he died."

"That sounds bad," I say. "But if this *is* Contil's Poison, then he's sure to have the antidote. So we'll have to—"

"I'm not finished," She interrupts. "Having a poison as lethal as this will not be enough to finish him off, which is why you need a weakness to exploit, something no one else but Contil would know about."

"You speak the obvious. But where and how are we going to get that kind of information?"

Harlow hesitates before answering.

"Do you remember everyone that belongs to the Black Flag?"

"Sure I do. But what does that have to do with—"

"Just answer the question."

"Alright. There's you, of course, Grimhild, Contil, Heabur, Vincent, Tegan, Nalu, Riston and Junn."

"And Amour."

"Well, yes. But Riston told me that she's been dead for years."

"He told you about her?" she raises an eyebrow. "Then he also probably mentioned his infatuation for her. How she was reckless, a good fighter, how she had a sharp tongue…" Harlow stands up and comes around the table. "…how good she was with concocting potions. How she didn't care what people thought about her, how her hair was so coppery red…"

My eyes widen and I inhale sharply.

"You're not saying that you're… that you—"

"I am," she says. "That woman who was part of the Black Flag in the beginning, the one that ran after Contil after the split — is me. I'm Amour."

I stagger back.

"If you are Amour, then why let everyone believe that you're dead?" I stammer. "Riston! How could he not recognize you? He should know that—"

"Have you already forgotten your vow?" She slaps her hand tight on my blabbering mouth. "A lot has happened between then and now and I've gone through great lengths to hide my true identity. He cannot know. No one can know. As far as the world is concerned, Amour is dead. If Contil discovered that I am still alive, he will come after us with every Bandit he's got."

I remove her hand.

"And why would he do that?"

"Because I am the only one that knows how to kill him."

CHAPTER 23

— The Ceremony of Starlight —

The late evening sun shines down over the scarred buildings and the bowed heads of the mourners as they make for the Square. Each man, woman and child holds a small, red paper lantern, keeping the long-held tradition of honoring our fallen, but never at this scale. This time, death and misery touched the lives of everyone, and they all gather in respect. There are no voices as we spill into the Square. Malory hobbles beside me, face grim and struggling to stay positive. She leans on my arm as we take our place amongst the shifting crowd.

Light begins to fade and the air turns cool. I look at all the sorry faces pressed around me, faces of men trying to stay strong for their families, faces of women that lost everything, and of children that do not seem to know what's happening. I was wrong. Back then about wanting them to know the truth about the Bandits, back before I understood that terrible truth myself. There is still time for them to have a fighting chance at a normal life.

"Do you know where…" Malory's voice trails off as she cranes her neck to look over the people's heads, an impossible task since her own is at chest-level.

"If he wanted to be here," I hold her tight, "then he would—"

"You lot talking about me?" Dale breaks through the crowd, holding a lantern carefully as if it might break at any moment.

Malory holds out her other hand to him and he takes it. We stand on her either side and for a long while we stand in silence. Someone begins to sob quietly. I notice Dale lean his head towards me. He looks ragged and drained, a bandage around the gash on his face, tanned skin almost glowing in the descent of the sun. He opens his mouth, but soon closes it. What is there to say at a time like this where nothing can ease the blow. Almost as if she heard my thoughts, Malory starts talking, more to herself than anyone else.

"…They might never know what he did for them," she whispers.

I see a family holding one another close. The little boy and adolescent girl safely housed between their parents' encircling arms.

"They might never know."

I look down at Malory, tears welling in her eyes and leaving clean streaks as they roll down her wrinkled skin.

"But we will," I muster a crooked smile. "Every laugh, every cry and broken heart, every time they pick themselves up… we'll know what was given for it."

She looks up at me with weary and sadness, but with a spark of hope and joy buried somewhere in her eyes.

"We'll know…"

She squeezes me as tight as she can.

Ahead, before the stair to the Great Hall, I see a man take his place in front of the crowd.

"Here we are, friends," Marcus speaks loud and strong, the bedrock we have been sorely missing for too long. "None of us have seen times as terrible as these, none of us spared from death's cold touch. But we will do as we have always done. It's time," he takes a red, paper lantern offered to him and he holds it respectfully; he clears his voice. "As we are about to send these spirits into your everlasting and accepting arms, we remember the shining light they were in our lives. They were extinguished too soon, but now they will lend their light to the heavens and will watch over us as we see them in the night sky."

I reach over and put my arm on Dale's shoulder. He no longer tries to hold anything back.

"So now, as the sun sets and the air is cold, our loved ones above shine bright as they welcome the number we add to their splendor."

I close my watery eyes and see Junn's face flash in the black. He smiles in the way he used to, the way that made you want to stick around him.

"The memory of their lives will never fade…"

Grimhild appears at Junn's shoulder, braided beard glossy clean, white teeth showing in his grin.

"…For they will be forever etched into the sky, secured in the heaven's tender care."

Countless more faces appear behind them and go into infinity. I open my eyes as Marcus raises the lit lantern above his head.

"The dead are not ever truly gone, the living will never forget, and we will meet again."

At this, people standing around the Square step forth and hold out open flames for those sending off their loved ones. One-by-one, the lanterns light and the Square illuminates with a soft, crimson glow. The multitude join together by their shared suffering, united in grief.

A man bearing a flame approaches us. Dale hesitates for a moment, our faces highlighted with the light of the lives we prepare to send away.

"We release them to you now and pray for their happiness unending and their lives without pain."

Marcus uncurls his fingers holding the lantern and lets it rise into the sky, carried by the smooth breeze. Slowly and each in their own time, the people release their families into the night like so many fireflies. I look away from the spectacle and see Dale still holding tight to Junn's little light. He lifts the lantern to eye-level and blows out the small flame. My eyes grow wide, mouth opening and closing, unable to articulate my surprise. Malory is as taken aback as I, for she let her lantern slip from her fingers where the wind casts it to drift amongst the others.

"Trust me," Dale says with a wink.

He starts to walk away, winding through the weeping and sobbing masses.

I share a look with Malory. What's he up to? With nothing left to do, we follow Dale away from the wake, through the rubble-strewn streets, and out of the Compound.

*

The air out here feels lighter as if the weight of our crushing grief was physically manifest within the walls. I look over my shoulder and see the last of the red lanterns leave their owner's care and float in a column of twinkling light against the pastel pink and purple onset of dusk. I return my attention to what's ahead. I support Malory walking beside me, weary from healing the injured. Her breath is labored, but she offers no complaint. Our walk through the rolling grasslands has a therapeutic effect on me and lightens the burden on my heart. It gives me a chance to think clearly and remember what led me to this moment, remember everyone who offered their help. I am so lost in contemplation that I almost do not realize how far from the Compound we ventured. Dale sloshes across the ford in the river snaking its way through the Resting Wood. I haven't visited here since… Is Dale taking us to…My sneaking suspicions solidify into hard fact when I lay my eyes upon the interlocking green, pink, and white boughs of my Family Tree.

"Dale," my voice sounds distant in my own ears. "What did—"

"Hush, now," he says. "You'll see in a moment."

I stop talking but my lips remain separated in silent disbelief. Dales takes us through the spattering of pine and evergreens, their scent tickling my nostrils, all the while I keep my focus on the Family Tree whose collective trunks I can now see is bathed in a warm glow.

Dale, Malory and I step past the last of the trees growing on the grassy hill and stand before a sight that will live on in both heart and memory until the day I die. Lanterns, similar to the ones used for the Ceremony of Starlight, hang from strings that run from ground to branch, highlighting the different shades of the magnolia, oak, and cherry trees bloomage. Dancing tongues of fire jump and leap from the shallow fire pit dug in the place where I last laid, before which is a wooden altar, stained a rich, dark brown. Harlow stands with her back to us beside the altar her hand resting beside a black, silky cloth concealing the shape of a man.

"What is… how did you…" I cannot find the words.

I've mentioned this place only to three people my entire life: Junn, Dale, and Malory, but Dale never once joined me when I used to ask him to visit. But he transformed it into this! My heart throbs in a confusion of searing joy, and deep, black sadness that keeps me in a strange place between weeping and shouting with elation.

"After you and I *talked* in Hector's Tavern," Dale says, "I needed to do something."

I gaze up and around at the simple beauty and overwhelming magnificence at Dale's gesture.

"You were right," Dale shifts in place, uncomfortably. "I was dishonoring his memory. So now, he'll be remembered."

Harlow does not turn from where she stands, but takes a few hard breaths through her nose, and says,

"I never would have taken you for the sentimental type."

She at last turns and faces us. Strands of her hair hang loose from their braids and fall in front of her glossy eyes, nose raw and red, skin partially drained of color.

"God, I'll… He will be sorely missed."

She steps away from the altar, but her hand lingers on its smooth and polished surface until the last of her fingers slide off.

"I thought," Dale looks down as he plays with his hands. "I thought that the table I was working on would be perfect for this."

"This is," I put both hands on his shoulders and wait until he looks up and meets my eye. "This is exactly what he deserves. Thank you, Dale."

He averts his gaze and his cheeks flush.

"It's nothing."

I look at Harlow while she is lost in the trance of the fire on the black silk.

"Did you know about this?"

"No," she says, sniffing loudly.

I approach her, my teacher, my mentor, and my friend.

"Besides myself, you might miss him the most," I pause for effect. "But don't worry. I'll keep your secret."

Harlow lets a smile pull at her lips and she laughs.

I stand in front of the altar, looking down at the rippling black sheet, and think about the man underneath. Malory lets go of my arm and comes to a quaking stop at Junn's head. Tears abound on her aged face as she stares longingly into the space where his eyes are hidden. She was his mother. From the time his real parents died, she was the one that watched he and Dale play, bicker, and grow. Grow into men of great deeds, both. She lost a part of herself. I look from her state of lament to the shape of Junn's body, then I feel a weight drop from the lump in my throat to the burning pits of my stomach, where the flames of my ambition burn wild and hot. Ambition to make sure none again feel the pain I feel, desire to drive the Bandits from Hyravon, and a base yearning for revenge. The flames in my chest swell, and from the fire blooms a featureless man and a name that rings like hammer on anvil: Contil.

*

The Black Flag do not sit at the broad table for lordly gatherings, but at a small round one off to the side, half-covered in shadow, each elbow-to-elbow with their neighbor. Tegan looks up as Dale and I enter the Great Hall, his face cast in the wavering light of a candle at the center of the table, a strand of his long black hair in front of his eyes. Dale, Harlow and I take the last three empty seats and settle into the group. I look around at those who have walked with me into hell and back. They, too, look at me and at one another, still bearing the scars of battle so freshly earned, red and scabbed trophies of a victory won through incredible odds.

Tegan takes a deep breath.

"My friends, we have come far, very far since we formed our organization. We used to be wanderers, outcasts. Now, we are brothers and our family has both suffered and prospered over the years. We have seen depravity hook its talons into the minds of our former companions and take them to a place where we could not follow; we have witnessed Grimhild, a well-loved and trusted man, fall for the sake of Junn only to see him, too, fall. And we have seen the waters of this life run red. Through pain and courage, I am sure we will see more hard sacrifice. But, we do not forget the accomplishments and heroism of the unpledged. Viper, Dale, you came to us with a simple request: to help save a life. A request we have since granted, though the credit is not solely ours to take. You were right there with us, both of you. You braved the sunless days and the harrowing nights alongside us, we who have walked this everlong and uncertain road for more days that I care to fathom, and have emerged entirely worthy."

Dale and I exchange quizzical looks.

"And, in our eyes," Tegan continues, "men and women of such an iron will and strength of heart that performs acts of heroism deserves recognition for them. I, on behalf of all present, would like to extend an invitation for you to officially become a part of our organization, to become a bearer of the Black Flag. What say you?"

"You honor me. I—"

"We accept," Dale blurts.

I shake my head at him. Dale looks back at me.

"What? You were going to take way too long to say the same thing. So, with that out of the way, what are we going to do about Contil?"

"Where would we be without you to keep us in line?" Tegan chuckles. "However, you are right. It is high time to discuss what shall be done."

"Viper and I spoke about this at length," Harlow states. "And we came up with an interesting plan. Viper?" She looks at me.

I nod my understanding.

"We did. And I think that the best way to get his attention is for me to travel to the western Compound alone."

"What, have you lost your mind?" Dale exclaims.

"If I go with an army, Contil will surely meet force with force. But if I go alone, he will have to meet on my terms."

"You would trust in the whims of a madman? A man that thinks himself a god?" Dale asks. "We should end this together. Fighting side-by-side."

"I would like nothing more than for that to be the way," I say. "But this is the best plan."

"Well, if you won't let us go with you inside," Dale says. "Then at the very least let us go with you on the road! We've come this far and now you want to just go off on your own?"

"I cannot," I say apologetically. "It has to be me that goes. No one else."

"And once you are inside, *alone,* what happens next?" Dale questions. "What stops Contil from killing you on the spot?"

"Nothing," I answer. "I trust in him that he will allow us to meet."

"You trust a man who slaughters innocent people?"

"I trust his ruthlessness and desire for power. Tegan, you heard Shalvok, how he praised Contil's strength. The Bandit himself was strong, but when Nalu severed his head, the hoard went running. The same will happen when the Master dies. And if I, a mere mortal human, challenge their god, he will have little choice but to accept. If he doesn't, he risks losing control."

"What about the real possibility that he kills you, dumbass?" Dale asks.

"If he wins, then it will only have been me that dies. But if I win, then we'll be rid of the Bandits for good. They believe that whoever swings hardest and longest is king, or in this case, a lunatic with a god-complex. Should I kill him, I will be their new king and I'll command them to return to the Northern Reaches."

"Your plan is bold, Viper. I've said it before," Tegan responds. "After everything that's happened I'd be a fool not to trust you. But this… relying on the religion of murders to grant you not only safe passage, but what sounds like ownership over the Bandits? Who would be the real fool?"

"You are right to doubt, but I see no other way that doesn't end in war. We haven't the man power to attack him outright and the people will not stand for us waiting idly by as we are put to the sword. No. It's this or nothing at all, and time is running out."

Dale and Tegan search for any possible alternatives, but eventually come up short.

"Very well," Tegan concedes. "May whatever you believe in watch over you. You all should get some sleep. It might be the last chance for it. It's a long road to the Western Compound."

Tegan tries to bolster us with a smile as we stand to depart, but it affects no change in our mood. We are too entrenched in our solidarity to see this to whatever end. I leave with Dale and we step back into the mild night. The mourners of the Cremony have left the Square and it stands silent and vacant. Vacant of the carts and stalls of peoples' goods or trades offered to one another, devoid of the sense of unification that presided over the countless interactions held here, at the heart of the Compound. The reconstruction process has the rubble from the attack in piles of both varying size and contents at the outer edge of this open place. The streets that were avenues to our fight for freedom, fought loud and hard as the resistance surged against Carver's Bandits, we now tread in silence. It is difficult to think or hope that things will completely return to normal, especially after the Bandits, the subject of every wives' tale and source of every nightmare, rampaged in the one place that was safe and sure. Dale and I come to a parting as we walk into our building. Dale goes down the hall to his room, and I to mine.

There is precious little chance that I will find rest tonight. I feel a weight on my mind that grows heavier each second I lie awake. It keeps my head pressed against my pillow and drives out all other thoughts. All that remains in the cool quiet is my restless body and the word that is the world on my shoulders: trust.

Harlow believes in me enough to trust me with this crucial plan. Tegan and Dale trust in my strength to see this plan through, the people trust in us to bring their vengeance to the Bandits. And all of them rely on me to see that their trust is not misplaced, wasted on a bright light that is soon to be snuffed out. My eyes slowly close as I drift off to the pleasant ambiance of chirping crickets.

CHAPTER 24

— A Long & Twisting Road —

The sun peeks out from the desert in the east and its light gradually rises from the floor to my bed where it falls onto my face. I uncurl my legs and arms into a full, rejuvenating stretch and look out at the small patch of blue sky from the window opposite of where I rest. I strip from yesterday's grime-stained clothes — which blackened the sheets — and put on fresh ones. I take my boots and slip them on. I turn and kneel in front of the little chest at the foot of my bed. I open it and first remove the under layer of the strong but light armor that Grimhild gifted to me. I hear his empowering voice in my head while I piece together the battle-gear's full set. I tie the last strap at my side and finally take from the chest my short, agile sword. Its polished steel shines glamorously in the daylight. As I slide it into its slick, dark brown sheath, I appreciate the work of Tao and his weapon smiths in their unquestionable ability to remove the gore and scars of war from the leather and metal. It looks as though it came straight from the forge this morning, not at all like the most cherished of my possessions: my small, silvered knife. It rests on the nightstand and does not rebound the light as brilliantly as it used to. I walk over and pick it up. The grip feels like home in my hand. I turn it over and inspect the details, thinking back to that day on the trek to Kandent, how Grimhild and the others told stories about how their weapons got their names, and how mine was nameless.

I remember how the blade flew through the air towards Junn, how it blazed in the fire like a piece of the inferno, a shard of light. Shard. I smile to myself at the name's simple beauty. I give Shard a flourish and insert the blade into its worn sheath at the small of my back. I walk the hall to Dale's room. I knock, enter, and see Dale stuffing things into an already crammed pack.

"I'm almost ready to go," he glances up from his hurried work. "Tegan said that it's a long way to the Western Compound, so I got you some extra things: whetstone, extra blanket, and more socks. Trust me, if there's one thing you'd wish you brought more of, it's socks. Can't tell you how many times my feet got frostbite because of wet socks. And the feel of 'em in your boots alone is enough to—"

"I'm not going with Tegan," I say.

"What's that?" Dale asks, not pausing.

"Tegan and the others want to accompany me through the Ironwood Forest, but I am going alone."

Now he stops and meets my eye.

"And why would you do that?"

"It's a little complicated."

"Marching off alone towards your own death seems a simple issue to me."

"Harlow is going to explain everything. For now, I need your help."

"You're somethin' else, you know that?" He looks at me with his dark brown eyes and shakes his head. "What do you need me to do?"

"Just keep Tegan and the others distracted 'til I get away. I think this time, I'll take a horse."

Dale smiles.

"Look at you, ready to conquer the world. Sure have come a long way."

"Just buy me an hour, tops."

"One thing before that," he reaches into his pocket and retrieves his special match-lighter. He holds it out for me, the smooth, dark wood has a sheen and its polished metal-plated corners show my distorted reflection. "You might need this."

"Oh, I can't," I splutter. "You should—"

"Shut up and take it. I'm trying to be nice."

I accept Dale's gift and try to think of something gracious to say.

"Now, don't get all soft with me," he chuckles. "Get goin' before we start sobbing like little girls."

*

Spring does wondrous things to the forest. It is one of life's smallest gifts, and one of my favorites. To see the sunshine lighting the green leaves, turning some gold, and falling to the grass-covered ground ignites a spark of joy in me and lightens the weight on my heart. The bark of the trees is a rich brown that will fade to grey come autumn, squirrels emerge from their hiding and chatter and leap in the treetops, shaking their emerald boughs. I look up at them as the hooves of my horse gently clip and clop on the hard-packed trail. I never could have imagined how much more pleasurable riding is to walking. So many times I've gone the length of the Ironwood on foot, and it's a cruel irony that this may be both the first and last time I'll have the luxury of a horse.

I uncurl the map Dale packed as I come to a fork in the trail. This is it. One path leads left, towards the Western Compound, and the other right, taking me north and away from trouble. I smile to myself as I think of Orbith's astute words. Trouble has no borders indeed. There's nowhere for me to escape even if I wanted to. Here is the moment of truth. I run the plan through my head over and over. It's going to work, it has to. Deep breath.

The moment I tread on the western road I feel a subtle change in the air, a shift in the wind, an alteration in the color of the trees, the quality of the soil beneath me. The horse doesn't seem to notice.

I shiver with cold as the light rain that has been falling since mid-afternoon falls more substantially while dusk settles over the Forest. Even though only two days have passed, I have already had to resort to following Dale's advice about the socks. Sticking weather. Just as the light disappears, so to does the lushness of spring, leaving the ground barren of grass that would otherwise buffer me from the pools of muddy water that the horse's pounding hooves occasionally sprays in my face. I can't go on like this for much longer unless I want to go mad, or freeze to death. I pull my drenched travel cloak higher around my head and hunch my shoulders, trying to pierce the sheets of rain for some kind of shelter for the night. I ride solemnly in and out of the spells of rain created by the dwindling trees around me, and then they, too, disappear. I come to a rocky outcropping and see a desolate, hilly land before me; I cannot see the road through gloom and rain. I encourage the horse forward.

"There's a good boy," I run my hand over his lean neck. "We'll find a place to rest soon. I hope."

The horse tosses its mane and flicks drops of rain all over. We wade through the field of rocks protruding from the empty ground, and as I am about to leave their sanctuary, I see a bright glow rising from behind a black boulder lighting a halo of rain around it. I tilt my head to shield my eyes. Who in the hell would be camped out in a place like this? Probably not unlike the reason I seek to do the same. Everyone wants to be dry. I veer towards the light. But what if it's one of Contil's Bandits, or Haebur or some other vile thing that's waiting for me? I reach under the folds of my cloak for the grip of Shard. I feel a small measure of safety with my fingers around the handle as I approach a very small and humble campsite with a tall, steepled tent, and a shallow — very wet — fire pit. I open my mouth to announce my arrival.

"Hello—"

"Ho there, stranger."

The voice cuts off my proclamation and sends a bolt of surprise shooting through me. I pull Shard from its sheath and glance towards the source and see a pair of black boots, slick and glossy in the rain, walking towards where I sit in the huddling light from the tent.

"There'll be no need to weapons, friend," the man holds up both hands, palms outward.

"Well met," I say, apprehensively, lowering the point of my knife. "I did not mean to scare you, I just wanted—"

"Scare?" The stranger lets out a bark of laughter. "I've not been scared for some long years."

He steps into the pool of feeble light and I see that he wears a green coat with its high collar pulled up to his ears, underneath I see the ringlets of chainmail glinting in the rain; the pommel of his sword peeks through the dark green fabric. He looks up at me and a smile touches his traveled face. His eyes are kind, but within them lingers a haunting air. This man has seen things.

"To what do I owe this very unexpected pleasure?"

"Well, I was looking for a place to wait out the weather," I return Shard to its sheath. "I'd hoped to find one amongst these rocks."

"Hope no longer, stranger," the man says. "There is space enough in my tent. What be your name?"

I separate my lips to answer, but quickly think better of it in case this man is not all what he appears; I see the man smile wider.

"Wise, that is. Let's become better acquainted, you and I, before we have the sharing of names. Come. You can stake your horse over there," he gestures towards a large rock behind the tent.

I dismount and lead the horse to the rock, feet splashing through sediment-filled water. The man ducks through the opening of the tent and invites me to follow. I oblige him and find the interior of the tent to be both spacious and dry, wonderfully warm and dry. A box of very strange design rests in the middle of the tent's floor. Veins and webs of silver and ruby course over its translucent surface, allowing the light and heat out into the tent. I continue to marvel at the object until at last I say,

"How is it that box makes such strong heat yet does not burn or smoke?"

The stranger removes his green coat and places it on a thin metal hanger beside the entrance. He turns his head over broad shoulders; a sigil of a rose is embossed on his back: bronze stem and thorns with silver petals.

"To answer that," he says, "you must know a great many things about the world. And I am afraid that neither of us can afford the time it would take to explain it."

"Then tell me, what is it that brings you out here?"

The stranger sits on a rough looking cot and gestures for me to take a seat on the stool next to the curious box.

"Duty," he replies.

I sit in silence and await his reply. When I realize none is forthcoming, I press on.

"What is the meaning of the sigil on your back?"

"Oh, this?" His left hand drifts over his right shoulder, towards the symbol. "It is the mark of a time long since passed. It is now recognized as the mark of a particular order of individuals to which I belong."

"The order that tasked you with your 'duty'?"

"Aye," he takes a good look at me, making me shift uncomfortably on the stool. His eyes soften and his eyebrows, met in concentration, relax. "You may call me Seeker, for that is the nature of my duty. Anything beyond that you must learn for yourself."

"And I am known as Viper," I say. "A pleasure to meet you."

"Curious name, that," Seeker ponders. "I once heard tell of a Viper from an old acquaintance of mine. A truly legendary warrior."

"I admit the name is somewhat unnatural. My brother gave it to me when he found me in a cave ten years ago, even though everyone wanted to leave me there."

Seeker's eyes widen. "Your brother, what was his name?"

I pause for a moment, wary of the eager glint in his eye. What's the worst thing that can happen?

"I have — had two brothers: Dale and Junn."

The spark of curiosity fades from Seeker's face, replaced with a shadow of despondency.

"Junn, he fell warding off the Bandit's attack on the Southern Compound."

"And that is what brings you to the edge of Hyravon," it is not a question, but a statement of fact. I nod my head regardless.

Seeker leans back and rubs the underside of his chin with his left thumb, deep in thought. I shift my gaze and look into the ornamented box close beside me on the tent floor. As I stare, I begin to see a writhing mass of white unidentifiable shapes that move in and out of vision. They claw their way to the surface and the box's orange and red rimmed edges and vanish as quickly as they appeared. What a strange thing.

Seeker sits forward and props his elbows on his knees, clasping his hands together.

"Junn was an honorable man, you have my sincerest condolences."

"You met him?"

"I did at that. Both myself and my order owe him much, though now he will never have the chance to hear our thanks."

"What did he do for you? I know very little of his life, sadly."

"I will tell you out of obligation towards your late brother, for what I am about to say has been a closely guarded secret for centuries. Though, I suspect that our secret is becoming more common knowledge of late. But, be that as it may, it does not decrease either the value or danger of knowing it. That box by your feet, it used to be something of a common occurrence. What resides in that box, the power that allows it to produce the heat you feel, the light you see, it is a power the people of the world once called magic."

I raise my eyebrows and feel my forehead line with wrinkles.

"Magic? Surely such a thing cannot exist—"

"For proof of its legitimacy, you only need to look down. The magic held within that box was harnessed from the molten earth itself. How I came to posses it is not your concern," Seeker quickly cuts off my unasked question. "All that you must know is that magic, a power thought to have been long, long gone, still abounds. One only needs to know where to look."

"Are there more like this box? Are you a spellcaster? Can you teach—"

Seeker holds up his hand.

"You misunderstand the nature of magic. But, as I already said, I have not the time to explain."

Magic. Who would have ever thought that it's real, let alone believe that I would stumble upon it completely out of the blue.

"Junn was instrumental in assisting my order to... reacquire this box. And through that aid, we have been able to make strides towards a better world," Seeker cups his hand around his ear, listening for the pitter-patter of rain. "However, there is much work to be done to reach that end. And I fear that you have much to do yourself. Revenge is a dark and twisting road, Viper. Ward yourself against it, lest you succumb to the lure of power."

This man knows more than he says, for how else would he know of my endeavor to exact my vengeance upon Contil can his Bandits?

Seeker rises to his feet and invites me to do the same. He graciously, but firmly, escorts me to the exit.

"I wish you the best of luck. I am sure that our paths will cross again in time."

I have so many questions left to ask. How is this the first time I am hearing about magic? What can it do, who can use it and how? How many other people know about magic and can they teach me more? But, as I have become used to, I am forced to shelve my queries as I trudge towards my horse. I slide my foot into the stirrups and jump onto the hard saddle. I turn to look at the tall tent, hoping for a last glimpse of Seeker, but no one is there. I do my best to rid my mind of my conversation, pitting all my focus on the task yet before me. But, as I begin to ride westward once again, I cannot shake the feeling that fate's hand led me here.

*

Light has come and gone on the fourth day and darkness is now complete. There are no more buds of flowers, no more towering trees, there is only sparse and resilient spindly trees, short grass and bushes that dare grow here, in the west of Hyravon. Nothing, not even the pale face of the moon witnesses my swift passage. As the long miles continue to drift by, I see the first real change in the terrain. I come upon a high ridge that was invisible in the dark until this moment. I ride past it and see a flat, barren expanse of land; layers of black sky and dark ground, each proceeding darker and darker towards an ominous sight. Red pinpricks of torchlight outline familiar high walls, behind which rises a slender tower. Wind from the south brushes the clouds away and unveils the moon, its light glinting off the metal spikes and barricades of the Western Compound. The mouth of the fortress glows menacingly from a small fire, attended by four guards, aloof in their secluded stronghold.

To plan for something like this is one thing, but to see it with your own eyes has a way of diminishing all the careful calculations to the ideas of a child. I look down from my steed at the Bandits, hoping that luck is still with me.

The wind shifts and my horse rears back its head, mane dancing as it snorts and stomps the ground. I spin around in the saddle, one hand clutching my sword. Then I hear them.

"Hold that light higher," a Bandit orders. "The tracks lead this way."

I look around for a place to hide, but this dead land offers very little. Through the shroud of night, I leap from the saddle and lead the horse off the trail, away from the approaching voices and their orange firelight.

"I say we turn back," a second Bandit says. "Master will never know."

"Disobedience is death," the first Bandits snarls. "This way."

The pair of voices are very close now. I see them emerge around the ridge as they search and peer into the darkness. The ring of light around their one torch is not strong enough to reach me, but the horse is still frantic. It whinnies in fear and the Bandits snap their focus onto the sound.

Shit.

"You 'eard that?"

"I hear nuffin' but the wind," says the Bandit with the torch.

The keen Bandit sniffs at the air and stands, leaning his eyes against the darkness for an eternity. My hand gripping my sword sweats with anticipation.

"Alright," he relaxes, "let's—"

My horse tosses its head and shrieks in fright, dashing away, deafening in the quiet.

The Bandits exclaim and watch the horse as it disappears into the night.

"Find the rider!" torch-Bandit orders. "He couldn't have gone far."

They split up. I stay still and flat as a stone against the ground, praying that their search is less than thorough. Fighting this close to the Bandits at the gate will surely draw their attention. I'd lose everything. I lay still as death and hold my breath. I hear their feet kick and scrape on the parched earth. Don't breathe.

A grizzly and guttural horn blasts its call into the mild air and the Bandits stop.

"Already?"

"Let's go," torch-Bandit says, voice sounding anxious.

They quickly retreat back towards the Compound. I take a breath. Stupid horse.

Crawling to my feet, I watch the Bandits return to the gate, wondering what called them. The pair reach the guards and come to a stop. The ordering Bandit with the torch waves his arms at the others, gives one of them a shove. The Bandit regains his footing and takes the offender by the shoulder and butts him in the head. The others gather around their fighting comrades and spectate as they shout and holler at the brawl. Eventually, one comes out victorious, the gate opens, and they drag the body of the defeated inside.

Well, didn't expect that. But, one less Bandit in the world only helps me. And that gives me an idea. But, I have to be very careful until I can get an audience with Contil.

I weave my way to the base of the Compound with a quickness and calculated precision, stopping only when one of the watchmen swivels his head in my direction. When I come against the wall, I can smell an overwhelmingly putrid stench. It seeps in the air and through the very stone that separates me from its origin. I try to shake my head free of the scent and the thought of what it must have taken to produce it. I walk along the wall towards the front and run my hands over it slowly. A few feet before I can see the Bandits around the corner I feel an irregularity. I stop and inspect it more closely. I feel letters etched into the cornerstone.straining my eyes in the dim light, I can make out the words carved in angled script.

To protect heart and home,

to shield you from the darkness.

To gather the peoples that roam,

to guard you from the heartless.

This must have been written by the Pau'larin when they built the Compounds all those years ago. How they would weep were they to bear witness to what has become of them. I remove my hand from the inscription and hear one of the Bandits speak.

"What do you think you're doin'?"

The whole of my body seizes.

"Get up! I'll be damned if I'm goin' to keep watch while you doze off!"

Something hits the wooden crate and the Bandit yelps as his comrade awakens him.

"It's not like we are goin' to see anything in this dark," says the lazy guard. "Even if we could, no one but us are wondering about."

I edge towards the corner and catch a glimpse of the scene in front of the gate. The resting Bandit stoops to retrieve his skeleton helmet while his enraged companion turns his back to him and resumes his scan of the onyx horizon, muttering insults. The other Bandit joins him as he puts on his helm and they stand staring in opposite directions.

I shoot my gaze to the ground underneath me and search for a rock large enough to fill my palm, useful little things. I soon find one and prime it to throw, waiting for the right moment. I flick my eyes from one guard to the other, where their heads are facing. I throw the rock passed the nearest Bandit and it lands in between them. They look towards the sound in unison, and as they point their weapons at it, I come sprinting around the corner. The farther Bandit reacts to my advance but he realizes too late. Before he can say the words of warning, I shove the nearer Bandit and run him through with the tip of his companion's spear that is raised in defense. The Bandit's body shoots down the length of the spear and gore paints the wooden shaft dark red. He rams into the wielder's body, causing him to teeter back and drop his weapon. He looks up and sees the point of Shard centered between his eyes. He freezes. We stand poised against one another for a breath before the Bandit reaches for something. I bring my knife around and drive it under his chin. His eyes go unfocused and he topples to the ground that greedily soaks up his blood.

I look down at their bodies and feel revulsion at the next part of my plan.

I am nauseated before my fingers even touch them. Kneeling down, I strip one Bandit of his bone armor, and try to keep my eyes averted. I don't want to look too closely and see they're human. Once I finish, I reassemble the armor onto myself. I bend and take the helmet and the spear from the corpse, shuddering as I look at the eye sockets; see, for a moment, a pair of green eyes looking back. I turn the helm around and pull it over my head, its interior warm and dank. If I'm going to pass for a crazed, bone-wearing cultist, then I have to do this right.

I drag the bodies out of sight, enter the gatehouse, and turn the winch so that the gate is barely open. I slip through that narrow space and slide inside the Compound. I now see the visceral practices of the Bandits laid bare before me.

My eyes follow trails of blood stained deeply into the earth that lead to mounds of bodies, piled high and low in widely dug pits all throughout the courtyard, their carcasses plucked and harvested of their bones for the Bandit's rituals; I can see through the layers of their rotting masses. Off to one side, where the bodies reach too high to pile any further, a lone Bandit reaches for a rope. It's attached to a vat hanging from a broad post that is driven into the ground next to the pit; the Bandit gives it a tug. The vat tips and from its brim spills a wave of black liquid that washes over the dead. The Bandit then takes from the post a torch and bends to touch its flame to the soaked bodies. There is a flash of blue and golden flames as an inferno devours the faceless multitudes. The Bandit departs to fulfill some other foul plot as black smoke curls from the depths of the pit and seeks to smother the moon in the sky. I look to where the Bandit is going and see blood-soaked wagons and handcarts, crafted in the Bandits' cruel fashion, stacked against the rim of the courtyard. Onward still I see the narrow tower, bathed in firelight, staring down on me like an observer of a gnat that is waiting to be swatted. Its black silhouette cuts a rift in the moon and renders down its malice onto the ground on which it is built. The tower splays its dominance wide and it spills into the surrounding architecture, molding and connecting the other buildings into a web. A path opens at the center and forms a trench that leads to a crooked stair, ending at a guarded, closed door.

It is then that I notice I am not alone. I dart my eyes to my left and see a tall, brawny Bandit looking at me. I jump in my skin and nearly turn away to escape before I remember that I am in disguise. He stares lazily at me for a second or two before he drifts his head aside and goes back to tugging and ripping splinters of bone from a disembodied arm. Without turning my head to look at him, I confidently walk by the Bandit and into the nightmare before me. While I was on the outside, the smell was bad. But in here? It is indescribable. As I pass ditch after ditch, pit after rotting pit, all filled with the dead, it is all I can do to just put one foot down in front of the other. The tangled nest of building lurking ahead of me makes the Western Compound feel smaller than the other two, for all around its radius the other structures that once existed are cleared and replaced with the pits and their scattered towers and thunderheads of black smoke. But from what I can see there is no more than a half-dozen Bandits roaming out here. I guess that most of them are inside the buildings, and as I get closer to them, I can hear muffled sounds of revelry. I peer in through the distorting glass and I see a horde of unarmored Bandits passing by one another. I continue to advance towards the door at the end of the trench ahead of me. Two Bandits stand guard, their hands resting on the hilt of their swords. As I come nearer the one on the right steps in front of the door and blocks it with his body while the other takes one step forward.

What do I say to get through? I can't say a word! The second I open my mouth they will realize that I'm not one of them. Too bad that I don't have the knowledge of magic that Seeker does.

Just twenty paces separate me from the door. I come up with an answer.

Closer and closer to the guards, the path I walk becomes increasingly narrow. Cracked and stained windows on either side show my reflection.

I am now ten steps from the guards, both of whom glare down on me with their weapons out and ready.

Five steps.

Suddenly, I feign my foot catching on a loose stair and I stumble forward. In my fall, I lunge with my spear and pierce the guard through the chest. The other guard blocking the door looks aghast from me to the bleeding sentinel. He opens his mouth, chest rising as he fills his lungs, but instead of sounds exiting his mouth, Shard enters it, burying deep into the back of his throat.

If Harlow had not been my teacher, I don't know how I would get by without knowing that the solution to most every problem is 'just kill it.'

I drag the bodies into a crevasse in the narrow corridor without a soul to witness. The way forward is clear. The door is right in front of me. I reach my hand out and pull it open. It glides on its hinges and a breath of sweet air washes over me. The contrast of the two aromas catches me off guard and I hesitate on the threshold before I enter the tower.

CHAPTER 25

— The Awakening —

The interior is wide and delicate, meticulously put together. Lavish tapestries depicting various scenes of conquest or celebration hang on the crisp, white brick walls, columns of dark marble hold up the vaulted, candlelit ceiling, and slender tables on either side of the open room, draped with violate silk, support polished gold and jade bowls that spill over the brim with vibrant apples and grapes. Embroidered carpets cover the flagstone floor and lead to a set of heavy, stained double doors; dark metal rings hang from each, and to either side rests a lit, gold and silver brazier. I silently creep towards the doors at the end of the room, my footsteps dampened by the carpeting, pausing as I pass the columns to make certain that I am alone. I step out from the last column and see a hallway on both the left and right of the large doors. I check them for anyone that may be lurking there. No one. But, I do notice that they lead from where I came. The ends of the passages are capped by doors are less extravagant than what I see around me. They must lead outside to the network of buildings, connecting them to this tower. I turn and face the large double doors and think. If these hallways are for the use of Bandits to come quickly in and out, then these giant doors must lead to somewhere important. I wonder if it has something to do with the horn I heard.

No sooner after finishing my thought when something slams in the room. I look around with a start, feeling adrenaline pump through my body.

Slam!

A second reverberating report shocks my nerves and then I finally realize that the side passages are being opened. I turn around and bolt for the concealment of the columns. Just as I take cover, I hear belligerent voices and their accompanying footsteps filing in. There is a deep and mechanical scrapping soon followed by labored huffs and grunts. I peek my head out and see the heavy doors opening. At first, I see nothing through the increasingly widening gap. I keep watch and am soon presented with the thing heaving the way open. The Bandit is gargantuan, larger than Shalvok and naked from the waist up except for his neck, where a circlet of skulls hangs. He wears blood red gauntlets on his hands. They come up to his elbows and end in a point that shines like a distant star. The Bandits flings the doors the rest of the way open with one large armored hand, his muscles straining against their weight. They thud on the end of their hinges and the gatekeeper stands to one side as droves of Bandits pour from the side passages into the opening. I duck behind cover and wait until I can no longer hear the procession marching through the tower. After some time the clamor dies down. I stick my head out once more and, in the mouth of the doorway, standing beside the gatekeeper, is Haebur. My chest swells with anger and hate. Harbur looks pleased and commands that the gatekeeper shut the doors.

Haebur departs and the gatekeeper brings the heavy doors to a close, one at a time.

I'll never be able to get in if they're shut!

Thinking quickly and looking around the room for something to stop the doors from closing, my eyes fall upon one of the many shiny, silver fruit bowls. I flit my eyes back to the gatekeeper. He already has one door locked in place, but I cannot move yet. If I do, he will see me. I have to wait until the second door conceals his face. I have to time this perfectly. The Bandit has the other door half closed and it hides him from view. I seize the moment and jump from behind the column in a flash, snatching the bowl from a table, and slide it into that slender opening with only a few inches of space remaining. The door closes on the bowl and twists the fine artisanship. I huddle down tight against the wall and pray that he did not notice, waiting for something to happen. The bowl rattles in the marginal space as the gatekeeper attempts to close the door fully. I prepare myself for the worst. Suddenly, the rattling stops as a voice calls out from behind the door. I hear a blunt, metallic thud as the door ring falls back into place on the other side, then, silence.

I exhale. That was close.

I steadily rise to my feet and face the doors. I clamp both hands around the door ring, plant my feet strong, and pull back as hard as I can. Slowly but surely, the door inches open. I slip through the space and seal the way closed behind me. There is a faint glow reflecting on the door. I turn around and see a circular, wide open room; low-burning lanterns are along its walls, and their light disappears in the dark recess of a spiraling stair in the middle of the room, winding up the tower and down below. I approach the brink of the stairs and gaze down. From the bottom of the steps wrapping around the circular walls comes forth a smoldering glow; I see the gatekeeper's figure peak in and out of view as he descends. Now and again, as I peer into the dark, I see shadows flicker and I hear a low rumble that grows more substantial each moment I give to the depths. I turn my head away and look up the height of the tower. I look back down and shake my head. I dread to think of what may be happening down there.

I descend the long stair. My footsteps scrape faintly on the filthy path, and the air becomes hot and thick. As I come closer to the base, the rumbling transforms into a coherent chant, uttered by myriad voices. I make it to the last step and come upon a wide arch that opens to a vast chamber. Empty cells and cages are on the fringes of the space with long hooks and pikes leaning against them or hanging from racks. Bandits of every size and brand of evil gather in the center, where the floor disappears, replaced with the glowing light. Some Bandits stand above the fodder, adorned with their grotesque outfits: helms of human skulls affixed with horns, cuirasses of fused plates of bone, dotted with patches of decaying flesh. The silhouettes of the assembled Bandits burn bright in the light from down there. I cannot see from where I stand at the entrance, but as I watch, their chanting reaches a climax and they shout a name: Merr'tyura.

A single, unfamiliar voice dominates the chamber.

"Merr'tyura, look upon us, your faithfully devoted, and show yourself to us! Gaze down and witness our gifts as we give them gladly to you, you who is wise and powerful above all!"

I can't see what's happening… I need a better view.

The voice continues to shout powerfully as I creep amongst the shadows towards the cages.

"But those have been the least of our offerings, for we have reclaimed your lost son! The living god, Merr'putra! Ended are his days of wandering and long nights of solitude, for he stands before you now!"

I climb onto a tall, metal cage with thick, black bars; spikes on the outside point inward. I look across the room and down. I can now see the place in the floor from which the light emanates is gouged out and tiered, creating five levels for the teeming Bandit spectators. I see them shouting and reveling in whatever ceremony is taking place. I look over the countless Bandits, the gruesomely, fantastically adorned commanders and chieftains, the foot soldiers and their nightmarish armor, all the way to the bottom where I see three men standing. One wears a cloak and I cannot distinguish his features. I instantly recognize Haebur. He stands between the other two around the fire, of what I now realize are burning bodies. One of the men still speaks and fills the air with his practiced words. He is of small build and his black hair is pulled back into a tight ponytail. He energizes the Bandits with broad gestures from his toned arms and silver words. Haebur steps forward and speaks.

"By the will of Merr'tyura and through much hardship, Vincent and I," he gestures to the black-haired man, "have found Merr'putra! Though, he is not before you in his own, physical form, he occupies the body of your most faithful disciple: Contil"

Haebur and Vincent then turn to recognize the third and tallest among them. He steps forward to stand in front of Haebur and Vincent as he uncovers his face. The hood falls away and reveals long, grey hair that falls over his broad shoulders like a sheet of iron. His face is strong and emotionless as he surveys his followers with emerald eyes.

He looks up and stares right at me.

A shudder quakes my body and I scramble from the top of the cage and crouch behind an upturned table. I barely breathe.

The chamber seems to fall into utter silence. My heart threatens to burst; a cold, mesmerizing voice slithers through the air into my ears.

"You can come out. I won't hurt you," it says after it silences the Bandits. "I must say, I am impressed that you were able to infiltrate this place. It is a remarkable feat. I wonder how you did it. Climbed the walls? Crawled your way in? Killed my guards and disguise yourself as a Kleph? I know you have been eavesdropping. Why don't you step out from behind that table and join us?"

How could he possibly know?! He must have found the bodies or guessed!

I stare frozen at the hard-packed earthen floor, unable to decide what to do.

I did find Contil, but fighting him in front of a hoard of Bandits is not the best-case scenario. Harlow would say to run, but what choice do I have?

I stand up, come to the edge of the pit, and look down at the assembly as they all stare right back at me.

"Wonderful," Contil opens his arms slightly. "Since you have very obviously gone through great lengths to be here, I presume that you are aware of who I am? Of course you do. Come down so that we may speak more candidly. I yearn to finally make your acquaintance."

The gathered Bandits murmur and become restless. Vincent whispers something to Contil, but he silences him with a gesture; Contil's cold glare does not break away from me.

I remain stationary on the brink of the pit, grappling with the uncertainty of my predicament. If my plan has any chance to work, I have to play along with Contil's demands.

At last, I conquer my nerves and I descend into the pit. I near the five tiers and the Bandits filling them that remain an obstacle to me. I come closer to them, but they do not make way for me. It is only when I feel the heat of their breath do they step to one side on the first tier.

"As fate would have it, you come to us at a very precise moment," Contil resumes. "As you have overheard, the god Merr'tyura is on the verge of being reunited with her long lost son. Long have her devout children been in search of him. And now, all of their toil and sacrifice will be rewarded…"

Second tier.

"…Yet, despite all the efforts of her faithful servants, there remains but one hurdle to our path: the awakening of Merr'putra…"

Third tier.

Vincent attempts to speak secretly to Contil once again, but he answers him with ire and strikes him into silence; he looks back to me.

Fourth tier.

"…Merr'tyura only accepts living offerings. So, it is only fitting that the blood that revives her son be of the finest quality, a requirement I previously filled by one with whom you are very familiar, Junn. It is a shame that he met his end fighting my lieutenant. Though fortune smiles upon me still, for it appears that there is another that is as worthy a sacrifice as he. And Merr'tyura has chosen that lamb herself…"

Fifth tier.

I stand on the bottom circle of the pit, face-to-face with the man responsible for the deaths of families, of livelihoods, of brothers.

"…She has chosen you."

The Bandits roar and bellow, so desperate to please their god. Contil settles them with an outstretched hand.

"You have saved me the trouble of seeking you out myself, and for that, you have my eternal gratitude. In that vein, I bid you to speak! Tell us, why are you here?"

Contil sneers, his green eyes daring me to answer. Vincent scowls at me and keeps a hand on the grip of his sword that hangs at his side. Haebur is behind them by the fire with his arms folded across his chest; his polished metal armor glints with every slight movement. I look Contil dead in the eye.

"I've come for revenge."

Vincent and Haebur's eyes snap to the sword at my side and draw their own. Haebur takes a step towards me, but Contil stops him with a word.

"Wait. I'd like to hear what this boy has to say."

Haebur looks at me and his nostrils flare from being denied the chance to put down the intruder. He lowers his one-handed battle-axe to rest at his side; Vincent sheaths his sword. Contil looks at me and cocks his head, his stare never losing its hold on me.

"You have come to kill me, have you?" he asks. "Well, here I am! Go ahead!"

There is a pause. Contil and his henchmen stand in front of the fire, and the Bandits are disquieted.

"Before that, I have a proposition…"

What are you doing? Do you honestly think you have a chance?

"…Take your Bandits and never show yourself here again."

Haebur and Vincent burst out laughing.

"You have surely gone leave of your senses!" Vincent hollers. "Who do you think you are to give orders to Merr'putra's vessel? We will not simply back away! My lord, allow me to strike down this insolent creature!"

"No."

Vincent hesitates and glances over at his master's stone cast face.

"If it is his desire to fight, then so be it. Long have I been separated from the real work."

Contil takes his hand and undoes the crimson clasps of his cloak, allowing it to fall and pile at his feet, revealing a long, slender sword that hangs from his engraved belt. He curls his fingers around its grip and removes it from its black scabbard, the steel rings as it is drawn. Vincent and Haebur step out of the pit, leaving me alone. Contil glares at me as the flames dance in his eyes. I take Shard from my belt in one hand and my short sword with the other, my entire body tenses. Contil steps forward, his weapon relaxed at his side; I move back.

"You come this far to recoil from me?" Contil mocks as we circle the fire. "I know all about your 'adventures,' Viper. How you and that band of mercenaries stormed my fortress in the north, how you have slain my lieutenants and saved your people time and time again. It is admirable how your heart aches for them. The world does need more men such as yourself to balance the chaos. However, the world, in equal measure, beacons to men with a greater purpose than those who derive fulfillment from acts of compassion. You see, what I have achieved here is the fruits of years of labor. I built this sanctum to Merr'tyura and opened a channel through which her followers can communicate; an olive branch extended to the lost, wandering souls to find new purpose. Because, in the end, is that not what all life ultimately seeks? To strive towards a goal greater than themselves? I have seen lost souls come to that light, wholly believing that their calling lies within the selfish satisfaction that is accompanied by giving. But the irony of light is that it blinds you. Darkness on the other hand, darkness allows you to see the truth. And I have led these beings towards that truth, that acting in one's own self-interest begets naught but the scattering of unity. Had I not stepped into their chaos, the Bandits would still be drifting in the Northern Reaches, thoughtlessly slaying one another in endless competition, never realizing the full scope of their potential."

"You know nothing of unity!" I continue to circle the fire. "If you did, then you would never have left the Black Flag, never turned on the ones that put their trust in you! You conjure your false principles of unity like a trickster's smoke, here for one moment and gone the next. I wonder how long it will take your followers to realize that your fabricated sense of brotherhood can be erased with the softest breath."

Contil laughs. His echoes reverberate in my head.

"And you believe yourself to be this breath? You are arrogant indeed if you think that your mere presence here and small words will be enough to shake their faith."

"No. All that I need to do is prove that you are a fraud and the Bandits will take care of the rest."

Contil stops pacing.

"When they see you for the snake that you are and realize that their god is a sham, they will lose whatever it is that keeps them inline and you will have more than just me to worry about."

Contil looks at me through the fire's floating embers with his penetrating green eyes; wisps of his iron hair squirm on the heatwaves. I plant my feet and redouble my hold on the grip of my knife. The ring of the enclosed pit and the Bandits slowly fall away until there is nothing left but Contil myself, and the fire between us. It all comes down to this. The planning, the killing, the loss, everything rides on the outcome of this—

Contil's sword rips through the flames in a flash of movement, slashing at me through the smoke. I bring up Shard and parry the attack. He is stronger than I anticipated and I almost allow my knife to slip from my grasp. The clashing of our blades cuts through my trance and brings my surroundings crashing back down around me. Contil scrapes his sword down across my own and flicks it aside. He raises it again to attack in one fluid motion, but I react and counter with my off-hand short sword.

Contil's face of stone breaks and shows wild ferocity as he spins around faster than I can blink. He drives his boot into my chest and sends me sprawling on my back. He looks down on me in the dirt, reveling in the pleasure of combat. He stabs down; I roll out of the way and spring back to my feet. He lashes out again and gives no quarter. I am on the defense as Contil probes my guard for an opening. I swat away his sword only to have it attack from a new angle, and with each successful guard, I find the next more difficult to execute. Is he getting faster?

Contil flurries me with a series of flashing strokes and pummels my short sword out of my hand where it falls to the dirt. Contil kicks it away as he moves in. I cry out and lunge at him with Shard, raising the blade to his heart. Contil laughs, flicks his weapon up and effortlessly deflects my attack, stepping to one side as I stumble by him. I look up and see his raised fist before it smashes against my face. Stars flash before my eyes and I once more find myself on the ground.

I feel something small and hard press against my breast: Harlow's phial of poison. Contil's boots shuffle in the dirt.

"I expected more from the one that has been such a thorn in my side," Contil gloats, brushing hair from his face. "It is a wonder how you made it this far, leaning so heavily on poor swordsmanship and sheer luck…"

I shift my body and carefully reach for the phial.

"Some credit must go to your friends, of course. After all, *they* were the ones that killed my lieutenants. And it comes to no surprise that they learned from my example after leading them to so many victories. It's a disgrace that none of that knowledge was passed to you…"

I claw and scrape at the phial towards my hand.

"I am afraid that it never will. Here is where your luck runs out."

I lift my eyes to look for Shard. I see it lying next to me, just out of reach. I need more time.

"There's just one thing that I don't understand," I roll to my back, closer to Shard. "How were you able to unite the Bandits? I've heard the tales about the savages in the north. How did one man bring together all of their tribes under one leader?"

Contil looks down on me. He is recovered from the thrill of fighting and resumes his face of stone.

"Such things are irrelevant to the dead."

"Then it should be of no consequence to speak of it."

Contil's eyebrows raise slightly. I inch over to Shard.

"You are tenacious, boy. Very well, I shall humor you before your end. As you so elegantly put it, the tribes in the Northern Reaches were in a state of anarchy, constantly locked in conflict with one another, each tribe claiming to be the one true herald of Merr'tyura. I simply managed and controlled that chaos, reshaping and bending it to make them realize that they fight for the same goal; that the blood spilt in civil war could be put to a better use. You see the results surrounding you."

I glance about the pit as Contil idly paces, a predator circling its prey; my knife is almost in reach.

"And they just blindly accepted you? How many did you have to murder before they saw things your way?"

"I saw them as a horseman sees a field of flowers. I could have trampled them underfoot. But, instead, I nourished them and allowed them to grow and spread; brought them to the realization that, together, they stood to be much more than mere tribes at war. They could be this!" he gestures to his bloodthirsty audience.

I stretch out my hand, take Shard, and tilt the phial behind my back to coat the blade with poison. Contil notices me and brings his sword level with my throat. I freeze with the container of swirling liquid poised over my blade. I feel wet soil. I hope I aimed right.

"What do we have here? He says. "One last-ditch effort to save yourself?"

He reaches down and takes the phial from me. There is a pause as Contil's persona goes from reserved superiority to surprise… anger from finding himself in the unknown. He turns to me.

"Where did you get this?" He asks, coldly.

"I found it."

Contil takes my collar and brings me up to meet his fist.

"Where did you get this!"

I fall back to the ground and spit blood.

"I… found it. Maybe you should keep better care of your things."

Contil bends down, his eyes cut through me.

"I so detest repeating myself. I'll give you one last chance to answer."

I look from Contil's stare over to Shard laying at my feet. There is no hope of me reaching it before Contil reacts. I have no choice. I meet Contil's gaze.

"Amour gave it to me."

Contil straightens up.

"How do you know that name?"

"What, for all your knowledge of my travels you don't know the answer?

Contil's face contorts with rage. He swings his foot into my side and knocks the wind out of me. I roll towards Shard and conceal it with my body.

"Amour is dead!" Contil roars. "Tell me where did you get this phial!"

"If I didn't know better," I wheeze, "then I'd say you're scared."

Contil cries out in fury and kicks me a second time, and a third.

"Haebur!"

"Yes, my lord?" Haebur answers.

"Take our guest to the annex."

I see the blur of Haebur's silhouette against the fire light as he follows his orders. I feel him grab my arms and drag me to the edge of the pit. He calls for Vincent to help. The last thing I feel, besides my head swimming, is the hard shape of Shard tucked into my boot.

CHAPTER 26

— Bad Luck —

The Bandits' chanting no longer fills the silence, the glow and heat of the fire in the pit is gone, replaced by the lavender haze of dawn. It filters down on me through a high window as I wake on a cold stone floor, removed of my Bandit disguise; I can feel the dried blood on my face crack as I sit up. I look around and discover that I am in a small room whose only way in or out is through a heavy, solid door. I stand, wincing when my legs take my weight upon them. I come towards the small window at the rear of the room. It is just above my head when I stand underneath it, but, on the tips of my toes, I am able to field a look outside, and it is then that I hear a familiar tune of rushing water. I gaze out and see the incandescence of the impending sunrise that will soon shed its light over the barren landscape, though the black husk of what once was the Western Compound corrupts its potential majesty. I turn south and see, far off and away, the snaking ribbon of the Nadi river, running from its frozen origins at Lake Winterpool. Its surface in the predawn is deep indigo and is in complement with the shadowed terrain over which it flows. I cannot guess where it ends, but on its course there, it seems to flow very near at hand if not directly underneath. The sound harkens back to that dreaded fortress in ice and snow and Junn's broken figure. A shudder runs through me; Grimhild's kind smile and infectious laughter imprint themselves in my mind's eye for a brief, peaceful moment. What would he do in my position? He probably would not have been stupid enough to find himself like this in the first place. I slump back to the floor and close my eyes, thinking about happier times spent with drink in companionship under roof or heavenly sentry.

I hear something on the other side of the door. There are no voices, only the shuffling of feet and a groaning as something hard scrapes over the floor. The bustling ceases and there comes a metallic sliding and a deep, hollow click as my jailor unlocks the door. It creaks open and reveals Haebur standing with two burly Bandits, each of whom are adorned with bones pierced through the skin of their brows, arms and noses. Haebur orders them to seize me, a direction they take to with gusto. With one at either side, the Bandits take me by the arm and yank me to my feet. My head swims and vision blurs from lack of food or drink. They drag me out of the cell, passed a grinning Haebur, and into a wide, circular room with similarly small windows cut into the walls at regular intervals. The light, stifled as it is, surrenders enough to my eyes to allow me to see a thick and sturdy wooden chair situated in the middle of the room, stained with what I can only guess is blood. Behind that sits a long, thin table, topped with objects of undecidable purpose. The Bandits take me to the chair and shove me down on it, using thick leather straps on the arms and legs to hold me in place. From an unseen recess of the room comes the sound of an opening door through which I count two more people. I see Haebur bow his head to the newcomers. I turn slightly to the left and see that the person to which Haebur gives reverence is Contil, followed in close proximity by Vincent. Vincent moves aside and joins Haebur. Contil stops before me, head held high in victory, exuding malice. He stoops low in front of me. I can count the dark grey stubble on his chin as he speaks.

"Were the amenities of your cell to your liking?" He mocks. "I find that a minimalistic approach to a place such as this has a certain effect on its occupants, wouldn't you agree?"

I do not respond. Contil's eyes flick from one of mine to the other.

"Well, in any event," he straightens and steps back, "I hope that now we might have a proper dialogue about something you mentioned yesternight."

Contil turns and steps towards the table. Haebur picks something off its surface and hands it to his master.

"You say that Amour lives, yet you share not her whereabouts, nor do you speak of how you were able to find that phial. The time for silence has passed. You will tell me what I want to know."

Contil turns back around, holding a gruesome device in his hand. It is some kind of glove, yet is something else entirely. Instead of fingers, the glove has long, thin spindles of metal adjoined to the hand, the leather of which cracks as the metal moves and clinks together. He hands it over to Vincent who, with eager cruelty, forces the device onto my fighting hand.

"Whether or not you give that information freely is up to you. Just know that whatever you decide, this will not be pleasant."

The stiff leather is rough and cold and forces my hand rigid; the metal is corkscrewed and the top ends are flat. One by one, Contil adjusts the spindles until their inward-facing points stop just shy of my fingertips. Contil's eyes search me for weakness with his hand on the spindle over my little finger. I offer none. Then, with each word, Contil turns the spindle until the metal burrows into my flesh.

"Where is Amour?

I cry out in pain. The sharp point of the spindle pierces my finger like a needle through a sheet of paper. I feel a hot trickle of blood issuing. And again, Contil speaks and turns the spindle, this time over a new finger.

"How did you get this phial?"

The anguish is unlike any I have felt or dreamt of. I can feel the spindle scraping and gouging the bone as it pierces my finger. It drives away any thought of reason and makes me writhe and convulse against my constraints. Vincent and Haebur sneer in the face of my agony. Contil continues to interrogate and torture me, each question instantly followed by the tightening of a spindle, and when all my fingers are spent, he drives them deeper and deeper passed the second joint and almost down to the knuckle. Crimson flows freely down the wooden chair and pools around its legs. Contil lets go of the glove and steps back, fury evident in his emerald eyes.

"You surprise me, Viper. Weak and pathetic though you are, you show resolve. You have gained my respect."

"If I came in search of your respect," I snap through gritted teeth, "then I'd have betrayed my friends long before this. Your respect means less to me than a worm in the dirt."

Something deep inside Contil snaps. A smile breaks across his face and he barks a humorless laugh. The smile vanishes. He raises his closed fist, strikes me in the face and stomach, the force of the blows rocks my head back and sends the chair with it. We both tumble to the hard, blood-covered floor. The back of my head smacks against the stone and for a moment, the shock of the impact blinds me. I hear footsteps approach. Vincent and Haebur raise me from the floor and stand on either side. Contil wipes blood from his knuckles.

"When I learned that the people of the Compound had staved off my assault, do you know what I felt? Not anger at losing to a bunch of grimy peasants, not regret having lost Shalvok. No. What I felt in that moment was pride. When word reached me, the news was not only about the defeat of my army, but also of the defeat of the defenders' leaders. Tell me, Viper, how much did you weep when Shalvok put down your brother like a rabid dog? Did that sting? Does it make all the effort it took to rescue him seem worthless? I have heard tales of his heroism, but stories oft fall short of reality. It is a shame that he'll never have the chance to prove me wrong."

"It's bad luck to speak ill of the dead," I grimace. "But, I don't suppose that you believe in that sort of thing."

Vincent, standing closely to my right, bursts out in laughter.

"What need of luck does a god have when he creates his own at a whim? No such luck did we need when we put your pathetic people to the sword!"

I shift in the chair and head-butt him in the stomach, knocking the air from his lungs. Vincent staggers and goes to retaliate, but Contil's raised hand stops him. Vincent's face contorts with rage as he turns to his master.

"Please, allow me to deal retribution! This cannot stand!"

Contil shoots Vincent a menacing look and he shies away.

"That's right," I ridicule. "That's a good boy."

Vincent reluctantly steps back, vehemently cursing me as he obliges to Contil's command.

"Do not try his patience again," Contil says. "I would be loathe to keep pleasure from him a second time."

Haebur walks over to the table and picks up another instrument of torture. "This should break him if it doesn't kill him first."

"No," Contil says without turning to look. "I still intend to offer him to Merr'tyura. And for that he needs to be whole. But, before that, I will get him to talk. If you will not do it for yourself, then perhaps you will for another. Haebur," he asks, "what was the name of the third brother?"

"Dale," he smiles.

"Yes. Dale. I am sure that the Compound will not be able to defeat my Bandits a second time. Find him."

Haebur bows and goes to leave, but before he can, the master calls his dog to heel.

"One more thing: take this urchin with you. I want him to watch as the bodies burn."

"Animal! Monster!" I shout. "Don't hurt them! They have nothing to do with this!"

"I am afraid that my mind has been made," Contil says. "Bandage his wound. It is not yet his time to die."

Haebur approaches me, and slowly and deliberately unscrews the spindles from my bleeding hand and crudely wraps it with coarse gauze. He removes the straps on my wrists and legs, and calls for the Bandits. They step from the shadows, pick me up and drag me to the door. I become faint from blood loss and hammering pain as I am taken from the torture chamber and through a dark, narrow hall, soon ending at a studded door. Vincent swings the door open and they bring me into a well-decorated room. The flagstone floor is laden with red carpets with gold frills on their borders, dampening our steps. Polished suits of armor stand sentinel in alcoves in intervals against the grey walls, occasionally broken by tall, stained windows. They bring me to the gate, a massive set of iron-reinforced double doors with a heavy plank barred across them. The Bandits hurry forward and open the way. From the steadily widening rift comes forth a draft of cold, dry air, imbued with the scent of water. They take me through the gate, their footsteps falling heavy on the stone bridge that provides safe passage over the river, coming ever nearer to the Western Compound. My head swims and I become nauseated from the careless escort and I shut my eyes.

In the space between their closing and reopening, I am transported from the bridge to a darkened room. A stifling air hangs about the place, seeming to draw the breath out of my mouth while the pungent scent of manure assails my nostrils. I must be in the stables, a thought no sooner had than proven true when I hear a restless neigh come from the shadows. The Bandits discard me, let go to fall on the filthy, hard packed dirt floor, strewn about with hay. Vincent and Haebur make ready their mounts. They return holding the reigns of their horses in tow. Large and beautiful they are to behold in such close proximity, their sleek black and grey coats glisten as they catch faint light.

Haebur gives an order to the Bandits and they hoist me up into the saddle of the nearer horse. My maimed hand smacks against the hard saddle and I grit my teeth. Vincent mounts in front of me and looks to Haebur whose red beard is back-lit by the light coming in from the opening down the length of the stable. He returns Vincent's look and nods sharply. Then and at once they whip their steeds into a gallop and speed off towards the unsuspecting Southern Compound.

The strong light of mid-morning splashes on my face and the wind whips through my hair, each hoof pounding against the earth sends pain down my right arm to the tips of my mutilated fingers. We make it no farther than the ridge a quarter mile from the Western Compound when Vincent's horse rears up and kicks at the air as its startled voice calls out in surprise. Neither Vincent nor I can hold on to the frightened beast and we fall backwards to the ground. The horse turns and bolts away. I see the cause of its alarm. Ahead on the road, laying still as death, is the second horse and Haebur's body pinned underneath; a white-feathered arrow juts out from the breast of the horse and the neck of its rider. Vincent scrambles to his feet and draws his sword, shouting at our attacker.

"Come out of the shadows! Come out and let us fight like men! Allow me to introduce you to my blade so that you might slake its thirst for bl—"

An arrow hisses and Vincent's taunting cuts short, replaced with a gurgling gasp for air. I see his body collapse and lay still. A panic wells up inside my heart. I'm next. I struggle to lift my head, to get up and run or fight, but all the strength I can summon is only enough to slightly lift my torso. I lay on my back, helpless to do anything about it. Then, all of a sudden, I remember. All the pain and desperation of the last several hours forced the plan from my mind. The sun shines down in my eyes, the fiery orb nearing its full and strongest. I would shield my eyes were it not for my momentary paralysis. A black figure appears and stands above me, holding a long bar in its hand. I stare up at the silhouette. It speaks.

"*'Face me like a man,'*" the voice mocks, a woman's voice. "I hate how they always assume I'm a man. '*Introduce you to my blade*' my ass! Look who's lying dead and whose left standing!" She walks closer to me and kneels down. Her body blocks the sun and allows me to see her face. A good fighter with a sharp tongue, her hair coppery red… Harlow.

My mouth can hardly form the words my heart yearns to say.

"Hey," Harlow turns to face someone out of my vision. "Come over here. This is no Bandit."

Moments later, a second black shape runs over and stands above me. This time I do not even need to hear his voice to recognize that Dale is here, too. Almost immediately, Dale exclaims at the sight of my wreak of a hand. He takes a knee, inspects my wound and sets aside his bow and quiver.

"What the hell did the Bandits do to you?"

"They tried to get answers out of him," Harlow says. "And answers they might soon get if we continue to talk like this in the open. Here, help me move him out of the road. The bodies, too."

They help me to my feet and lead me off the road and out of sight of the Bandit stronghold. Once I am safe around the corner of the ridge, they lay me at the hooves of a pair of brown horses, tethered to the ground. Harlow and Dale dart for the dead men and their slain horse and return to me.

"He's lost a lot of blood," Harlow says. "It'll take a miracle if he ever uses his right hand again."

"Will he live?" Dale asks, anxiously.

"He won't die. Though, this bandage is of little help. But that is an easy fix."

Harlow undoes Haebur's poor handiwork and reveals the scope of my injuries. My hand, from the puncture wounds at the tips of my fingers down to my wrist, has turned black, and the blood veins spidering across the back of my hand and over my blotchy red and sickly yellow forearm are dark blue. Dale averts his eyes as he spits curses at Contil and the Bandits; Harlow does not even flinch. She pulls out and uncorks a wide-mouthed jar containing a pasty cream substance. She scoops some on two fingers and lathers it over my wound. The paste stings when it contacts my skin, but after a short while, I feel a warm comfort radiating from my hand. Harlow wraps fresh strips of clean, white material around it and ties it tight around my wrist.

"That will be enough to keep you going," she says. "Getting you back to the Compound must wait."

"And why is that?" Dale asks. "We came here to save him and save him we have! So let's get a move on!"

"I told you our plan! We can end this!"

"Coming in for a surprise attack *was* the plan. Just look at him. Do you really think he can handle it? As much as it kills me to let Contil go on living, Viper is more important than revenge."

"It's not just about revenge!" Harlow reasons. "It's about protecting the lives of other innocent people like Viper. You'll be helping him as well as the others back home."

"She's right," I say, abruptly. "We might not get another chance like this again."

Dale stares at me.

"You're clearly delirious," he says. "All that blood must have drained from your head! We should get him back home, to safety."

"Things did not go entirely as expected, but I'm not through yet," I say. "I've trained with Harlow enough to use my left hand just as effectively as my right. The plan will still work."

"And how can it?" Dale argues. "Contil's defenses are up now. Harlow told me that we were to follow you in the Western Compound and beat Contil three-to-one. We have lost the element of surprise so now it's time to fall back and regroup."

"Listen to me! By coming alone I was able to convince Contil that he is still two steps ahead of us. Yes, he harmed me and that cannot be undone. But just think about it. Here we are, at the threshold of Contil's domain, his two most loyal and trusted allies are dead and I am thought to be well on the way to the Southern Compound. We still have a chance to actually *surprise* him. This is the only chance we'll have to kill him. If we can sever the head, the body of the serpent will wither and fade. The only choice left to us is how to go about it."

Dale stands wordless, mouth agape. Harlow speaks up.

"Viper is right. And I have a thought as to how we can draw out the snake's neck." She places a hand on our shoulders. "I will go and meet him. There is no doubt that he will be unable to pass at the chance to see Amour. You—" she stops Dale's rising objection with a raised finger, "you and Dale are to stay in my shadow. Contil, as you said, believes that you are in the company of his servants, so you should remain unseen until the time comes."

"Amour? Who's Amour?" Dale asks.

"She is part of a past life," she responds, simply. "And this will be her last day."

"Be as it may, that still doesn't give us a way in," Dale counters. "How do we slip passed the guards?"

Harlow smiles and gives him a hardy pat on the back. "Exactly how we always do."

With that, Harlow pulls her thick, coppery braids out of her face and off her shoulders into a black chord, fastening her hair at the back of her head. Dale pulls his Warhammer out of the sling at his side; patches of blood stain its hard, pyramid head. We look at one another one last time before we turn and face the road. Home and loved ones are at our backs, death and journey's end lie ahead.

CHAPTER 27

— The Head of the Snake —

In the broad of the day, we three go side-by-side, solemnly towards the unguarded gate looming ahead of us. Harlow's proud, warrior pose on horseback is a magical sight. The woman that was my tutor could very well be a deity, sent down to earth for righteous retribution long overdue. When the last one-hundred paces separate us from the entrance, Dale and I duck out of sight, off to the side of the road behind unorderly mounds of earth, just as I did one night prior. Dale follows my lead as I find a hiding place high enough for both of us to be completely concealed. We peek out and watch as Harlow carries on alone; her stature tall and noble, her staff held aloft in her right hand. She continues riding up to the heavy gate, pausing briefly, quickly collecting herself. Harlow proceeds and enters the open maw of the Compound, disappearing inside. Dale and I slowly rise and go in pursuit of our companion. The unbearable reek of the forsaken Compound greets Dale in the same fashion as it did me when I first set foot inside the walls. He covers his nose and mouth with the crook of his elbow and coughs, a string of profanity falling from his covered lips.

"It smells like all those who have ever died are here and rotting!"

"It's just a small taste of what the Bandits are capable of. Of how far Contil is willing to go," I say. "Here, get out of sight."

Dale slips into one of the mass graves and I crouch behind a stained wagon, spectating as Harlow marches ever onward. Her progress continues unimpeded until she reigns the horse to a stop at the beginning of the tapered road that leads to the base of the tower, fastened between the network of mangled buildings on either side. They all appear to be emptied. Harlow gives a quick look around.

"I have returned!" She calls to the silence. "Amour has returned to see her unfinished business to its end!"

A smothering silence greets her challenge. I wonder if Contil has closed the ever-watchful eyes of his domain, momentarily turned to the task of gathering his army. For all his strategy and cunning, he could not bar one he so sought from standing in the heart of his hateful fortress. Harlow looks up to the top of the tower looming down on her, jumps off the steed and plants her feet on the ground. She looks so small in the wake of the shadow before her and the death and destruction around her. But still she stands unwavering.

The silence breaks. All the doors and gaps of the buildings burst open and out from them pour the Bandits' teeming hordes, large and threatening they are, all clad in their hideous fashion. Harlow tenses up and brandishes her weapon, its pulverizing metal ends glint in the hazy light of the late morning. The horse panics and bolts away from danger. Still, she stands; still, out come the monsters of the north. She has nowhere to go. Dale and I look on anxiously as the Bandits enclose Harlow who is entirely unwilling to show despair in the wake of such terrible odds. A slam rends the air. Up ahead, at the end of the tapered path, the door to the tower bursts open and in its gap stands a man of tall stature and iron-grey hair; green eyes flashing with insidious purpose. Contil strides down the path, slow and deliberate, never swaying his gaze from the prize standing surrounded before him. He comes to a stop and places a ringed hand on the silver hilt of his sword peeking out from his midnight black cloak; crimson clasps catching the light. He looks down at Harlow, head held high, as a sneer pulls at the corners of his mouth. But it is Harlow who has the first word.

"It appears that you've let time get the best of you. If we had passed on the street, I would have taken you for an old man who lost his way to the grave."

"Cocky words oft come from the mouths of those bereft of hope. Is that not why you are here? To end your pitiful life? Ever have you come short of adequate.

Your misplaced judgment all those years ago bore the penalty of death — or so I thought, and now again. Had you arrived just one day sooner, you may have had a chance to see your pupil off to meet his bitter end."

"He learned from the best," Harlow states. "It seems that your solitude and fraternization with mindless barbarians has dulled your edge. While your skills have become stagnant, mine have only grown, and Viper is of no exception. He —"

"He is the most auspicious of us all, for he — even before myself — will see the dawning of a new world. He is the key and you," Contil's eyes smolder with fury and his nostrils flare, "you are just in the way. You have come too late to do the world any last, vain good. It matters not how you were able to elude me for as long as you did, for now we meet at luck and fortune's end."

He brushes aside his cloak and draws his sword.

"I thought that when the day came, when we were to meet again, I would feel something," Harlow says. "Something from the life I once had and the man I once knew. But I feel nothing but pity. Pity that you let yourself fall into this depravity, pity on the men you've deceived. A man that commits atrocities such as the deeds you have wrought deserve little else than what they have delivered unto others."

"The woman that followed me so closely should know that the only way up in this world is by standing on the necks of lesser men," Contil responds. "Though, it seems that placing yourself in meek company has softened you and driven that truth from your mind."

"I am baffled that I ever looked up to you. I see now, though, that you have always been this version of yourself. But this time, unlike that day, I will not fail."

"Oh, Amour," Contil hisses. "You could have been so much more."

Contil lunges at Harlow with great speed, the tip of his blade aimed true at her heart. Harlow brings up her staff to parry, but Contil changes direction at the last moment. He spins around, maneuvering to one exposed side and slashes her right arm. She lets out a cry of anger as she makes a low, sweeping kick directed at Contil's feet. The attack shoots up a wave of dusty earth and Contil takes a step back. Harlow advances and they exchange blow after blow, battering one another's guard. They come closer and closer to the pit in which Dale hides. For a moment, they battle at the pit's edge above Dale, quaking with the urge to join the fray.

Harlow stops Contil's downward slash with her staff and pushes back with a grunt, about to strike at his exposed chest. But she falls to one knee, clutching at the cut on her arm. She looks up at Contil.

I tentatively stand and edge my way over to the throng of watching Bandits to see more clearly, keeping one hand on Shard.

Contil runs his blade along the fabric in the crook of his arm, cleaning it before he slides it back into its sheath. He stands triumphantly before Harlow and bends to her level.

"So valiantly fought, but still yielding nothing but your own defeat," he gloats. "Time may have changed many things, but it seems to have left you the same. Weak and predictable."

Harlow meets Contil's eye.

"Poison? This is a cheap way to end a fight! Give me the antidote and let's finish this!"

Contil laughs in her face and stands. He reaches for a small sphere hanging on his belt and removes a tiny phial of clear liquid.

"I assume that you are referring to this? I'm afraid that it has already been spent." He uncaps the phial, up-turns it, and spills its contents before Harlow. "Your foolish student was kind enough to return the last of my poison, making this worthless to me."

He looks down on her, expecting to see her pleading for mercy at the sight of her only hope of life soaking into the ground. Instead, he sees her giving him a sly smile.

Several things happen in the next few moments: Contil's expression of dominance shatters into anger and he draws his sword to attack. Harlow snatches up her weapon and blocks Contil's blade. Dale comes out of hiding and bursts from underneath the bodies, brandishing his Warhammer. In one crushing blow, he swings his hammer at the post that holds up an ironbound vat of pitch and topples it, dousing a cluster of nearby Bandits with a viscous, black wave. He shouts my name, and I instantly understand. I reach into my belt, take Dale's match-lighter, and throw its lit body into the writhing group of Bandits. A searing blaze engulfs them instantly and they run hither and thither in a blind panic. The surrounding Bandits back away in fear of the raging inferno, unable to impede its progress as it burns through their ranks. Contil duels with Harlow and has her on the defensive in the midst of the pandemonium, driven further into madness from the wall of fire encircling him. Advancing towards Contil, I slip between the Bandits as they frantically try to regroup; Shard held close. Dale steps out of the mass grave and enthusiastically adds to its numbers, swinging and pulverizing line after savage line of Bandits charging him. I come nearer and nearer towards Contil who hacks and slashes at Harlow with an animalistic brutality. His sword chips away at Harlow's staff, finally at the end of its usefulness. It breaks.

Shard gleams hungrily in the smoke and fire.

Contil sees panic building behind Harlow's eyes and draws back his arm for the final blow. He lunges with his sword but Harlow claps her hands around its razor edge and stops its tip from finding its way to her heart; blood drains from her clenched hands like a river flowing unabated.

"Always so rebellious!" Contil shouts. "Even at death's door you resist! Abandon your hope! It's done nothing for your benefit."

Harlow bares her teeth through the pain. Each inch the sword cuts through her hands towards her heart compels my feet to carry me faster. I come into Harlow's view from behind Contil's back, and for the smallest space between seconds, her eyes flick over to me. Even in a blind rage, Contil is sharp and perceptive. He pulls back his sword out of Harlow's hands and whips around to face me, but is too late to block all of my attack.

He flicks his blade up and deflects the point of my knife, sending it instead to nick his upper arm. In the same motion, Contil reverses his sword and drives its brutally hard pommel under my ribs. I gasp for air and drop back a few feet. Contil comes at me, his long black cloak and grey hair catching in the heatwaves; emerald eyes ringed in fire, devoured by wrath and mayhem. He poses to cut me in two; there is no hope visible. But it is an invisible hand that stops him.

Like so many men before him, fathers, husbands, the young and defenseless, Contil feels at last the same pain he once inflicted. The poison of his own devices courses through his veins from the small cut on his arm. It pumps into his black heart. He freezes before his sword can fall on me, clutching at his stricken arm before hitting the ground; laying on his back in the same fashion he once thought so amusing. The crisp, blue sky and the black smoke from the burning bodies that seeks to fill it hang above Contil and crush him like the bottommost depths of the sea. I step closer and stand over Contil as he fights to draw in breath.

I tear my eyes away from him and face the Bandits. Some are still attempting to put out the fire burning their comrades while others try to overwhelm Dale, who is still standing unscathed in the protective reach of his Warhammer. One Bandit, wearing a golden mantle about his torso and up his spine, a winged helmet resting on his head, notices Contil's fall.

I speak out.

"Your leader is fallen! Merr'putra is slain! I command you to leave! Go back to the Northern Reaches!"

The gilded Bandit, along with a few others in earshot, walks towards me. This pest is bluffing, surely. They look to the ground, at Contil's body that lies there unmoving. The Bandit's wild eyes bore into me, the only thing staying his hand is the religion that binds him. He turns around, snarling and storms out; Bandits in his wake look after him in surprise. No Bandit has ever walked *away* from war willingly. But, one-by-one, they come to realize that a new leader is in command and new orders have been given. They leave the Compound like a strangling hand wrenched away from a throat. I return my attention back to Contil as he laughs with what little air he is able to draw in.

"There is so much potential in chaos," he wheezes. "You see that it is volatile, so easily manipulated with a word… a sword. Over years, my whispering has drained the Bandit tribes of their contempt for one another; my sword sharpened their obedience. But, when I'm gone, what will come to befall you and your home? Who will be the one to shout anger and war back into them? No one will be there to stand between you and the sleeping beast in the north, as I have done. One will waken Merr'tyura and once that happens, no force in this realm can stop them."

"That will be for us to deal with. Your time has passed."

I watch as the poison completes its course through Conti's body. His limbs shake and quiver uncontrollably as the veins on his neck and face bulge and his skin turns crimson, then a sickly dark shade of violet; a green foam seeps out of his mouth and his body wracks with one last convulsion before he lies still. Harlow and Dale join me. Harlow holds the broken halves of her staff in her hands, Dale stands with his hands on his knees, chest heaving from the battle. He turns his head up to look at Harlow.

"So," he pants, "Amour is immune to poison, huh?"

"Amour died her last death today," she smirks and punches him, playfully.

"And so has he," I turn away from the body. "Let's go home."

As the pungent stench of the Western Compound recede from our senses, Dale stops. He looks back at the burning wreckage of Contil's fortress and heave a great sigh. I pause and give him a curious look.

"What's the matter?" I ask.

"You know how long I spent on that?"

"On what?"

"The match-lighter, of course! That took me months to make, from sketch to a working model. And you just went and threw it into the fire," Dale throws up his arms and groans in anguish.

Harlow laughs as Dale turns back around and resumes walking.

"That's what you're most concerned about?" Harlow asks. "I swear, men and their toys…"

CHAPTER 28

— The Shadow's Passing —

The air is quiet and the sky turns dark as we come upon the last stretch to the Southern Compound. My right hand still throbs painfully, but my wounds, as well as Harlow's, have closed thanks to her medicine. We ride on companionship; Harlow has a steed to herself while I sit behind Dale's formidable bulk. The forest thins and from their spaced branches I see wispy, cobalt blue clouds scrapped against the pastel pink sky that is rapidly sinking into red and then black as stars come out to shine more brightly.

"I've been wondering," Dale breaks the long silence. "What other secrets do you have, Harlow? Contil cut you with the poison, same as Viper did him. So why are you not dead? And you," he turns to me, "you also have some explaining to do. Why was I left out of the planning?"

I open my mouth to answer but Harlow speaks first.

"We didn't want to cause any alarm."

"Alarm?" Dale exclaims. "You saw what we did back there. I think some alarm is justified. Hell, we may have had an easier time at it with the rest of the Flag there."

"Listen," I intervene. "I would not have been able to get in and speak with Contil had everyone been present, and we had to make him believe that he remained two steps ahead of us. The smallest group possible would be best, and that came out true."

"Then I suppose you had a change of heart when you brought me along?"

"You were in mind from the beginning," Harlow answers. "Besides, someone had to set those Bandits on fire."

"You still could have told me you were immune to his poison."

"Not immune," she admits. "I'm just good at what I do."

"Have it your way. Next time, just tell me about the crazy shit before I'm knee-deep in it."

I laugh and we continue to ride as light fades and memory guides our steps towards home.

Our bodies ache and our heads are heavy on our shoulders when we finally come into view of the Compound and its friendly lights that dot the ramparts. The thought of a peaceful night's rest is quite overwhelming. As we close the distance, I am able to pick out sentries against the black canopy of the sky, especially around the breach caused by the Bandit's war machine. One of the sentries spots us and a bell rings; a horn blows. In the time it takes us to come within shouting distance of the Compound the summons of the horn attracted dozens of patrolmen, armed with bow and arrow.

"That's far enough!" shouts a guard from the wall. "State your intentions!"

Dale and Harlow reign in their mounts.

"We are the Black Flag," Dale answers, proudly. "And all we want is a night's rest."

There is a commotion and the assembled watchmen disappear from sight. I hear shouting from within and soon the gates open; Dale nudges me with his elbow.

"It's never going to be the same after this," he says.

"How do you mean?"

"You're a hero! And as soon as they discover that, you'll never have a moment's peace."

"What you did is something to be proud of," Harlow leans forward to see me from the other side of Dale. "And speaking as your teacher, I expect you out in the courtyard before sunrise for the second half of your training."

I roll my eyes at her.

"But for now, enjoy yourself," she points towards the gate and the people of the Compound issuing from them, "because they're all here for you."

At the forefront of the crowd is Malory, wearing a grimy apron and her blue ribbon that retains her unkempt hair. I slide from the saddle. Her face lights with joy and relief, and when she reaches me, she takes me in her arms with no prospect of ever letting go.

"Thank the stars you made it back!" she exclaims, kissing my cheeks. "Never in all my long years have I tossed and turned under my sheets as much as I have these last few nights."

The people swarm around me, shouting and cheering as we enter the Compound. Over the masses, I see the courtyard and streets leading from it being lit in welcome. Soon, the light drowns out the stars and the praise and merriment replace the peaceful ambiance of night. People fill every space available as they all want for the same thing: to celebrate. The crowd swallows Dale and Harlow; Malory departs to fetch a new bandage for my hand.

I feel someone grab my shoulder. I turn around and look into Marcus' weary eyes. The wrinkles on his face deepen as he musters a smile.

"We cannot thank you enough – I cannot thank you enough. I am so sorry for all the damage my actions caused."

"The best apology you can give isn't with words, but what you do with the second chance given to you. The things you did came from a sense of duty to protect. I know that. Now they need to know that."

Marcus' eyes well up with tears. He looks away at the scene of victory around us, at the women and children, men and sons reveling in the Shadow's passing. He chuckles to himself.

A path opens in the packed courtyard and Tegan and the Black Flag issue from it. I depart from Marcus and get the attention of my companions.

"There he is, at last! The man of the hour!" Riston says. "I feel a feast is in order! Where is Hector when you need him?"

"It's nearing midnight already. Do you think that a feast is necessary?" I laugh.

"Of course!"

"I am usually not one for overt celebration," Nalu says. "But these circumstances are… special."

"I'll drink to that!" Riston says.

Tegan smiles and shakes his head at Riston, who is already on the prowl for Hector and, undoubtedly, his delicious ale.

"It is hard to believe that it's all over," I say. "It feels like the passing of a nightmare. Only, the wreck and horrors followed us into the morning."

"But so did the victories," Tegan replies. "The war is won. If only all those that started it could see its end," he looks up at the sky bleached clear of stars. "I know that they're all happy, and all the happier to see that their sacrifice was not in vain." He looks back at me. "So, what happens now? Will you remain with the Flag?"

"There is little help I can offer," I gesture to my ruined hand. "Besides, I think it's time that I put down the sword for a while."

The Compound's warning bell chimes loud and sharp over excited voices and everyone falls into an anxious silence. Are there Bandits around seeking revenge? I look about and see Riston and Nalu standing on the wall, holding brimming flagons of ale, the dark liquid showering down on the spectators.

"Everyone!" Riston shouts. "Tonight is a night of revelry and glory! The storm has passed and we who have weathered it stand proud!" The crowd cheers. "That being said, there was one last battle to be fought, a battle I am pleased to inform you was won. The battle of Hector's tavern and the victory of a feast. Go, now! Eat and drink until you can't stand!"

Riston tilts his head back and downs the entire flagon in one go. The people laugh, applaud, and go in search of food and drink.

Malory returns and sets to replacing my bandages with fresh ones. She unwraps my hand and breathes in sharply when she sees the extent of my injury.

"Oh, my poor boy! What happened to you?"

"I'll get by."

"I dare say you won't! I cannot see you managing anything but a spoon with your hand in this state."

"I'll get by," I put my other hand on hers and she stops.

"Your spirit has always been strong. But, I think all is not lost."

"What do you mean?"

"Well, in my years of being a healer, I've heard many strange tales and stories about knights and noblemen fighting and such. Now, I don't want to put your faith in a myth, but I believe there is one that can make you and your hand as good as new."

"Come on, then! Be it true or false, I'd hear anything with such promises."

"Now don't say that I didn't tell you so if it turns out to be nothing but a folk's tale. But, I hear tell of a man – a sage – that lives in the east that can cure all sick and mend broken bones with nothing but a word. I don't see how that is possible, but if there is even a little chance it's true, you should take it. I would hate to see you constrained so by this hurt."

"A sage in the east, huh? Riston once said something about a Sage."

"That's right. Across the Bymore, in Thalvia in the land beyond. It will be quite the journey, but I think that you're well-versed in 'journeying' by now," she cackles and ties my new bandage with a neat bow. "Now, what do you think about joining the feast?"

Malory starts to lead me by the arm to follow the last of the people heading for the tavern, but I hold back.

"You go on ahead. What I want more than anything in the world right now is peace, my pipe, and a warm bed."

Malory smiles and nods her understanding. She comes back, takes me in her arms and kisses me. She turns and heads for the sounds of euphoria.

The empty streets on the way to my room feel more welcoming than ever. Scarred and beaten though they are, the blight of war can never truly conceal the happy memories of its people that lie underneath: escaping from Hector's cellar, stealing Dale's boots and those quiet nights when I snuck back inside the Compound from being at the Hill. Even though those memories come from the Northern Compound, I continue smiling and remembering as I walk through the hall to my room. I open the door and find that it is not empty. Dale is sitting on my bed and Harlow stands looking out my window.

"I told you that he would come here," Dale says to Harlow as I enter. "He wins a war and won't even show up to his own party."

Harlow turns and flicks a coin at Dale, who does a poor job at disguising his pride at winning.

"You bet over whether or not I'd come to my room?"

"We bet over if you'd come *and* if you'd look terrible when you got here," Harlow corrects.

She sits on the chest at the foot of my bed and gives Dale a mean eye as she does.

"You said I'd look terrible?" I turn to Dale. "I expected that from her, but you? I'm hurt."

"We've been spending too much time together. I think she's starting to like me."

"Shut up," Harlow smacks Dale's leg with the back of her hand.

"You see?" Dale smiles.

We share a silence in camaraderie from our common experiences; I join Dale on the edge of my mattress, gingerly keeping up my broken hand.

"So," Dale says, "what happens now?"

"Don't know," I reply. "It's going to take some time to make things go back to normal. We have to clean up the wreckage from the streets, rebuild everything that was destroyed durning the attack… After that we should probably resettle the Northern Compound."

"Why?"

I lean forward to look at Harlow.

"Why what?"

"Why would you want to live inside walls any longer? They were built for a threat that is no longer present. I say we rediscover the lost villages and towns, make our country free and strong."

"You think people would want that?" Dale asks. "I mean, maybe some day. But there are so many of them — even me — that belong here. The Compounds are all that we know."

"You misunderstand," she stands from the chest. "I say that *we* go and *we* find those forgotten places. There's no telling if any Bandits are still hunkered down in them, unknowing that their deity has been slain. I say, we go inform them."

"I follow your meaning," Dale strokes the scar on his chin with his right thumb. "But now, though," he claps both hands to his knees and stands with a huff, "I could use a drink. Anyone else?"

"Riston did appear very full of himself, drinking on the wall like that," she grins, slyly. "I think I should remind him that humility is a virtue."

Dale and Harlow rise and step out of my room. Dale hangs back and stops outside of my door frame.

"You coming?"

I look up at him, thinking.

"You know," I say, at length, "after everything that's happened, all I want right now is peace and a moment to myself. Go and enjoy the party. I'll be fine right here."

"I could not be more proud you," he cheeks flush. "You've done some hard things. And if Junn could see you now, he would say the same."

Dale walks away and I stare after him until the sound of his feet on wooden boards fade from hearing. I walk inside my room and gently close the door. I lean over and open the drawer of my nightstand where I find my simply carved smoking pipe and the small tangle of dried herbs of my favorite blend: Skullcap and White Sage for relaxation, and mint for flavor. I pack the well-used pipe and ignite it with a match. I kick off my boots, toss my clothes into the corner, lean my head back and take a long drag from the pipe. The smoke provides a cool sensation; I blow it through my nose and feel the frosty bite of the mint while the Skullcap and White Sage smooth all sharp edges the events of the last few days filed down. I close my eyes, my mind clear of worry, my ears filled with the joy filtering through my window.

THE END

EPILOGUE

The trees over my head whisper as a small breath of air blows through their leaves. I breathe deeply as the wind gusts and I can almost feel my lungs absorbing the vibrant, rich, beautiful atmosphere that hangs over the overgrown huts and small, grey brick houses. A paved road that nature has reclaimed winds through the abandoned town from one end to the other, and vanishes back into the deep of the forest. I look back the way I came, passed the decrepit bell tower, and see Dale meandering from one decaying building to another while Harlow watches him. She shifts her weight from one foot to the other, hands on her hips, looking at Dale with the sort of twinkle in her eye a mother has for her adventurous little boy.

I can hardly believe we were actually able to find this place. When Harlow suggested that we rediscover all the abandoned towns I thought it would be as easy as hunting down a missing boot or misplaced spoon. I was so terribly wrong. It took over a month for us to even begin searching. After the defeat of Contil and the routing of the Bandits, Marcus needed every strong pair of hands he could get to commence the process of rebuilding, which obviously excluded my own. I've been able to find my own way of helping, though. Malory says I've been '*a joyous addition to her staff.*' I think she just says that because she knows how badly I wanted to aid in the hard labor. But, after three weeks, all of the rubble from the battle has been removed and the major damages to the buildings have been repaired to a livable level. Not soon after that, Harlow and I delved into any maps and records we could find about Hyravon and her settlements. We found close to none from the stores in the Southern Compound. Tegan found out about our plans and offered his own personal knowledge. I never would have thought he knew so much about the land, or hoped that his memory would be so detailed.

We encountered the first village of Auster a few weeks ago, just north-east of Lake Tave. It was a quaint place with wood-reinforced clay huts, a dilapidated fence around its perimeter and a fickle climate. The wind from the distant Bymore Desert would sometimes drive away the pleasant cold coming from the peaks of the Southcap Mountains. After carefully marking our maps, we made for the port-city of Darpas, on the other side of the Southcaps, on the coast of the Summer Seas. I knew when I proposed we go there that it was not a lost place, but I wanted to see what an ocean looked like. Harlow was quite descriptive when she told me just to imagine a very, very, very large puddle. Dale has been there once before and said that Darpas was a magnificent city, that he'd like to visit again. So, we departed from Auster and set our horses towards the eastern end of the mountains.

The road and weather on the way to the sea was pleasurable and predictable. With my mind removed from the shackles of doubt and anxiety the Bandits presence instilled, I was free to take a leisurely pace and sometimes — quite literally — stop and smell the flowers. There is a meadow full of perennial flowers like Daisys, Cat's-ear, and Red Clover and Buttercup, just before the eastern end of the mountain range. We trekked through the verdant field and quickly came to an unexpected stop. Here, amongst the trees that dress the foot-hills of the Southcaps, lies an uncharted town. Dale carefully consulted Tegan's maps, but there was no marker over the place for the town. Driven by curiosity and duty to keep to our mission, we ventured into the settlement.

The wind gusts again as I look up towards the bell tower, at the empty space where the bell itself surely used to hang, and say,

"This is a big town. Wonder why Tegan didn't know about it."

"I can think of a few reasons," Harlow struts towards me. "The first and most obvious of which its that Tegan isn't half as clever as he fancies himself to be. Another is that this town could be too far away for Tegan or your Compound's cartographers to take notice of. But what I think is that this place was built to recently for it to be widely known or plotted."

"But who would risk that big of a project with Bandits wandering about?" Dale asks, giving up at last on peeking into every empty shell of a house.

"Perhaps they thought they were safe enough to build it this far from the Northern Reaches."

"I don't think that the architects were very concerned with safety," I make a general, sweeping gesture. "There are no walls or gates. They must have felt safe indeed."

"Very well observed, Vipe," Harlow sarcastically claps her hands.

"So, what purpose did this place have?" Dale taps the head of his warhammer with a fingernail. "If not for protection, then what?"

"Maybe the people of Darpas built it along a trade route?" I say. "It's about half-way from the Southern Compound to the port-city. They might've used it to trade with others before reaching the middle of Hyravon."

"That begs the question of why we've never seen one of their trade caravans before. If this place was built recently, then we should have seen at least one cart."

"You know what I think?" Harlow lethargically strolls down the grass-sprouting cobble road. "I think that none of that matters. This places empty and there's no real point in trying to sniff out the answers, which might be endless."

"I suppose you're right…"

"…As usual," Dale and I say in unison.

Harlow exhales sharply through her nose.

We lead our horses on foot through the town. We come around a gentle bend in the road and see a house on the corner, slightly higher than its neighbors due to its patch of elevated earth, that is not woven with shoots of ivy or encroached upon by tall grass. Is someone living here?

"Who do you reckon is staying there?" Dale asks with a hand resting on his hammer.

"I'm done with guessing games," I march towards the distinguished house. "There's one good way to find out."

I wade through the bedraggled lawns until my feet touch the well-groomed grass of the peculiar house. A sweet fragrance hangs over the property. I glance up at the empty sockets of the windows and see nothing that suggests ongoing residency. I unconsciously raise my hand to knock on the front door, then shake my head clear of proper, neighborly etiquette and instead reach for the handle and push the door open.

One of the first things I notice is the smell of freshly tilled soil, and an underlying one of some herb or plant that I do not recognize. I take a few steps into the house and see two padded armchairs tucked into a rounded corner with a fireplace and a small table between them. Farther into the space I see daylight splashing its bright rays into what I imagine is the kitchen; well-used pots and pans hang on hooks from the plaster ceiling. My boots thump on the scuffed floorboards as I head for the kitchen and the broad, waist-high countertop in the middle of the room. Pantries, closets and cupboards encircle the counter. Some have doors of glass and I see bundles of dried spices, corked and sealed jars and bottles holding objects soaking in some marinade or another. I turn my head and see a square dinner table nestled against a tall and wide bay window that yields a sight into a garden. Once bright tulips now on decline, hydrangeas and sunflowers dot plots of the ground where a stone path weaves around them.

I turn at the sound of feet behind me and see Harlow and Dale impassively inspecting the house; Harlow runs her index finger over the countertop, leaving a streak of clean wood on the dusty surface.

"Looks like they've been gone for a while," she observes.

I take another look around and notice the same. A film of dust clings to every surface of the kitchen.

"Not that long ago, right?" Dale rummages around the kitchen's many cabinets. "Or else the lawn wouldn't be so tidy."

"If that's the case," Harlow turns to face Dale, "then I'd stop making a mess of their things. They might be back soon."

"I don't think that they will," I say. "Take a look at this."

Harlow and Dale join me beside the dinner table where a note written on a square piece of slightly stained paper rests on its dirty surface. Harlow picks up the page and quickly runs her eyes over the script as she reads.

"'*To my dearest,*'" she reads, aloud. "'*Upon your return, you will find that I have moved on. There is business in Thalvia that requires my immediate attention. It turns out that the Cromwells are in over their heads in the Kingdom's politics. I've left the home well stocked with all the provisions you might need, you'll even find a surprise in the garden that you've been hinting at. I will be staying at the Ruin Inn for a few days if you decide to join me. But, until then, you have my thoughts and my love, yours forever, Mylin.*'"

Harlow returns the paper to the table with a huff.

"Wonder what the surprise might be," Dale cranes his neck to look out the widow into the garden.

"Really?" Harlow says. "Thats the part that grabbed your attention?"

"Politics bore me," answers Dale, already on his way to the back door. "But surprises are exciting!"

Dale swings the door open and lets in the outside warmth and salubrious aroma. Harlow and I follow him out and walk the stone path, raking our eyes over the flowers for some kind of hint to what the surprise might be. We come to the end of the yard and see a wooden lattice in front of a wrought-iron fence that encircles the garden. The soil beneath the lattice is a fresh dark brown and thorny stems wind up and around the arch, bearing few buds, but one is in the infancy of its bloom. A blood-red rose is growing at the crown of the lattice like a sun setting over a hill. I stare at the beauty of the rose, picturing the time when all the buds will be fully realized.

All of a sudden, I recall an image of a bronze rose with petals of silver, and a strange conversation with a mysterious man.

I whirl around in a frenzy, startling the quiet Dale and Harlow. I blabber a stream of nonsensical, unconnected words, trying to articulate my excitement.

"Would you please think before you speak?" Harlow asks. "I take pride in my ability to teach, and you're becoming a very poor example of my talents."

I take a breath and collect myself.

"I cannot believe I forgot!"

"Forgot what?" Dale demands.

"On my way to the Western Compound, I ran into a man that called himself Seeker. He had this glowing box in his tent that was bright and hot like fire, but did not burn or smoke. He told me that it was magic, and he knew Junn! And he —"

"Whoa, slow down," Dale says. "Magic? Aren't you a little old to believe in that sort of thing?"

"You didn't see what I did. You'd believe if you saw it, too."

"You said he called himself Seeker?" Harlow questions.

I nod.

"And that he knew Junn?"

I nod again.

"Yes."

"Tell me," her lips curl in a smile, "did he have a symbol of a rose somewhere on his clothes?"

"He did! How did you know?"

Harlow lets out a cackling laugh.

"Oh, how times have changed!"

"You know him?"

"I do," she wipes a tear from her eye. "He must fancy himself quite a bit with a name like Seeker. He is the one that wrote that note; he is Mylin. Junn and I met him when he was just a scribe to the monks at Buruaren. I guess that I should've taken him more seriously. He was going on and on about discovering magic, researching tirelessly. I departed his company when I thought he lost his mind. But Junn stayed. Looks like Mylin was actually on to something."

"So, magic *is* real?" Dale asks. "How 'bout that. You know," he looks at me, "I remember seeing that symbol before."

"Really?" I raise an eyebrow. "When?"

"During the night Junn found you. There was a fight near the cave, but the bodies didn't belong to the Compound, and some had a bronze stem and thorns with silver petals on their clothes. I didn't think anything of it at the time. But now, hearing all this about monks and magic, maybe there's more to it than I thought."

"You said you met Mylin at Buruaren?" I look at Harlow.

"I did."

"Where is that?"

"On the eastern side of Mahadvala, close to Thalvia."

I put my hands on my hips and think; I look up to stare at the lone, budding rose. I look back at my companions.

"How do you feel about another adventure?"

Made in the USA
Middletown, DE
11 September 2021

47118354R00190